M…

AND LAUGHTER LINES

Carol E. Wyer

Published in 2011 by YouWriteOn Publishing

Copyright © Carol E Wyer 2011 asserts the moral right under the Copyright, Designs and Patents Act 1988 to be identified as the author of this work.

First Edition

All Rights reserved. No part of this publication may be reproduced, stored in a retrieval system, or transmitted, in any form or by any means without the prior written consent of the publisher, nor be otherwise circulated in any form of binding or cover other than that in which it is published and without a similar condition being imposed on the subsequent purchaser.

All the characters in this book are fictitious, and any resemblance to actual persons living or dead is purely coincidental.

A CIP catalogue record for this title is available from the British Library

To my husband for his infinite patience and understanding.

INTRODUCTION

When I started this novel, I had no idea what a blog was, let alone how to write one. During my research and attempts at writing my own blog I discovered that there is an enormous world-wide community of people of all ages and backgrounds who write regularly about their passions, interests and lives. Not only do they welcome you to their space and come and visit yours but their blogs are highly entertaining and beautifully presented.

I would like to thank all my followers, who have become great blogging friends, for their tireless support and encouragement in this venture.

Special thanks to EmptyNest, Thisisme, Desiree, DizzyC, fishducky, Trininista, High Heeled Life, Lavi, Craziness Abounds and Eva.

CHAPTER 1 - JULY

WELCOME NOTE

Welcome to *Facing 50 With Humour* the blog that gives you laughter lines. And, clearly, very bad tag lines. I was going to call it *Facing 50 With Fear, Trepidation and a Bottle of Chardonnay* but I think that title was already taken. I suppose it's like a diary only anyone with internet facilities can read it. For me it's more than a diary. This is the only way I'll stop myself from going insane, or indeed committing murder. I hope you enjoy it. Please feel free to leave me a comment.

ABOUT ME

My name is Amanda Wilson. I like chick flicks, wine, romantic novels, wine, 1970's and 80's music, chocolate and wine. I am a very desperate housewife. I live in a village in rural Staffordshire, populated almost entirely by elderly people. Even the local window cleaner is in his seventies. I used to have a life and a job. Nowadays, I seem to spend most of my time acting as a referee between my husband Phil -who since he retired - has become the grumpiest of grumpy old men, and my son. We waved him off with a fanfare to university a couple of years ago but he returned to the nest almost immediately, having turned into a complete drop out. Life is a tad on the dull side at the moment. However, there are changes afoot, very significant changes and that is why I am writing this blog. By the way did I mention I like wine?

Monday 5th

My very first blogging entry and I for one, am rather proud of myself. It's taken five days to work out how to do it, but here I am at last. Where shall I begin? I could start by complaining about my rotten life and how last night, my revolting son brought back several of his drunken friends to our house after we had gone to bed. They made so much noise that at 2am I had to go downstairs and ask them to leave. This morning I got up to find toast crumbs and jam spread all over the kitchen tops where they had tried to make some food and someone had left me a floating present in the toilet.

.....Or, I could rant about my crotchety husband who spent breakfast reading the back of the milk carton, ignoring my conversation about what we could do for the day. He withdrew to his study without a word. I might as well have been invisible. However, that is all far too depressing.

How about beginning with the subject of birthdays? My life has been turned completely upside down this last year for a variety of reasons. To cap it all I have reached a serious crisis point this month because I am going to turn fifty. How depressing is that? The big five oh.

No one prepares you for this. You trundle along merrily with your daily business, striking off birthdays as if they were cricket scores, thinking nothing of it and then one day you look in the mirror and see your mother staring back at you. You wonder how this can have happened without you noticing before. Your expiry date is just about up. You are going to be half a century. In cricket terms you are going to be fifty but hopefully, not out, not just yet.

When it was Phil's fiftieth, nine years ago, I pulled out all the stops in an attempt to celebrate the event. Part of me believes you should embrace these occasions and be spoilt by those who love you. In those days I hadn't quite realised how depressing it was to actually be facing fifty. I arranged a surprise trip to Dubai. I cajoled a free upgrade from economy class to business class on the flight by playing the *It's his Big Birthday* card at the check in desk. Actually, I think the woman checking us in took pity on him as he stood in silent embarrassment while his noisy wife divulged his age to the world. I did the best I could to make it special. So, when Phil announced a few months ago that he would help me celebrate my birthday by arranging a surprise trip I initially got very excited in spite of the usual anxiety that one feels at hitting a milestone birthday.

Last year it poured down in torrents on my birthday. It rained, non-stop, from the moment I woke up to moment I sank back into my bed in a semi-drunken stupor. As usual, nothing special was planned for the day. Phil is just no good at planning birthday surprises, and as he despises parties, I can't even plan one for myself. It was too wet to go out anywhere. It was such a shame because I used to love my birthdays and the excitement that surrounds them. Unfortunately, it's been some time since I've felt excitement about anything.

The novelty of going away and being spoiled rotten for a few days is beginning to wane slightly as the big day creeps nearer, and I consider just how old I actually am. I am as old as *Coronation Street*. I can remember miniskirts the first time they became fashionable. The problem is that I don't really believe I am all that old. I still consider myself to be fairly young. Last month though the realization hit me, well more thumped me squarely on the nose. Almost immediately, I began to feel old. I don't suppose my newly discovered depression is due solely to my forthcoming birthday. I have just realised how unimportant I have become and how dreary my life is. Still, there is no point in being too depressed about it and going away will be such a treat.

I've been in preparation for four months, cutting down on food and cutting out chocolate. I tried cutting out the odd glass of wine too but that made me fractious. I have been a slave to sit-ups every night in an attempt to look good in my newly purchased Karen Millen shorts. I know it may seem as if I am making an enormous deal about it but it is such a novelty to be going away let alone making a trip abroad.

We haven't been away since Tom dropped out of university a year ago. One minute we were looking forward to Phil's early retirement, doing some travelling and having 'us' time and the next, Tom had returned from university with a hillock of debt (thank goodness he didn't stay the full four years or it would have been an Everest sized mountain of debt), and a huge attitude problem.

He has transformed from a nice young man into a hideous selfish oaf. He spends most of the time lazing about in bed, down at the pub or on his mobile phone. I almost don't recognise him as the dear boy he used to be. Whatever he learned at university in that year will certainly be of no use in today's job market, unless there are vacancies for young men to test out free beer and cigarettes. I'll certainly be glad to abandon him for a few days.

Phil won't tell me where we are going but he looks very pleased with himself and keeps whistling, *Oh! We're going to Jamaica.* He also whistles, *Tie Me Kangaroo down Sport* so maybe I'm reading too much into that especially as we are only going away for six nights. However, he knows I do not want to get rained off this year and that I love the sea so he'll surely have booked a trip to the South of France or Spain. In fact, anywhere sunny would be acceptable.

Posted by Facing50Blog.com - 0 Comments

Wednesday 7th

This morning I woke up at four am to find Phil's side of the bed empty. He normally gets up early but even by his standards four o'clock is suspiciously early. I wondered if he was feeling alright as he's been having trouble sleeping recently and so got up to make sure he wasn't being sick or indeed, nothing worse had happened. He wasn't in the bathroom, or the office where the computer lay dormant blinking its sleepy little red light at me. There was no sign of him in the lounge or the kitchen, and by the back door I discovered his slippers. No, he had not left home. I knew immediately where he would be. I made him a cup of coffee, got a coat and boots on and made my way down to the bottom of the garden to the paddock.

Phil was sitting on his haunches dressed in his old blue anorak and pyjama bottoms. In his hand he had a large shovel. He saw me and motioned for me to be quiet. I tiptoed as lightly as possible to where he was squatting. He pointed nearby to a mound of earth which was moving slightly. It stopped and then the earth moved again. Phil leapt up and smashed the mound with his shovel passionately, yelling obscenities but I think we both knew that the mole causing th destruction of our paddock with its molehills had disappeared into the labyrinth of tunnels and would be back to torment him later.

The mole arrived four months ago. If you could see our garden you'd think there were at least twenty moles in residence, not just one. It started one Sunday afternoon. Phil had just spent his usual two hours walking up and down what we call the paddock; three quarters of an acre of grass overlooking fields. It was meticulously trimmed with smart green stripes resembling a well kept bowling green. He'd cleaned his mower, oiled it, placed it back in the shed in its space between the ladders and the leaf blower, and gone for a shower.

When he went out to admire the field after his shower, and to hang out his towel to dry, he discovered a large mound of earth right in the middle of the paddock destroying the neat illusion he'd created. He immediately got his spade and neatl replaced the earth, jumping on it all to make it flat again and attempted to replace the grass which had also been pushed up Twenty minutes later and the mound had been pushed up again. Phil fetched his spade and flattened the earth. All was quiet until the next morning when he discovered not only was the mole hill up again, but so were two others at the far end o the paddock, and so he flattened them all and replaced the grass with ferocity and much cursing.

Since then it has become a battle of wills. The mole is definitely winning. We now have a paddock with so much tunnelling under it that Phil can no longer mow it properly. The lawnmower lurches from side to side in a drunken fashion as it falls into the dips. It is impossible to make the grass look tidy. Each morning he or I go out and flatten the hills. By lunchtime they are all up again. We repeat the process in the evening. Wednesday, I put back twenty-six hills before he could see them and rage even more. The garden has been annihilated.

Naturally, we've tried to get rid of it. At first, I thought we could simply discourage it from coming into the field. We put anti-mole products on the lawn and a sonic tube that emitted a noise which moles are supposed to loathe. Our mole put a hill up right beside it, so it must be deaf. We dropped moth balls into the tunnels as apparently they are sensitive to certain aromas and dislike the smell of moth balls. The mole continued to put up its hills. A neighbour suggested that moles hate the smell of blood and volunteered to get me a few buckets from the local abattoir but I couldn't face pouring it all over the garden. It would look like something from a horror film. I read moles were haemophiliac. Phil cut down small branches from the pyracantha bush to shove down the hole and prick it to death. I ripped my fingers to bits shoving them into the tunnels and bled all over my white top. When Phil wasn't looking I pulled all the pieces out again. It was too horrible a death, even for an irritating mole.

Eventually, what with the devastation it was causing, and the annoyance factor I became worried about Phil whose blood pressure was going sky high, and called in a pest controller. It cost a fortune but he put gas pellets down all the tunnels, assured us we would be rid of the mole, and he'd come back to check progress in a couple of weeks. Two weeks later the mole was more active than ever, presumably it was hyper on all the gas it ingested before it put on its own little gas mask. The pest controller declared it a mystery. He gave up after the sixth attempt.

Phil the hunter, is determined that he will catch this mole. He is often to be found sitting with his shovel in one hand and his fork in the other. Each time he sees a shudder of earth he spears the mound with his fork, and hits the hill with his shovel. The mole is almost a metaphor for what is happening in our lives. We are stuck in a repetitive, frustrating pattern. Phil is getting increasingly irritated by it. I know how he feels.

In the meantime I'm looking for a mole catcher, one of those individuals who'll catch it and transport it away, preferably to Greenland. You'd think living in the country there would be hundreds of mole catchers but apparently it is a dying art due to pest controllers who now deal with moles. I think I'll have my work cut out to find one. On the bright side at least it's given Phil something to do other than check his share portfolio all the time.

Posted by Facing50Blog.com - 2 Comments

SexyFitChick said...Hello! You sound like a desperate housewife alright. It gets to us all in the end. I'm a fan of chick flicks and wine too. I thought I'd leave a comment and hope you get the little varmint sorted. I mean the mole, not Phil, although it sounds like he needs sorting out too. Next door's dog seems to keep critters away from my house. Good luck with it all. I'll be checking back to see how you are

getting on. In the meantime I'm raising a glass of Australian Shiraz to you. We have some great wines here.
Facing 50 said...I am so pleased to meet you. It's so nice to know there is someone else out there who understands my frustrations - and pleasures – cheers!

Friday 9th

Yesterday, I received a card and a cheque for twenty pounds 'to indulge myself' from my mother. She is a widow and struggling on a pension. She grows her own vegetables, brews her own repulsively strong wine which she insists on glugging straight from the demijohn before it is ready, and only spends money on cigarettes which she absolutely refuses to give up.

I've noticed that of late she has become increasingly like one of Marge Simpson's sisters: Patty or Selma. She's always got a drink in her hand, a cigarette in her mouth and growls rather than talks. Actually, to look at her, she looks more like Grandpa Simpson or one of those wrinkly dogs - a Shar Pei. Still, she is my mother and I remember her when she was very beautiful and looked like a glamorous Joan Collins. I saw a photograph of her taken when she was a young twenty year old and she was an absolute stunner.

Feeling very fond of her at that precise moment, I decided to spontaneously telephone her instead of waiting for the usual Sunday call.

The telephone emitted a sickening screeching noise. I almost dropped the phone trying to cover my ears.

"Hello? Mum?"

"It's you," replied a rather disappointed gravelly voice. "I thought you were one of those nuisance calls. I've had nine in the last forty-eight hours so I nipped next door this morning and borrowed an old chalk board from Bernard who teaches Art. I've been waiting all day for them to ring again. When I answer the phone I drag my nails down the board to put them off. I've been dying to know if it works.
She demonstrated again and I experienced another ear deafening screech.

"I can assure you if I were a salesman, I definitely wouldn't phone you again after that row."
I waited for a response. There was a lengthy pause while she dragged on her cigarette.

"They always seem to ring when I'm upstairs in the bathroom. I have to rush down the stairs only to be greeted with: 'Congratulations, you have won a prize,'" she drawled in an American accent which brought on a fit of coughing. "I'm sick of them. I thought I'd managed to get them stopped by using that telephone service but these calls are coming from abroad."
There was another pause while she coughed, not just a cough, a revolting hacking stomach turning cough. She starts every day like that. It's like an old engine coughing into life each morning. It's horrible.

The tirade about cold callers continued for a further seven minutes, at which point I began to wonder why I was even bothering to phone, when she suddenly barked,
"Anyway, why are you phoning? Did you get my card and money? I sent it yesterday so it should have reached you today. I hope it hasn't got lost in the post. I sent it early so yo

would get it in plenty of time and be able to take it away with you..."

That was that. She was in full flow. You can't get a word in sometimes with her. She barely pauses for breath. Steam filled the kitchen as the kettle boiled. I put the phone down on the top and poured hot water over my tea bag. I let the flavours infuse and removed the bag. Cup of tea in hand, I retrieved the phone.

"...I put a first class stamp on it too so it would get there in time. What a price they are. I remember when it only cost six old pence."

I seized the opportunity as she paused to take another drag, to break into her monologue.

"That's why I'm phoning. I thought you'd like to know I'd received it. Thank you for the money too."

"Well, it's not enough for a toy boy or a yacht," she chuckled throatily. "Mind you, you're too old to know what to do with a toy boy now. You'd probably just sit him down with a cup of tea."

There was more raucous chuckling followed by a coughing fit.

"Anyway looking at your last photograph you sent of yourself I thought you could probably use it to get some of that buttocks stuff. After all, you're not getting any younger are you?"

What was she waffling on about? Jennifer Lopez had had her buttocks lifted. Is that what she meant? Mine need more than a lift. I think they reach the back of my knees. No, she couldn't mean a buttocks lift. I mused about it while she launched into a further monologue about the past.

"Do you remember that time when you broke the door handle and we couldn't get out of the lounge for hours?"

"Oh and what about that time you fell down the stairs and landed on the vicar who had just popped around."

"I'll never forget the time - you'd have been about fourtee - you got stuck attempting to climb though the tiny open kitchen window because you had lost your house keys and couldn't let yourself in. When we came home from work, there you were, bottom in the air. Ha, ha, ha!"

I just added the odd 'yes', still curious as to why I needed stuff for my buttocks. I've always had a large backside. No one has ever suggested I needed it enlarging. It was sufficiently large, hence I got stuck all those years ago trying to get through the window. Her ability to recall events from thirty and forty years ago astounds me. I pondered further on what she might have meant. Maybe old age had caught up with her at last and she was just talking gibberish. She continued her personal trip down memory lane

"Mum, what do you mean 'buttocks stuff?" I asked as she inhaled deeply on a freshly lit cigarette.

"For your wrinkles. You know, injections that freeze your face and stop your laughter lines from becoming too pronounced, buttocks injections " she emphasised getting back on to the subject in hand, which at that point was my inability to cook and how I had boiled a pan dry trying to cook an egg when I was a teenager. She really does live in th past. I hope I don't get like that. Mind you, I can barely remember what I did last week. All the days seem to blend into one dull and pointless one

Posted by Facing50Blog.com - 2 Comments

SexyFitChick said...What a character! Is she for real? My mother spends all her time on the beach wearing a large hat and worrying about her SPF cream. Still, she doesn't remember much about what I was like as a teenager – thank goodness. I was a bit of a tearaway.
Facing 50 said...Yes, she's always been like that. She loves to criticise me. I'm suppose I'm used to her put downs now. She can be quite funny though when she's had a few drinks and is telling a story. My mother used to put olive oil on her skin to get a suntan. She looks like a walnut now. At least your mother is sensible.

Saturday 10th

Goaded by my mother, anxious about my waning looks and depressed about getting older, I spent this morning staring gloomily into the magnifying mirror while wearing my reading glasses to get a better look at myself. She had a point about my laughter lines. They are quite obvious around my eyes but deeper lines are etched into my forehead through years of squinting because I refused to wear my glasses. 'Ah, vanity thy name is woman.'

I also appear to be sprouting hair all over my chin and sides of my face. I'm going to turn into one of those hirsute old women that I used to laugh at when I was young and hair free. What do you do about this problem? Do you pluck the hairs? No, I read somewhere that makes it worse. I'll have to look it up on the internet. In the meantime, I'll leave it alone because Phil's eyes aren't so good anymore and he might not notice. Crikey - what's happened to my eyebrows? I know I had an unfortunate experience with a threading session last

year but there seem to be hairs all over the place and I look like Sam the Eagle from *The Muppets*.
Posted by Facing50Blog.com - 0 Comments

Thursday 15th

This morning I got some terrific news. For the first time in a year I was going to be able to go to the shops alone. On my own. By myself. Just me. Since Phil retired I feel like we're co- joined (not in all matters of course. We do go to the bathroom separately). Ordinarily I can't leave the house without him.

"Just off to the supermarket dear."

"Oh, wait for me. I'll come along and carry the bags."

"I'm going to get my hair done. I'll be about three hours."

"Wait for me. I'll come and wait on the bench outside the hairdressers' and read my paper."

I don't really mind him coming with me, but I hate the comments about my driving:

"So, you didn't see that pothole then?"

"You're too close to that car. Slow down."

"Don't forget that the indicator stick is on the left. Feel free to use it any time you overtake."

"You might want to pull over here to let that ambulance that has been trying to get by you for two miles go past."

"Turn right here, no, the other right."

Most of all, I hate the fact that he sees everything I buy. There are no more 'secret' purchases. No more "This old thing – I've had it in my wardrobe for years." At first, I tried hiding new additions to my wardrobe in an old supermarket plastic bag, but he rifled through it one day in the hope of finding a cake for afternoon tea, and nearly choked when he saw what I'd paid for a blouse. A few months ago I had a better idea. I'd been torn between a Marc Cain beige jumper with a large leopard printed on the front and a flattering Cashmere Cardigan in Crimson.

"I'll take them both," I decided.

The shop assistant looked approvingly at my choice.

"They are beautiful, aren't they?" she cooed.

She caressed the cardigan as if it were a cat. It might even have purred.

Would you mind just folding them up in tissue paper for me? I requested.

The assistant looked at me puzzled.

"I don't want my husband to see them," I explained. "I want to put them in my bag."

She gazed at my bag and looked at me as if I was about to commit a heinous crime.

"They won't fit in there," she spluttered.

I looked at my large bag. I had brought it along deliberately to hide goodies.

"If you fold them up into small packages, I'll be able to stuff them in, under my glasses case and my purse," I explained.

She glared at me and held the cashmere cardigan protectively to her bosom.

"Maybe you should just take one item today and one next time you come in. Otherwise they'll be ruined. You can't crush items like these."

In the end, I agreed and just bought the leopard jumper. She continued to glower as she folded it into a tiny tissue enveloped parcel and handed it begrudgingly to me. As I left the shop, I'm positive I heard her talking to the cardigan telling it what a narrow escape it had had.

I have resorted to more devious tactics since then. Now, I always carry a large recycle bag. Phil thinks I'm doing my bi to save the planet. I'm not. I'm saving my sanity. I pile ordinary stuff like toilet rolls on top of any new garment which lies hidden neatly at the bottom of the voluminous bag

Of late though, there hasn't been any money for special purchases and I spend more time looking in the shop window than buying clothes. Today, I felt liberated. Today, I granted myself the freedom to buy whatever I wanted, within reason. After all, I am going to be fifty.

Euphoric, I accompanied Freddie Mercury on Queen's *I Want to Break Free,* which blared from the car radio as I drove to town. I saved Phil the trouble of having to agonise over choosing a suitable present for me and bought a new dress with the joint credit card, one that did not have to be squashed up in my bag. On the way back to the car I was inexplicably drawn to a new shop offering Cosmetic Services

I opened the door and nervously looked around. A fresh faced receptionist looked up and asked if she could help me. I edged towards her and explained that I might like to have a procedure.

"No trouble," she said smiling pleasantly. She didn't seem to find my request at all bizarre. Now, here's a form to fill in and if you'd like to sit over there and complete it I'll let Nurs Younger know you are here. Yes," she added when she saw the look on my face. "She is called Younger and her first name is Eve, Eve Norma Younger."

Chuckling, I dropped down onto one of the leather chairs which squeaked rudely. Younger by name and Eve N. Younger by nature it would seem as a woman in her late twenties with a porcelain wrinkle-free complexion met me in the treatment room. She needed no treatment. She was perfect. I gazed in admiration as she assessed me.

I won't go into all the details here of what was done. I didn't feel a thing when she injected the stuff into my forehead. It was all quite painless and strangely pleasant.

"I hope this makes me look as youthful as you," I quipped as I prepared to leave.

"It should do. I use it regularly and I'm forty-eight," she replied.

This could be the tonic I need. I've recently been lacking in confidence. Phil never looks at me. He's certainly not interested in me physically any more, probably because I'm turning into an aged crone. I am undeniably getting old and let's face it, regardless of what magazines may say: that you are still beautiful at fifty or fifty is the new thirty, if you don't feel good about yourself then you are going to be unhappy.

I'm not completely convinced that I've done the right thing but if it helps to eliminate those hideous lines between my eyes and makes me look a little younger then...I also had my eyebrows shaped and tinted. The gorgeous young beautician, who was presumably put off by my continuous anxious babbling, has arched them a little too much, giving me a permanent look of surprise (which could be useful when I open my birthday gifts).

I was advised to frown a lot for the first few hours. That isn't a problem as I constantly frown, usually because even to this day I refuse to wear my glasses unless I absolutely need to read. The last time I went to the optician's he warned me that if I didn't put them on for driving I would be driving illegally. He looked so sternly at me that I thought for one moment he was going to report me to the police, so I promised I would wear them more and then spent the next hour walking backwards and forwards past his shop in them so he could see me wearing them.

Phil was distracted this evening and didn't notice me frowning all the time at him. He seems to be distracted more and more these days. Some days I feel I should try and get his attention by striding about wearing nothing but a thong and thigh length boots. Sadly, I'm convinced that it would just backfire and he'd just look right through me. He does that more and more these days. He doesn't see me anymore. No, it's a bad idea. Besides, I don't think even I would want to see me in just a thong and boots these days, not with this cellulite and these flabby bits.

I pointed out the tinted eyebrows just in case he wonders why I look different when the 'buttocks' works. I told him about the present he's bought me which seemed to cheer him up. Maybe he's simply relieved that he doesn't have to think about it anymore or maybe he's just pleased that I didn't spend too much on it. I checked in the mirror before bed but the lines are still there and I can still frown deeply.

Posted by Facing50Blog.com - 1 Comment

SexyFitChick...Can't wait to see if it works. I'm going to get some if it does. No point in looking your age if you don't have to.

Friday 16th

This morning brought disaster. Okay, I admit, that is an exaggeration. It was not quite disaster. One of my eyebrows has lost its tint overnight leaving me with a comically quizzical look. I tried using my eyeliner to fill in the gaps but it was too coppery and now I have one slightly ginger eyebrow and one dark brown and I can still frown deeply.

Phil was a little grumpy, in fact he is always grumpy. If you met him you would invent a new verb 'to grump' as in 'Phil grumped to the shops'. He epitomises grumpiness and if he were a character in an A.A. Milne story it would undoubtedly be *Eeyore,* whereas I am definitely *Tigger* - an irritating, effervescent, bouncy *Tigger*.

Last night, in a moment of madness, probably due to post buttocks hysteria, I insisted on starting my birthday celebrations early and opened last year's birthday present – a bottle of Lanson Rose Champagne. I should have drunk this sooner as it had lost its pink tinge and looked more like Lucozade. Having been off the drink for a while, Phil was soon the worse for wear. He dozed off in the chair and had to go to bed at 8.30 pm leaving me to attempt tipsy sit-ups in front of the television which swam in and out of focus. Well, I do want to look good for this birthday trip.

He was also crabby today because it is Friday, and we do not go out on a Friday. Actually, we don't go out much anyway but Fridays Phil flatly refuses to drive. He just can't face the traffic which he complains about every single time we go out. For some reason the road that goes past our house is absolutely jam-packed on a Friday with heavy goods vehicles, caravans, motor-bikes, tractors, vans, and cars.

To cap it all, this morning at 7.30am, a procession of Vintage Steam Engines puffed past followed by about six miles of traffic stuck behind them. The house shook as they rolled over the potholes causing Phil's lips to tighten in a thin line. Tomorrow, there's going to be a Vintage Steam Fair in the next village which is three miles away. The speed they were going, they might just make it there in time if they don't stop for lunch.

Fridays are also a drag because Tom doesn't normally work on a Friday. This means we have to put up with him lying in bed, or as Phil calls his room, *the Pit,* until midday and then stinking out the bathroom before disappearing to the pub. At least when he's at work we have some respite. Whatever happened to him? Before university he was a normal teenager. I thought we'd grown through the difficult period but apparently not. Since he's come back, it's just been one unending nightmare.

I had a really bad night's sleep, and not just because of the champagne. Phil likes to go to sleep with the radio on and I hate it on. A creature of habit, he goes to bed at 9pm on the dot and puts the radio on a timer to turn off at about 10.30pm, which is roughly when I go to bed. Last night, not only had he mistakenly set it to turn off at 11.30pm, but it was playing dance music.

Dance music is fine when you want to dance, not when you are trying to get your beauty sleep. I had just listened to the extended version of Donna Summer's *Love to Love You Baby* with accompanying panting, and was about to get up and pull the plug out of the radio because I couldn't find the remote control to silence it, when it went off with a loud ‘phut!’ I eased back into the pillow, breathed a sigh of relief, and then Phil started snoring, gently at first but then louder and louder. He sounded like a pneumatic drill. The walls reverberated with each snore. I kicked him, of course, but that only stopped him for a moment or two and each time he restarted, he was louder.

My brain began to whir in time to the cacophony of snorts coming from next to me. In the darkness anxieties assaulted my tired mind. As the minutes turned into hours I started to worry about Tom and wonder when, or if, he was going to come home. It was now very late and all the pubs would be shut. He had only gone into the local town. There were no nightclubs there or all night bars. He was hardly likely to be hanging out at the all night supermarket. I worried about his safety. Maybe he had had his phone and money stolen. He might have been involved in a brawl and was now sitting in Casualty. Worse still, he could have had an accident. Was he sitting on a pavement in town in the cold too drunk to remember where he lived? Those ridiculous fears, that mothers all over the world experience when their children are out at night, gnawed at me relentlessly. The stupid thing is that while he was at university, no doubt drinking his body weight in alcohol, and hanging out in the most frightening places in Manchester, I didn’t worry. Now that he’s back in the nest, I fret every time he goes out, even if it’s to the shops.

I thrashed about for a further hour before eventually dozing off. A stomach ache caused me to sit bolt upright in bed. It was probably due to all the anxiety. Many illnesses are caused by worry. I agonised that I could even have something serious like appendicitis. Those thoughts and fears always seem ludicrous in the daylight hours, but at 4am, laying awake alone in the dark, everything gets out of proportion. I cursed Tom. I wished he'd behave normally, and at least let us know he was okay. Unable to stay in bed any longer, I got out for a glass of water. My mobile phone was flashing on the bedside locker. Tom had mistakenly sent us a text intended for his girlfriend:

'Hi Babe. Soz. At Dave's. Bit pi**ed. C u SatSun? Miss U xx'

So, the inconsiderate 'so and so' was at a friend's house, and he hadn't even thought to let us know that he was safe. I got up carefully ensuring I didn't wake Phil. The phone flashed again.

'Hi SexyBum. Fancy a romp in the car wiv me again? Luv u Xx'

Oh Lord, should I tell him he's texting the wrong person? Wide awake by now, I went online and checked my symptoms on the internet at one of those very useful health clinic sites. My stomach gurgled and knotted up with pain. The phone flashed.

'SexyBum R u cross wiv ur Hunny Bunny? Txt me bk. Miss u n ur soft boobs xx'

I wiped the message off. I don't want to know about Tiffany's breasts. The knot in my stomach grew. I clicked a few more websites. Another flash and another text message.

'Hunny Bunny is feelin randy –wish u were here to hold me up lol'

Rather embarrassingly my symptoms seemed to indicate I had trapped wind. Great, I'm apparently turning into a flatulent hairy old woman. The phone flashed

‘Hunny bunny needs his sexysexyBum. Dave is sleep n I lonely xXxX’
I switched it off and my stomach growled. He’d probably forget he had sent the texts in the morning. He sounded completely sozzled. Had a glass of red wine to settle my stomach and went back to bed.
Posted by Facing50Blog.com - 2 Comments
SexyFitChick said...Thank goodness I don’t have kids.
Facing 50 said...Some days I wish I didn’t have one too.

Saturday 17th

Finally I’ve managed to produce a header for this blog. It’s taken ages. Tom told me about something paint on the computer and after many attempts I’ve succeeded in producing a picture for the blog. I chose a champagne bottle with a cork flying out of it, and painted the number 50 on the cork. I’m rather proud of it. It is a minor achievement in my otherwise dreary life. I emerged from my room bursting with enthusiasm shouting “ta dah!” Phil looked blankly at me as I bragged about my new found skill and asked why I would want to write a log. I attempted to explain what I was doing but he had resumed reading the business section in *The Telegraph* in a dismissive manner. I finished the bottle of wine from last night in celebration. Well, one or two won’t hurt after all.
Posted by Facing50Blog.com - 0 Comments

Sunday 18th

Over the weekend, the rest of Europe sweltered under the hottest conditions for decades and we stared gloomily out of the window again, watching torrents of rain fall against the panes as it overflowed from the gutter. We even considered lighting the fire to cheer ourselves up. Roll on Birthday trip and, dare I say it, roll on sunshine. I endured the weekly phone call from my mother. The phone rang at 4pm on the dc and I was greeted by the sound of the usual drag on a cigarett and...

"Hello."

It was going to be one of those difficult conversations where I don't know what to say and there are horrible long pauses. I only spoke to her a few days ago. What on Earth wi I manage to say today?

My mother is one of those people who believe that life for me stopped the second I left home. She steadfastly refuses to acknowledge anything I have done since then. As a consequence, conversation is limited to things that happened between 1960 and 1979. It's been difficult between us for decades. We haven't seen each other for years and only dare communicate on the telephone. It's better that way for both o us. Either we are too similar or too different. I can't work it out, but we still manage to rub each other up very easily.

It was the same for Phil and Tom when Tom reached the age of sixteen. He only had to walk into the room and Phil would start bristling with annoyance. It seems to happen at about the time when the child gets taller than the adult. I remember my mother got twitchy when I zoomed past her tin five foot nought inches. She took to wearing the most enormous platform shoes. They were like the ones Elton Johr wore in the film *Tommy.* Goodness knows how she managed to stagger around in them, but she did, and thereafter, when they were no longer fashionable she would wear ginormous heels instead.

A similar thing happened with Tom and Phil. Luckily, Phil didn't take to wearing platform shoes, but he suddenly got prickly and starting pulling himself up to his full height when Tom was around. They are very different. Phil is the tidiest man I know: he puts his socks in colour-coded order in the drawer. Tom throws his in a smelly pile on the floor and under the bed. Phil is very careful with money, having worked so hard for it, and having built up his business from scratch. Tom seems to think it's to be spent as soon as he can get his hands on it, earned, and borrowed or whatever. Phil has a very strong work ethic whereas Tom...well you get the idea.

My mother was particularly ratty today.

"So, the gardener said he couldn't stay as he had a bad back and left me with the 280 plants to put into tubs on my own," she complained taking short angry slurps from a glass in between sentences.

"I didn't know you had a gardener."

"I don't now. I fired him. He was no use. He only managed to pull up a few weeds and make a mess of the vegetable patch. And, he was always taking coffee breaks and scoffing bacon sandwiches."

"Did he bring sandwiches with him for two hours gardening?"

"No, I made them of course. You have to keep the workforce happy. It made him too happy. He spent more time sitting at the table drinking coffee and eating bacon sandwiches than working."

She cursed as her lighter ran out of fuel and her voice faded as she rummaged around looking for another to light her cigarette.

"So the upshot was that I planted all 280 plants myself," she continued, banging down a glass.

The glass was filled again. "It shouldn't have taken him two hours to cut that patch of grass either. I can do it in twenty minutes. I know I'm a bit younger than him, but that's no excuse. If you say you are a gardener, then you should be able to garden."

"Mum, how old is the gardener?"

"Oh, I don't know, about eighty-five, I suppose."

I gave up. She was just going to be hard to please. Letting her drone on about people's standards declining, I put the phone down, got a packet of biscuits out of the cupboard and poured my own glass of wine. She didn't notice I had disappeared for a while.

Eventually, she terminated the one sided conversation with a begrudging, "Well, have a nice birthday. I don't suppose I'll get to talk to you next week."

... As I'll hopefully be hundreds of miles away, and she probably won't phone me while I'm abroad, I guess not.

'Happy Birthday to me.'

Posted by Facing50Blog.com - 0 Comments

Monday 19th

Good news - I can't frown as much. The bad news is that I've started to screw my eyes up from the bottom instead. So that's how it works. You get your wrinkled area treated, which in turn

makes you overuse the muscles in another area, which means you have to get them treated and so on until you have a face full of the stuff and can't employ any facial muscles. I think I'll leave well alone in the future. As they always write on *Facebook* 'Six more sleeps until we go away'. Opened a bottle of Chablis to celebrate and drank the lot after Phil went to bed grumbling about the mole.
Posted by Facing50Blog.com - 2 Comments
SexyFitChick said...Maybe I won't try it then. I might get one of those machines that make your facial muscles work by twitching them with electricity. It'll be better than standing in front of the mirror for hours trying to do facial exercises.
Facing 50 said...That sounds like a better idea. I'm not getting on very well with the buttocks treatment. This stuff always seems to work on celebrities though.

Tuesday 20th

Phil is miserably staring at the computer screen in his office. He hides in there most days. Since he sold his business earlier this year and invested all the money into shares, he has become the most morose man you can imagine. Not only does he miss the cut and thrust of the business world but the shares are performing appallingly. He made the mistake of investing in BP and then of course there was that dreadful Deepwater Horizon disaster in April. Eleven men were killed, oil spilled out into the Gulf of Mexico causing a natural disaster, and BP shares tumbled. They've been tumbling ever since. Phil bought them on his stock brokers' recommendation as they provided a good income, but apparently that is being cut, and there will be no more income from them. The share price has dropped so low that Phil dare not sell them. He keeps hoping they'll recover. It's knocked him badly. His Lloyds' banking shares are also no longer yielding and I think Phil is worried that we'll soon run out of money.

The continued malaise of the Global economy is also doin nothing to improve the picture and, like many other people facing retirement, we simply do not have the income that we thought we would have. Tom returning home has further impinged our expenditure as we have to keep supporting him because he only works three days a week on minimum wage. He can't afford to run his car or to buy food. Mind you, he'd afford quite a lot more if he stopped spending his cash down at the pub or on cigarettes.

This is not how I had envisaged the future. I had hoped tha we would finally be able travel all over the world. I'd looked forward to spending time together doing fun things, taking up hobbies, have adventures and enjoy ourselves. Phil has worked so hard and had so little time to enjoy himself but nov all we do is sit at home, surf the internet and go out once a week to the shops, where we might have a piece of cake between us and a coffee each. Retirement is not for sissies.
Posted by Facing50Blog.com - 0 Comments

Wednesday 21st

At last something nice has happened in my dull little world. It concerns my neighbours and their moggy. When I first saw *Robocat* it was a week after our neighbours had moved in. I was staring out at the front garden which all three properties share, thinking I should clean the footpath when th cat flap next door opened and something tumbled out. It stooc up, shook itself and promptly fell back on its haunches. It looked like it had just been let out of the spin cycle on the washing machine. Its fur stuck up in clumps and its tongue was half sticking out of its mouth like it was blowing a raspberry.

Clearly arthritic, the cat, for indeed that was what it was made its way slowly and robotically across the stretch of garden that could be classified as its own onto my patch where it sat down and looked bewildered.

"What is that?" Tom asked as he joined me at the window.

"I think it's the new neighbours' cat."

"Looks like *Robocat*," he guffawed. And so the name stuck.

After acclimatising itself *Robocat* decided that he would use our part as his toilet area, not his part or indeed the third section which belongs to our other neighbours. From that day on he would stagger out daily, wobble over to our area and do what he needed, generally in the small area where I had carefully planted primulas and daffodils to look attractive. It obviously smelt nice there for him. Of course, I never caught him and therefore couldn't 'shoo' him off. On the rare occasions when I saw him making his approach, I would leap out and he would sit down, tongue between teeth, and pretend he was bird watching or looking at the sky.

My neighbours, who are very sweet, apologised about it profusely and volunteered to clean up the mess but they are elderly themselves and, well, you just have to get along with people especially when you live so closely. *Robocat* was also very old, seventeen in fact. And he was much loved.

"He used to be such a great mouser," said Fred his owner, patting him hard on the head. I thought the cat's head would roll off to reveal a long coiled spring, and prove, in fact, it really was a robot.

"He loves birds," continued Ethel, his mistress.

"Don't all cats love birds?" I replied.

"No, he genuinely loves them. He likes to sit and listen to them and watch them. He's never chased one," she said caressing the top of the cat's patchy head.

"Tyson used to be such a handsome chap."

"Tyson?"

"Tyson, after Mike Tyson, the boxer. He was so big all the other cats were scared of him."

It was difficult to imagine this mangy creature as king of the cats. Tyson looked at me, tongue out, lost in the world of memories.

"He's a blue Persian. Used to have lovely fur but he's like all of us who are getting older. He's losing his looks," chuckled Fred, rubbing his own bald shiny head.

Poor old Tyson. In an effort to be neighbourly I cleared up his mess daily but, as he became older, he developed a penchant for performing his ablutions directly under our post box which is to the side of the front door. I'd go out to fetch the post, unlock the box and hey presto the post would fall ou landing in, well, you can imagine. The cat was becoming more incontinent with age. Yuck! I tried to put him off using the area by leaving prickly mohonia leaves among the flowers, but he scratched them all up along with the flowers and still managed to perform. I read you could get flowers tha were unappealing to cats so I bought some and planted them out. *Robocat* ate them.

"I say," said my other neighbour when we met outside. "I wonder why he only goes to use that part of the garden. He never comes over here," he announced somewhat gleefully. Phil loathed the poor animal.

"If I catch it, I'll boot it up the backside."

Tyson sat by his cat flap listening to the blue tits in the tree with his funny tongue sticking out, oblivious to the wrath next door.

Last week my neighbours had to visit a sick friend in Bristol and asked me to look after Tyson for a couple of days. I was just to give him milk and tuna and phone them if he died. Those really were my instructions. Tyson is now nineteen and creaks appallingly when he walks. They left in the afternoon and I went to check Tyson in the early evening. I unlocked the door and heard sad, mournful mewling.

"Tyson, where are you?"

He wasn't in his basket in the kitchen. I couldn't see him. I followed the noise and there was Tyson stuck on the landing of the stairs. I presume he had gone looking for his owners and having struggled up the stairs, couldn't get down again. He was trembling. I got his blanket and carefully wrapped it around him to carry him down.

"You know me Tyson, I'm the lady from next door. You like my flowers," I crooned. "Now don't worry, they are only away a couple of days."

I sat with him for a while until he looked calmer, then got him some food. I even scratched his head although cats make me sneeze. I checked him again an hour later but he was asleep in his basket.

Next morning he was waiting by the cat flap for me.

"Yowl, yowl, yowl, yowl, yowl," he said falling over in th effort to show me how pleased he was to see me. I picked hin up.

"Morning Tyson. You feeling better? "

"Yowl, yowl, yowl."

"Oh that's good."

I spent an hour sitting with him, talking about the birds in the garden, and stroking him. He tried to wash himself and lurched off the blanket bed. I picked him up. He really was quite a character. I could see the beautiful animal he had once been when I looked into his azure green eyes. He was quite animated and even accompanied me to the door. He creaked outside, one foot at a time, and sat beside a pansy which he sniffed. He looked pleased with life.

"I'll see you later, Tyson. I'm just here if you need me," I shouted as I re-entered our house.

Phil thought I'd lost the plot completely.

"If you are bonding so well with Tyson, maybe you could ask him to stop using our front garden as his toilet," he huffed

That evening I had a long chat to Tyson about our garden. explained that it really was a nuisance and how the flowers were all dying as a consequence. He listened with his tongue out then licked me. It was like being rubbed by an emery board.

"Anyway, Fred and Ethel are back in the morning, nice and early so I won't be coming around again," I explained.

"So, just think about what I said and look after yourself." I stroked him gently behind the ear and sneezed.

Guess what? Yep, since I've looked after Tyson aka *Robocat* there has been no more mess under our letter box or in the flowerbed. I did, however see my other neighbours yesterday looking rather cross and clearing something away into a plastic bag. Tyson was sitting by a large pot of pansies listening to a group of long tailed tits gathered around a seed feeder hanging from a small tree in his part of the garden. Just call me Doctor Dolittle.

I've been trying to guess where I'm going for my birthday. It will be somewhere warm, not too far away as we're only going for a short break and hopefully by the sea. I've been 'Googling' destinations. I've just found an article about Monte Carlo. It sounds very glamorous. I fancy myself on board a yacht with a glass of champagne in my hand. I wonder if Phil has planned a few days in Monte Carlo?
Posted by Facing50Blog.com - 2 Comments

SexyFitChick said...I have a galah. I bet Tyson would love him. He can sort of talk. I've tried to teach him to swear but he can't seem to get the hang of it. I wanted him to protect the house and shout out at burglars. He's too dim for that though. He's quite good at squawking though so that'll do the trick. Nice story.

Facing 50 said...Thank you. Nice to know you are reading. I'd love a parrot. Phil says I sound like one maybe that's why I like them so much. At least it'd be something to chat to!

Thursday 22nd

I spent all morning on the internet and discovered there were approximately 297 021 321 arc second minutes (I'm no sure what an arc second actually is though) remaining until the trip. I really should have done some housework, or something useful, but I was looking for remedies for facial hair and got sidetracked.

That's how it often happens. I'll pop on to check my emails and then just take a quick look at *Facebook* where I'll get carried away playing some stupid pointless game. Time flies when you have to milk your virtual cows, tend to your virtual vegetable patch and collect your virtual crops. I'm avoiding *Facebook* at the moment. That is to say I'm desperately trying to not log onto it. There's something there that I'm not sure I can face at present. I'll be able to handle it better after I've been away.

Normally, after checking my virtual farm, my virtual coffee shop and my virtual tropical island I'll tweet about what I've been doing so my five followers are up to speed with my life. Oh no, I only have four now. @Sellingyougarbage is no longer following me. After being a virtual farmer and a virtual waitress I'll mess about with my blog for a while trying to get the layout right and before I know it, it's time for lunch and I've done nothing in the house.

It's particularly bad if you make a bid on *eBay.* You can't leave the computer alone and keep checking to see if anyone has outbid you. I spent two entire days on it not so long ago trying to buy a Concorde clock for Phil. He kept wondering why I shiftily disappeared into the office every ten minutes, and in the end got annoyed with me and told me to sit still at which point some person outbid me and the clock sold.

I couldn't find a remedy for the hair problem. I don't fancy laser treatment and, quite honestly, after this month's cosmetic procedure it's probably better if I stay away from that sort of thing. It transpires that people use bleach but mine is already blonde. I suppose it'll look better with a suntan.

Posted by Facing50Blog.com - 0 Comments

Friday 23rd

Believe it or not my mother phoned again. I don't know what's got into her. She was chuffed to bits with the DVDs I sent yesterday. During Sunday's phone call at some point between the silences and the grumbling about plants I had managed to get her to talk a little about TV programmes she had been watching. When *Strictly Come Dancing* is on she can talk for an entire hour about how awful the dancers are as she used to dance very well, almost professional level. On Sunday, she mentioned that she had loved the film *Gremlins*.

"I really liked the gremlin that was wearing a Macintosh and 'flashing' and ..."

There was a pause for a choking cough whilst I held the phone away from my ear and grimaced.

"...the one with the ten cigarettes hanging out of its mouth," she wheezed.

I refrained from making any comment.

Yesterday, I was familiarising myself with the latest music releases, in my continued quest to stay on Tom's wavelength. I was browsing through the 'M' section when my eye was drawn to the stack of reduced DVDs on a shelf nearby.

Gremlins was one of them, so I bought it, went to the post office next door to the shop and posted it to her.

Since Dad died, she's been amazing with her ability to become technologically literate. She got herself a mobile phone and can text faster than I can. She bought a GPS so sh wouldn't get lost going to the shops, as she hadn't driven for long while. Last year, she purchased a small DVD player for travelling. When she goes to Cyprus, which she does regularly, she takes it with her to watch a film. It helps take her mind off the fact that she has to sit on the plane for four o five hours without a cigarette. It's lucky they serve alcohol o the flights or she'd be really stuck. So, I thought *Gremlins* would amuse her on her next trip and no doubt all her fellow passengers who'll be able to listen to her noisy laughter followed by a hacking cough for ten minutes. To them I apologise in advance.

Mum was in fine form, having been put in a good mood b my thoughtful action.

"I've just got off the phone to the insurance company. The sent me a renewal and they've put my insurance up from £18 to £350 per annum with a £350 excess."

If anyone from the insurance company saw my mother driving they would probably refuse point blank to insure her.

She continued, "...so I phoned around a few companies an got a cheaper price, £258 with £200 excess. Then I phoned my company back and told them if they didn't match the pric I'd been given, I'd take my business away. I've been with the ten years and I've never had an accident."

She stopped talking to take a sip from a glass. I could hear ice cubes tinkling in it. There was a further pause as she lit a fresh cigarette.

"So, you got it knocked down to £258?" I asked admiring of the fact she was so feisty even at seventy-six years old.

"No, I told them I'd been quoted £169 and they believed me. After all I'm only an old lady. Who wouldn't believe me?" she chuckled wickedly. "Old age has its perks you know."

Posted by Facing50Blog.com - 1 Comment

SexyFitChick said...I love that word chuffed. I'm going to use it today. Maybe I could teach my galah to say it. Your old lady sure has some guts.

Saturday 24th

At last it is almost time to go. My case is bulging. Maybe it is a little overfull for such a short trip. I've squeezed in the lovely new dress that I/Phil bought for me, along with my shorts which now fit after all those sit ups. I still don't know how they managed to get a black spot on them just through trying them on. Why does that always happen with white clothes? My fake tan looks passable for the beach, although I never get it to look like models do. There's always an element of streaking or a patch missed. I've tried on the sarong thing with jewellery and those sandals that tie up your legs in a Grecian fashion and the effect is quite good.

I maybe should have targeted the bingo wings before yesterday. I've had trouble raising my arms today. It was probably a little ambitious to do sixty repetitions with 4lb weights in each hand.

My face doesn't look younger, but there is a certain cheery youthful element in there somewhere and, after I used a proper eyebrow pencil my eyebrows looked quite good. I think I'm ready to face fifty. I wonder if we'll celebrate it on the beach under the stars with the ocean romantically sighing in the background. I set the alarm for 5am but I bet I don't sleep. I'll be far too excited.

Posted by Facing50Blog.com - 2 Comments

PhillyFilly said... Hi I'm your newest follower. I love the way you write about facing up to getting older. I had some work done on my face last year and didn't regret it. Not sure what 'crikey' means. Is it an English expression? I'm from Florida myself. I hope you have a great time and keep posting. Can't wait to hear where you are going.

SexyFitChick said...Don't forget your factor 30! You don't want to look like a walnut do you? Sixty reps was way too ambitious. You should have practised by raising your wine glass a few times to your mouth then swapping hands and raising it again.

Sunday 25th

I've had to log on and blog this as I got up at 1am to repack the wretched suitcase, and now I can't go back to sleep. Just as he was about to go to sleep, Phil told me our holiday destination because he couldn't keep it a secret anymore. No, it's not Monte Carlo or one of the Balearic Islands. We're off to the land of efficiency and nice motor cars. We're going to the city of sausages, pumpernickel bread, large beers and the BMW factory. No wonder he was pleased with himself. It's his perfect holiday. We're going to Munich.

Now, I’ll have to hunt out my umbrella as the forecast is somewhat grim there. I wonder if I’ll look good in Lederhosen?

Posted by Facing50Blog.com - 2 Comments

PhillyFilly said...“Hahaha! You make me laugh.

SexyFitChick said...What a galah!

CHAPTER 2 - AUGUST

Sunday 1st

The fiftieth birthday celebration holiday is definitely over. I'm back to my usual world of gloom and chaos. Luckily, I'd stocked up on red wine before we left. Looks like I need to drown my sorrows again. It rained, of course, but we didn't mind too much. In fact, at one point Phil romantically put his arm around my waist and led me around the puddles, whilst sheltering me with the umbrella. We sat on trams and went all over Munich to avoid getting wet.

The BMW factory tour turned out to be quite entertaining as it happened, although I did keep hoping Phil was going to surprise me at the end of the tour by saying:

"Here's your real present – a lovely BMW 3 series Convertible."

Instead he said:

"Come on we're going to the Hofbrauhaus?"

The Hofbrauhaus turned out to be the main brew house in Munich where you sit on long benches with jolly strangers and drink huge glasses of beer whilst listening to an 'Oompah band'. It was actually quite good fun, and Phil looked the most relaxed I've seen him since he retired. I wish we had more experiences like that.

We went out for dinner on the big day itself. When I was younger I would always get spots just before an important event, a party or going out with a boy for the first time. That stopped as I got older but now whenever I want to look my best, my stomach blows up like a football, no, not the size of a football, more like the size of a stability ball, making it almost impossible to choose an outfit. The only options are stretchy skirts or trousers with elastic waists. Fortunately, I don't go out any more so the problem rarely arises.

It's not just my stomach that refuses to behave as it shoul now even my hair rebels. It used to be sleek and long and blonde. Now, cut in a much shorter style to suit my aging fac it sticks out at weird angles. It won't lie down flat and sleek. Oh no, it sticks up and defies brushing or wetting or spraying with hairspray so now I look remarkably like my mother. On my all important 50th birthday, my hair rebelled due to the rain. My stomach blew up to giant proportions, which I managed only to hide by wearing a long cardigan over the to of my new dress, somewhat spoiling the effect. Still, Phil didn't mind. He was actually enjoying himself.

Celebrations now over, I returned home a fifty year old woman. On the return journey I was overwhelmed with anxieties about aging which now displaced the excitement of going away. Phil was gazing mournfully out of the window. He had lost all interest in me again. I expect he was thinking about his shares. I was not looking forward to coming back home. Coming back to reality is always hard after a nice trip, even a short one. Coming back to reality when it is as dull as mine is even worse. We were greeted at the airport by Tom who had been under instructions to meet us.

"Hope you had a good time."

He gave me a quick peck on the cheek and managed to avoid my gaze.

I've been Tom's mother for over twenty years and you jus know when something is being hidden from you. Children don't realise that we truly have a sixth sense about things, an all the way home Tom was, as far as I was concerned, behaving shiftily. For one thing he talked nonstop about work. The fact he was speaking at all was in itself bizarre, as we normally have to take the lead in any conversation, cajoling him into monosyllabic responses.

I soon found out why. The back door was almost off its hinges although someone had attempted to prop it back up with large lumps of *Blu-Tack*. The kitchen floor was horribly sticky. Several of our bottles of wine had mysteriously disappeared and there were some cigarette burns on the hall carpet. During our absence he had managed to hold a party, which I later discovered had lasted several days.

His mates had disturbed our aging next door neighbours by banging loudly on the dustbins, which were lined up tidily for collection outside, as if they were drums until someone from over the road had yelled at them to be quiet. I had to go around to everyone and apologise. Pity he wasn't here. I'd have liked to have banged on his head like a drum.

Before we had left for our short break I had taken Tom to one side and showed him an article about a girl who had held a party at her parent's house while they were on holiday. She had posted the event on *Facebook*. Hundreds of people she didn't know had turned up and the house had been completely ransacked. I had voiced my concerns and extracted a promise from him that he would look after the house and invite no guests or friends over in our absence. He had looked at me wide eyed with innocence and said

"Trust me; I'll look after everything for you."

He knew he had overstepped the mark this time, but he disappeared as soon as he dropped us off. One minute he was there the next he had shot off at speed. Obviously, he hopes that by the next time we see him we'll have calmed down and won't be so mad at him. I'm not sure if that will be the case.

Phil is the most furious I'd ever known. Looks like I'm going to have to placate him, but I fear it'll take a long time. I tried to go onto some websites dealing with teenage problems whilst Phil marched up and down the house examining it for further damage, but it seems that really Tom should have gone through this teenage strop, years ago. He is nearly twenty-one after all.

I drew a blank so tried leaving a message about what to do on *Twitter* but no response as yet. Phil is so angry he refuses to even discuss it with me. If I so much as mutter the name Tom, he glowers at me as if all of this is my fault. So, at the moment, it is like living in a library where no one is allowed to speak. Every time you open your mouth, someone stares daggers at you. Good thing I have the internet, and a large bottle of Chianti.

Posted by Facing50Blog.com - 1 Comment

Fairie Queene said..... Give him a good hiding. Tom, I mean, not Phil, although he could probably do with a telling off too. It never did me any harm. Just do what Tom is doing and wait for Phil to calm down. It always worked when I rowed with my boyfriend. He would sulk for days and I would leave him alone until he decided to behave again. By the way, glad you had a good time. I'm your latest follower.

Tuesday 3rd

After the expenditure last month and now the repairs we'll have to make to the door, carpet and the broken window we discovered after Tom disappeared to his girlfriend's house for three days, it is time to retighten our belts. Phil has been most verbose about this and has been walking around the house in the dark at night time so as not to use electricity. He banged into the bedroom door tonight and swore loudly. None of this is helping his mood to improve. There are a few reasons, other than Tom and the mole, as to why he has become annoyed again so rapidly.

We've spent the last six months going completely square-eyed examining every estate agent's website possible looking for a new home. Living beside, what has become over the years a very busy A road is just horrendous. Neither of us sleep properly any more as heavy goods vehicles hurtle through the village all flipping night As they come past our house, they rattle over the ever-deteriorating road surface, vibrating the house and disturbing our light sleep. Of course, we've complained to the Council but, since the whole of the UK seems to need funding for road repair, there are 'insufficient resources' for our road.

We have tried various remedies including earplugs. You have to roll them quickly and firmly between your fingers and ram them into your ear before they start to expand. That takes several efforts. You end up shouting at each other because you can't hear each other and what a passion killer – you look like you have orange earwax sticking out of your 'lugs'. I tried some herbal pills - effective but addictive and they also leave you feeling a bit hung over and bottles of red wine (same result as herbal tablets plus stained lips) Eventually, we decided it was probably time to move. We looked at hundreds of properties on the internet and by employing our demanding criteria: must have garage, not be next to any road, be detached, and must have a nice aspect, we managed to narrow the choice down to only six. Three of them were somewhere in The Cotswolds, at places we've never even visited.

Phil was a complete pain at the viewings even though I really liked two of the houses. One was an ideal chocolate bo thatched cottage. He vetoed them all, coming up with pathetic reasons as to why he didn't like them: they were too big, not big enough, overlooked, too isolated, too square, yes I know, even I couldn't work that logic out -too expensive, much too expensive, not light enough and so on. He walked around eac property determined to hate it. He wore his special cantankerous look normally reserved for car salesmen, financial advisors, and estate agents who he calls shafters and who he believes don't work hard enough for their money. He's very critical of double-barrelled named salespeople. Especially after one incident, when he asked to speak to the agent who was handling the sale of a house that interested us.

"I'm sorry but Simon Cauliflowerears-Rhubarb(Rhubarb) is too busy on his very important 'Raspberry' to speak to 'Rif Raff' like you," he mimicked after the conversation and let out his own accompanying raspberry which resulted in me making all further phone calls to agents.

Personally, I'd have thought putting up with fractious Phil for half an hour was enough to guarantee a bonus at the end o the month, let alone their wages. Phil could not be swayed at all, even though in the main it had been his idea to move. He declared that he actually liked our house and if it weren't so noisy he wouldn't consider moving. I think that he suddenly realised that it would be very expensive to move and got cold feet, but I wouldn't dare tell him that. Now he has come up with his own solution to the noise problem: special secondary glazing.

I let him sort it out and, like a man on a major mission; he researched for days until he found just the right company. Based in the South, they have fantastic testimonials from major banks, universities and important institutions. They weren't exactly ordinary secondary glazing merchants for houses. He phoned them and they got a sub-contractor from Chester to telephone him as we live out of their patch. In order to get a quotation Phil had to measure all the windows which proved to be rather entertaining. I was pretending to be far too busy in the office to assist him but was listening to him with my door slightly ajar. There was a fair bit of expletive and yelping as he tried to juggle the phone to read out measurements from our rather ancient metal retractable tape measure which retracts brutally and without warning. Measurements finally given and sucking his sore thumb he came to tell me the good news looking really rather delighted with himself.

"There that will sort us out. They'll be no more noise and I'm sure the men will do an excellent job of putting in the secondary glazing. They have extraordinarily good testimonials from clients who recommend them."

About an hour later I heard an impressive groan as he logged on to his e-mails. The quote had come: £10.000.00 plus VAT. It looks like we are going to have to try the earplugs again.

Posted by Facing50Blog.com - 2 Comments

Fairie Queene said... Typical man. You should have made him move. I love new houses. Getting new curtains and carpets to match and choosing fabric is such fun. I love decorating.
SexyFitChick said...Can't you use your feminine charms to get your own way? That's what I resort to. Oh sorry, I forgot, this is Phil you are talking about!

Friday 6th

Since we got back I've had a continual run of bad headaches, no doubt brought about by the distinctly awful atmosphere every time Tom turns up, and walks into the same room as Phil. Tom has kept out of the way and has been staying at Dave's, or his girlfriend's house, regularly. He appears to think everything is back to normal after the episode with the party. I have been feeling quite annoyed the last couple of days though, especially as I can't find my headache pills. I can take any other sort of pain but not headaches. They make me feel awful. If I don't stop the headaches in time I get a continuous migraine for days.

I'm not a wimp. I spent a lot of my youth in hospital being attacked by needles and suffering tortures thought up by doctors and surgeons. I was on traction for thirteen weeks when I was seventeen years old. A year later and after undergoing two major operations, I spent six months in a plaster of Paris cast covering my body from my neck to my hips looking like a huge tortoise. Then, I got some giant screws attached to my decaying spine and kept setting off scanning machines at airports and, worse still, at the library where they have metal tabs in all the reference books to stop people stealing them. I would get to the exit machine, set it off and a huge guard would shake me down to ensure I hadn't stuffed a copy of the Encyclopaedia Britannica down my jumper.

As a consequence, I can abide most pain, but I simply can't endure headaches. My stash of pills has disappeared from the bathroom cabinet so I highly suspect that bloody Tom has used them all to get over his far-too frequent hangovers. I'll have to drive ten miles to town and buy some more and that is a complete fag.

Posted by Facing50Blog.com - 1 Comment

SexyFitChick said... I know a good cure for headaches!

Tuesday 9th

So far this is turning into a month of annoying pains. Phil and I had just sat down for afternoon tea on Sunday. This is the only part of the weekend that Phil enjoys. He loves desserts and cakes and on a Sunday he is allowed a large slice of a cake of his choice. For a short while he is almost content. The house phone rang just as we sat down and Phil groaned.

"It can't be her; it's only 3.30pm."

He was, of course, referring to my mother, who as I mentioned last month, always phones on a Sunday between four and five o'clock and will be on the phone for fifty-nine minutes and fifty-nine seconds exactly. She has recently signed up to a tariff offering her one hour's free talk time on a Sunday.

If I don't answer the phone immediately I get into trouble. The longer I leave it to ring, the worse the greeting will be. If I leave it too long I'll be greeted with,

"Oh you are actually there at last are you?"
This will be followed by a painful silence while I try to think of a plausible reason as to why I haven't picked up when I know she usually phones at that time. Having got my excuse out she'll say "Hmmm," in a manner that tells me she doesn't believe a word I've said and the conversation will be an icy one.

If I answer almost immediately, I'll get a choice of greeting from 'Hallo Pet.' Hailing from the North, this regional greeting usually indicates a nostalgic mood so I know we'll be talking about the past. 'Hello Sweetheart,' usually indicates she has had too much to drink. 'Oh, hello,' reveals her to be in a bad mood. The worst category of greeting is 'Oh you're still alive then.' This is usually reserved for when I've avoided her calls for two weeks. The greeting is an important indicator of the tone of the conversation and I can then try to placate or cheer up as required.

Such was the case this particular afternoon.

"Hello Sweetheart."

Oh bugger! That means the conversation can go in any direction depending on how much alcohol she's consumed.

"I thought I'd phone."

There was a long pause while she took a lengthy drag on the ever present fag. Phil got up in disgust and went outside.

"Hi Mum."

There was no point in saying anything further. I just let her ramble on for a while and interjected with "Oh, really?" and the odd "Uh- huh."

"Well..." she finally growled after some monologue about the weather and how Simon Cowell was an absolute cad on

Britain's got Talent. She might only be five foot high (and about five foot wide at the moment) but she terrifies most people and certainly still terrifies me. My Dad was away a lot when I was young so it was like being brought up by a single parent. Boy did she rule me with a rod of iron. Even now I'm frightened of upsetting her and she can still push all those buttons. A fifty-year old woman I may be, but put me in front of my mother and I'm fifteen years old again. She still treats me as if I'm fifteen too, which makes it even more difficult.

"...Well?" she growled again. "What have you been up to?" she demanded, which was a cue for me to say,

"Oh, nothing much."

Thus, allowing her to carry on with her diatribe against Simon Cowell - poor man. Today, however, because I was still upset about Tom and the lack of headache tablets which resulted in the aforementioned migraine I casually mentioned Tom's thoughtlessness, untidiness and general bad attitude.

"Ha!" she exclaimed. "You were just the same when you were younger."

I was dumbfounded.

"No, I wasn't," I argued.

"Oh yes you were."

What was this - a pantomime?

"You always left your room in a mess and you never let me know when you would be back."

"Mum, I was never allowed to go out."

The phone crackled. A glass thumped back down on the small hall table. There was a long inhalation. She exhaled. I imagined the cloud of smoke which would be enveloping her. It is absolutely true to say that I rarely went out alone. When I was eleven, I went to a Girl Guide camp at the other end of the town where we lived. I couldn't sleep for days beforehan due to excitement. It was my first time away from home and was going to spend a week under canvas with other girls my age. My bag was packed four weeks before the camp began. arrived at the camp at ten in the morning and by four in the afternoon my mother had turned up to make sure I had washed properly and tidied my clothes away in the tent. She told me off for having dirty feet.

"You look like a member of the Black Foot Tribe," she announced loudly making everyone near me hoot with laughter and immediately they started to make fun of me. My mother then proceeded to visit every day to make sure I was okay and hadn't caught dengue fever. The annoying thing wa that all the girls really liked her.

She would turn up in her glamorous fake fur coat with a cigarette in a holder looking like a film star and the girls would cluster around her while she would regale them with stories of what a dreadful child I had been, making them roar with laughter about how clumsy I was and so on. How many girls have been on a camp where their own mother, not only turned up every day, but stayed to sit around the camp fire, and sing *Ging Gang Goolie*? I was dragged back from my musings by the sound of a hacking cough.

"Anyway," she continued. "Your room was very untidy. Your clothes were always thrown on the floor and I always tidied them up."

And so the conversation went on. One hour and fifty-nine minutes later I was drained. I'd been chastised for all my teenage inadequacies and obviously Tom has clearly inherite all my faults. I was accused of having been lazy and selfish at that age. Well, Tom didn't get his laziness from his father, that is true. As I've said before, Phil is the tidiest man I know, probably the tidiest on the planet, with maybe the exception of James May from *Top Gear*. If truth be told I have only become neat since I've known Phil and even now my wardrobe frequently needs tidying as things keep mysteriously falling on the floor.

I decided to try even harder with Tom. That proved to be incredibly difficult as Tom headed straight out again after returning from his girlfriend's house, stopping only to get changed and pong the house out with his aftershave. To cap it all, he managed to block the toilet the following morning which promptly overflowed onto the bathroom carpet, and because he didn't want to be late for work, left his father and me to clear it all up and unblock it. Phil is furious. No, Phil is beyond furious, and nothing I can say or do placates him.
Posted by Facing50Blog.com - 3 Comments

Faerie Queene said... Your mother sounds brilliant fun. I'd love to meet her.

SexyFitChick said... Singing *Ging Gang Goolie* around a camp fire. Now that takes me back to my camping days. We didn't sing around a fire though. I'd have been about seventeen. I'll leave it up to your imagination as to what we were doing. Hope Phil calms down soon. He'll pop with annoyance. That'd solve your problems.

Facing 50 said...FQ - Everyone seems to like my mother. I wish she liked me a bit more. SFC - I can guess what you were up to. I haven't got amnesia just yet, although sex is fast becoming a distant memory these days.

Thursday 12th

We're both mentally exhausted. I can no longer mediate between the warring parties. I don't even remember when the warring started. I remember one day everything was fine and the next minute they were at each other. Probably, as I mentioned before, about the time that not only did Tom reach six foot tall, and for the first time started to tower over his father, but also got very broad chested. He would walk into the room and fill it up while both Phil and I would seem to shrink and diminish in stature. It was almost like watching rutting stags as each vied for territorial rights. Phil considers himself the Master of the House and I think he felt that role was being undermined by the suddenly stroppy and unapproachable Tom.

We were really pleased when he went to university as it gave us all breathing space. For Tom it provided the tantalizing taste of freedom and independence, so now he's unwilling to abide by rules. He wants to be independent again and Phil, well Phil wants the rules of the house to apply. That includes looking after the home he has provided, and respecting those who have provided it. I've tried explaining Tom's point of view to Phil and vice versa but although they nod and even sometimes agree with me, if you put them together in the same room then you need to dive for cover very quickly indeed. So when Phil was in an absolute horror of a mood this evening. When Tom returned from work I tried to warn him by indicating with my head like a mad nodding dog but he breezed past me.

“Evening Papa,” he said, in what he intends to be an affectionate tone, but what actually comes across as patronising. Suddenly, I wished we still back in the days when Tom was just a young boy. Now, I must have some headache pills somewhere. Failing that, I know I have one last bottle of Chianti in the back of one of the kitchen cupboards.
Posted by Facing50Blog.com - 0 Comments

Monday 16th

I’ve had to blog this moment as I am somewhat confused by it. Something peculiar occurred today. Phil and I always go to town on a Monday for a coffee and cake (Phil’s other weekly treat- he does seem to be obsessed with cake at the moment) and a couple of hours separation time (my treat). The town is large enough, and our shopping interests diverse enough, for us to manage to not see each other after we agree on a time to meet outside the department store. I will stand at the appointed time, and Phil will invariably be late, leaving it just to the last minute of the car park ticket running out, so I’ll have to jog up the stairs to make sure we don’t pay for the next hour.

Once we’ve had our cake, I’ll head in the direction of my favourite shop and check out the fashion there, or head off to the music shop, where I will acquaint myself with the latest films, actors, artists and music so I don’t seem to be such an old Fuddy Duddy to my son.

It started when Tom was younger. In fear of having nothing at all in common as he got older and needing some common point of interest I made an effort to ‘gen up’ on the sort of music he liked. I prided myself on knowing all the latest releases and which artist was 'flavour of the month'. I even liked some of the noise that escaped from his room so much that I bought CDs for myself to put on my personal stereo player, and to this day I like 'The Killers', 'Elbow' and 'Muse'.

One day I was attempting to retrieve some washing from Tom's bedroom floor and he had something recognisable on his stereo. It sounded like Malcolm McClaren's *Buffalo Gals.* I even
knew the lyrics and was singing (badly) along as I tried to take my mind off the disgusting aroma that was permeating the room. Tom was rifling through some boxes and looked up in surprise.

"You know this?" he asked suspiciously.

"Oh yes," I replied, happy to be considered hip for a while. "I like this one."

"It's by Eminem," he continued.

"It's very good," I repeated having no idea who, or what, Eminem was. I was more enthralled with my new Cool Mother status that I had awarded myself. My son actually thought I was with it. What a sense of achievement.

Well, it backfired spectacularly at Christmas. Tom bought me the latest Eminem album. I tried to look suitably delighted to receive it as I unwrapped it. After all, he had made an effort to buy me something he thought I would appreciate. Phil looked at me with a bit of a gleam in his eyes. He knows when I'm faking and picked up on my discomfort.

"Oh great," I enthused. "It's an Eminem CD. It's exactly what I wanted."

I hugged Tom tightly, pleased that he had attempted to be so thoughtful. No one had picked up on my deception, or so I thought, until he suggested I play the CD there and then and Phil joined in.

"Yes, come on," cajoled Phil. "You love *M&Ms*." (The idiot.)

He knew full well that he was putting me on the spot. The CD was inserted and Phil desperately tried to keep a straight face while I nodded my head along to the latest Slim Shady rap. When it got to the bit about 'humping a moose' and 'my bum is on your lips', I really didn't know what to do. I could hardly sing along. Phil was enjoying himself thoroughly by now, which is in itself a miracle given he hates Christmas, but, after I gave him a pleading look, he told Tom to turn it down a bit. Luckily, Tom was distracted by a text and went off to phone his girlfriend and the CD was turned off.

Today, I had it all planned: first a quick stop off to the ladies powder room and then off to the department store for a quick try on of the latest fashions. I have, in recent years, become one of those people who miraculously puts on a cloak of invisibility when out. Younger women manage to run pushchairs over my feet, or walk right into me, without seeing me. Gangs of teenagers, oblivious to my approach, walk straight at me until I dive for cover in a doorway. Doors are banged shut in my face. Shop assistants don't see me waiting patiently for them to finish their chat about their hair or nails. I frequently get sales assistants saying, "Sorry to have kept you waiting," as if just noticing me for the first time. I don't really object to this though. I quite like my cloak of invisibility. It enables me to spend lots of time looking at things, or trying out makeup, without someone rushing up to see if they can help. I bet I could walk out of a shop with a whole pile of stolen goods in my arms, and a giant striped lampshade on my head, and no one would notice me. Today, however, a spotlight appeared above my head and a loud voice announced my presence to the entire world.

I was just on my way from the toilets through the children's wear department towards the stairs when I noticed a furry *Jemima Puddleduck* (the character from Beatrix Potter's books). I stopped to pick it up. Before Tom was even born Phil and I had purchased a toy duck like this. Up to that moment, I had flatly refused to buy anything for the baby in case it invited bad luck, so we had no cot for him to sleep in, no clothes, no equipment, in fact; nothing. One particular day however, we had been together in Sheffield, and walking han in hand, because in those days we were young and still madly keen on each other, we had seen a *Jemima* duck that played a lullaby. We looked at each other. An unspoken thought passe between us, and instantly, we knew we had to get it for the little life that was inside me.

As I reflected on that moment, without any warning whatsoever, a huge wave of nostalgia hit me. Tears welled and broke the banks of my eyes. They would not stop. They cascaded down my face. I had no control. I was aghast. I couldn't comprehend what was happening. I am not an emotional person. Life is just a huge joke to me; to be taken with a large pinch of salt, a slice of lime and a shot of tequila. But today, holding a yellow toy duck, in the middle of the department store I looked like I had suffered a tragedy. Wors still, people were beginning to notice me. There was a genera uncomfortable air as expectant mothers stopped and stared at me. Where was Harry Potter when you needed him? One anxious elderly lady came up to me.

"Are you alright dear?"

"Yes, thank you. Just something in my eye," I sobbed, and headed as quickly as I could, back to the toilets.

I stayed there for the majority of the two hours we had allocated ourselves. Finally, I regained my composure and stopped the leaking tears from flowing. I had a twenty minute wait while the eyes lost their puffy red look and so played games on my mobile in the toilet cubicle. I made my way back downstairs to wait for Phil. Sure enough, he was late. I checked my watch. Time was about to run out on our car park ticket. Then I saw him grumpily approaching, carrying what looked suspiciously like a supermarket carrier bag, no doubt containing some cake for afternoon tea. I watched him approach with affection. Just as he was at the entrance to the store I hugged him.

"What's that for?" he moaned.

"Oh, no particular reason. Just because I can," I replied and half jogged towards the stairs to get the ticket stamped before our time elapsed.

Posted by Facing50Blog.com - 2 Comments

FaerieQueene said...Oh I almost cried when I read this. Loved Beatrix Potter stories when I was younger. My boyfriend bought me a Peter Rabbit. It still sits on my pillow.

SexyFitChick said...Sounds like you need a glass of my favourite Shiraz. It was just a blip. You'll be back on form tomorrow.

Wednesday 18th

The tearful episode on Monday was somewhat explained last night. I was asleep dreaming of being on a warm beach. The sun was beating down and I was getting very warm. I woke up with a jump. I was actually pretty hot. It was a cool August evening and I am notoriously freezing cold at all times. Phil hates my freezing cold feet and freezing cold hands. When people shake my hand they always remark abou how cold they are. I even have to wear two or three layers in summer, but tonight I was warm. No, I was hot. Then it hit me. The average age of menopause is fifty-two. I could be starting to go through it; the menopause. Was this a hot flush

Well, if was a hot flush, then I didn't know what all the fuss is about. It was nice to be warm for a change. The temperature went up another notch. I was a little uncomfortable. It went up again. I felt light-headed. It was happening again. I kicked off the bedcovers. I was still too hc and, yes, starting to sweat. This was one of those times when wish I had some female friends to talk to instead of an emotionally stunted husband. I couldn't discuss this with him I only have to say time of the month and he scurries off, so if he thinks he has a menopausal wife with lunatic hormones, he'll head for the hills. I'll have to check it out on the net. I'll keep quiet about it. With a bit of luck he won't notice.

Posted by Facing50Blog.com - 2 Comments

SexyFitChick said... Welcome to the club. It's all downhill from here.

PhillyFilly said... See a doctor. I think you had a night sweat, dear. We American women experience hot 'flashes' at this time of our lives. I guess they are the same as a hot flush. I now have some hormone replacement patches and I feel so much better.

Saturday 21st

Tom came home with his girlfriend Tiffany tonight. Normally, they just call 'hello' and race off giggling to his room but I noticed Tiffany was carrying a very smart small suitcase.

"Er, is it okay if Tiffany, like, uhm, stays the night?"

What could I say? Tom had spent a year at University and I'm sure he had girlfriends there, although he appears to have spent so much time drinking there that he maybe didn't have time for relationships. I know that I would never have dreamed of asking my parents if a boy could stay the night when I was his age, but this is a different era. I bet that when Tom stays at the Henderson-Smythe mansion he doesn't spend the night in the guest room as Mr Henderson-Smythe presumes. Phil obviously had similar concerns and looked like he was about to voice his protest, but I got in first. After all, you don't want your son to lose face in front of his girlfriend, and she clearly had permission to stay out.

"Yes, no problem. I'll come and get some clean towels for Tiffany."

I headed off to find my best towels and to make sure the bathroom was clean and hadn't been left in a foul state by Tom. Tom and Tiffany raced off as usual, him chasing her up the stairs and her squealing like a child. Phil rolled his eyes.

"Great, now we have two of them to deal with."

About an hour later the thumping bass tones of one of Tom's CDs resonating from the bedroom amplified as he opened his door and thundered downstairs with Tiffany now wearing one of his hooded tops. It looked like a short dress on her revealing long blemish free coltish legs. Her face glowed and she smiled shyly.

"Just getting Tiffany some food," he announced. He's somewhat of a stranger to the kitchen when it comes to cooking, so loud banging and crashing ensued, as he galumphed around the kitchen, whacking plates onto the tops and banging every cupboard door, looking for ingredients to make sandwiches. Phil could stand it no longer, threw down the television remote control and without a word, disappeared to the bedroom.

"Dad gone?" enquired Tom almost immediately, his mouth full of sandwich, other hand clutching Tiffany's while she looked up at him in an adoring fashion.

"Yes, he's not feeling too good," I declared apologetically.

"Not to worry – we're off now. Just come to say bye. We'll see you later or probably in the morning."
I smiled at Tiffany.

"Sorry about Tom's Dad. He's a bit out of sorts."
"No probs. My Dad's like that a lot too. It's an age thing."

I sat for a while reflecting on how I too had once looked like Tiffany. I had possessed a slim figure and blemish free legs, not like now, where one or two varicose veins were starting to appear. I too had had long hair and bright eyes. I don't remember when I started to change, but it seems to have happened very rapidly. Good thing my eyes are so bad because at least I'm unaware of some of it. I couldn't help but feel envious of the gorgeous Tiffany and her youth. I was jealous too of the effect she had on Tom. Phil hadn't looked at me the same way Tom did Tiffany for years, even two decades now, and I began to feel miserably old. To cheer myself up after cleaning up the explosion of mess in the kitchen I switched on the computer as there was nothing worth watching on television.

I'd been avoiding this for over a month. I knew I shouldn't do it but well, I'm just so fed up with everything in my life at the moment. I logged onto my *Facebook* page and as I clicked on the little icon at the top I felt that same heady rush that I'd experienced the first time I read it:

'Friend Request – Todd Bradshaw'

I first met Todd in the romantic Moroccan city of Casablanca. Technically, I had encountered him before that; at the airport where we all had gathered for the flight to Rabat. There were twenty of us all assigned to various schools in Morocco as part of a large project to introduce English into the Moroccan curriculum. Recruited from all over the UK none of us had met before this day and were to be sent all over Morocco.

You couldn't miss Todd. He stood out from the group of chattering teachers gathered around the board which displayed the name of the company we were to work for. He was wearing a pair of tight jeans and a white shirt hinting at a perfect physique. Sunshades were perched on his golden head and he was smiling confidently. He had a smile that would make you succumb to absolutely anything he asked. I felt weak-kneed the first time I saw him. I joined the group and stood nervously hoping I hadn't forgotten something important for the next two years of my life.

When he eventually spoke to me, asking where I was to be working, I was completely tongue-tied. I burbled incomprehensible gibberish. I was hardly a good advertisement for a teacher of English. He smiled again kindly and asked me if I would do him a favour. I nodded willingly. Thanking me and gracing me with another heart stopping smile he went off to the cafe for a coffee with another colleague, a striking girl who had legs that went up to her armpits, leaving me to look after his suitcase.

Although we were both stationed in Casablanca, it took one drunken night at an ex-pat party before we really got to know each other. He'd been coming out of the bathroom as I was trying to go in. I lurched into him against his well-toned body. Twenty minutes later, someone banged on the locked bathroom door in frustration and we emerged, hand in hand, as a couple.

It was the most exhilarating sixteen months of my young life. We had picnics on a deserted sandy beach at weekends; sat on the balcony overlooking the sea watching the magnificent purple sunsets and then the sparkling stars. We caught a coach to Ceuta in the North, travelling through the Rif Mountains and Todd bought an old car. We then travelled the length and breadth of Morocco in our vacations.

We journeyed South through the Atlas Mountains during our vacation period where we watched goats climbing Argan trees, ending up at the edge of the Sahara desert, where we rode camels and climbed sand dunes to watch the sunrise together. We stayed in riads in Marrakesh and mingled with the exotic sounds and sights on the Place Djemaa el Fna. Gradually, I fell deeper and deeper in love. Todd was a born adventurer. With him by my side I felt I could conquer the world. He had so many plans and places he wanted to explore. We were going to have the time of our lives.

The contract in Morocco ended and Todd was offered a fabulous job in Kuwait but I couldn't go with him as there were very strict employment rules about women in such a devout Muslim country. We needed two wages to fulfil our plans and dreams of travelling and opening a language school in Turkey, so I took a job in a private school in the UK, and Todd headed east. I can recall that last parting to this day; the passion that enveloped us as we clung to each other at Heathrow before he slipped away through the gate and away forever.

He was due back at Christmas. We spoke every week on the phone. I wrote to him every day. The week before Christmas he announced he couldn't get time off as it wasn't a recognised festival by Muslims. I couldn't get a flight out as all the seats had gone by then. The phone calls lessened and he didn't reply to my letters. Eventually, he confessed that he was seeing someone else there, citing loneliness as the reason they had been drawn together. I stopped writing. My heart shattered into a million pieces and in spite of him making several efforts later to beg forgiveness and to ask me to have him back, I couldn't get over his deception. Two years after the event I met Phil. He was solid, dependable and made me laugh. He was right for me and we got married.

So here he was again, back in my life. Todd Bradshaw. Without any further consideration I pressed 'Confirm' and was directed to his *wall*. I clicked on his photographs and there he was muscular, smiling, suntanned, and just as I remembered him. He'd hardly aged. He'd posted quite a few photographs of him on his travels: Hanoi, Bangkok, him cycling The Great Wall of China. There was one of him in hi diving kit having passed his PADI exams. I clicked on anoth one of him waving a trophy in the air, smiling that smile I knew so well. And finally, there was a wonderful photograph taken at dawn of him and a cattle dog running along a golden beach. He'd posted some great status too: 'Life begins at 50' 'Just won my first veteran's race – I was the youngest there' 'Blown away by the art at the Guggenheim today' 'Cried at *The Deer Hunter'*.

Like me, he was a film buff. We used to go to the cinema every week and watched all the latest releases in both English and French. We sat snuggled against each other in the darkness of the cinema, clutching hands and living each moment of the film as one. After the show we would stay up late into the night discussing it, reliving the best bits and planning what we would see the following week.

Phil hates films unless they are *James Bond* films. And even then, he only likes only the ones where Roger Moore plays the character James Bond; not Daniel Craig. He doesn't approve of Daniel's hair colour, calling him James Blonde. The last film we watched together at the cinema was *Fatal Attraction*, a 1987 film with Glenn Close and Michael Douglas, about a married man's steamy affair and how it comes back to haunt him. Phil fell asleep during the sex scene on the sink and snored throughout the film.

'Lovely photos' I wrote and pressed 'send'.

Posted by Facing50Blog.com - 1 Comment

SexyFitChick said... Quite right too – go for it girl.

Sunday22nd

My laptop has been beckoning me all morning but I didn't dare log on. I'm torn between wanting to hear from Todd, and wishing I hadn't sent that reply. I tried to distract myself by doing some cleaning, but I didn't want to start up the vacuum cleaner in case I disturbed Tom and his girlfriend, who stayed in bed most of the day. Phil went outside and cleaned his car to stop himself from yelling at them to get up. Then, he cleaned Tom's car which made him even more irritable. I took him a coffee and a bourbon biscuit.

"Lazy little sod," he grumbled, meticulously leathering the car dry. "I bet he hasn't even got up yet."

"Why didn't you just leave it for him to do?"

"Because it would never get done. It would be permanently filthy. I know it's not brand new but that doesn't mean it shouldn't be looked after. I can't abide filthy cars. He's an ungrateful monster. If my parents had been kind enough to buy me a car at his age, I would have made sure it was looked after. He takes everything for granted. I should make him catch the bus to work and sell this. We could do with the money."

I didn't think we were so badly off that we needed the few hundred pounds that Tom's second-hand car would fetch. I guess I'm going to have to be more cautious with regard to spending now and that will be difficult, after all, aren't we women programmed to shop? I can't go into town without wanting to buy something, not necessarily even for me. My mother does that too. She was rather excited this afternoon about a new supermarket that's just opened up near her.

"I've just returned from the new store. It's vast. They gave each customer a small map with all the aisles labelled so you could find your way around. The assistants are all on roller skates and help you when you get lost. It's quite good fun. They have some fantastic reductions. I got some trousers for two pounds, honestly two pounds, can you believe it, two pounds?" she enthused.

It was the most excited I'd heard her for a while.

"They've got dresses for five pounds as well. Those wide skirted ones. The material alone would cost that. I don't know how they do it."

I refrained from discussing child labour in foreign countries. The conversation was punctuated by the sound of a lighter igniting a cigarette.

"Were you tempted to buy a dress then?"

"Oh yes, I bought six and four pairs of trousers, I thought they'd look good when I go on holiday."

See all women of all ages love a bargain and love shopping.

"You are off to Cyprus again, are you?"

Judging by the tinkling ice cubes I could hear, I would say she was on whisky and water.

"I'm going tomorrow, for two months. I'm ready for a trip. It's a bit boring here. Some of my friends are going out there for their annual holidays now, so I thought I'd meet up with them. Might be fun."

Great, no hour long calls for two entire months.

After Dad passed away, Mum was invited by friends to go and spend a few weeks with them in Cyprus. While she was there she bought herself a holiday flat. It isn't a little flat in a retirement block of ex-pats who play bridge every night, as you might expect, but located in the heart of Larnaca. It is not a conventional choice for a widow. The cranky lift often breaks down. Rusting bicycles adorn the stairwells waiting to trip you up. Washing permanently hangs on all the balconies. Strange aromas leak out into the streets. Greek Cypriots yell constantly at each other from one balcony to another. Each morning, the cars outside cough into life loudly, and people scream off on noisy mopeds racing to get to work. It's like living on a foreign council estate, and Mum adores it. She loved the authenticity of the place the first time she went there and so bought the flat with a view to spending half the year there, rather than be stuck in the UK especially over the cold gloomy winters.

Credit where it's due, my mother has become an absolute hit in that particular area of Cyprus. Locals in the community adore her. She gets invites to their homes, or goes out to restaurants to share in big family celebratory meals. She has people dropping in all the time, sometimes even bringing local dishes for her to reheat in her microwave. She has even been invited to their children's birthday parties. She complained about the last one she went to though. It was for a three-year-old and was full of old Greek ladies, dressed in black, sitting around in a circle, and worse still, there was no alcohol at all. Normally, she has a fabulous time each time she goes to Cyprus rarely staying indoors.

I don't know why she doesn't just live there full-time. It is such a far cry from the lonely life she has back home where she only ever sees the next door neighbour, or maybe the window cleaner. She has little to occupy her here in the UK. She only ever seems to entertain herself by doing old

crossword puzzles, or watching the TV, that is when she isn'
in the garden complaining about having to maintain it. It
always surprises me how well she gets on in Cyprus. She mu
love going there because she is even prepared to give up her
precious cigarettes for the duration of the journey. Although,
how bad tempered she is at the end of the trip, having done
without for so long, is anyone's guess.

Last time she was away she arranged for a friend to pick
her up to go out to dinner. All dressed up to hit the town she
had a couple of glasses of wine while she waited. Her friend,
Fizz phoned to say she was en route, so my mother made her
way down in the rickety, slow old lift to meet her outside.
When she finally reached the exit, having spent several
minutes chatting to some neighbours she had encountered on
the way down, she emerged into the half lit street to discover
Fizz's car right outside the front door of the building.

"Yoo-hoo darling," she shouted and yanked on the
passenger door handle. It wasn't Fizz but a young Greek
Cypriot man, who clung to the door handle in alarm,
convinced that my mother was a lady of the night. She didn't
twig it wasn't Fizz and kept pulling at the door shouting,

"Come on, let me in."

The young man finally yelled out in Greek for her to clear
off and leave him alone. She suddenly realised what was
happening and watched bemused as the young man sped awa
into the distance, missing his gear change in an effort to
escape. She thought it was hilarious. When Fizz turned up tw
minutes later they guffawed all the way to the restaurant
where she even phoned me to tell me about her experience.

All I could hear were snorts of laughter, muffled chortles and lots of coughing.

I would love to be able to ask her about these changes that are occurring to my body, after all she's been through it, and most of the websites tell you that you'll experience similar symptoms to your mother. We just aren't close enough. She's so old school that she'd tell me to stop whingeing and get on with it like she and many others have. If one of the symptoms of the menopause is short-tempered irrational outbursts, then I reckon my mother went through it for about twenty-five years. She certainly was quite volatile so I really hope that won't be the case for me. Maybe I should try some phyto soya or equivalent after all Asian women are supposed to experience less difficulties and it is presumed it is because they eat so much soya. Yes, I'll sort it out myself with some help from the local health food shop. I'm sure they have to deal with women like me all the time.

Whilst I was pondering on all of this, and deciding how to deal with the inevitable aging of my body in a mature manner, whilst not inflicting those around me with tantrums and histrionics like my own mother, Phil stomped into the room. He looked at me in a long suffering manner and I immediately felt nettled.

"Yes?" I snapped.

"Have you seen my glasses? I've put them down somewhere and I can't find them."

He is always losing his spectacles. Like me he hates wearing them, and leaves them lying about after he's used them. He always misplaces keys too. I spend hours every week looking for keys that he has shoved in a pocket of an old coat, or put in the wardrobe instead of putting them where they belong, that is to say in the key drawer, and now he's started doing it with his glasses. He'll leave them in the shed or on top of the car. Last week, I found them under a pile of clothes on top of the washing machine. Honestly, a bloodhound would have trouble finding them. It's maddenin

"If you put them back in the glasses case, where they belong, we wouldn't have to go through this rigmarole fiftee minutes, three times a day, would we?" I retorted, somewhat sharper than I had intended.

Phil gave me a look mingled with hurt, surprise and suspicio

"Don't bother. I'll find them myself."

Oh dear. I think I may need to start on soya or something pretty quickly.

Posted by Facing50Blog.com - 4 Comments

SexyFitChick said...Exercise and sex are good for women going through the change. Up to you which one you choose but from what I gather, you should maybe buy a pair of trainers.

Facing 50 said...Very funny. At least your comment made m smile.

Faerie Queene said...What is it about older men? They always lose things. My boyfriend was forever losing his glasses too. I bought him a chain so he could hang them around his neck. He looked very distinguished with them. Your mother is so much fun. I'd love a night out with her.

Facing 50 said...That is a good suggestion but Phil will certainly not wear a chain. He despises jewellery of any description. He doesn't even wear a wedding ring.

Monday 23rd

Checked *Facebook* this morning but there are no new messages. Maybe he's given up.

Posted by Facing50Blog.com - 2 Comments

SexyFitChick said...I'm hoping that he hasn't. He probably just doesn't check his emails too much – too busy staying fit.

Facing 50 said...I hope he hasn't too.

Wednesday 25th

Wretched Tom has scraped his car and knocked the wing mirror off it. He claimed he didn't know how he did it. He said he might have done it when he was turning around in the pub car park because he thought he remembered hearing a noise. Phil blew yet another gasket. It's not so much the damage to the car that has annoyed him but more the fact that he thinks Tom might have been drinking and driving.

He confiscated Tom's keys and gave him a lengthy lecture about drinking and driving. He went over the facts, time and time again. It was like listening to a track on a CD stuck on repeat. In fact it was nothing short of torture. Tom sat stony-faced, apparently listening, and nodding every three minutes. He didn't defend himself at all. He interrupted Phil's flow only to add noises of agreement accompanied by further nodding. I knew he wasn't paying a blind bit of attention to Phil. After he went up to his room I followed him to lend my weight to Phil's argument. Maybe if he heard it in stereo he wouldn't do it again. He was on the phone.

"I've just had an ear-blasting from the Rents. Yes, it was about the car. Yes, it was about the mirror you broke when you tried that three point turn. Look I know I said I'd help you

with your driving before your test, but I don't think I can do it again. Dad went bananas. No, I won't tell them it was you. Yes, don't worry. I'm sure you'll pass your test anyway without my help. Yes, me too. See you tomorrow.
No, you'll have to get your dad to drop you off at the pub. I'll meet you there. Love you. No, you go first. No, you hang up first. No, go on..."

Phil sat slumped in his chair.

"Can you believe it? I know Tom's badly behaved but I didn't have him down as a complete idiot. After all the talks we have had about driving. I've told him time and time again not to take the car when he goes to the pub. That boy has no common sense and no sense of loyalty. After all who bought him the car?" he growled.

"I'm pretty sure he won't do anything as stupid again.'

"How can you be certain?"

"I overheard him," I confessed.

Phil glowered at me.

"You've been eavesdropping again, haven't you?"

"Unintentionally. Don't you want to know what I heard?"

"No, I don't. It's not my business. And, it's not yours. No good comes from eavesdropping," he said huffily.

Maybe not, but at least I can rest in the knowledge that Tom can be loyal and that he isn't drinking and driving. Children don't tell you everything and sometimes, for your own sanity, to have to resort to other measures.

Posted by Facing50Blog.com - 2 Comments

Vera said...Whilst I don't agree with eavesdropping I have to agree with your statement. You never find out about your children unless someone lets something slip.

Faerie Queene said...Love makes you do all sorts of strange and illogical things. I once drove all through the night to my boyfriend's house to leave a red rose on his doorstep. Just so it would be the first thing he saw when he got up and would make him think of me.

Monday 30th

Bank Holiday Monday and Tom is stuck at home with us because he still isn't allowed to use his car. He's been here all weekend and it's driven us nuts. He's been playing his music full blast and clattering about in the kitchen making sandwiches which he takes back to his room. I nipped in there while he was in the bathroom to retrieve all my plates which were strewn on the floor and under the bed with bits of decaying ham on them. Phil keeps huffing and glowering every time Tom appears.

He got up late again today. The overpowering stench of Lynx filtering into the kitchen alerted us to the fact he was up. As we were sitting down to lunch he marched into the room and asked if Tiffany could come and spend the afternoon here, as he hadn't seen her for three days. Phil grimaced at the thought, got Tom's car keys and told him he could have his car back if he promised never to drive after a drink again. Tom promised and scarpered faster than you could say 'Alcopop'.

Posted by Facing50Blog.com - 2 Comments

SexyFitChick said...Any news yet from You Know Who?

Facing 50 said... Not a Dickey Bird - or even a Kookaburra.

CHAPTER 3 – SEPTEMBER

Friday 3rd

August went out damply. September started more brightly. That's more than I can say for Phil, who I found sitting glumly in front of the computer. The pension funds are performing badly and it is having a further damaging effect on his already bleak mood.

"I wish I hadn't sold out when I did," he complained, not for the first time. "If I had only waited, I wouldn't have invested at such a bad time, and we wouldn't be looking at such a depressing picture. If it continues like this one, of us might have to go back to work."

He looked at me pointedly.

"Well, I am almost sixty and completely unemployable unless you'd like me to try and get a job stacking shelves at *B&Q*"

I tried to imagine that for a moment. Phil in a DIY store, snarling at some poor unsuspecting customer who just wants to know where he can find some hooks or 3 ply wood, and realised if one of us had to return to work, it would have to be me. However I am equally unemployable.

It's been quite a few years since I've taught and my translation business was struggling due to the advent of the internet, instant translation services and *Babel fish* years ago so I too would be hard pushed to find work. That's the problem at our age suddenly you are on the heap. You need a job but can't get one because you are too old or overqualified and old.

When I used to teach I remember the older teachers alway got the flack whereas I, who at the time was young, and dare say it, reasonably good looking, had the pupils eating out of the proverbial hand. I think some of them found me entertaining, although quite unintentionally.

I am somewhat prone to malapropisms, especially if I'm not really paying attention to what I should be saying. Not a good trait in a teacher of English. One day I was trying to giv my very reluctant class of sixteen year olds a synopsis of William Golding's *Lord of the Flies*, one of their G.C.S.E. se texts. I had a class of twenty sixteen year old rugby playing boys who really didn't like English lessons but put up with me; possibly because I was one of only three female teachers in the entire school. I must have been a little distracted as I was burbling away, reading my prepared notes about the first few chapters of the book:

"At the beginning of the novel we learn that a group of boys being evacuated by plane from the UK are shot down and ejaculate onto an island," I droned.

There was a palpable frisson in the room and twenty head looked up simultaneously with ever widening grins as they watched me mentally recap what I had said and waited for m to blush, which of course I did, a spectacularly deep magent

"Eject," I said in a small voice. "Eject, er, not ejaculate."

I gained in popularity from that moment and the group all managed to pass their G.C S.E. English exam. Nowadays, it would be a different story. I wouldn't be on their wavelength at all. I don't know anything about what teenagers watch or listen to. I am officially out of touch and that makes me feel old too. I'm still in contact with some of those I taught who are on *Facebook*. It seems that social networking sites are no longer the domains of the young. I have fifty-nine friends, most of whom are over thirty years old. Tom refuses to be friends with me. That would of course completely ruin his 'street cred'. Ironically, six of his best friends from school are actually my friends too on *Facebook*. Good thing he doesn't know.

I'd be lost without these sites. I find myself checking *Twitter* and *Facebook* several times a day. Obviously, now I write this blog daily. Hardly anyone reads it, that is, apart from my dear new blogging friends PhillyFilly, Fairie Queene and SexyFitChick; but it acts as therapy for me. It keeps me from screaming at the walls. And, it's cheaper than going to a psychiatrist. It's a bit like talking to yourself. If I started muttering out loud, Phil would really think I'd lost the plot. So, these sites are the closest I get to having proper relationships with people.

Once you no longer work, but your old chums still do, you have much less in common and so you lose touch. You no longer all meet down the pub on a Friday night and moan about the week at work, or laugh about what the boss did today. It's all very well talking about taking up hobbies or travelling, but what you don't realise is how expensive it all is when you don't have the salaries coming in. Even going out for a coffee is pricey when you also take into account the fuel to get to town, the car parking fees and then the actual cost of the coffee. I don't know how some people manage. I don't know how my mother manages. She must spend most of her time staring at the wall.

In general, Phil and I get along remarkably well. We both seem to manage without too much interaction with others. I feel sorry for Phil though, because he was always out at meetings and having business lunches, or going to factory and warehouse inspections, and now he just seems to sit behind the computer trying to work out how to get the best from the finances we have. At the moment he's preoccupied with 'Operation Austerity'.

I hope he'll forget about one of us returning to work. I'll cross my fingers that stock markets will rise again, shares will increase in value, and we'll continue to be able to draw enough money from Phil's pension to keep us going.

Posted by Facing50Blog.com - 2 Comments

Vera said...Hello. I loved this post. I used to teach too but many years ago. I taught at a girl's school so no problems for me. I've enjoyed my visits here so I've just signed up to follow you. Keep laughing at life.

Facing50 said...Nice to meet you Vera. Thank you very much for visiting. I am always surprised how people find these blogs.

Monday 6th

Last month I wrote about the devastation that the mole was causing. Following that post I received an email, from a very kind anonymous person, who gave me some very helpful information. I contacted an accredited local humane mole catcher. Based in the area, he has an extensive client list but assured me that he would get to us as soon as possible. I explained that the mole was causing me to have a nervous breakdown so he prioritised us. He's been visiting for the last few days. He comes to check his traps daily for the mole, but the wily little bugger keeps avoiding them.

Earlier today, I was in a process of buying a cow for my virtual farm when I was interrupted by a loud knocking on the back door. It was the mole catcher. He stood beaming at me. He had discovered not one, but two moles in our field. A breeding pair no less. One was slightly smaller, the female, and according to the mole man, undoubtedly pregnant. The other was larger and a male. The mole man is very knowledgeable and went to great lengths to explain the mating habits of a mole. Apparently, they only have one day to 'get the job done' (in his words) and then the male disappears. Looks like this one had been caught on his way to the pub. Ha!

The mole man stood with the tube-like traps aloft, admiring the moles. He was busy showing me the male, telling me that it actually has the most number of teeth of any mammal; forty- four to be precise. It has teeth like a tiny underground shark. At that precise moment there was a sound like a champagne cork popping (I'd recognise that sound anywhere) and the female mole flew from her trap, onto the garden, where she navigated the shrubs and bushes with the precision of a champion downhill slalom skier. She disappeared down a small rabbit hole amongst the rose bushes right outside our lounge window. I thought they were supposed to be blind. This one seemed to have better eyesight than me, and motor skills for that matter.

The mole man stood transfixed. His mouth made a perfect 'O' shape. You know that moment when everything seems to happen in slow motion? As the female mole hurled herself down the rabbit hole like a pneumatic drill, the mole man dropped the other tube, which tumbled to the floor and opened. The mole man said “Noooooooo!” Then, everything speeded up again and the male mole emerged like a mini rocket, sped down the path just like a formula one driver, executed a superb right turn at the top of the path, and headed for the farmer’s field next door, where he disappeared before you could say ‘Well, I’ll be...’

The poor mole man, who only gets paid per caught mole, has had to lay his traps out again in an attempt to recapture them, or at least catch the female. He’s a little anxious that they have got wise to him now and will avoid the traps. They are quite intelligent you see. So, we’ll no doubt have hundreds of baby moles born soon under the rose bushes, and that’ll cheer up Phil no end. He’s under a lot of pressure at the moment so I’ve decided not to burden him with this piece of information. I just hope the mole man can capture the mole before it starts annihilating the flower beds.

Posted By Facing50Blog.com - 1 Comment

PhillyFilly said...We have gophers. I’m guessing they’re the same sort of varmit. Good luck.

Friday10th

Flipping economy measures! Phil has bought a present for me, more accurately, for himself. It is a grooming kit with a razor and a set of attachments for various lengths of hair. He announced that it will save ten pounds a month on his hair cut bill. I’d better not tell him what I spend a month or he’ll use it on me. Highly commendable, but I will have to do the trimming and, in a nutshell, I am rubbish at cutting anything in a straight line. I have astigmatism which means I really can't see straight lines.

My students always had to sit with their heads cocked to one side in an attempt to read my writing on a board, as it sloped alarmingly upwards. You'll know if I've put up a picture because apparently it'll be at an angle. This can be very frustrating for people. They'll straighten the picture and I'll come along, think it's wonky, and re-straighten it and so on. You think Phil would have known better, but he was chuffed at his attempt to economise, and as he said "Any muppet can do it." I wondered if he was hinting that my eyebrows needed doing again.

He insisted we had a go immediately and sat down on a kitchen chair in readiness. I had no time to protest. I picked up the comb and the dreaded device. My hands began to shake because I knew I'd be for it if I got it wrong. Phil held a hand mirror and supervised me. When he is in this sort of frame of mind it is quite daunting. He loves being in charge. It reminds him of his days at work and he barks instructions at me as if I were one of his minions. He can get extremely cross when he feels someone is incompetent, and at that moment, I was pretty certain I would fall short of the mark. First, he insisted on giving me a lengthy tutorial on how to cut hair as if I were very dim, which immediately irked me.

"You do it like this!"

He kept shouting, while simultaneously showing me how to put a comb through his thinning hair, and run the device over it. After several minutes and waning patience, I assured him I would be capable of holding the comb and doing as he requested. No sooner had I manoeuvred the comb into his hair with trembling fingers, than he jerked his head away, and declared I hadn't put it in properly. This continued for a few further attempts. Every time I carefully positioned the comb, and was about to run the razor over the end, he moved away and demonstrated yet again how to do it, which in fact was exactly the same way I had just done it.

I became frustrated with him, all that shouting and snatching the razor away from me every two minutes, to poin at where he wanted it. It's difficult enough to trim in a straig line. Having
a grown man wriggle about like a five year old is just plain annoying. I bet he didn't behave like this in the hairdressers. Hot and bothered, I succeeded in grabbing the comb from hir and told him if he wanted it done he was to leave me to it, or he could just do it himself. I put the comb attachment onto th end of the device and pushed it up over his hair at the back o his head with renewed irritation. Uncomfortable and hot I jus wanted to get the job done.

"Yes, yes!" he said. "That feels right."

Emboldened, I played it over the area again, and more hai tumbled down onto the kitchen floor. I was getting the hang c it now. On the fifth attempt Phil, who is not renowned for his patience, decided he wanted the front bit to be cut before I'd actually finished the back, and started wriggling about again. Before I realised it, I'd shaved a huge chunk out of one side c his head.

"How's it looking?" he chirped up, oblivious to the fact that I'd just made the most awful balls up.

"Oh it's okay. Looking good," I offered and attempted to even the style up.

Whatever I did after that didn't detract from the huge shaven line he had at the back of his head. Fortunately, Phil could only see the front. I finished. I was so hot and sweaty that the grooming device almost slipped from of my hand. I didn't think it was hormonal this time. Before Phil could even consider examining the back of his head closely I rushed off with the hand held mirror which I promptly hid in the bottom of my wardrobe.

Phil only able to see himself from the front, and having preened himself in front of the mirror for a while, decided I had passed the test. By evening I'd calmed down. Phil had forgotten all about his haircut and didn't notice me wincing every time I looked at it. All was going well until Tom came breezing in. In spite of me trying to catch his eye, shaking my head and pointing as if performing a deranged form of Charades he stared straight at the back of his father's head which was bent over the sink while he did the washing-up, and commented gleefully.

"Crikey, Dad, what happened to your hair? All you need to do now is dye half of it purple. You really need to change your hairdresser; she's only managed to give you half a Mohican! I'd ask for half of my money back if I were you."
Posted by Facing50Blog.com - 2 Comments
Vera said... I couldn't stop laughing at this. It's hilarious
Fairie Queene said...I did my boyfriend's hair for him with one of those machines too and he got very angry about how short it was. I threw the machine away after that.

Tuesday 14th

I have spent the last few days hiding from Phil. I made sur I was always busy in a different room to him. I apologised of course. He demanded to see the damage and then refused to speak to me. He barely managed monosyllabic replies to any of my questions, just like Tom. I hate being ignored. In that sort of situation I talk even more than normal which exacerbates the situation. Phil will normally glower at me. This results in me nervously burbling or attempting to tell funny stories in an effort to get him back into a good mood, when really, what I should do, is be silent. Unfortunately, I don't seem able to stay quiet.

Today, he told me in no uncertain terms to 'shut up'. I was trying to engage him in a conversation about something I had read on the net while he was trying to watch *Quest means Business*. Admittedly, it was incredibly foolish of me to speak during the programme, knowing how Phil becomes positively glued to anything remotely financial on the radio or televisior Fed up with it all I pulled imaginary woollen balls from my jumper and sulked. Great, now all three of us are behaving like a bunch of teenagers.

Immediately after being told to be quiet, the damn phone rang.

"Hello Sweetheart!" shouted my mother. "Just a quick call to tell you I won't be able to phone on Sunday because I'm going to out for lunch with Mario and his family. I'm going out to dinner at the Marine Club with Eliana and her friend, and then we're going on to a bar. I won't have time to phone you."

I heard music in the background and laughter.

"I'm sorry I've not phoned this week. I was out at the *Aphrodite* last night with some friends who have a place in Paphos, and last week I was out every night except Friday, when everyone came back to mine. We stayed up until 4 am drinking Metaxa and playing *Charades*."
More laughter.

"I'm afraid I rather upset the neighbours that night, but after they banged on the door the third time, I invited them in and we all had a great night. Angelos (a gnarly sixty year old) taught me how to dance to *Zorba the Greek*. We're all going to his granddaughter's wedding next weekend, where we'll no doubt practise it."

I hadn't managed to get a word in at this point, as per usual. I sat mesmerised by the image of my seventy-six year old mother in one of her Demis Roussos sized dresses, no doubt worse for wear, due to the vast volumes of alcohol she'll consume, whooping it up at a Greek wedding. I hope they don't let her lose on the plates. She'll have them all smashed before people have finished eating. Before I could say anything at all I heard her shout,

"Yiassou!"
This is apparently the Greek for 'hello'. I thought it was the name of her friend.

"Yes, it's open. Come in. I'm just on the phone. No, don't worry I'll be finished in a minute. Oh lovely, Ouzo, my favourite, you shouldn't have."
I felt like I was listening to a radio show and not part of the conversation at all. I waited patiently for the muffled chat to end for her to return to me.

"Got to go. Lena and her friend are here. Talk soon. Bye."

I looked at the buzzing phone's receiver. Who are all these people? What is she up to? 4am parties in her flat. Brilliant, now there are four of us behaving like teenagers.
Posted by Facing50Blog.com - 1 Comment
SexyFitChick said...Sounds like your mum knows how to have some fun. Who do you take after? LOL.

Thursday 16th

I got a message in my *Facebook* 'Inbox' this morning. It read:

'Mandy. At last I've found you again. Isn't *Facebook Finder* wonderful? I understand from what I've read that you are now married. Any kids? I'm still single – I let the right gi for me slip away. I live near Sydney with only my dog, Digit, for company. I try and surf most weekends and do some cycling. By the way, you look as beautiful as ever. And I remember you **very** clearly. I'm still so sorry about letting you get away from me. X'
I replied:

'Hi Todd. Yes, been married 22 years to Phil who has recently retired. I've got a lovely son called Tom. You'd like him. He's very sociable. Not up to much these days, just housewifey things. Don't worry. It was a long time ago.'
I got a reply immediately even though it was two in the morning over there in Australia.

'It might have been a long time ago but you were the most important thing in my life and I realised that too late.'
I didn't reply. Maybe I will later.
Posted by Facing50Blog.com - 3 Comments

SexyFitChick said...Cor! he sounds gorgeous. I live near Sydney too. Maybe I should go and check him out. Find out some more and let me know.
Fairie Queene said... Go on, it's only a message
Facing50 said...I'm not sure about all of this. I knew him such a long time ago. I don't want to start something I can't finish.

Friday 17th

Oh dear! I logged onto *Facebook* this morning and Todd had left another message for me:

'I only ask for you to spend a little time with me. Join me for a game of *Scrabble* for old times' sake.'

The last few days I have been regretting my decision to befriend him. I don't really think I should start a relationship with him, even if it is on the internet. However, those thoughts were immediately brushed away. I adore playing *Scrabble* and haven't played since those hedonistic days when we would pull out a set, and make up the most sensuous words we could think of with our letters.

I still love a challenge, and I knew I would be able to beat him easily. I always could. I went to the *Scrabble* application, and sure enough, a board was waiting for me, with our little profile pictures facing each other. Mine is the only decent photo I have of me. I'm smiling and wearing sunglasses, which not only hide my wrinkles, but have the added bonus of making me look younger. His revealed an Adonis in trunks, holding a surf board under his arm. His still blonde hair was swept back from the sea and he sported the whitest smile.

I looked at my letters. Drat! I had the letters e-e-e-e-l-a-o, I was hardly going to be scoring highly with that lot. I played ‘eel’, having decided ‘ale’ was too common, and’ ole’ would probably not be allowed. Playing *Scrabble* on *Facebook* is quite easy. They give you a dictionary next to the board and even a list of words that contain two letters. How simple is that? I stuck with ‘eel’ and played. It wasn’t long before a little message appeared next to the board, where you can hold a conversation at the same time as playing:

‘Morning Gorgeous. Just been dreaming about you’

The word ‘lick’ appeared on the board. I tingled. If I said ‘lick’ to Phil he would immediately fantasize about ice cream but I knew exactly what Todd would be thinking. I sent a smiley face not trusting myself to actually write anything, and played ‘eek’.

Posted by Facing50Blog.com - 2 Comments

SexyFitChick said...Sounds like fun. He must have been quite a guy in his day.

Facing50 said...Oh yes, he was.

Sunday 19th

I wasn’t expecting her, but at 5pm today the phone rang shrilly. I picked up to the sound of muffled laughter. It had to be her.

“Hello Sweetheart! I just thought you might be bored today and would like to hear something funny.”

I was about to say that I wasn’t bored at all, that my life was very interesting, actually, but looking at the pile of ironing I still had to finish, and all the washing up that Tom had left me, I was forced to agree that I wasn’t having the best of days.

"Oh we had such a hoot last night. You'd have loved it," she continued in an almost girlish tone.

She went on to regale me with her latest exploits, periodically breaking off for a cackle and cough. The night before, the usual crowd had gone back to her flat, having had a very good night out. They opened another bottle of wine and Fizz, as bubbly as her name would suggest, rallied everyone for a game of *Twister*. Somewhat worse for wear, they had just managed to get themselves into a complete tangle. My mother was, as always, up for it, and had managed to get herself into some impossible position, which involved a leg over Felix, a 70-year-old barman, and another over Bernard, a retired Ex Pat, who was playing under the watchful eye of his wife Margery. It was Bernard's turn and on being told he had to move 'right hand yellow' he suddenly piped up

"Margery, Sweetheart, I don't seem able to move."

"Of course you can, you clot" she retorted. "There's a space there," and indicated where he should move too. Everyone laughed. Poor old Bernard he'd obviously had too much wine.

"Uhm, no dearest. I can't seem to move at all. My back has just gone out."

Consequently, Bernard remained pinned by my mother, Felix and a third player, the voluptuous, and very large, Maria.

It took them ages to untangle themselves, particularly my mother who had to be helped by everyone to get her legs back to their normal place. Bernard had to be carted out of the apartment block on a stretcher by two medics and all his friends lined the street to wave him off with a drink in their hands, then went back up to my mother's flat to continue the party.

"We've just been to visit him at the clinic. We took him a bottle of brandy, for medicinal purposes of course. He says he'll be out tomorrow so we'll probably have a party for him. Better stick to *Charades* this time though," she chortled.

Posted by Facing50Blog.com - 7 Comments

Vera said...Oh I love your mother. She really takes life by the horns doesn't she?

Facing50 said...Yes, that's one thing I can say about her. She's always up for it when the occasion presents itself.

Faerie Queene said...She's so much fun. You should go and join her out there. It would do you good.

Facing50 said...No; I think I'd cramp her style. I never played games, even as a child.

SexyFitChick said...I don't believe you. You seem to be quite keen on *Scrabble*!

Facing50 said...That's different. It doesn't involve getting your legs stuck around a stranger's waist.

SexyFitChick said...If you played it properly, and not just on the net, it might result in getting your legs around someone's waist. (Wink, wink)

Facing50 said...Now you're just being very naughty. I'm older and less supple now remember.

Monday 20th

I completed my first game of *Scrabble* with Todd this morning. He stayed up nearly all night so he could play in 'real time' with me. I won, even though he kept trying to put me off by writing messages in the sidebar.

'What are you wearing?'

‘Jeans and a shirt’
‘No, what are you wearing **underneath**? What sexy underwear are you wearing? You always had sexy knickers. I remember those red silk ones you had with tie ups at the side.’
I thought about my greying comfortable granny knickers, which hold in my stomach, that I was wearing at that moment.
‘Black lace halter neck body’
‘Mmm. Just imagining it on you. Bet you look delicious. Can’t play properly now for thinking about you in it’
The conversation continued in that vein for a while but I still managed to beat him 320 to 260 and played a full word into a triple.
Posted by Facing50Blog.com - 3 Comments
SexyFitChick said...For goodness sake ditch the granny knickers. Buy something sexy. I’ll send you a link to a couple of websites.
Facing50 said... There’s no point. No one sees me in my underwear. I have a couple of special items that I wear to try to get Phil interested in me, but they barely register with him. I even tried wearing a thong and stockings. I strutted about the bedroom in them striking a sultry pose. Phil asked me if I was alright, and worried that the knickers might be uncomfortable wedged up my bum as they were.
SexyFitChick said...They are pretty uncomfortable. Buy some new stuff and try that. Failing that, pack a suitcase of underwear and catch a plane to Australia, where I’m sure you’ll get noticed.

Tuesday 21st

Tom is an absolute wretch. Every morning, I make his sandwiches for work. If I didn't, he'd only have a cigarette fo lunch. Phil told me to stop making them, and let the lazy little beggar get them himself. I don't like to think of him not eating properly. One morning, he got up too late to prepare them and went to work clutching a box of cereal for his lunch. Some dormant maternal instinct kicked in. I felt guilty and I just couldn't let that happen again.

Yesterday, I had had one of those motherly moments. The ones where you want to do something nice for your offspring. I'd splashed out on some of his favourite food as a treat. I'd envisaged him opening his lunchbox and finding all these tasty treats. There were sausage rolls and chocolate bars. I'd made up smoked ham bagels and even bought his favourite crisps, the more expensive ridged ones. He hadn't descended by eight for his breakfast, and by eight-fifteen there was still no sign of him. I thought I'd better check on him.

"You okay?" I half whispered, as I tapped on his door.

"Uhmmmm?"

"Tom, it is quarter past eight already. You are going to be late for work."

"Uhhhh uhmmmm."

"What?"

"I 'm tired. I can't be bothered to go to work."

"What?" thundered Phil, who had appeared from nowhere

"Get out of that bed **now**, you hopeless waste of space!" he bellowed.

I hate confrontation, so I scarpered. I could hear them screaming at each other. Tom was really going for Phil.

“I’m sick of you trying to tell me what to do. I’m nearly twenty-one you know; not a child.”

“Well, start behaving like an adult then.”

“You’re just mad at me because **you** haven’t got a job.”

“If I had one, I wouldn’t be lying in bed like you, you lazy sod.”

The commotion continued. There were some angry mutterings and grunts. A door was slammed. Phil entered the kitchen a cross between furious and shocked.

“He’s just shoved me out of the room,” he stammered in disbelief. “How could he?”

Five minutes later Tom, now dressed for work, stormed out of the house without a word. He slammed the back door behind him loudly, and stomped off to his car. It was only after he had gone that I saw the box of sandwiches.

Phil shut himself away in his office straight after, and now he won’t talk to me. I can’t even get him to come out for morning coffee, and so here I am blogging away as if it’s an agony column. I send my apologies to everyone who is reading this blog, as I’m a bit out of sorts today. I must have been very out of sorts actually, because I clicked onto Todd’s latest message which I really should have avoided after all that wicked flirting yesterday:

‘Morning Sexy, Just been awoken by a very erotic dream about you. It made my day. Hope yours is good too. XXX’

Posted by Facing50Blog.com - 3 Comments

PhillyFilly said... You need some fun girlfriend.

SexyFitChick said...Result!

YoungFreeSingleandSane said... ☺

Thursday 23rd

Phil, who is still in a foul mood with Tom, has really been taking austerity to the next level. He is cutting down the amount of hot water we use. I'm not to use the washing machine daily or twice a day as I sometimes have to. We aren't allowed to run the hot water to wash up. We have to wait until the kettle has been used to make coffee, and then ti the remains into the sink to use as washing up water. As far a I'm concerned one good thing has come out of it though. No that I'm only allowed to use the washing machine on cheap rate overnight, twice a week, I can't wash the mountain of dirty clothes that are strewn on the floor of Tom's bedroom.

Up until now, I followed the same routine daily. I would hold my breath, race into Tom's room scooping up everythin in sight. I would then rush to the machine with it, finally exhaling as I bundled it into the machine, and slamming the door on it before it escaped. He has an inordinate amount of washing. He seems to wear an entire wardrobe on a daily basis. Every week I find myself washing several pairs of pants, tops, t-shirts, hoodies, tracksuit bottoms and since he started exercising at the local gym, some rather repulsive sweaty socks and shorts appear with regularity. Phil's decision to cut back though means I am now liberated from this onerous task. It will also prolong the life of my poor machine.

Now that I'm no longer doing his washing, it has been decreed, in his absence, since he has not yet returned home, that Tom should be responsible for his clothes, and take them to the local launderette every Saturday. Sadly for him, the launderette shuts at 12pm on a Saturday, so if he wants clean clothes then he'll have to actually get up in the morning and not loaf in bed for most of the day.

Phil has a whole list of wretched ways to save money. Some ideas have been more successful than others. Last winter our house sprung a leak in the heating system. Even though we've tried digging up bits of the floor we couldn't find the leak. Apparently, some chump laid all the copper heating pipes in concrete, so we'll probably never find it unless we dig up the entire house.

The upshot of this was that the boiler wouldn't work. We had no heating and we were freezing cold all winter. I spent most afternoons huddled under a blanket on the settee with a hot water bottle, too cold to do anything, except shiver. Honestly, it was perishing. Even Phil, who radiates heat, looked blue-nosed. The sole benefit of that situation was that Tom spent as much time as possible out of the house, rather than lie in bed watching his own breathe clouding up in front of his face, and he stopped bringing friends home at all hours.

Phil decided to have a log burner fitted so at least the lounge would be warm this coming winter. In anticipation of the event Phil ordered five tonnes of coal, while it was being sold at the summer price. To ensure we would have sufficient fuel he also ordered some logs. The logs were brought round by a neighbouring farmer while we were out. He dumped them onto the driveway and shoved a bill for them in our letterbox. They have come from an ancient oak tree and are massive. Approximately two feet in diameter they are completely useless. We can't offend the chap. You have to be careful with locals, especially locals, whose families have lived in the village for generations. Phil is now planning on chopping the logs into more manageable sizes. That is going to be fun.

Still, he's pleased with the coal. In his opinion it was wortl buying in bulk because it would have cost us so much more tc order it after August. It's been spilling out all over the garden from behind the shed for weeks. There's a colossal heap of it. It looks like we've been mining the stuff. We can hardly see the garden for it. I don't think he realised how many bags there would be when he ordered it. It took two burly men to offload the black stuff. The flowers that used to grow where the coal now resides have suffocated under the weight and withered. Phil maintains that the price was right and therefore it was worth it.

The men came yesterday to fit the little burner. After two cups of tea, they set to work. Their first task seemed to involve dislodging an old bird's nest which was in the chimney. This caused an entire chimneybreastful of old coal dust to tumble into the lounge. Clouds of dust rose into the air and settled over all the furniture. It was obvious what I would be doing after they left. Three more cups of tea, some panting and lots of sucking of teeth later, the log burner was in and ready to ignite. Phil would clearly be chopping logs for a very long time because the door to the burner was miniscule. He didn't need logs so much as large matchsticks.

"One last thing," said the man who'd installed it. "I noticed you had rather a lot of coal outside. I hope you weren't planning on using it in this burner. You can't use ordinary coal in it. Make sure you only use smoke free coal."

I don't think Phil will be able to get a refund on all his coal but at least he'll be able to use some of his pent up frustration chopping logs.
Posted by Facing50Blog.com - 2 Comments
PhillyFilly said...I liked this post. I can just imagine the look on your poor husband's face. As black as the coal he had purchased. Hope you stay warmer this winter. You could always buy a fur coat!
SexyFitChick said...You could always snuggle up together to get warm. Or, maybe you could consider moving somewhere warmer. We have summer here in Australia when you have winter. You could always come to visit an old friend.

Friday 24th

Tom has finally returned. Since the set to with his father, he has not been home. He sent me a text to say he was staying at Tiffany's house. I bet Tiffany's parents have been delighted about that arrangement. He came in tonight, and stormed off immediately, to his room. Phil has been in an absolute stinker of a mood since the whole episode, and we've hardly spoken. I tried to put across Tom's point of view; how he probably feels oppressed at times. He had just got used to independence and the freedom that university affords. Now he was expected to fit back into our mundane routine, and the way we live, but Phil rejected this theory.

"He does exactly what he wants, when he wants. He comes and goes as he pleases, and has no consideration for us, or for what we have done for him."
He went on and on and on.

I went to Tom's room, knocked gently on the door and stuck my head in.

"Look, your Dad is really upset about what happened."

"So he should be, shouting at me like that, and shoving me."

"I thought you shoved him?"

"Yeah, well he shoved me first, and I shoved him back."

"Oh for goodness sake, just try and see it from his perspective. He only wants you to do well in life. He wants to see you take advantage of all the opportunities that are out there. He can't bear it when he thinks you are not fulfilling your potential," I continued.

"He treats me as if I'm a huge disappointment to him."

"No, he doesn't. He isn't disappointed in you at all. He just wants the best for you, and you have to admit you haven't really tried to achieve yet, have you?"

Tom looked sheepish. I continued for a while longer, and then left him to think over what I had said. Phil was fiddling about in the kitchen, attempting to repair a light switch over the cooker which wouldn't light any more, when Tom came down.

"Sorry Dad," he murmured, looking quite upset.

Phil regarded him quietly. I thought he might blow up again.

"It's alright son. It must be a little difficult for you sometimes. You probably feel a bit oppressed; after all you have been used to your freedom, what with being at university. It can't be easy coming back here, and having to get used to living the way we do. We're not your age group and we have our set ways. It's hard sometimes to adjust.'

They shook hands and semi hugged. Maybe they should shove each other about more often. It obviously helps them see sense.

Posted by Facing50Blog.com - 3 Comments

The Merry Divorcee said...Hi. I'm a new follower. Maybe they should both go into therapy. My eldest needed a whole year after my first husband and I split up.

Facing50 said... Sorry to hear that. I think Tom will be okay. Phil and I don't intend separating.

SexyFitChick said...Really?

Saturday 25th

It was a relatively quiet day today. Tom went to the launderette with his washing. He was collecting Tiffany to help him with it, and to keep him company while it whirs around in the machines. Poor Tiffany! It's hardly an exciting date.

I took advantage of the lull to check out an Ann Summers underwear website. If I wanted to wear some of that stuff I seriously need to lose weight. I'll stick to the granny knickers for the time being.

Checked the board but Todd hadn't played a word. He had left a message though.

'Taken Digit to the beach for the day. Wish you could come too. Remember those afternoons in Morocco in the sea?'

Oh yes, I remember them alright. I might just start an exercise regime again. I'd like to think I could look good in that underwear on the website; even if I never buy any.

Posted by Facing50Blog.com - 1 Comment

Faerie Queene said...You should buy underwear for comfort my boyfriend had a dreadful furry thong. He thought he looked very sexy in it but it just made me want to giggle whe he wore it.

Sunday 26th

If Phil discovers my latest faux pas, he'll divorce me for sure.

I decided I ought to have a clear out of the kitchen cupboards. Heaven knows what's lurking in the back of those I tackled my task with gusto and my spectacles so I could see the dates on the tins and packets.

Removing all the jars of jam that Phil had bulk purchased, in case the world ever runs out of jam, I discovered a bottle o red wine hiding in the back of one of the cupboards. It was one which had been given to him for his fortieth birthday. It would obviously seem sensible to dispose of the said red win as it had probably gone off by now.

Out of the two of us I am more the wine connoisseur. I say that glibly, because I actually know very little about wine, bu I seem to enjoy and appreciate a good red wine more than poor old Phil, who can't drink the stuff as it gives him a headache. He usually sticks to the tried and tested Pinot Grigio or a nice little Petit Chablis. I love red wine. I can sit for ages savouring the flavours of red fruits or oaky notes.

My discovery of this particular bottle of red wine was a bi of a coup because I'd just finished my last bottle of Chianti. Phil won't let me share his white wine which he makes last for months by not drinking them at all. I sought him out and found him in front of the computer, growling about some fun he had bought into that was floundering. All our shares seem to flounder and lose money.

"Uhm, there's a bottle of red wine in the cupboard. It's technically yours, but as you don't like red wine, can I have it tonight to go with the pasta?"

"Erg, grump, hurrumph!" came the reply, which I took to mean, "Yes, have it with my blessing. I hope you enjoy it."

I dusted it off and put it on the kitchen top for later. I continued throwing away out of date tins. I knew how they felt; past their sell-by and undoubtedly, no longer tasty. Just as I put the last tin in the bin Phil emerged from his office grumpily, and stomped into the kitchen where he stood and stared at the bottle.

"Where did that come from?"

"I already told you. It's yours. It was a birthday present from your work colleagues for your fortieth birthday."

He looked horrified.

"My fortieth? Gosh, that's a long time ago. This is a 1983 wine. Shouldn't this have been drunk years ago? Crumbs, I hope it's alright. It'll be like vinegar by now. Oh well, you could always put it in your cooking if it isn't right. It might improve the flavour of your coq au vin."

I screwed the corkscrew into the bottle, pretending I was screwing it into Phil. The cork came out with a pleasant 'plop' sound.

"No, I think it'll be okay," I announced, savouring the rich aroma that emerged from the bottle.

Phil peered at the label.

"Chateau Margaux. Isn't that supposed to be a good vineyard?"

"Yes, I think so. Chateau Margaux is one of the well known Chateaux in Bordeaux."

Phil, however, lost interest in the wine and went off outside to check the air pressure in the car tyres.

Later that evening I poured a large glass of the wine and settled down with it. It was lovely and fruity.

"You should try some of this. After all, it was your presen It's very nice. Not at all heavy. In fact it's very fruity. I don't think you'll dislike it," I insisted as Phil wrinkled his nose. He reluctantly let me pour him a small glass.

"Mmm, it's quite nice for a red wine. You should check u on the internet about it. Maybe we could get another bottle. It's rather tasty."

I glugged another glass, and then another. It really was rather smooth, beautifully fruity and frightfully moreish. Soon, I felt pleasantly relaxed. Even Phil had a slight glow to his face after his thimbleful.

The following morning I woke with no aftertaste, no red lips and no hangover. What a great wine. Pity we hadn't got a couple of bottles of it. I logged on and *googled* it.

The winemaker notes said

'*The 1983 Margaux is a breathtaking wine. The Cabernet Sauvignon grapes achieved perfect maturity in 1983, and the result is an astonishingly rich, concentrated, a typically powerful and tannic Margaux.*

Anticipated maturity: 2000-2030.

96/100 pts. (Robert Parker)'

Aghast, I read all the reviews I could find. Apparently it is 'the Bordeaux of the vintage'. I sat mouth open and checked out the price. It currently retails for approximately £521.65p ($649.99). Oh damn and blast! We should have kept this bottle as an investment. It would certainly have been a better investment than some of Phil's funds. It's entirely my fault. I'm going to punish myself by giving up wine for a while. Which just leaves one question; should I tell him?

Posted by Facing50Blog.com - 5 Comments

PhillyFilly said...No, no, no. Some things are definitely best kept secret and this is one of them.

Fairie Queene said... I think you should keep this to yourself. He'll be furious if he finds out how much it was worth especially with the way he is trying to save money. Forget all about it and be pleased you had the chance to drink and enjoy an expensive wine. My ex had a wine cellar. When we split up I hid a couple of the best bottles for me to enjoy alone.

SexyFitChick said...You could always put some cheap plonk back into the bottle and try and sell it on *eBay*. Well, it's worth a try isn't it?

Vera said...My dear; I suggest you keep quiet about this little episode. If you are lucky he will have forgotten all about the wine by now.

YoungFreeSingleandSane said...I agree with the others. Best to let sleeping dogs, or in this case, empty bottles, lie.

Monday 27th

I have taken your advice. I've thrown the empty bottle of expensive wine away so there is no evidence in the house, and ergo, no reminder for Phil. Having now given up wine for a while I have decided that it's time to look after my health. I have been to the health food shop where I bought a vast amount of *Well Women* tablets. I was a bit embarrassed at first, because the shop seemed to be full of young fresh faced men looking at body building powders. I whispered some of my symptoms to the very young assistant and suggested that thought I might be menopausal and what could she recommend. She looked at me blankly, chewed her gum then yelled out at the top of her voice:

"Gloria, there's some middle-aged woman here who want to know what to do about getting all hot and sweaty in bed, and having a hairy face."

The young men looked sympathetically at me. I suppose they'd love to have my hairy face. Fortunately, Gloria turned out to be much more sympathetic, and having glared at the girl, whisked me off to a special section for aging women. Sh apologised profusely for the young girl's behaviour, explaining that she was in fact the manager's niece, and was on work experience.

"Not for much longer though," she added darkly.

My goodness, there are so many things you can take for hot flushes, night sweats, mood swings or getting your libido going again. Now, that's an issue too. Phil has never been what you may call a passionate man. However, since Tom came home he doesn't seem interested at all. Phil goes to bed too early and gets up too early for there to be any contact in bed. There is no spontaneous sex in front of the telly, or on the kitchen table, actually I don't think we ever gave that a gc even before Tom returned. Phil says that his lack of libido is down to Tom's return.

I know that Phil's has never been over enthusiastic in that department. His idea of foreplay seems to consist of a tap on the shoulder and the romantic word 'Well?' I think he is using Tom as an excuse so maybe that Horny Goat's Weed added to my basket of goodies could be the answer. I could crumble it up into his food. I bought some useful supplements for me too: Soya Isoflavones, vitamins, Black Cohosh for night sweats and some Evening Primrose Oil; a sort of starter pack for the premenopausal woman.

Gloria was very helpful. She suggested I check herbal remedies out on the internet, or get advice from an assistant in the shop (clearly not the young gum chewing woman) before I rushed in and bought too much. She also recommended I see my doctor. Hmmm! I'm not sure about that.

I only go to the doctors when it's completely desperate. Besides, you have to wait three weeks for an appointment to see our local doctor. I've usually recovered by the time the appointment date arrives. It would seem that I'm now prepared for this new stage in my life.

I put all my little pills in the bathroom cabinet and glanced in the mirror. I was pleased to note that I couldn't frown properly and the lines that were over my nose and between my eyes were not as deep. I double checked with my glasses on. Excellent! Maybe the 'buttocks' treatment was worth having. Yes, what with that and the pills, especially the Horny Goat's Weed, I'll be fine. Cheers!

Posted by Facing50Blog.com - 3 Comments

SexyFitChick said...You need something to spice up your life. I think a light flirtation with an Australian ex Englishman might just do the trick.

Fairie Queene said...I hope that rude girl gets the sack. I wouldn't stand for such behaviour at my boutique.
Facing50 said...Haha SFC-You are really very naughty. FQ-understand that she will not be employed there for much longer. Apparently, she wants to become a social worker.

Wednesday 29th

Amidst the austerity and gloom a minor miracle occurred this late this month. There is a little ray of sunshine on the horizon. Tom announced yesterday evening, just as he was about to go out, that he was going to go back to college.

"What?" spluttered Phil. "After all the money and time yo wasted last time? I'm not paying for you to enjoy yourself lik that again."

Tom had the grace to look shame-faced.

"Er, no, I was thinking of doing an HNC in Business Studies at the local college after work, two days a week. In two years I'll have a decent qualification, and I might get promotion at work if I can show them I can work hard."

Our work-shy boy is starting to realise after several month of stacking boxes in a warehouse that throwing away his education wasn't a good idea. Amazing! A glow filled that space in my heart that had started to become barren.

"Just one problem," he continued. "I need nine hundred pounds to pay for the course. I will pay you back in instalments every month though."

Phil didn't hesitate. Austerity month or not, at last his son was seeing sense and every penny that went towards that course would at least not be wasted down the pub.

"I'll come with you tomorrow," he declared. "We'll get you signed up for the course."
He sat back in his chair and, duly dismissed, Tom scooted off, no doubt to celebrate down at the pub.
Posted By Facing50Blog.com - 2 Comments
Vera said...See there is hope after all.
Facing50 said...It's early days though, Vera, early days. He hasn't got a good track record when it comes to commitment, or studying so we'll have to see how this turns out.

CHAPTER 4 – OCTOBER

Friday 1st

My mother has bought a new mobile phone. It is one with an integrated camera. I keep receiving photographs of her and her friends in Cyprus. It was bad enough imagining what she was up to. Now, I get to see it in clear pixelated detail. There are photos of her in restaurants with large groups of people I don't know at all. They are grinning, and waving glasses of wine about, looking as if they are on an 18-30 holiday, well to be more accurate, a 68-80 holiday. I'm dreading getting one with the whole group 'flashing'.

There are pictures of her at various weddings and parties, dancing. I wonder why she doesn't seem to be using her walking stick on those. Suspiciously, there seem to be a lot of photos of her with a gnarled old Cypriot who has a shiny gold front tooth, and a young man who looks, as Tom would put it, 'fit'. My mother is now texting and photo messaging more than Tom, who can't live without his phone.

She has sent me a peculiar text too, which reads:

'Bin 2 the Trodos Mountains with Grego. Was beaut day. Sun was shining but there was snow on tops of mountains n children were sledging. We stopped off at a Taverna on the way back n listend 2 the cicadas then walked along the beach Luv X'

Just what am I supposed to make of that? She sounds quite unlike my mother. She's normally very particular about her spelling and refuses to abbreviate a word. She told me off for using 'l8ter', saying I didn't need to drop my standards just because I was texting, so now I have to write out full sentences, with correct grammar, which takes ages. I have no idea who Grego is. Maybe he's the man with a gold tooth. Ordinarily, she stays around the flat and only goes to the beach to read her book, so going to the mountains is unusual for her. The text even smacks of romance but that's highly unlikely. Maybe she just had too much Cypriot wine in the Taverna. However, I have an uncomfortable feeling that something strange is afoot in Cyprus.

Posted by Facing50Blog.com - 2 Comments

SexyFitChick said...How cool is your Ma? Fancy photo messaging at her age.

Faerie Queene said...Those phones are so useful. I took a photo of my boyfriend coming out of a hotel holding someone else's hand. I used it to confront him. He confessed of course and then we broke up. I sometimes wish I hadn't seen him and photographed him though.

Saturday 2nd

Since retiring it's been an uphill battle to get Phil interested in anything or indeed to encourage him to take up any hobby. He insists he doesn't need one, and I'm convinced that he does. He spends far too much time in front of the computer.

After Tom went to university, I decided I would make the most of my newly discovered free time to try something new. I bought several tins of coloured pencils and taught myself to draw. I was extremely pleased with the results, and the more drawings I completed, the prouder I became. As I had the drawing bug I forced Phil to share in my new found passion. One afternoon when all he seemed to want to do was wash hi car and check some share prices on the internet, I sat him down with some charcoal pencils, and told him he had to draw something for me. For inspiration, I had dragged out some of his photographs of birds

In my opinion, Phil is quite a gifted photographer. One, who loves nature, and he has taken some extraordinarily good shots of wildlife in the past. Admittedly, he still uses an old Cannon A1 camera containing film, as he can't bear new technology and refuses to even look at a new digital camera. He likes to fiddle about with the lenses and filters on his old trusty camera. He's also one of those photographers that takes so long to set up the subject, just the way he wants it, that, in the case of a bird, it's likely to have made a nest, laid and hatched several eggs and flown south by the time he is ready to press the shutter.

Having poured through the photographs I had offered him, he finally settled on one of some magpies squabbling over some seed under our Acer tree, and drew it. It was very good indeed. Having done it, he gave me back the charcoal pencils and asked if he could go and wash his car.

A few weeks ago, thanks to Ethel, I discovered that our local village holds an art class for the residents, both male and female, every Friday afternoon. The afternoon is taken up with drinking tea or coffee, eating biscuits and cake and sitting drawing, or if you prefer, painting. It is run by an accomplished artist who advises you on your technique and helps you achieve a better standard. It's also a very good way to meet folk and as we still only know a handful of people here it seemed like a jolly fine idea.

I informed Phil that we were going. He refused point blank. I had a complete wet out on him and told him I was sick of doing absolutely nothing with my life. I told him he was a boring old git. I told him he was never open to suggestions. I sulked. I cajoled. I wheedled. It was only the promise that he only had to come once, and that he would ge a piece of cake, that swung it in the end. We were to take some work we had already done with us to be judged of a good enough standard to join the group.

I routed out Tom's old portfolio case. He had used it for transporting his artwork when he was at school. I blew the dust from it and slipped my treasured drawings into it. I foun a suitable cardboard A5 folder for Phil's magpie picture and off we went.

The Village Hall was packed out with women of all ages.

"I thought it was for men too," whispered Phil.

"Oh, it is," said a loud voice and a striking woman with bright pink hair and large orange earrings in her fifties stood before us. She beamed at Hubby. 'They just haven't turned u today. I had planned a surprise for the women in the group. You don't have to stay. Phil looked ready to bolt. I grabbed him by the arm, and informed the woman that he would be keen to stay. He glowered at me. I knew better of course. He'd be glad that he'd come. I was pretty certain, that under that gruff exterior, lay an artist.

"Now, as you are both new to the group, I'd like to take a peek at some of your work. Just so I can get an idea of your standard."

Obviously, this was the famous artist who would help us improve and interest us in art.

She took out Hubby's magpie sketch.

"Oh yes, this is very good. You've captured the mischievous spirit of the birds beautifully," she commented, her purple framed glasses perched on the end of the nose. "Yes, you have a nice sense of proportion. You'll be fine for this afternoon's class if you are sure you want to stay. It'll be easy enough for you."

Phil looked pleasantly surprised. Before the artist could examine my work, he was whisked away by a sweet elderly lady, dressed in an artist's smock who promised to find him some cake.

"It's so nice to have young men come to this event, isn't it Mildred?" she cackled to her friend, who sported a jaunty beret, and Phil was dragged off to the tea table.

I glanced down. The artist was staring at some splodges on a large sheet of paper.

"Oh sorry," I said. There's some work in there that isn't mine. My son did those when he was still at school."

"That explains it," she said. "They are clearly less accomplished. I've put them to one side."

To the left, were my wonderful drawings sitting in a neat pile.

"Now this, this however, is superb. Very like a Jackson Pollock. Resembles his *Convergence* I'd say. I'm very impressed with this piece. It'll be interesting to see what you make of the subject today."

With that, she smiled a toothy grin, handed me back my Tom's splodgy picture and clapped her hands together.

"Ladies, and gentleman," she added looking pointedly at Phil who was sandwiched between two blue-rinsed haired ladies, holding an exceptionally large plate of cake. "As you

know, every month, we try to test your skills a little further, by giving you something different to paint or draw. Something that you might not have considered attempting before."
I glanced around for a clue as to what we might be painting today; maybe there was a bowl of fruit hidden at the back under that tablecloth.

"Please get your materials and gather round in the usual circle. Put up the easels where you would like, and those of you with pads, help yourselves to the desks."

We duly collected easels and tables, and shuffled forwards with them forming an extremely large circle. Phil was going down a storm, helping all of the giggling ladies with their materials and stools and desks. He even looked like he might be enjoying himself. The two old ladies from earlier got him set up between them, right in front of me.

This class was hugely popular. There were at least forty women set up. They were all very interested too. This artist had certainly worked up their enthusiasm or someone had put a large bottle of brandy in the tea they'd been drinking. They were clucking at each other and there was an air of excitement.

"So, Ladies and Gentleman," said our artist hostess. "Get your pencils and paints ready for today's subject. I promised you last week that I would give all the ladies a present, for all the effort you have made, and here it is..."

Into the room sauntered a young, extremely fit young man wearing a dressing gown. There was a collective intake of breath. Turning slowly around the group, his eyes finally resting on Phil, the hunk gave a suggestive wink to him and dropped his dressing gown under which he wore nothing. He draped himself on a chair to show himself off to the best advantage ready to be sketched.

The room fell silent and although you could see appreciative smiles on the faces of the women nothing else could be heard apart from the sound of Phil's charcoal which hit the floor and broke.

Posted by Facing50Blog.com - 6 Comments

SexyFitChick said...I'm packing my bags and art materials and coming to stay with you. You are going to carry on with the art aren't you?

Facing50 said...It was a one-off. I don't think I'll be going back. My drawing looked like a Picasso without talent. I don't think the artist was impressed. Phil had to leave. He feigned a coughing fit and shot off home. He's still cross about it.

Vera said...What a shame your mother wasn't there. She'd have thoroughly enjoyed it.

Facing50 said...I might tell her about it. The trouble is that she isn't interested in anything I do, so she'll probably pay no attention to me.

Vera said...Try her out.

Faerie Queene said...My boyfriend used to be a model too. He was horribly gorgeous but very vain.

Sunday 3rd

Phil has informed me that if I have any more hair brained schemes like that one, I'm to keep them to myself. He now thinks he's the laughing stock of the village. I think people have got other things to do with their time, than think about Phil. He spent the day in the garage blacking his car tyres and messing about.

I sent Todd an email about the art episode and got one back. I is far too suggestive to post it for you to read but contained the words: painting, nude, chocolate and licking. I'll leave yo to imagine its contents.

Posted by Facing50Blog.com - 3 Comments

YoungFreeSingleandSane said...I always thought it was women who were supposed to like chocolate. I do. I get through several bars a week while watching TV dramas.

PhillyFilly said...Phil needs to loosen up. Buy him some chocolate.

Facing50 said...Thanks girls, but I'd better leave him alone for a while. He'll get over it. He usually does. PhillyFilly – I might just get him a bar of chocolate to say sorry.

Wednesday 6th

Phil has a Swedish mistress. Ever since he first saw her he has been smitten. I have even seen him caress her fondly when he thinks I've not been looking. As you may recall, last month Phil had a log burner fitted. We also have an enormou pile of dry ash logs to use, none of which will fit into the burner. Now it's starting to get cooler on an evening, Phil has decided that the pile needs to be used. The logs require cuttin to a size where they will fit through the aperture of the tiny log burner. We tried to purchase a log splitter but they were hugely expensive, costing far more than the wood itself, and so we settled on purchasing an axe. It transpired that at this time of the year, axes were rarer than hen's teeth but finally, after much searching on the internet; I discovered a DIY store that sold log chopping axes.

The DIY store is over forty miles away and only had one axe remaining in stock, which I reserved and paid for on line. We collected the axe the same day. It took an age for the dopey young man at the enquiry counter to serve us, and even longer for him to even understand what we wanted, and find the order number on his sheet. We stood fuming while he put out a message over the tannoy system:

"Could someone from garden please come to the tills?"

"It's not really my department," he explained. "I'm normally on paint."

No one arrived. I asked the young man to make a further announcement. Phil began to chunter about the inefficiency of it all. Had I not already paid for it, we would have walked out. He then began to bristle with annoyance, and I could sense he was about to demand that a senior figure be brought down, when, at last, the person 'from garden' appeared, wiping sandwich crumbs from his mouth. I explained again about ordering the axe, and handed my order number over, yet again. He looked at the number, then under the counter by the till, and pulled out a very long axe.

"Gavin you dopey prat! It's here, under the counter. How did you miss it?" He said to the young man.

"It's not my department," reiterated Gavin with a shrug.

We drove home in rush hour traffic. No sooner had we pulled up, than Phil was tearing the cardboard off the blade, and was headed purposefully towards the pile of logs. Within minutes I heard a tremendous 'thunk!' and rushed out to see him holding a handle without an axe head.

"It flew off!" he said in disbelief.

Sure enough, there was the axe embedded in the wall of the wooden garden shed. Fortunately, it had missed Phil's beloved car, and indeed Phil himself. We drove straight back the next morning with the axe, and the head, where it took a further hour to explain to Gavin, why we didn't want it, and demand a refund.

Since then I've made several attempts to find a suitable replacement, not, as Phil put it, 'a Mickey Mouse one'. Yesterday, though, I hit pay dirt. Somewhere in the recesses of my brain, I recall watching a bush craft programme which was presented by Ray Mears, an expert on survival in the wild. He would know where I would be able to find a proper long handled log splitting axe. I 'Googled' him and discovered not only had he got his own website, but an online shop, where I could purchase, pause for a fanfare, a handmade, Swedish, long handled wood chopping axe! I phoned up the number on the site and spoke to a very helpful girl who advised me on the best axe to buy - a *Gransfor* axe. It would come by special delivery the next day, and had a ten year guarantee, along with a booklet all about its history. I told Phil whose eyes began to shine. He was transformed into a small boy waiting for a new toy train set to be delivered. He paced in front of the door all morning waiting for the van to deliver it.

The axe arrived at eleven. By five past eleven Phil had unwrapped it, breathed the heady sigh of a man in love, and taken it outside to oil it and try it out. He spent the rest of the morning reading the booklet, and admiring the photographs o the man, who has personally made the axe. It is, in fairness, beautifully crafted and Phil loves excellent workmanship. Th

axe is now resting in the lounge, propped up against Phil's chair. He won't part with it at the moment. He looks so content it would be a shame to shatter the moment. Ah, little Swede! How did you manage to win his heart so easily? How can I compare to one so beautifully made as you?
Posted by Facing50Blog.com - 1 Comment
The Merry Divorcee said... He hasn't been watching *The Shining* has he? Be careful!

Thursday 7th

Tom went to college tonight. I felt it was like his first day of school. I kept asking him dumb questions like

"Do you have enough paper and pens?"

Phil told me to lay off and leave him to sort himself out. I still bought him a new folder though to put his work in.

His class was straight after work so we had a relaxed evening knowing he wouldn't be back until nine. At midnight, I was woken up by a noise; a thud against the bedroom window. It happened again. I looked out and there was Tom waving at me.

"Soz," he whispered as I let him into the house. "I forgot my keys."

"You're quite late back from your class. I thought it finished at nine."

"Yes, it did, but we all thought the class was so dull that we deserved a few pints at the pub to cheer ourselves up. Thanks for letting me in. Hope I didn't wake you."

I remain unconvinced about Tom's commitment. I shall of course mention nothing to Phil, who was fast asleep and heard nothing.

Posted by Facing50Blog.com - 1 Comment
Vera said...I hope the course gets better. You should try tying his house keys around his neck to stop him forgetting them.

Friday 8th

Eureka! I have finally found an interest for Phil. Following on from the axe episode, Phil has been on the Ray Mears website, and discovered that they do weekend survival courses. Guess what? Yes! He wants to go on one. I have no interest in lying on damp forest floors, trying to light a fire with two twigs, and drinking my own urine. Phil is going to go on his own as his pre-birthday treat. Normally, you can't get on one of these courses for a couple of years. They are surprisingly popular, but someone has dropped out to go on an expedition to the North Pole instead, and Phil has been offered his place in April. Fantastic! An entire weekend to myself, and something for Phil to gen up about before he goes. What a result.
Posted by Facing50Blog.com - 3 Comments
SexyFitChick said... Maybe you could spend the weekend playing *Scrabble* with a certain someone.
Facing50 said...I'm sure I can think of better ways to spend my weekend though.
SexyFitChick said... Yeah right, of course you can. Bet you spend it on the *Scrabble* board though.

Monday11th

Since I hit the big five oh I seem to have become more obsessed with my appearance. When I was younger I never cleansed, worried about my eyebrows, put on carefully applied foundation, or made sure I wore cream day and night. I used to chuck water at my face, slap on some lipstick and rush off out. Of course, that's half of the problem. My face is now revealing the lack of care that I gave it during my twenties, thirties and even forties. Unless I want to look like a piece of leather parchment in my sixties, I suppose I'll have to give in and do something about it now. Even Phil is becoming more aware of the ravages of time. I discovered some eye cream for men and tooth whitening paste in his bathroom cabinet last week.

Bearing that it mind, I headed off to the new make up shop in town. It has weird and wonderful potions for every type of skin, and person. I'm a complete klutz when it comes to makeup. I just never learned how to use it. I wasn't one of those girls that would hang around in the school toilets enhancing their eyes with thick purple eye shadow. I was the boring one. I was the one who did her homework on time. Others, who had an active social life even at that age, copied my answers in the changing room, just before lesson started. As far as I was concerned, I already knew I looked hideous, so make up wasn't going to help me. Also, wearing glasses isn't conducive to putting on makeup. Once your eyes get as bad as mine have, and you have to wear your reading glasses in front of the magnifying mirror, you know you have problems. How do you get mascara on without hitting the lenses?

I explained to one of the girls in the shop that I didn't know what I needed. That is always fatal. She brought out pot after pot, jar after jar and pump after pump. She lined them all up, then scrutinised my skin while I sat on a tall stool, like the one used in a classroom for the class fool.

"Do you use a night cream?"
I shook my head.

"Well you should. I recommend this one. It has retinol in it. It's very good for aging skin."
She moved one of the pots forward as if we were playing a game of chess with them.

"Day Cream?"

"No."

"You need this, or this. This one is the better one, and retails at £110. That one is okay, and it costs £38."

"That one," I said pointing to the cheaper one.
She frowned slightly but moved the next chess piece forward

"What do you use on those broken capillaries around your nose?"

"What broken capillaries?"
She pointed out bright red marks near my nose.

"Soap and water."
She gave me a look that was a mixture of both pity and scorn

"You need some concealer," she announced and headed of for yet another pot.

After an hour she had an entire chess board of pieces lined up. She'd shown me how to put on concealer around my nose thus hiding the red spots. She evened up my skin tone with powder and a brush. My eyes were highlighted; my eyelashes minked and my thinning lips were made to look fuller and voluptuous. I was quite taken by the minking. You coat your eyelashes with brown mascara, and then administer a touch o black, just to the ends of the lashes. The effect is dramatic, instant lengthy, seductive eyelashes.

"Much better," murmured Natasha, the beautician who had opted to work her miracles on me.

"Now you look like you have eyes. The mascara has opened them up."

She handed me the mirror and waited for my reaction. I didn't disappoint. I felt glamorous.

I had to be careful with what I chose though. I had squirreled away some of the housekeeping money this week, so I had enough money to buy some cream and mascara. I also had a little of my 'emergency fund' which I keep from Phil's prying eyes. This allowed me to get the concealer too. Prior to this visit my face certainly counted as an emergency. The girls declared me presentable at last, gave me some samples, and a facial/neck massager. I can't even begin to describe it. It has two rollers, which you balance either side of your face and neck, connected by a wishbone shaped flexi piece of plastic. Apparently, it'll help me get rid of my double chin which is, according to Natasha, very aging but in spite of her best efforts, even I drew the line at a jar of neck cream for £220.

The massager resembles a sex aid; not that I know anything about sex toys. Clutching my bag, I marched off confidently to meet Phil. I felt super sexy (not because of the massager you understand). Surprisingly, he was standing outside the department store, waiting for me. I smiled. He looked at me quizzically. He looked at me some more.

"Have you had an accident? Have you been hit in the face?" He asked. "You look like a panda that lost a fight."

Guess I won't be minking my eyes much then.

Posted by Facing50Blog.com - 7 Comments

Faerie Queene said...Don't listen to him. I bet if you dressed up in something sexy and minked your eyes he'd notice you.
Facing50 said... No chance. He wouldn't notice me if I danced naked in front of the log burner with a tamborine.
SexyFitChick said... I know someone who would notice you. Have you spoken to him recently?
Facing50 said... He left a message for me, but I daren't open it.
YoungFreeSingleandSane said...Get your eyelashes dyed that'll make them longer. ALL men like you fluttering eyelashes at them don't they? Especially, first thing in the morning.
Facing50 said...Maybe he'd be more interested in YOU fluttering your eyelashes. I think when you get to my age, men like Phil, suddenly become more interested in reading the backs of cereal packets in the morning, than staring into your eyes.
SexyFitChick said...For goodness sake, read the message that Todd left.

Tuesday 12th

This morning I attempted to recreate the sultry effect that Natasha managed, completely in vain. The concealer is in blobs around my nose, and I've missed my lip line completely. I bet my mother has the same problem as me. What's the point in trying?

Todd has sent me a link to an article about him. I read it through a couple of times. It's about him winning a surfing competition. It accompanied by several photographs of him posing with his board and a cup.

I must say, Todd does look very good for his age. I've decided that children age you. I should have had a cattle dog instead. At least that wouldn't have broken my favourite seashell by resting a beer bottle on it. It was only a shell, but it was a shell that Phil had found on a beach, one romantic weekend many decades ago. He washed it off for me saying the colours were as pretty as my eyes. I'd treasured it because it reminded me of that moment, and now it's in pieces in the dustbin. Is that symbolic of our relationship, I wonder?
Posted by Facing50Blog.com - 2 Comments
Vera said...I'm sure that isn't the case, dear. The memory is still there after all.
Facing50 said...But fading with time I fear.

Friday 15th

I seem to be getter older by the day. I didn't feel like getting up at all today. I was completely lethargic. My stomach has blown up again, and I'm spotty. I thought you were supposed to have all these problems when you were younger, and thereafter it was all fine. Maybe I'm allergic to all that cream I bought at the shop last week. I am, to put it bluntly, racked off.

I haven't seen Phil all morning again. I think I heard him talking to the stock broker about mining stocks, which seem to have resurged now that the Chilean Miners have been rescued. I was glued to the set yesterday, watching each of them being rescued. It was immensely moving.

The poor souls have been trapped underground since August 5th. Phil seemed genuinely interested and moved. I discovered later that evening, that his interest was not entirely in the human side of the ordeal. *The World Mining Trust* fund which he purchased on August 6th, when the mine collapsed and all the mining stocks dived in price, has made some significant gains. I suspect it earned him a healthy profit. Judging by the gleam in his eyes, he is not just happy for the rescued miners and their families.

I attempted some housework but didn't have the heart for it today. I hate feeling like this. I compensated for my lack of love, by eating all the chocolate I could find in the house. Phil has his own small cupboard in the kitchen, which is filled with various bars of chocolate. He is the chocoholic in the family, and even Tom wouldn't dare to take any of Phil's chocolate, but I just desperately needed it today. Ordinarily, I have no desire for chocolate. Now, if the drawer was full of cheese or sausage rolls or cooked pasta there might be a problem.

I sneaked into the kitchen and, as I still couldn't find Phil, opened the drawer and wolfed down an extra large *Mars* bar. That didn't do the trick, so I had to follow it with a family sized bag of *Maltesers* and a double *Twix*. I felt much better after that. Unfortunately, Phil also had a chocolate craving and was dismayed to discover his chocolate had gone. I had to confess, then race up to the Post Office to replace it. I think the walk must have done me good because I felt much better when I got back. I should have tried that first.

Posted by Facing50Blog.com - 3 Comments

The Merry Divorcee said... I adore chocolate, especially that chocolate body paint.

Vera said... A good walk always makes you feel better, blows the cobwebs away.

SexyFitChick said...Both increase your level of endorphins, the hormone that makes you feel good. One is fattening; the other promotes stamina. Guess which does which?

Saturday 16th

Okay, as they say nowadays,' my bad?' I couldn't help myself. He'd left the *Scrabble* board wide open to play it and I had the following letters: g-a-o-r-m-s-s. It might have been partly because I was losing, and a full word meant points, or I was just feeling wicked. I blame you SexyFitChick! I played 'orgasms' on a double word too. Within seconds he had written:

'I wonder if I could still give you multiple.......'

I didn't know how to reply to that so I sent an exclamation mark and a wink. Anyway, I feel a lot better now. I can even face Phil, who has only just emerged from his room, and keeps going on and on and on, about Tom. I don't know what he expects me to do. I just let him chunter and thought back to those days in Casablanca.

Posted by Facing50Blog.com - 3 Comments

SexyFitChick said ... See, now you feel great, don't you?

Serene Siren said...Just found your blog. Your life sounds interesting. Just become a follower. By the way – you should always play to win.

Vera said...Oh I say!

Sunday 17th

Apparently, it's not just my mother who is enjoying life to the full at the moment. I was washing the windows which overlook the front courtyard, when I observed Ethel, squatting

on a stool taking a photograph of old Fred. He was attemptin
to get his leg over the saddle of a shining Triumph motorbik
Several attempts later he sat astride it proudly. I had to find
out what they were up to.

"Hello, what's going on?"

"Oh, Fred has treated himself to a new motorbike for his
birthday next week. We're taking a picture for the
grandchildren. Then we're going to send it to them on his ne
Pea Pod," explained Ethel.

"Pea pod?"

"Pea pad? Something like that," she explained. "Fred got
one for his birthday from the children. He's found all sorts o
webs. We bought the bike from one web, what's it called?
bDay? We had to put in a bid for it. Fred was up all night,
weren't you dear, waiting to see if our offer was accepted?"

I wished them well, took a photograph of them both sitti
on the bike, and returned to my windows. I later saw them
putting on some leathers. Ethel wound her arms tightly arou
Fred's waist and, as they set off, I'm sure I heard her shriek
with glee.

My mother is back from Cyprus and rang me to let me
know she was back safely. She certainly sounded a different
woman to the one who has been phoning the last couple of
months. She said she was tired. I guess that's why she was a
bit deflated. She seemed to have been whooping it up daily
out there. I would like to have her stamina when I'm her age
don't have it now though, so it's not very likely. She said sh
would send me some more photographs of her friends.
Posted by Facing50Blog.com - 1 Comment

Vera said... You are never too old to have fun, well, to try and have some fun

Thursday 21st

This morning some men came to put in our secondary glazing. Yes, we eventually ordered it. It transpired that the quote Phil received was wrong. It had been intended for another client. Phil pointed out that all workmen need copious amounts of tea to get a job done, and we had no milk. He refused to go and buy some himself as he was going to oversee the job. By oversee, I presume he meant, chat to the men for hours and put them off what they should be doing.

The only shop in the village is in fact also a post office. It sells absolutely everything you could wish for, especially if you are an old age pensioner here in the village. There are brightly coloured balls of wool for knitting or crocheting and thread for darning. There are half bottles of whisky, obviously for medicinal purposes, aspirins and cough mixture. There are old fashioned jars of wine gums, aniseed drops and other boiled sweets. In one corner, you can find second hand books. In another, is a large rack containing various birthday cards. I found cards with 'Happy Birthday - 65 today', 'Happy 80th', and even 'Congratulations now you are 100'. There's a section with 'In Deepest Sympathy' cards for those who don't live to be a ripe old age. One shelf in the shop is full of baked beans and cans of corned beef, so if we ever get cut off by a plague, like the people of the village of Eyam, we'll have enough provisions to see us through. You can purchase a lottery ticket there too, and of course, you can buy milk.

We live at one end of the village and the Post Office is at the other. So what? You may say, well for those of you who don't live in a rural village like ours, let me explain. We have lived here for twenty-three years and I now know eight peopl to talk to in the entire village, and two of those are our next door neighbours, who are from the North originally and were relocated here due to work. The villagers, having been born here, married locally and lived here all their lives, are reluctant to accept newcomers. In their eyes we are still newcomers. We are the outsiders who bought the barn from Farmer Jones. In fact, almost everyone here seems to be calle Jones. When we first moved here, the locals would traipse around to stare at what had been done to the old cow shed tha we had purchased, without even introducing themselves. The would just stare and suck their teeth, looking depressed at the loss of yet another good farm.

Getting to the Post Office should take only ten minutes, bu inevitably I will meet one or more of the only eight people I know in the village. Each one will stand and gossip for ages. Consequently, it always takes forever to get to the other end of the village.

Today, I met 'Old Pete' (Jones). He spends all day walking up and down the village hoping to bump into people like me. He's incredibly lonely and always wants to reminisc about his days in the Army. No sooner had I managed to extract myself from him, than Mrs Featherlite (used to be a Jones but married) scooted out from her house, two doors down, where I swear she had been waiting for me to go past. She'd had a letter from her son in New Zealand and wanted t tell me all about his new job, his wife, her four grandchildren their dog and a holiday they had recently been on. She then went onto talk about her sister's knees and lastly about the noisy road. We all love to chunter about the road in our village. Just when I thought she'd finished, she got the same letter out of her pocket.

"I got a letter from our Nigel today," and off the conversation went again.

I finally made it to the Post Office where, as always, there was a queue of mobility scooters. Personally, I would be terrified of driving along these roads and the pavements are so sloped it must be nigh on impossible to balance in comfort on the seats of these things, however this is the generation that survived World War II and they won't let a juggernaut bearing down on their tiny scooter frighten them, so they manage to shoot up and down the road with relative ease. I was just about to go inside, when my phone made the beeping noise of a text coming through. I looked down to retrieve the text, only to discover it wasn't my phone at all. It was Mrs Turnpike (not a Jones but a cousin of the Joneses) reversing on her scooter, which promptly ran over my foot.

"Didn't you hear me?" she yelled, as she sped off down towards the road, darting out in front of a huge petrol tanker, which squealed to a halt.

The queue in the Post Office was lengthy. The wait was made longer by the Post Mistress chatting to every single one of them, about their weekend, the weather and the other members of the village.

"Oh yes, and Doris had to call the doctor at two in the morning because Bert had pains in his stomach."

"I heard he wasn't feeling too well."

"Yes, Charlie and I think he's got an ulcer. You can never be too careful at our age."

"Oh yes, I know. Stan had an ulcer. He couldn't eat red meat for weeks."

"Does he get his meat from Fred?"

"I think so."

"We had some of his beef last week, and I couldn't chew it."

"His chops are super though, aren't they?"

"We had a chicken from him too and it was delicious. Had it with some of Ted's new cabbages."

"Did Mildred try those chicken breasts I got for her last week?"

"Yes, and she said thank you; they were lovely."

I almost gave up the will to live. Eventually, I got the milk. I managed to pass the new hairdresser shop that has just opened in the village without further encounters. It's called *Chic Styling*. Still, in this village blue rinsed hair and perms are considered chic, so it probably is aptly named. Every Friday morning, you can see old ladies making their way up t the other hairdresser, which unsurprisingly is called *Jones'* to sit under the hairdryers, and cluck away, each one emerging an hour later, sporting a tight blue rinsed perm. Hope the new hairdresser isn't expecting to cut and shape the latest style from Paris or Milan here.

I struggled through the group of gossiping old ladies, spilling out onto the pavement by the bus stop, all pursing their lips in disapproval even though I said good morning to them. I had started on the home straight when a microscopic furry bundle charged at my ankles, yelping and attacking.

Rufus, the ankle biting mutt, belongs to Edna. She is another member of the community who has decided we have lived here long enough to now pass as honorary locals. I had to listen to tales about Rufus, and what they have been doing since we last met. I tried to pat him in an effort to be friendly, but he obviously doesn't think twenty-three years here is long enough and attempted to snap at me.

One hour thirty-three minutes later I reached home clutching the bottle of milk, which by now was getting warm, to find the men standing in a huddle drinking tea from plastic mugs. They looked at the bottle and smiled.

"Oh thanks Love, but you needn't have bothered," they said. 'We always bring our own tea in the flasks.'

Posted by Facing50Blog.com - 1 Comment

SexyFitChick said... Were they good-looking workmen?

Tuesday 26th

I logged onto *Scrabble* today, but Todd hadn't played a word, or left a message. I have to say I felt a little disappointed. Maybe I've frightened him off by being so forward and flirty.

I am happy to report that after using the face massager for several days I have noticed an improvement in my face. It feels tighter and I might have less of a jowl, although that's difficult to ascertain, as you keep moving your head around to check, and it creates new folds around your chin. Be warned though, if you use it too much, you really do get jaw ache. The first few nights I had pains in my gland area. I woke up after a horrendous nightmare in which I was growing huge lumps on my neck, which resembled hyacinth bulbs, and could be plucked off. It was quite terrifying but I persevered with the contraption and feel I am making progress.

That is more than I can say for my body. I've let the rigid exercise routine fall off. I must make more effort, but it's difficult to get motivated on your own. I think I'll investigate the possibility of a gym, and maybe I'll be able to encourage Phil to go. He could really do with a hobby. He spends far too much time on the internet researching funds. Periodically, I'll hear mumbled tones as he talks to the stockbroker who handles his pension. He'll come out of the office, grab his briefcase and go back in again to mumble. I tried to cheer him up today with a joke:

"How do you make a small fortune? Start with a large one."

It didn't work.

I was checking my game scores on *Facebook* this afternoon, when the little red light came on, announcing a message had arrived for me.

'Hello Gorgeous. Sorry I couldn't play with you earlier. I've just come back from a cycling race. I came first, so I'm on such a high. It's better than sex. Well, it's better than sex, unless the sex is with you.'

The heat that crept up my neck wasn't from a hot flush.

'Congrats. I've not been cycling for a while.'

The light flashed

'So no good rides then recently?'

I could picture him grinning and grinned too.

'Fancy a quick one?'

I typed and opened the *Scrabble* board.

Posted by Facing50Blog.com - 5 Comments

SexyFitChick said... At last. Now, get yourself in shape again.
Mamma Mia6 said...Be careful. You don't want to go down that path.
Facing50 said...It's only a game of internet *Scrabble* (and some mild flirtation).
PhillyFilly said...He's definitely hot, no wonder you flushed

Thursday 28th

Sit ups are a chore. I managed twenty today and then strained my neck. Why isn't there an easier way of getting a flat stomach? I got so depressed, I wolfed down all of the cheese that was in the fridge, and now I can't do any more sit ups to wear it off, because my neck hurts too much. Pity Phil can't massage it for me. I bought him a small massage ball, with a cute face printed on it, ages ago, in the hope we could have some fun with it. It just sits on the top behind the bed, mocking me. However, I have discovered that the facial/neck massager is very good, especially if you try to use it against the sore parts of your body. Maybe a glass of wine will help.
Posted by Facing50Blog.com - 1 Comment
SexyFitChick said...You need to buy a stability ball to use for sit ups. Or maybe you could get Phil to curl up into a round shape and use him.

Saturday 30th

I've found myself hovering about on the *Scrabble* board all day in the hope that Todd would join me. I don't think this behaviour is very healthy. I tried to challenge Phil to a game of Backgammon but he snorted, and when I suggested cards,

he laughed, and asked me if I was any good at 'Snap'. He is just no fun anymore.
Posted by Facing50Blog.com - 2 Comments
Fairie Queene said...You should take up reading instead. I have some great recommendations on my blog....*Lady Chatterley's Lover* is always a good choice.
SexyFitChick said....Strip Poker is one of my favourite card games.

Sunday 31st

My mother called at four. I have to admit, in a strange sor of way, I think I missed her regular calls. That's probably du to me feeling sorry for myself again. This is an alien feeling t me. Well, not completely alien but I'm not normally prone to bouts of woe. I found myself sniffing at the film *Casper the Ghost* last night as I watched it alone in the gloom of the lounge. Phil was tucked up in bed. I was overcome by loneliness. So today I picked up the phone with something akin to pleasure, and even experienced a fleeting moment of fondness for my mother. I had planned to tell her about the ar class and had a few things to chat about. The feeling was quickly dispelled.

"Hello Mum," I piped up before she could say anything.

"Well, what's the matter with you then?"

"Nothing? Why do you ask?"

"You seem odd; out of sorts."

How could she detect that from a quick 'hello'?

"No, I'm absolutely fine. Now, are you going to enlighten me some more, as to who is on these photographs you have sent?"

"Well, there's no need to sound like that?"

"Like what?"

"All accusatory, as if I've done something wrong. May I remind you that I'm your mother, not your son? I don't need that kind of tone."

How had I managed to stuff up the phone call so early on? I had even been looking forward to hearing about her friends. It was not to be. She got quite shirty with me and told me she'd speak to me when I was in a better mood. I wasn't aware I was in a bad mood. I am now though.

Posted by Facing50Blog.com - 2 Comments

PhillyFilly said.... Maybe she is feeling a little guilty and doesn't want to discuss it with you. Attack is the best form of defence.

SexyFitChick said...If you are feeling aggressive may I suggest boxing? It helps alleviate tension and improves muscle tone. How about using Phil as a punch bag?

CHAPTER 5 – NOVEMBER

Sunday 7th

Sunday – the worst day of the week. A day absolutely detested by Phil. It's the one day of the week when you can guarantee he will become completely morose. Or should I say even more morose than usual? Yes, I know most people can't wait for Sunday. Starting each Monday morning, they count down to the weekend. They dream of being able to have a lie-in, go out for a drive, or maybe go to the shops. Some yearn to be with their families or to sit with a nice cold beer and watch football. Some can't wait to meet up with friends and go to the pub. Others will sit happily on a sofa with their loved one and watch a DVD in the afternoon, or play on the Nintendo 'Wii', and that, in a nutshell, is precisely why Phil hates it so much.

It stems from his working days, before he became retired and dull. To him a day away from the office was a day completely wasted. No money could be made on a Sunday, so he would prowl around the house like a caged tiger. He'd waste the day waiting gloomily for Monday to arrive. 5am Monday morning Phil would be in the shower whistling. Booted and suited he'd speed off to work at 7am on the dot to eagerly await the ringing of phones, each heralding new orders. His hatred of Sundays continues to this day, accompanied every weekend by his grumbling refrain 'I don't like Sundays' like an inaccurate Boom Town Rats song.

He hates Sundays now, more than ever. Every day is like a Sunday to him, but at least weekdays he can occupy some of the time checking the financial markets. He refuses to go out anywhere over the weekend, on the grounds that that is exactly what everyone else will be doing. Those of us who ar long-suffering partners of grumpy men like Phil, know you don't even suggest such a ridiculous idea.

The most exciting activity we can manage is a walk aroun our village. Phil quite likes that. He can vent his anger and exercise simultaneously. The whole process usually starts at the bottom of our drive where we need to cross a road. Inevitably, at the moment we wish to cross, a dozen cars or vans will come careering around the blind bend at speed. Phil glares at every one of them, even those doing the speed limit often yelling at them.

"You... You're not doing 30!"

I hardly think that the drivers are going to be bothered by withering look from an apoplectic 'Grumpy', especially as half of them are going so fast they probably haven't even see us. The traffic is a constant source of grumpiness. During the week he can complain for hours, really he can, about the larg heavy goods vehicles that thunder through the village. Recently, they have taken to mounting our curb in an effort not to bash into each other, when passing on the bend by our house, which has meant our entire grass bank is now destroyed. Weekends, he has the added pleasure of complaining vociferously about the wretched motor bikes, which insist on accelerating past the house, and whose dreadful whine is heard for an eternity, as they screech through the village.

Finally, he is coaxed across the road where he launches into a tirade about the dog mess all along the pavement. Som irresponsible local has taken to letting their dog foul the pavement quite badly, even though there is a meadow opposite and this has become the latest 'bête noir' for Phil. Each time we negotiate the piles along the pavement, and slalom our way up the street, I fantasize about following the said owner, and returning the said mess to them, via their letterbox. Phil insists on pointing out every single poop pile, and accompanies each find with a loud "Disgusting!" or even louder rude comments about the owner in the vain hope I expect, that the owner will hear and feel truly rebuked. Hitherto, the only recipients of this tirade have been elderly people making their way to church.

The dog mess finally diminishes in amounts and we arrive at the bus shelter. This is currently bestrewn with rubbish dropped by local teenagers who sit there each evening. Inevitably, this will lead to a rant about the youth of today and by now we will have reached the far end of the village and the pub which is currently advertising Christmas Day meals and yes, as you may have guessed, sends him into the predictable speech about commercialism. Mercifully, nothing else bothers him for a while now and we complete thirty minutes in compatible silence enjoying the fields and nature, unless speeding traffic forces us to leap into the hedge rows.

The rest of the day is spent gardening if it is nice, or sitting behind the computer trying to work out what financial markets will do the following week. It is the dreariest day and each Sunday has got worse and worse recently. Phil is becoming almost impossible to put up with. What with him grumping about, and Tom loafing about it, it is hardly surprising I spend my time here in the office blogging to you all. My mother didn't even call me today. I tried to ring her

but the phone was engaged every time I rang. Sorry to be so depressing today. It's just Sunday blues.
Posted by Facing50Blog.com - 0 Comments

Monday 8th

It's been one of those misty days where you just feel like staying in with the heating on. We can't do that of course, because the heating doesn't work. I spent the morning on the internet simultaneously hugging a filled hot water bottle. Phil was fed up too. Not because of the cold but because he'd missed a buying opportunity. Since the episode with the A38 Airbus which had an engine cut out on its way to Australia, the engine manufacturers, Rolls Royce are under pressure to resolve the problem. If they cannot sort it out in time they could suffer dire consequences and of course their share price is currently down. Phil saw the potential in this scenario. He believed Rolls Royce would rally, solve the problem and the share price would climb. He phoned the stock broker and told him his thoughts. The stock broker was inclined to disagree with Phil, who finally decided to accept the advice and wait to see what might happen. Naturally, the problem was resolved today and the share price leapt five percent. Phil is furious that he has missed out.

"If I had invested on Friday we could have recouped so many of the losses we have made recently in one day," he chuntered.

He complained all morning, periodically coming out of his room to bang some drawers and to give me a running commentary on the share price which continued to climb higher and higher. It's such a shame he didn't make some

money on those shares. Maybe he could have made enough to get this heating fixed.
Posted by Facing50Blog.com - 1 Comment
Vera said...Hindsight is always 20/20 vision.

Wednesday 10th

I feel under the weather yet again. This is becoming too much of a habit. It's mostly due to my inability to sleep, and the pounding headache which prevented me from lying in bed quietly, which is why I am posting this at five o' clock in the morning. I got up at three o'clock and took some headache pills but they refused to work so I took another couple. I know you shouldn't do, that but I felt rotten. Tom's bedroom door was open indicating he hadn't come home and as usual I started worrying about him.

He's probably at Tiffany's house, although I'd be surprised if Mr Henderson-Smythe would allow him to keep staying there. He is rather fond of his one and only daughter. I heard that he is desperate for her to become a surgeon, like him. I fear that won't happen if she continues to see Tom. She'll never find time for her studies. The headache finally eased but then I became a little hyper, probably due to too many pills, so I thought I'd come and complain to the laptop. What a dear friend you are. You let me rant and listen to my moans uncomplainingly.

Last evening Tom came into the lounge, marinated in Paul Smith, and announced he was going out. I decided to take advantage of his absence and attempt to have a romantic night in with the ever-distant Phil. I had bought a filled Yorkshire pudding each. I am ashamed to admit that I just cannot get the hang of Yorkshire puddings. My mother used to produce some of the finest for Sunday lunch, crisp and huge, but light as a feather. I loved eating them with mint sauce, made from fresh mint in the garden. I have never been able to emulate he in that respect and so I cheat by buying my puddings, as they are one of Phil's favourite meals.

Phil fetched some wood to light the log burner we had installed earlier this year to make the room cosy. He prepared it all at six o' clock. By seven o' clock he was in an absolutel foul mood. The log burner refused to light. He tried firelighters, paper, small sticks of wood, and many curses, bu to no avail. The log burner just kept going out. Meanwhile, the Yorkshire puddings were cooked and I called him through for his meal.

"In a minute," he grunted, ripping up several sheets of the *Financial Times* in a further attempt to light the reluctant fire.

"They're ready now," I emphasised.

"Okay, two minutes," came the reply.

Ten minutes later he arrived sooty faced.

"Damn thing. It doesn't like the wood we've got. It's too hard for it. It just can't burn it. I'll have to order some more wood."

Bearing in mind we have an enormous pile of wood that was not good news. Just for good measure the Yorkshires were dry and burnt. We ate in silence.

I tried to rescue the evening by letting him watch something stimulating on the television. I had recorded a programme about the UK's national debt. Apparently, we are indebted by 4.8 Trillion pounds. To get an idea of how much money that is, if every single house and flat in the UK were to be sold, and the money used to pay off the debt, we would still owe one trillion. It was a very good programme, but we both sank deeper and deeper into depression.

"I wish I lived somewhere else," declared Phil as the credits rolled. "Mexico or Canada or just anywhere, other than here. There are times like this, when I remember I'll soon be sixty that I ask myself what am I doing staying here? Shouldn't I be doing something interesting with what's left of my life?"

He stood up, plumped up his cushion, and without a further word went to bed. It was only eight thirty so I stayed up for a while, but his words echoed in my ears. I wish he would do something interesting with his time, and I wish we could do something more interesting together.

Posted by Facing50Blog.com - 4 Comments

Vera said...Sounds like he's going through the male menopause. Watch out he suddenly doesn't decide to buy a Harley Davidson motorbike, or get his ear pierced.

Facing50 said...I think I'd quite like to see him in leathers.

PhillyFilly said...A trip to the surgeon does wonders for cheering you up. My chap has just had his pecs done. He feels like a million dollars now.

YoungFreeSingleandSane said...Buy him some more chocolate to eat.

Friday 12th

I gave in and made an appointment to see the local quack, or doctor, as he should be appropriately addressed. I've not been to see him since Tom was a baby. The headaches are just not going away and I'm getting crotchety.

The last time I went to the surgery, sometime in 1990, I was greeted by a sour faced receptionist who ticked off my name on a list, and barked at me to wait my turn in the hot stuffy waiting room, where you could pass the time reading magazines from 1970, or listening to *Pan Pipe* music. Every ten minutes the door to the waiting room would fly open, an a doctor, there are three at the practice, would stand in the doorway with a wad of notes in his hand and call you forwar It has all changed since those days.

I forgot I'd made the appointment and was carried away on the *Scrabble* Board about to play vixen in a triple word. Phil banged on my office door and suggested I might like to get a move on if I still wanted to see the doctor. I snapped of the computer, and since the surgery is half a mile away I sprinted there. In truth I sprinted, jogged, puffed, hobbled an staggered my way up the road. As the car park there is alway stuffed full of cars there was no point in dragging the car out and the exercise was bound to do me good.

Red faced and puffing, I arrived at the surgery, a few minutes late. I launched myself at the door only to find it refused to open. I pushed again; nothing. I couldn't get into the surgery. Then I spied a screen to the left of the door over which was a large sign saying 'Enter your information here before entering'. The door would only open once you had pu in the correct information.

I wasn't wearing my spectacles so I couldn't see the scree clearly. I haphazardly put in what I thought it wanted, only t discover it was the wrong information and the door remained firmly shut. Fortunately, Edna and a dejected Rufus came by to collect a prescription.

“Hello Dear! Is everything alright?” she asked. Rufus perked up on seeing me and got ready to bite my ankle.

“Yes sort of. Er, Edna, I wonder could you help me with this machine.”

“Oh yes, of course, no trouble, now let me see, it needs you to press male or female, that’s easy. Now it says to put in the month of your birthday.”

“July.”

“July? That’s the same month as Rufus, isn’t it, sweetie?” Rufus growled and circled my legs. I bent down to pat him and he showed me his sharp pointed teeth.

“Now now Rufus, be friendly. You know Amanda, don’t you. She’s a friend.”

Rufus decided that he would have a scratch instead, and sat down scrubbing his hind leg against his ear, giving me time to move and continue my checking in process with Edna.

“Which date is your birthday?”

“27th”

“Right I’ve put that in, and, bingo!’

The door mechanism whirred into life. The door to the waiting room opened with a noisy click. I thanked Edna who waved airily at me.

“No trouble at all. These new electronic machines can be very confusing for older people.”

I glanced around the waiting room for a chair. It was heaving with people. Surely they weren’t all here to see the doctors. I’d be here until the afternoon if they were all waiting. Half of the village seemed to have gathered and were chatting about their families, or discussing each others’ ailments. One or two of them actually nodded at me before going back to their conversations. It was worse than the post office. Mrs Featherlite emerged from the door having been to see a doctor. She waved a prescription in the air.

"Same time next week, Gladys," she shouted to her friend.

"Yes, I'll book the same time and then we can have a good catch up again," replied Gladys.

It appeared that they were using the waiting room to see their friends. Most of them had already been into visit the doctor and were just hanging about in the warmth. It was a surprisingly cheery atmosphere. No doctor came out with a wad of notes but I heard a disembodied voice over the tannoy system interrupting the tinny 1960's music that had been playing.

"Mrs Amanda Wilson to Dr Bright.... room three please, Mrs Amanda Wilson"

I knocked politely at the door of room three and entered. Dr Bright was perched on his chair behind a computer. I prefer him to Dr Misery Guts or Dr Just Take an Aspirin (and come back if you are no better). Dr Bright and Breezy looked perplexed. His thick glasses were perched on the end of his nose and he was squinting at the screen.

"Your records need to be brought up to date. I can't seem to find anything about you on this."

"When was the computer system installed?"

"Nineteen years ago."

"Then there'll be nothing on it about me, I've not been to see you for twenty years."

"Really, are you sure? I'm sure I saw you only a few years ago."

"Well, we do see you regularly when we are out walking and as you are driving to work. You did, in fact, also see me last week when you almost drove into me on the road outside the butcher's shop and again a few days ago when you nearly squashed us flat against a hedge in the lane. But, no, it's definitely been twenty years since I came here, just after the birth of your little girl. How is she by the way?"

"At university, training to be a GP like her old man, I'm afraid. She's just passed her driving test too. Hope she doesn't drive like her old man,' he grinned. Gosh, doesn't time pass quickly?"

Doctor Bright gave me a thorough examination and checked my blood pressure. He remarked about my high colour and I had to explain about running to the surgery. He nodded in a wise manner.

"It's fairly obvious that you are in good enough health. Statistically, you are reaching that time in your life."

I knew what he meant by 'that time'. I'd expected him to talk about fluctuating hormones and treatments that would assist. I'd spent weeks on the internet ticking off my symptoms and had already come to that conclusion myself.

"The headaches could be attributed to hormonal changes," he continued. "But, in this case I think you are far more likely to be suffering from tension headaches caused by stress. You can take medication, but unless you dispose of the problem, you won't get rid of the headaches. Do you think you know what might be causing it, and can you get rid of the problem?"

I thought about Phil, about how miserable he was and how unhappy it was making me, I thought about Tom and the mess he left behind each day and the tension between him and Phil.

I reflected on how much anxiety I felt about the way Tom wa turning out, and how frustrating he was with his lazy, don't give a damn attitude.

"I think I have an idea as to what may be causing it, and I would love to get rid of the problem, but it isn't going to be easy."

He told me to 'chill' more. He thought I should take up Yoga like his wife, and have regular massages to relieve the tension in my neck, which is partly to blame. He even suggested that I drink a couple of glasses of wine occasionall which cheered me immensely. He said relaxation therapy and breathing techniques might also assist. I don't know if they'll help but I'll have a go. It would be much easier though if other people just sorted themselves out.

Posted by Facing50Blog.com - 2 Comments

SexyFitChick said...Come check out my blog. There are some ideas on it that may help.

The Merry Divorcee said...You need a holiday – from your men.

Sunday 14th

I waited for my mother to call again today and when I still hadn't heard from her by five I gave her a ring. I thought she might still be annoyed with me for asking her about her friends. She answered cheerfully enough though. I soon founc out why. She had booked herself another trip back out to Cyprus for a couple of months.

"There's no point in hanging about her. It's cold and grey. I'm not going to waste what little time I have left sitting in every afternoon watching Noel Edmonds and his twenty-two boxes," she wheezed. "I'm planning on going on Wednesday. I've been discussing with my friends about having implants done. I'm going to get them done in Cyprus. It's cheaper there and they are very good at it. Two of my friends have had it done. They've recommended someone I should use."

I struggled to comprehend what was being said. My mother, sat around a table with octogenarians, discussing the merits of falsies. Besides, my mother was perfectly well endowed. She didn't need any new boobs. It was ridiculous. If anyone needed a new pair; it would be me.

"Mum, I've heard that sort of surgery can go wrong. What if they blow up on the plane when you came back?"

"Blow up? How can teeth blow up? I've been having trouble with these crowns of mine. I lost a front tooth last month. My other teeth are all yellow now. Probably due to all the coffee and smoking," she laughed hoarsely. "I really would like to have nice teeth again. I look like an old crone," she continued.

She prattled on about teeth and new implants for the whole conversation. Last week, she bought a dental repair kit at the chemist to stick a crown back in. She shut herself in her bathroom with her reading glasses, a magnifying mirror and a glass of wine to help steady her hand as she attempted to rejoin the broken crown to the stump. Of course, it wouldn't stay in. After numerous attempts, another dental kit, some more wine and a few phone calls to friends, she succeeded in getting the offending tooth back in. It fell back out when she was queuing at the bank, leaving her to smile a gummy smile at the young cashier. Exasperated by it all and several further failed attempts later, she has managed to get it back in. How?

Superglue! Goodness knows how the dentist will get it out again. She's organised treatment for the day after she gets ou there.

"Mum, are you sure you want to have this done?" I asked. "Shouldn't someone be with you? You know, in case you fee bad, or can't eat properly."

"Oh for goodness sake Mandy, I'm a grown woman. It's only some teeth. Besides, I have loads of people who will look after me. That's one of the reasons I'm getting it done there. Better there than here. So, stop your mithering. I'll sen you some photographs of them when they are being fitted. That way you won't miss out."

Posted by Facing50Blog.com - 2 Comments

PhillyFilly said...She'll be fine. I love mine. They're all shin and white.

Fairie Queene said...Isn't she wonderful? What a character your mother is.

Monday 15th

Yet another day in the Amanda Wilson household, that isn't all *Sunshine, lollipops and rainbows...* It used to be 'Sunshine, wine gums and rainbows' until I discovered that not only did they rot your teeth, but they weren't made out of wine – what a letdown. No, some days I get up and think I'm Tom Cruise in *Mission Impossible.*

"Today Amanda, aka Facing 50, your mission, should you wish to take it, is to prevent Phil from self combusting with annoyance. This message, like Phil himself, will self destruct in a few seconds."

This morning began with one of those predictable *Mission Impossible* messages. Phil had got up in a funk. I knew he was annoyed because he'd spent the last three hours huffing, and turning over in an exaggerated manner, which was really to ensure I was awake and know he was cross. I pretended to be asleep. The last thing you want at four in the morning is a complaining man. I can only deal with it in daylight hours.

Unfortunately, as I was part of the reason he had got up annoyed. I thought I'd better do the tender loving wife thing and get up to try and improve his mood. I tiptoed into the kitchen where he was throwing pieces of paper about and snarling. What could possibly have caused this mood? Well let me explain.

For years, no, decades we have had a mobile phone contract. It started when Tom was at school and had his own mobile phone to use for emergencies. I got one too so we could be in touch at any time. If he needed me and I wasn't in the house then he could get me on the mobile. Of course, Tom never used the phone to contact me, but succeeded in running up large bills texting and phoning his school chums.

Later, Phil decided he didn't want a house phone bill, as well as a mobile bill, so we only used the mobile. He happily used it to make his important and often very lengthy phone calls, to his stock broker and accountant. It was a simple phone. It was very large. It was like a brick and had large easy-to-use buttons; one to speak, another to end the call, and Phil was happy. When the contract ended we replaced the phone with an updated one. This one had smaller buttons and could send text messages. Phil didn't like the text messages.

"You use a phone for a conversation not to write to each other," he would complain. And then he would ask me to sen a text to one of his friends, as he didn't know how to use it. Years passed and he finally managed the art of opening a tex and reading it. He never actually mastered text sending.

At the end of that contract we replaced the mobile with a new even smaller phone. This one not only could text but ha a radio and a camera. I loved it and took photographs of Phil glowering, and used the headphones to listen to the radio in the garden, and drown out the noise of him complaining abo the weeds that I had failed to remove. Phil couldn't fathom why anyone would want to take a photograph with a phone when they could use a nice camera. As for a radio well didn' we have one in the house?

And so, onto the present day. After a two year contract, w were officially allowed to change our phone for something more modern. Ours is looking very old now, and used; a bit like me. The buttons are faded and the casing is scratched from banging around in my handbag with my lipstick. I've been wittering for weeks about getting a more modern phone and so, beaten down at last by my persuasive nagging, Phil said I could sort out the phone and get whatever I wanted provided it was still the same monthly deal.

I love gadgets and all that modern stuff, so after an hour with a gorgeous young salesman in the phone shop on Saturday, who showed me all of the new technology, and made it all look so simple, I emerged the proud owner of a smart phone. Shiny and black it is the all singing, all dancing version of a phone. I won't bore you with all that it can do, but suffice to say, it only falls short in two categories; it can' make a cup of tea or massage my feet. Apart from that, it can do everything.

Phil met me at the car park and casually asked if I'd got what I wanted and for the same monthly deal. He looked slightly nervous and then began to go ashen when I pulled out the phone listing the amazing things it can do. By the time I'd got to 'browse the internet' and 'download music because it is an mp3 player too,' he looked quite ill.

"Does it make phone calls?" he asked hesitantly.

"Oh yes, just like the last one," I replied confidently.

And therein lays the problem. It isn't at all like the last phone, or the one before, or the one before that. It is so complicated. You have to unlock it every time you want to use it. You have to use the touch screen and have no buttons to press. You can voice command it to dial a number. It tells you what the weather will be tomorrow. The front keyboard is full of *apps* (He was completely bewildered by that piece of information). Nothing is where you'd expect to find it. The text messages are typed on a small keyboard which automatically spell checks them. There is no more need for text speak like 'c u l8r'. It is a marvel of technology, which can only mean one thing; Phil quite simply loathes it.

Part of this dislike comes from the fact that I adore it. I shut myself in my room immediately with it learning how to put all my photos onto it and download my music. I bought it a ringtone. I cleaned it. I caressed it. I 'oohed' at the sheer cleverness of it. And, of course, after I learned all about it I wanted to share it all with Phil. He, alas, was not at all interested. I tried to show him how to make a call. He backed away as if it might bite him and when it rang and he heard the dulcet tones of Enrique Iglesias singing *I like it* he looked horrified.

Thus this morning he got up in a mood. I had thought I'd be able to drag him into the twenty-first century, after all he can now send an email, and it only took me four years to teach him. The phone however, was proving to be a problem. When he's in a funk it can take all day to cheer him up but today, after feeding him several chocolate biscuits that I was saving as a treat, and cooking him a nice breakfast, Phil's mood improved. I put Abba on the stereo for him and asked about his chilblains. I listened to him rant about the new world and technology. I was sympathetic.

An hour or so of pampering paid off. The problem of the new phone has been resolved. Phil has decided that he will purchase a 'pay as you go' SIM card for the very old first mobile phone that we used to own, and which he has kept all these years. He likes things as they were. He likes the old ways. He doesn't subscribe to technological advances. I'm not going to complain, after all, I get to play with my new toy, and I get to use all the free minutes – I just need some friends to call now and all will be well.

Mission accomplished.

Posted by Facing50Blog.com - 2 Comments

SexyFitChick said...Of course, you can download photographs onto your computer now from this phone and share them with your friends. Your special friends, I mean. Your special friends from Australia. LOL.

Facing50 said...I don't think that's a good idea. He'd see what I really look like. It's not a pretty sight!

Wednesday 17th

I continue to feel the ravages of time. This week, I have had to collect a new pair of glasses, or spectacles to give them their correct name. These are not 'reading' glasses, as I gave in to having those a few years ago; just after Phil caught me shining a torch onto some spice jars which were being held right up to my nose, as I tried to work out which one was cinnamon, and which one was chicken seasoning. No, these are for all the rest of the time when I'm not reading. They are to be my 'seeing' glasses.

I was very glum about the whole thing as I absolutely loathe wearing glasses. It stems from my childhood when my teachers, and my mother, decided I couldn't see properly after I had just started at the all important Primary School. I was hiked off to some old fossil of an optician in the town who put eye drops into my eyes rather brutally, making me cry, and then prescribed me some glasses. They had lenses like the bottom of milk bottles and were in round tortoiseshell National Health frames. I hated them with passion. It was well before the advent of Harry Potter, who has made such hideous items fashionable, and I wonder how much my life might have changed had they been fashionable then. I duly wore them to the new school where I was the only pupil to have glasses.

I was instantly taunted by fellow pupils who would laugh at me at best and at worst shout out "Owly!", "Four Eyes" or the dreaded "Speccy!" I hid the offending glasses at the bottom of my school bag and didn't wear them anymore. I continued to hide all subsequent pairs too, until later in life, when I would keep an emergency pair to wear when I had ba headaches, and no one else could see me wearing them.

Recently it has become obvious that my eyesight is failing considerably. I can't see clearly. "Pothole? What pothole?" I'll say as we drive into a crater-sized hole in the road. I've also starting falling off the edge of pavements as I can't actually judge where the edges are. Phil started to remark on my ability to knock over objects, and when I actually walked into the television, he decided I needed to see an optician. He even made the appointment for me at a newly opened establishment. He accompanied me there, me, resembling a reluctant dog on its way to the vet for a jab. We were greeted by a movie star lookalike and told to sit on rather glamorous chairs beside a glass topped table, adorned with smart magazines. I sat gawping at all the labelled cabinets containing prestigious glasses made by *Dior* and *Swarovski*.

"Mrs Wilson?" called out a velvet voice, and there stood my new optician, a gorgeous dark haired man, aged about thirty-five.

"Yes," I yelped, knocking into the coffee table as I leapt up, and dislodging all the magazines onto the floor. Phil rolle his eyes.

Anyway, the whole experience was rather pleasant. I was closeted in a dark room with a young man staring into my eyes; a situation I have not found myself in for many years. My astigmatism has become more astute and hence all the walking into things. My eyes have deteriorated sufficiently fc me to require glasses full-time, and especially for driving. I must point out here that it is completely inconceivable that I could consider any form of laser treatment, or contact lens, to correct my vision. Even typing that sentence has made me wince. I am ultra squeamish about eyes. The only solution is to wear glasses.

Next step was to choose some frames, and I was left in the hands of the same glamorous girl who had welcomed us, a striking blonde from Scandinavia. She was wearing a fantastic pair of stunning red frames that set off her face beautifully. What an advert for wearing glasses! To cut a long story short I let her choose my frames, and she settled upon a pair of handmade French glasses made by *JFRey,* called *Boz Eyes* (Ha ha, 'ow zee French are so funny).

I collected the glasses yesterday. They came in an amazing pony hide case, which has little straps like a mini-handbag. It is ultra cool. I shall use it to carry my lipstick and mobile when I go out. The glasses look cool too. They are copper coloured on the outside and bright lime green inside; a real contrast to the old National Health specs. Phil supportively told me I looked good in them, and when I drove home I avoided all the potholes. Then the problems started. When I got home I realised that the cupboards were all filthy, and scrubbed them all. So were the windows, so I scrubbed them too. Phil insisted they were fine but no, I could see they were not. Phil had a mark on his shirt.

"It's microscopic," he insisted as I whipped the shirt from him and washed it. Then I went into the bathroom. Up until that moment I had thought my hair was blonde, but on closer inspection I discovered it was grey. I must an appointment to get it coloured.

"Why?" wailed Phil "It's blondish."

I made an appointment to get my eyebrows done too as they were horrendous.

"There's nothing wrong with them," said Phil in exasperation.

Worse came though when Tom saw me in them.

"Nice specs Mum. You look a bit like Madame Trichet."

Madame Trichet had been his French teacher, a dear old sixty-five year old lady, with her hair in a bun and very loud glasses. I put the glasses in the drawer. Phil didn't seem to notice I wasn't wearing them. I'll wear them for driving. Th world is sometimes better viewed without glasses, rose coloured or otherwise.

Posted by Facing50Blog.com - 2 Comments

Vera said...I hated my specs too but you get used to them after a while and Harry Potter has made it cool to wear them

Trinny said...Hi! Just popped by to say hello. I've had glass all my life too. At least there are some smart styles out there, and the French are chic, so put them on girl.

Thursday 18th

I've given up with the exercise facial massager after discovering dark patches on my chin. They turned out to be bruises after my over energetic rolling of the apparatus. I'll continue to use it to ease my neck which still aches. I've als noticed that my face is even hairier than before and I wonder if I've over stimulated the hair follicles with all the rolling. It's either that, or I've started to absorb the testosterone that flies around the atmosphere here at home. I think I'm going t have to make another appointment to see Dr Bright and Breezy about this.

As I have mentioned before Phil is a very neat practical man. His socks are laid in formal rows in the drawer and coded according to colour. At the weekend, he patiently pulled apart an old brick wall, chipping off bits of cement and redoing it, humming to himself and spending hours on his knees uncomplaining, making the wall look perfect.

A practical man he may be, but one who cannot operate the DVD recorder, a microwave, work the CD player or indeed use a computer. You already know about his reaction to new technology and mobile phones. When Tom went to university he left behind his old Toshiba laptop that he had used at school. He didn't need it for university as there were huge computer libraries for them to work in. I expressed surprised when Phil laid claim to it.

"I can check out the share prices," he informed me.

I duly showed him how to turn it on, and set up relevant favourite pages for him to just click on when he needed them, and showed him how to turn it off. By now you will have gathered that Phil is just not very good with technology. Each time he needed to use our old fax machine there would be howls of rage and expletives emanating from the office.

"This ruddy thing won't work!" he'd screech. "It's useless!"

I would race down and press the appropriate button usually the one marked 'On', allowing it to whir into life. Machines hate him - apart from cars. The old printer would faint each time he attempted to print a document. It would freeze every single time, until I went down and gave it some smelling salts, then it would work. I refuse to let him near my precious laptop. I'd lose all my documents.

All has been well with his laptop. I generally maintain it, check updates, make sure it has no bugs etc. Phil turns it on. It allows him to look at his share prices and it has been fairly harmonious until today. It wanted to update some security software. Phil thought he could manage to do it without any interference from me. It wasn't long before I heard an exclamation of annoyance, followed by the furious punching of several keys, followed by some swearing, followed by more furious tapping. I went into the room to find Phil pressing every single key on the keyboard like he was banging out a 'Honky Tonk' tune on an old piano.

"It won't work."

The screen had frozen.

"I'll fix it," I placated.

"No, it's useless. You can't fix it. I've tried."

He bashed at it some more.

"No, leave it. I can sort it," I insisted.

Phil ignored me and started hitting the keys with his fist.

"Bastard thing!" he yelled, suddenly losing his rag completely.

"They are useless, pointless, irritating, annoying machines!"

He was rapidly turning into the character Basil Fawlty of *Fawlty Towers* in the episode *The Gourmet Evening* when he thrashes his car because it won't work. I couldn't bear it any more. I left him to it.

The noise and shouts got worse and then there was a thump, and then more thumps, followed by a crash. Phil came into the kitchen.

“That’s fixed it good and proper,” he commented looking flushed. “It was useless anyway.”
He went outside and started up his mower. The computer was lying on the floor. I tried to give it the kiss of life but it had given up completely. RIP little Toshiba.
Posted by Facing50Blog.com - 1 Comment
Serene Siren said....Poor Little Toshiba indeed. I hope I don’t come back reincarnated as a laptop and sold to Phil!

Friday 19th

We ‘buried’ Toby Toshiba, which meant a drive to the local recycling centre; a mission in itself. The queue to get in was enormous. There was a huge bouncer type in a high visibility jacket who insisted we all went to the appropriate skip to throw away our rubbish. The problem arose when people didn’t know where they should put their various items. I saw a couple of men lugging a huge mattress over to one skip, only to be shouted at by another man in a high visibility jacket, who insisted they carried it a further 250 metres to a different skip.

“That one’s almost full,” he yelled.

It didn’t look at all full to me, or to the poor pair carrying the heavy mattress, who were forced to puff and pant their way between parked cars, and hoards of people, also disposing of old chairs, fridges, televisions and general waste.

We finally found the appropriate metal container for the computer. It was stuffed full of old computers. I had to stop Phil from trying to pick one up and take it home, in the hope it still worked.

"Look at that one," he said gleefully, pointing at an old Apple Mac. "That looks brand new. I bet it still works."
I dragged him away.

Phil then decided that, in spite of dwindling finances, he'c like a new computer. He claimed the reason the old one wouldn't work for him, was because it had slowed down witl age. I know how it feels. I was reluctant to let Phil buy a new laptop. Not because I begrudge him having a computer, or indeed spending some money on himself. It's just I know he' break it, even if it's brand spanking new. He insisted it was vital to his research. He needed to track the share prices and check out funds. He was adamant about this, and when he suggested that maybe he could share mine instead, I gave in. don't want him anywhere near my laptop. It's my lifeline to the outside world and my friends.

We mooched around several stores today. By the fourth store Phil still looked baffled.

"What's Intel Pentium and why would I need Windows7?'
The array was bewildering. I loved the new iPads but, not only were they too pricey, but Phil couldn't get his head around them at all.

"Can you make phone calls on them?"

"I think you may be mixing them up with iPhones, like th one we've just got."

"What's a tablet used for? Don't you have those for your headaches?"

"Don't be silly."

At the department store where we normally have coffee, there was a promotion on laptops. With the help of a salesman, who, after we left, must have gone into a dark roon to have a breakdown, we finally settled on a super Toshiba Satellite A660-1DW with 4GB RAM and a 16 inch display. It had £100 pounds off the price. Having spent over an hour with the salesmen, asking pointless questions, which only revealed him to be completely ignorant about computers, Phil seemed pleased with his choice. The salesman exuded relief, wiped the sweat from his brow and hared off to package it up. When he got back to the till, Phil had disappeared. We found him in a side room looking at some televisions and computers that were on the shelves.

"What's that?" He barked at the man, pointing at a laptop that indeed, looked remarkably like the one he was about to buy.

"It's a second-hand one, Sir. It has been returned to us. Maybe the customer didn't like it, or changed his mind, and it has been sent back to us. It's been checked and works but there is no booklet with it, or box to carry it in and I think some of the USB leads are missing."

"But it works, doesn't it?"

"Oh yes Sir, and it has a two year guarantee with it."

"This price tag says that it is half price."

"That will be because it is missing all the instruction manuals. You would need to know how to set it up and use it, or you could maybe go online to order a manual."

Phil licked his lips and his eyes took on a familiar look. I knew what he would do. Sure enough we took the half price laptop. Phil was delighted to have got such a bargain.

"Tell you what Mandy; it's much more your thing, than mine. You have this new laptop, and I'll take the old one. You'll be much better at sorting it out and getting it going."

I have spent all the time since getting it set up. It has tested my patience, but we are getting along nicely now. My old laptop is trembling at the thought of going into Phil's office but I've told it as long as it behaves, and doesn't slow down every time it sees Phil, it'll be safe.

Posted by Facing50Blog.com - 2 Comments

Vera said...I have an Apple Mac. I love it. It's like my best friend. Hope your old laptop survives Phil.

SexyFitChick said...Shame there isn't a recycling bin for husbands. You could have chucked Phil in and chosen a new model. One that doesn't take so long to get going!

Saturday 20th

I could brain Tom. He put a whole pile of washing into my machine last night and turned it on when I was in bed. He didn't check any of the pockets, and now everything is covered in bits of damp tissue; masses and masses of it. He's not supposed to use the machine. He's supposed to get up on Saturday and go to the launderette. His heavy hooded tops have also been put in, and now the drum is dislodged. I'll have to call for an engineer to fix it. I sent Tom a text since he's never around to chastise. It's difficult to convey how cross you are on a text. I got a reply back:

'Soz. Had 2 use machine as goin out 2nite to party at Buxton. No time 2 do washin. Luvya'

I can't get all the rotten paper off the clothes. I shook them outside but it's clinging to everything. I tried to pick it all off but can't remove it. I used a lint remover roller which was also useless, so in the end I dumped it all back in Tom's room on his bed with a note:

'Make time next weekend and sort this mess out. Luvya'
Posted by Facing50Blog.com - 3 Comments
Vera said...Good for you.
YoungFreeSingleandSane...Another reason I don't want a boyfriend. They are generally so messy.
MammaMia6 said...Children never grow up. My eldest is almost thirty and still expects me to do his washing for him.

Sunday 21st

Tom came back late this afternoon. Phil told him to tidy his room. He muttered something about needing to do an important assignment for tomorrow and went to his room, supposedly to do it. I scurried off before Phil could start snapping at me about the fact that Tom, knowing he had an assignment, had still gone out for the weekend. As I went past to the bathroom later, I heard snoring. I suppose he'll ask for an extension on the assignment.

My mother phoned just as I was taking the chicken out of the oven.

"Get that!" I shouted to Phil.

"No way, you know who it'll be. You get it."

I tried to hold a conversation with the phone under my chin and serve dinner simultaneously. She chatted nonstop about her first appointment with the dentist. Full of excitement about getting new white teeth, she didn't notice that I was no longer listening. I had dropped the phone in the gravy boat and had to rinse it off under the tap. When I got it back to my ear, she was still chatting away about what she was going to do in Cyprus.

I just caught the end of one of her sentences ..."so he'll drive me to the surgery every day while I'm having this treatment. He'll, sort of, hold my hand though it all. And, he said he'd make soup for me each evening. What a sweetheart he is."

"Who?" I asked, probably rather suspiciously.

"Honestly, Mandy, I've just told you twice. I'm not going to repeat myself again. You really should listen more. Now, I must go. My dinner is almost ready. Talk to you when I can. Bye for now."

I looked at the congealed gravy and carrots floating about on the dinner plate. I no longer had any appetite.

Posted by Facing50Blog.com - 3 Comments

SexyFitChick said...It sounds like your mother has much more fun than you. I think I'd fancy getting my teeth whitened. It certainly makes you look younger. You want to watch out for your mum. Is she getting her teeth done because of a fella?

Facing50 said...No, that's not likely is it? She's almost seventy-seven.

SexyFitChick said...So? I'm not exactly twenty-two myself.

Wednesday 24th

Finally some 'me' time. I thought about Doctor Bright's advice and booked myself in for a haircut and colour. They give great head massages when they wash your hair, and I thought some time trying to make myself look better, might be therapeutic. It takes about three hours and I don't normally like spending that amount of time at the hairdresser because staring at oneself in the mirror, while tin foil is put in your hair, is boring and demoralising. However, having discovered a handful more grey hairs this morning, I figured it was time to get it done.

Marcus tied the black gown around me. Black is unflattering. I stared out from my hollowed eyes and looked in the huge mirror at the old woman I was becoming.

"So, what are we doing today?" asked Marcus camply.

"I want you to make me look at least ten years younger. No, make that fifteen," I joked.

Marcus giggled charmingly and ran his fingers through my mousy grey hair.

"I know exactly what you need," he announced, after staring at the reflection for a few minutes.

"A fortnight in the Caribbean?" I asked.

He squealed in delight.

"You are so funny. No, I think you need a pep up. Just leave it to Marcus. I'll soon have you looking glam, girlfriend."

Had he been watching Gok Wan on television again?

Three hours later I emerged, my newly striped head gleamed like a tiger. I was a mixture of blonde, brown and copper; a sort of mixture of all the *Desperate Housewives* put together. It looked striking. It also matched my coat perfectly, and you couldn't see where my head stopped, and my coat began.

Phil didn't notice my hair, even though he knew I was having it done, after all he'd just spent three hours waiting for me. He had spent the time very wisely, seeking out bargains in the supermarket. Phil cannot resist a bargain. If something is on offer he will buy in bulk. Today he had cornered the market in mini *Shredded Wheat.* He'd procured twenty boxes.

"I couldn't resist at that price," he said gleefully. "What a bargain. I bought all the remaining boxes."
The car boot was stuffed full of king size boxes of mini *Shredded Wheat*.

"Phil, do you actually like *Shredded Wheat*?"

"Well, no, not much, but I thought you might like them. They were such good value."

"By the way, I like your hair," he added.
I forgave him instantly. It looks like I'll be eating *Shredded Wheat* for the rest of the year, and well into next year too.
Posted by Facing50Blog.com - 2 Comments
SexyFitChick said...Go get them tiger, growl!
MammaMia6 said...At least he does the shopping. Mine watches television all day, wearing nothing but a vest and jeans.

Thursday 25th

I've got a text late last night from my mother saying she had just had the first part of her treatment.
'Look like an old witch – just missing a broomstick. Pity it isn't Halloween. I could frighten a few children. Will be worth it though. Staying in with girls for a quiet night. Love Mum X'
She's quite courageous isn't she?
Posted by Facing50Blog.com - 2 comments
Vera said...It was nice she let you know. She obviously doesn't want you to worry about her.
Facing50 said...I think you are right Vera. I'll send her a text back straight away.

Friday 26th

The phone warbled at lunchtime and a barely recognisable voice gave me the latest on the implants. She was full of praise for the dentist who had undertaken the task. I couldn't work out if she was unintelligible due to the treatment or too much wine. I got the gist of the conversation though.

Apparently, the treatment was lengthy, and as the dentist had to keep stopping for my mother to go and have a cigarette up on the surgery roof, it took more time than either of them thought. She is currently without her old teeth and is awaiting the final implants.

She's been too embarrassed to go to her usual haunts. She didn't want to be seen by the crowd she hangs out with. Fortunately, she has some very good friends who decided that she couldn't possibly sit at home like a seventy-seven year old, watching television, knitting or reading books and a group of them invited themselves around to her flat for an impromptu party. She soon forgot about her appearance and they've all decided to throw a party to show off her new teeth when they are finished.

"Oh that's nice. Just a few friends at your flat then?" I said.

You would think I'd know better by now wouldn't you?

"No," she said offhandedly. "I've booked a taverna for all my friends. There'll be about a hundred and twenty-four, no make that twenty-five, Helena is bringing her boyfriend. Oh no, make that a hundred and twenty-seven. Bernard is out of hospital, and said he wouldn't miss it for the world. We're going to have a fancy dress party, 'Greek Gods and Goddesses'. I'm going as Aphrodite," she ended triumphantly.

Posted by Facing50Blog.com - 2 Comments

Fairie Queene said...If your mother wrote a blog she'd have hundreds of followers.

Facing50 said... She's far too busy for that. You'll have to put up with me instead! LOL

Saturday 27th

Todd is off on his travels again. He always seems to be going somewhere.

"Don't you have a job to do?" I asked in response to his email saying he was going away to the coast for a few days.

"No. I invested all the money I earned from working in Kuwait, into gold funds, and I've made enough money to allow me to loaf about and have a good time. I don't work anymore, just have fun."

I checked the spot price of gold and discovered that gold had gone up 188% in the last five years.

"Did you consider buying any gold for your pension fund?" I asked Phil who was glowering at some notes he had written.

"I wish I had. It's raced away. I'd have made a killing if I'd invested in a gold fund or an ETF. Whoever had the foresight to sink money in gold, when it was on its lows, will have made a fortune," he continued staring wistfully into space.

Well, well, good looking, fun, fit, single and rich. Now that is interesting.

Posted by Facing50Blog.com - 1 Comment

SexyFitChick said...Send me his address. He sounds perfect.

Sunday 28th

We appear to have been invaded by Russia. Well, by their weather certainly. We have an abundance of snow outside and it is, without doubt, perishing cold. Thank goodness we had the log burner put in. I've been sitting inside at the computer wearing my new *Ugg* earmuffs. Actually, they are not proper *Uggs*. I think the correct term is knock offs. They have *Ugh* on the label instead. Good thing they don't say *Mugg.* At least they keep my ears warm. I hope it doesn't last too long and we get holed up for weeks. It's bad enough being inside with Phil most of the time, but all of the time would be too much for me to bear.

Posted by Facing50Blog.com - 3 Comments

SexyFitChick said...You wouldn't mind being holed up if it were with a fun loving, good looking bloke from 'down under', would you?

Facing50 said...You're right. I bet he'd think of some way to keep me warm.

PhillyFilly said...Could be snowed in here too. I'm going to check myself into a clinic for a couple of weeks and get some work done to myself ready for next year.

CHAPTER 6 – DECEMBER

Wednesday 1st

I used to love December. All the excited preparations for Christmas, the promise of snow that never arrives on the day, dark evenings snuggled in front of the fire with candles lit and Christmas tree lights sparkling. I'll burst into song in a minute about chestnuts and *Jack Frost* just recalling it all. Well, now I'm older, I don't like December as much. It's cold. It's dark and I can't see anything after three o'clock in the afternoon without every light in the house blazing away. The roads are horrendously busy and towns are heaving. From the beginning of December, trying to find a car parking space in town is like finding a golden ticket in a *Willy Wonka* bar of chocolate. If you do strike lucky, top floor, last space, wedged in between a people carrier and a clapped out old Ford, you can't actually get around the shops for people milling about.

As for buying something, well let's hope you've paid for six hours car park time, because you'll need it after queuing in each shop to pay for goods. December usually means preparations for Christmas as there isn't much else to look forward to, apart from work parties, but being retired means there are no more great nights out with the girls and boys from the office. I miss those old days of going out to clubs and dancing all night, while swigging bottles of tequila after a meal, where everyone wore a silly paper hat and got plastic useless toys out of a cracker. Sadly, one of the only highlights of December for me this year, appears to be the six monthly trip to the dentist for my check up.

When I was younger I had an unfortunate encounter with a 'one-armed bandit'. Nowadays it is called a fruit machine. If you pulled the large metal handle down on one side of the machine, three wheels would spin and show three different fruit. Certain combinations resulted in wins and coins would clatter down the Shute. On this particular afternoon, my parent had reluctantly allowed me to play the fruit machine with one of their friends at my father's Mess, a social club for the Military, while they had a little social time at the bar. The friend fed the machine with coins and let me pull the handle which stuck at first and then suddenly dropped down hitting m with its huge head smack bang in the mouth. My front teeth were smashed completely out. This meant that at the age of ten I had dentures.

Not only did I have to suffer taunts through wearing glasses but now I had to keep my mouth closed, which for a chatterbo like me, was incredibly difficult. I got used to the plastic dentures over the years but they were a nuisance. They got loose and often they would fall out when I was talking. On one occasion, during a German lesson, they shot out when I abruptly sneezed, landing in front of the teacher, Herr Cuts, - honestly that really was his name, -who almost trod on them. It affected my love life too. Having finally bagged myself a boyfriend at school when I was sixteen, I managed to lose him two hours later, when my teeth got stuck in a bread roll at lunch. I scared men off in nightclubs, where under the fluorescent tubes of the disco lights, my front teeth would glow green as if I had radiation poisoning. The teeth had their upside I got the role of witch number three in the school play *Macbeth* on account of my very long hair and the ability to remove my teeth. I was considered a natural, even though my acting skills weren't the best.

I have Phil to thank for changing my life. After he started going out with me, I confessed about my teeth, just in case they fell out or worse still, broke. He sent me to his dentist. When I arrived for my first appointment there was a bunch of flowers waiting for me from Phil along with a message saying 'Good Luck.' It was in the good old days when he was trying to romance me. The dentist bridged my teeth for me and I never looked back as they say.

That dentist has now retired and both Phil and I have a new dentist- Big Bertha from Poland. I think she's from Poland. Her surname consists of a lot of consonants, largely 'k' 'z' 'w' and 's'. She looks like an ex-wrestler, or a champion shot putter, and she is fanatical about keeping teeth clean. I don't want to lose any more teeth so I religiously floss and brush, rinse and use mouthwash after almost every meal. Phil, who is not so meticulous, is terrified of her. She thumps him on the arm each time he leaves and wags her finger at him.

"No eatings or drinkings now after all hard work I do to make you shiny!" she will tell him.

The trip today to the dentist was ghastly. The roads were abysmal due to all the snow that has been falling for days. It doesn't seem to have prevented many people from going out though. We both had an appointment. Phil went first. I sat in the crowded waiting room anxiously waiting for my turn. I'm afraid I've over flossed in recent weeks in order to escape Bertha's wrath, and my gums now bleed. Phil came out, rolled his eyes and sat in the waiting room while I went into the surgery. Bertha was scrutinising a sharp blade and motioned me to sit down. The chair shot backwards. A bib was tied tightly around my neck and a slurping sucker thing shoved in my mouth. I tried to explain why my gums were bleeding as she prodded them with her sharp instrument but she just grunted and prodded harder.

"You need good clean," she concluded darkly having checked all the teeth. She opened her metallic drawers and hauled out an array of implements.

The pain was excruciating. She scrubbed and scoured my teeth so much I thought she would remove the enamel. For the first time in years I suffered as my oversensitive teeth were attacked, scraped and plaque drilled away. Eventually, she stopped.

"Rinse!" she commanded. "Okay, you can go."

I leapt to my feet. Just as I got to the door, she thumped me on the top of my arm, and wagged her finger.

"No eatings or drinkings for you, either. I work very hard today to get you shiny. You don't want to make me cross, do you?" and she laughed a hearty laugh.

I joined Phil in reception. He looked as shaken as I felt.

"Let's get out of here," he whispered. "I really need a drink."

Posted by Facing50Blog.com - 2 Comments

The Merry Divorcee said... Ex number one got his teeth knocked out by me when I found out about his new girlfriend.

Vera said... Ahhh!

Sunday 5th

What a picture it is outside. The snow has been falling yet again and it looks very Christmassy. I tried to get Phil to come outside and make a snowman with me. He looked at me as if I were two stops past Barking. Who wouldn't want to make a snowman? It was perfect weather conditions out there; sunshine and snow. It reminds me of when I younger, not a child, but just younger. It gladdens the spirit. Well, it obviously doesn't gladden Phil's spirit. After a couple of sneaked glasses of wine at lunchtime, I went outside on my own to build a small snowman. My neighbours were out there too, getting some logs for their fire. They came to help and we managed an excellent effort. It certainly made them youthful. Cedric threw a snowball at me and his wife, Shirley, laughed and joined in, shoving snow down the back of his shirt until he squealed like a girl. They are both in their seventies. I saw Phil glowering out of the window at us and chucked a snowball at the window, but he merely drew the curtains together.

Posted by Facing50Blog.com - 2 Comments

SexyFitChick said...Phil's a 'Party Pooper'.

Faerie Queene said... Some people are just dull, dull, dull. Albert and I loved snow ball fights. He always squealed like a girl too.

Wednesday 7th

Another text from my mother and a photograph. Her teeth are incredible. Her mouth looks twenty years younger. She's understandably delighted. I gave her a quick call but forgot that she was two hours ahead. She was in a bar.

"Yesh, I'm very pleashed with shem. They look so white. Everyone here thinks I look yearsh younger. Shorry, I can't hear you too well. I'll shpeak to you shoon. I need shome more time to break shem in though."

I presumed the slurring wasn't due to several brandies. Hopefully, she'll break them in soon. She is somewhat renowned for her tenacity.
Posted by Facing50Blog.com - 1 Comment
Vera said...I think I might look into getting mine done. I'd love to have nice teeth again. I'd be willing to go to Cyprus to get them done if I could stay with your mother.

Friday 10th

"Oh the weather has been delightful, but the pavements have been frightful. There's no post 'cos we're on go slow, let it snow, let it snow, let it snow."

As you can see I'm getting cabin fever. I've been stuck inside with Phil now, for what feels like an eternity. He's in the lounge, conversing with the log burner, and I feel like I'm having an affair with my laptop. Tom went to visit Tiffany days ago. He can't get back here because of the bad weather. I bet Tiffany's parents are thoroughly enjoying having him as a house guest.

The weather was great to start with. It was festive and cheerful, but then the temperature dropped. Then, it got icy and cold; very cold. I mean -10 degrees and -11 degrees centigrade. We are just not used to that here in the UK. Rural Staffordshire, where we live, has gradually become cut off, due to impassable untreated roads. I hope it clears away soon as we intend going away later this month.

As a consequence, I've been blog hopping, and getting to know my new blogging friends. Phil has been reading financial reports and watching *Russia Today* on the television – no, even I can't work that one out.

A couple of days ago I realised we were running out of food. Help came from my dear computer. I logged onto my favourite supermarket stores' website and ordered enough food for a month long siege. It was delivered by a young man in a balaclava, who managed to get through the snow in his sturdy van. Admittedly, it had taken him a few attempts to reach us, but like a true knight in shining armour, or in his case, a huge coat and scarf, he appeared late in the afternoon.

"It's been crazy. Everyone is ordering online," he informed us, as he carried all my bags of food right into the house for me. He placed them by the fridge. I thought he was going to unpack the stuff and put it away.
Phil looked pleased, especially as he had spied some mince pies in the first bag.

"It's the weather, no one can get out. At least there isn't much traffic on the roads," he declared cheerfully to Phil, who had to push his truck back down the snow covered drive, after it stuck, and the wheels started to spin.

It's amazingly quiet out there. We haven't had any post for days. Last week, I saw the poor postman slipping about the main street, opposite our house, with an overstuffed mail bag. He looked like a veritable beast of burden. He had so much post, which had built up over the days, he couldn't deliver it all. He could only manage a few houses in the village and ours wasn't one of them.

Yesterday, I heard knocking at the front door. I was ecstatic.

"The post," I screamed in excitement, partly because I was going to make contact with another human being, other than

Phil. More importantly I've been expecting a CD for his Christmas present for over two weeks, since before the snow fell. It's *Elaine Page and Friends...*yes, I know that is desperately dull, but hey, he likes her. I got the key for the door, unlocked it and yanked the door open, only to hear a tearing sound. The postman stood like a slightly defrosted snowman on the doorstep with an armful of mail just for us. Maybe the noise was his arm falling off due to the weight of th post and cold.

I grabbed the mail and attempted to have a conversation with him. I think the cold had glued his lips together because h didn't seem to want to linger. He looked lop-sided due to the weight of his mail bag. I watched as he slipped and slid his wa back up the drive. The icy air poured in and, as I tried to shut the door, I discovered what the noise had been. All the wood from the door had pulled away. It had been stuck; iced to the doorframe due to the freezing weather. I had to fetch Phil from his hideaway to try and glue it back, but it's impossible and now we have a massive crack in the door that lets in even more cold air.

To make matters worse I discovered that I had been sent the wrong CD. I hadn't even been sent a CD. I am now the proud owner of *Casablanca* which has been digitally remastered on DVD. Todd will love that.

The forecasters have announced a slight let up in the temperature soon. Tonight, is only going to be -5 degrees but then temperatures are set to drop again. I guess the snow will stay, along with the fog and the frost for some time yet.

Phil adores his log burner and sits huddled in front of it every afternoon with a hot mince pie and a cup of cocoa. I'm going to keep my laptop company. It is without doubt my very best friend and companion.

"Let it snow, let it snow, let it snow..."

Posted by Facing50Blog.com - 2 Comments

SexyFitChick said...I knew a Russian once. He was a body builder. He was called Vladimir Squashiovsky or something like that. You could drop some brandy into Phil's cocoa to get him warmed up a little.

The Merry Divorcee said...I like the sound of your delivery truck boy. I wonder if he could deliver some goodies to me. He sounds more useful than my current hubby. Stay warm Honey!

Saturday 11th

After eating on an evening we normally settle down for an hour or two of television viewing. We're not big TV fans. Actually, I am, but Phil who hates films, decent music, theatre and musicals, is not. Phil's latest favourite programme is *Russia Today* which we watch from seven until eight so he can get his fix of world news. Then, I take control of the entertainment as he only seems to want to watch documentaries to do with finance. He'll normally let me put on something easy for him to follow, maybe a short murder/mystery (invariably we only watch half of this and often don't discover who the murderer was), a nature programme or maybe a light hearted comedy show.

I ensure I have a stock of pre-recorded DVDs of shows he might like to watch. He can get distracted far too easily so half hour shows are ideal. After he goes to bed, I am left in peace to watch whatever I fancy.

Since we bought the television eighteen months ago, after our old set exploded spectacularly, I have had sole usage of th 'zapper' or remote control. Phil is, as I've explained before completely useless with anything electronic. You may recall th episode with poor old Toby Toshiba. Only yesterday, he managed to send six blank text messages from the mobile, while attempting to read a text that Tom had sent. Get the idea For years we had a simple television control with only a few buttons, but the new TV came with a remote control displayin many buttons, and requiring a degree in technology to comprehend them all.

Last night, I discovered Phil had sneakily commandeered this control which he was hogging in his chair. The television was set up for the usual programme. I don't know why he like it but it affords me an hour of tranquillity while he sits glued to world news. I stare into space and dream of faraway places. I was languishing on a sizzling beach with Todd, who was showing off his muscled bronzed body, feeling warm and suntanned, instead of hugging a hot mug of cocoa, freezing cold with a blue running nose. The presenters waffled on abou gas prices, financial terrorists and the score in the hockey matches played the night before.

After *Russia Today* had finished I leapt forward to gain control of the set but, too late, Phil had picked up the control and wouldn't hand it back. I tried to snatch it from the arm of his chair but he grabbed it and held it at arm's length from me glowering at it, and then pummelled all the buttons. He managed to make the TV turn off, then onto standby, and at la back on again. All the time he was fiddling, I was tutting and making exasperated noises, which just made him all the more determined to keep me away from the control. Next, he succeeded in making the DVD player spring to life with accompanied whirring noises.

Phil became more frustrated and muttered incomprehensibly, all the time waving the control at the television and pushing every button possible. The volume was turned up to ear deafening proportions. The brightness and contrast were altered several times. Strange messages appeared and disappeared on the screen. The subtitles were put on and it took several minutes to work out how to remove them. He refused all help, finally discovering the correct channel changing buttons, and that most masculine of pleasures, channel hopping. Unable to watch any of the 700 channels for longer than thirty seconds and accompanied by expletives and comments such as:

"Rubbish. Codswallop. That's rubbish too. Drivel. Nonsense. Garbage!" the next hour went something like this:

'Tomorrow it will be icy again in the North East with temperatures dipping below freezing. Don't forget to wrap up warm'...

...'with a large belt and of course the obligatory pair of matching high heels, Girlfriend looks dramatic and ready to go out to hit the town...'

...'following the large group of baboons sauntering through the forests. Always cautious the alpha male'...

...'was taken into custody in connection with the discovery of the Kalashnikovs at his premises on Thursday morning and charged with'...

...'bringing the milk to boiling point...'

...'but Monsieur Poirot, who is the murderer? Well, my chil
it was not obvious from the start but I always suspected'...

...'The Russian President Vladimir Putin, after he took to th
stage last night with a rendition of Louis Armstrong's
'Blueberry Hill' at a children's concert'...

... 'Dozens of thugs subjected the convoy to an attack in
which the Duchess was jabbed in the ribs...'

...'with a cloth and left to cool. Next take three oranges '...

...'which the baboons use'...

...'for driving around bends at high speed. Next week on *To
Gear* the new Ford driven around the track by'...

...'a wandering albatross'...

...'in a diamond encrusted waistcoat'...

...'add two litres of'...

...'arsenic, which I found '...

...'in the glove compartment of the Toyota Landcruiser.
There is nothing to compare to the comfort and style of this
vehicle which has the looks of'...

...'Aunt Dorothy. Then the murderer crept towards the
kitchen'...'

...'in a figure hugging black dress topped off with those all
important heels'...

...'eating the cactus fruits along the way'...

...'with French onions and garlic'...

...'looking sleek and'...

...'frosty again tonight in Scotland'...

...'But Monsieur Poirot how did you know that'...

...'Watford would score'...

...'with a baboon from the rival troop'...

My patience at the end of its very lengthy tether, I could stand it no longer and was about to leave, when the television was snapped off by a peevish Phil, who threw the control down in disgust.

"Doesn't seem to be anything on this thing worth watching," he moaned and went off to check up on the financial news on the internet, leaving me to watch a terribly dull film peacefully without interruption. Time to hide the remote control I think. It's a pity they don't have remote controls for irritating husbands. Mine could do with being put on standby at the moment.

Posted by Facing50Blog.com - 3 Comments

The Merry Divorcee said...All my husbands were the same. They all need mute buttons. The one I'm with now is fine but his children could certainly do with mute buttons.

SexyFitChick said...I would hide the control down the front of my jumper or blouse. Maybe, he'll turn off the television after he has looked for it.

YoungFreeSingleandSane said...Yet another reason to stay single.

Sunday 13th December

"We've been invited to a party," I told Phil, who was busy looking at cars on the internet.

"Oh yes," he replied unexcitedly, gazing lustfully at a picture of the new CLS Mercedes Benz. I wish he'd look at me like that.

"Fred and Ethel have invited us around for a Christmas Party this evening."

Phil groaned.

“They’re well over eighty years old, what sort of party can you have at an eighty year olds house? Won’t they need to be i bed by six?”
I gave him a withering look.
“That’s pretty good coming from someone who can only manage to stay awake ‘til nine each night,” I retorted.
Suitably chastised he clicked off the page harbouring his latest desire.
“Okay, I admit that was a bit mean but they are quite elderly, aren’t they?”
“Well don’t worry because we’re not the only ones invited. They’ve invited our other neighbours too; Shirley and Cedric.’
“Better and better. What a fun night it’ll be. With us there, we’ll dilute the average age down to about seventy then.”
I really like Fred and Ethel. You may recall the episode wit ‘Robocat’, aka Tyson, earlier in the year. I feel a little sorry fo them. After all, it is Christmas time, and we should show our fellow man warmth and friendship at this time. They must get lonely at home all day – I do.
We arrived at Ethel and Fred’s house at the appointed time six thirty. I took them a box of chocolates as I know they are teetotal, and so a bottle of wine was out of the question. Ethel squealed in delight opening the door dressed as a cowgirl, in hat, cowboy boots and a holster.
“I thought it would be a bit of fun if we dressed up,” she explained, handing Phil a jesters’ hat and me a clown’s nose and hat.
“What would you like to drink? Tea? Coffee? Cocoa? Water?”

I must have looked mortified because she pondered a while and added,

"Oh, there's some homemade Elderberry wine somewhere too I think. I made it some time ago so I'm not sure what it'll taste like."

Phil, who can only manage a bottle of lager before he falls asleep these days, was about to opt for the cocoa, but accepted a dusty glass from Ethel, who poured something transparent into it.

"Isn't this nice?" she added and dragged us through to see Fred who was sitting in the lounge with our other neighbours, wearing a large headdress of feathers and dressed as an Indian. Fred was regaling Shirley, sitting uncomfortably in a chef's hat, with some incomprehensible tale and Shirley was looking bewildered.

"Fred, put your teeth in," said Ethel. "He doesn't like wearing them you see. Where are they Fred?"

They spent the next few minutes looking for Fred's front teeth palette which they discovered on a bookshelf. Fred put them in reluctantly.

"Cheers everyone," Fred announced raising his mug of tea and clinking it against Cedric's cup of coffee.

"Shirley, try this," offered Ethel, and gave her a large glass of the Elderberry wine.

"Cheers, Merry Christmas," we chorused, and simultaneously took a sip of the wine. At first I thought I'd ripped the roof of my mouth off, but when I recovered sensation I realised it was still there. Obviously, I wasn't alone as both Phil and Shirley looked like they had drunk lighter fuel. We couldn't be rude and so we all finished our glasses. By gum, it was potent stuff. It wasn't long before Shirley had a dose of giggles when Fred took his teeth out again and hid them in a plant pot so Ethel wouldn't find them.

Phil was looking quite pink after one glass and I found that suddenly the atmosphere was lighter. In spite of our protestations, Ethel filled up our glasses and got out some mince pies to enjoy with them.

"And now we should play some party games," she declared. "That's what we normally do at a party isn't it Fred."

Fred mumbled something through a mouthful of pie, so it was anybody's guess as to what he had said.

Before you could say 'play' Ethel was scrabbling about on the floor standing up a tiny matchbox and brandishing a pencil.

"Now where is it? I had it earlier," she muttered.

Shirley giggled and jabbed me in the ribs, which made me snort. Phil tried to look cross but couldn't. Ethel found what she was looking for in the cat's basket and proudly held up a ping pong ball.

"Right, we're going to play cricket," she announced. "The rules are as follows: any hit counts as two points, a hit as far as the fireplace is four points and anything else further is six points. You, your hubby and Shirley are on one team, and Fred, Cedric and I will be on the other. You can field first and we're going into bat."

With that she dropped to her knees like a thirty year old, waved the pencil about in front of the matchbox, which apparently were the stumps, and asked who'd be bowler. We elected Phil who by now, after two glasses of wine, was ready to hibernate, let alone sleep. He got up and attempted to 'bowl' the ping pong ball at Ethel.

Well, I think I know how Fred and Ethel spend their days because she whacked it for six all right. It smashed into the picture over the table, ricocheted onto the window and was sent hurtling backwards into the kitchen behind almost taking Tyson's eye out.

"Six," she shouted and tapped the floor with her pencil.

She managed to clock up seventy-two points before a very tipsy Shirley succeeded in catching the ping pong ball as Ethel hit it yet again with force. Our team applauded Shirley, who curtsied and almost fell over.

Cedric was next to bat. He couldn't connect with the ping pong ball for love nor money. His Mexican hat kept falling over his eyes, but Ethel insisted we all kept our hats on as part of the party spirit. Shirley and I thought it hilarious and couldn't stop laughing. Phil managed to get him out after a few attempts, actually hitting the matchbox and knocking it over. Shirley and I cheered and clapped Hubby on the back, hi-fiving each other. Ethel got us some more of her homemade wine. Fred was as formidable as Ethel. He clocked up a few 'runs' but declared himself out after a while.

"Not as young as I used to be," he said grinning revealing his one good remaining tooth.

Our side was in to bat. By now we were guffawing and snorting like a bunch of teenagers out for the night. I was first. As I bent down my knees made that popping noise they always make, sending Shirley into another paroxysm of laughter. I couldn't connect at all either with the ball. I couldn't even see it hurtle towards me. I waved the pencil around and missed badly. A few goes later and even with Fred trying to bowl gently for me, I was caught out by a triumphant Cedric. Shirley was as bad as me and couldn't hold the pencil for giggling. Phil managed to knock up a few points but we were a dismal bunch.

After that Ethel had lined up a game of 'Pictionary' which was even more hilarious because Shirley and I couldn't see what Phil was drawing, as neither of us was wearing our glasses. We guessed wildly at his efforts

"A cow?"

"A car?"

"A mermaid?"

"A fire extinguisher?"

Shirley got a fit of hiccoughs through laughing, and had to have another glass of wine.

Ethel's team, being sober, guessed Ethel's masterpiece, which was a gingerbread house and they surged ahead on the points table.

Several hours later, having played a range of silly games including 'pin the tail on the donkey' and consumed some mor of Ethel's lethal wine, we were ready to leave. Our team had lost all the games and Ethel's side victorious, but magnanimou in victory, said we should have a replay. I saw Fred putting his teeth in the fridge as we left. He put up his hand, mouthed "Shhh!" and waved goodnight. Cedric took Shirley home in Fred's wheel barrow as she couldn't stand up any longer.

"Shhluvley night, merry crossmouse," she managed before being bundled into the ancient contraption.

Phil was clearly worse for wear. He got stuck trying to take his socks off.

"That was great wasn't it?" he said as he fell backwards onto the bed. "Nice to know you can still have fun when you'r old," and fell asleep.

Posted by Facing50Blog.com - 4 Comments
SexyFitChick said...It sounds like Phil can have a good time when he tries.
Facing50 said...He had such a rotten hangover today. He was even worse than normal. I still can't work out how the donkey's tail ended up attached to the back of his trousers.
Vera said...You should both get out more. It would do you good.
Facing50 said...I think after last night neither of us will ever go out again, especially with elderly responsible, non drinking people.

Monday 14th

Phil and I have agreed to adopt a Christmas 'stuff it' policy this year, and I don't mean the traditional turkey. We're only going to buy one small gift each, and up to five small stocking fillers. These consist of simple presents: chocolate shaped reindeer, small paperback book, key ring etc.

In bygone years I used to buy quite a few presents, especially for Tom. I would wrap each one with meticulous care to disguise it in matching wrapping paper, with appropriate matching ribbons. I created a homemade tag for each one, with a cryptic clue cleverly written on it. The game was to try and guess the present before you opened it.

Last year, Tom had one with: 'Santa hopes this will make things clearer for you this coming year'. It was a special blade to use to clean his car windscreen. Come to think of it, I don't think he's used it at all. It usually took until lunchtime to unwrap the gifts, then we would all settle round the specially prepared table, for the traditional meal, normally a large farm chicken as we don't like turkey.

Last year, Christmas was an unmitigated disaster. I stupidly decided to get Tom involved in an attempt to make him more responsible. Phil was not convinced it was a good idea, claiming Tom wasn't capable of performing even the simplest task. I decided that it was to be Tom's job to buy the food for the Christmas lunch. He was fine about it.

"Yeah, yeah, large chicken, biggest I can find, enough for a of us."

"Yes, for all of us. Don't forget, you eat enough for five people, just on your own."

"Ha, ha," he replied good-humouredly whilst simultaneousl texting Tiffany, who he had known for three weeks.

"So, you are sure you know what to buy? It's all on the list, and here is the money."

"Yeah, yeah!" he repeated tucking the list and money into the pocket of his jeans.

Ordinarily, I would have sent him to our village butcher bu I had made that mistake the previous year. A month before Christmas, I ordered and paid for a large chicken, some bacon and a dozen sausages. I was given a receipt informing me I should collect on the 22nd December.

On that day I walked up to the butcher to collect the order. As I walked around the first bend I bumped into Mrs Featherlite's back. She was at the end of the queue for meat, which was stretching the entire length of the village. It moved so slowly that halfway along there was a stall manned by three old ladies, who were selling hot soup, mulled wine and hot dogs in rolls. As we shuffled by in the freezing cold, we all bought polystyrene cups of soup or wine to stay warm. There were various grumblings and mutterings. People complained to each other and swapped stuffing recipes as we crept closer to the butchers' shop. There was a distinct lack of festive spirit. At one point the vicar appeared and tried to get us all to join in some Christmas Carols until someone threw a bread roll at him.

"Sorry, vicar," shouted the guilty party, an elderly man wrapped up in a muffler, standing with some of his cronies who were chuckling. They were on their fifth or sixth cup of mulled wine.

"It's alright Fred. I'll see you in church on Christmas Eve and you can stand with the choristers as punishment," replied the vicar.

Fred smiled happily.

"Can I wear one of those funny gowns then? I'd look dapper in one of those."

I can honestly say that between the 22nd and 24th December the queue continued to snake around the village, as fresh customers added to the tail end, to collect their orders. After Christmas, the owners of the butcher's shop shut up for two weeks and went off to South Africa on safari, probably on the proceeds of all the sales they had made those few days. Three ladies put up a sign in the post Office to let us all know that they had taken £2,270 for charity over those same days, due to the enormous success of their sales.

It was so successful that they were planning to open their stall again every year and would be offering mince pies and sausage rolls, in addition to their hot dogs, in anticipation of even greater sales. I decided that I would no longer support my local enterprise but instead, would send Tom off to the nearest supermarket, some ten miles away. It seemed a simpler solution. Besides, if he stood in queue where mulled wine was served, heaven knows what he'd return with. His list was not too long. He only had to buy some bacon, a few sausages, potatoes, parsnips, carrots and compulsory Brussels sprouts, even though we don't really like them. It seems to be obligator to eat them at Christmas. And, of course, he had to get one, very large, free range chicken. It was a simple enough task.

Tom finally tore his eyes away from the phone and decided he'd go and get the food. An hour after leaving, I received the first text message from him:

'Big pots or lil ones?'

'Medium'

'How many parsnips?'

'Eight' I replied.

'Do u want carrots wiv green stuff comin out of tops?'

'No'.

'Do u want a chocolate log?'

'No'

'The chocolate log looks nice'.

'No'

'It's not xpensive'.

'No'

'Please'

'No'

'It'd be better than Xmas puddin'

'No'

'It's on offer'

'OK - get it'

‘Got V large chicken n sprouts ☹ standing in long q – must be 30 peeps here in q’

‘Well done’

Four hours later Tom returned, having stopped off to visit Tiffany en route. He threw all the shopping onto the kitchen draining board, and disappeared for a shower. I checked through the purchases. The bacon was unsmoked, not smoked, as stipulated. The sausages were enormous and certainly not the chipolatas I had requested. Half of the chocolate log had already been consumed and chocolate crumbs lay amongst the vegetables in the bag. The parsnips were soft. The carrots were fine. The Brussels, well, they looked like large green bullets. At the bottom of the bag was one huge large chicken.

“Tom!” I yelled up the stairs.

“Yeah?”

“What date is Christmas Day?”

He poked his head out of the room.

“The 25th,” he declared cautiously.

“Why have you bought a chicken whose sell by is up today, the 22nd?”

“Oh! My bad?” He said untroubled, shutting the door to continue getting ready for his shower.

Phil entered the kitchen from the office where he’d been hiding all afternoon, to find me throwing all the frozen meals out of the freezer along with loaves of frozen bread, in an attempt to find room to house the chicken until the 25th.

“Well, I warned you,” he commented and walked out again.

The day itself was absolutely diabolical. Tom got up so late he missed opening the stocking presents, which really wasn’t the same without him. After giving me a perfunctory kiss, followed by 'Happy Crimbo' to us both, he shot off to the pub and reappeared at four o' clock. By this time, the chicken, which was already dry through freezing, was overcooked and awful. The meal was a disaster. The only levity was the opening of my Eminem CD when Phil actually smiled for the first time that day. Tom then cleared off to Tiffany's house. Phil detests the commercialism surrounding Christmas anyway and only suffered it while Tom was young.

This year as I mentioned earlier, it is to be scaled down dramatically. We shall have an early meal together and Tom will go to Tiffany's for another meal in the evening, while Phil and I sit in front of the log burner with a glass of something fizzy. Instead of presents, Phil and I are going to treat ourselves to a trip away before Christmas, getting us away from the madness and lousy weather that has descended upon the UK.

I have found a villa company on the internet advertising a very nice villa in Mallorca for a ridiculously low price. We could really do with a holiday. Tom has been told if he has so much as one friend around, we'll throw him out into the snow filled streets where he can spend Christmas in a doorway, unde a piece of cardboard. Phil told him that so convincingly that even I believed him. I don't think Tom will misbehave this time.

The villa looks wonderful. The photographs show a beautiful, flower filled front garden. It's got a pool with a view of the mountains, and archways covered in wisteria. It has three bedrooms, a ping pong table, satellite television and heating throughout. In fact it looks ideal. Sunshine and luxury, what more could we ask for? Facing50 will not be blogging for a few

days as she has to prepare to go away. I'll tell you all about our trip when I get back.
Posted by Facing50Blog.com - 3 Comments
Vera said... Oh bless him at least he tried
SexyFitChick said... Bon voyage. Lucky you, going away from the cold and snowy UK. It's boiling here though. Might have a bbq on the beach.x
Lostforwords said... Hello I'm a new follower. Hope you have a good trip away.

Thursday 23rd

We returned late last night from our trip. It didn't go to plan. Tom had been ill all the week before we left. He felt lousy and looked dreadful. Phil insisted Tom still went into work under the impression that Tom's bosses would think he was swinging the lead to get time off to do his Christmas shopping. Tom struggled on. In fairness he's very good about being ill, unlike Phil, who, the second he gets a light cold claims he has influenza, the worst type of flu at that. You know when Phil is genuinely ill, as he doesn't complain, but if he's slightly ill then he'll look at you pathetically, croaking "Nurse," and demanding that I fill up a hot water bottle for him, and spoon feed him his food, while he stays in bed. It's become a joke between Tom and me. He will occasionally tell Phil he thinks he's getting a cold and cough at him, just to watch Phil's frightened reaction. Predictably, Phil will immediately cover his mouth with his hand and order Tom out of the room, all the time complaining that he is vulnerable to colds.

Tom may be a pain to live with, however he rarely complains about feeling ill. This time he looked rough. He looked grey and walked as if it were an effort. His nose ran constantly and he went straight to bed from work, rejecting an offer of food. He didn't even go out to the pub. He also coughed all night. I was awake listening to him suffer. He clearly couldn't sleep either.

"Are you sure you're well enough to go to work?" I asked him as he coughed so much at breakfast, that I thought he was going to break a rib.

"Of course, he is," shouted Phil, from the next room. "It's only a cold. He's young. Mandy, stop fussing over the boy." Tom blew his nose and left his cereal. He wasn't hungry. I heard him hacking in the bathroom. Phil emerged from the lounge.

"Has he left for work yet?"

"No, he's just getting some more tissues."

"Right, I'll come in for breakfast when he's taken his rotten germs away with him," replied Phil and, covering his mouth with his handkerchief, shot off to his office.

As a precaution, I took to disinfecting the kitchen and bathroom I share with him, each time he vacated it. All door handles were sprayed liberally too. There was no way I was going to let Phil come down with this before the trip. My life, such as it is, would not be worth living if Phil caught so much as a sniffle.

Tom seemed much better by the morning of our departure, and insisted he drove us to the airport. However, I had that familiar tingling in the throat, heralding the start of a nasty cold. It was not helped by the fact that Phil insisted on driving, all the way to the airport, with the window down so he wouldn't get any of Tom's germs. I sat in the back with the cold air blasting about my head.

I'm one of those annoying people who must arrive punctually for any event, or preferably early for everything. Phil is the complete opposite. When Tom was at school we were always late for any school event. We would tiptoe into the school concert well after it had started, and invariably missed Tom's solo performance on the tuba, which we would later hear from those who had arrived on time, had brought the audience to its feet in appreciation. We have been known to arrive at hockey pitches in time to watch the team leaving the field, slapping each other on the shoulders, and going off to celebrate their victorious win in a championship hockey match. Phil just can't be on time. I used to tell him he had to be somewhere half an hour before he really did, but he now factors that time in, so we are still always late. However, when it comes to airports I'm allowed to dictate what time we leave. We once missed a flight to Rome because Phil was trying to contact the office about something before we left. We then we got stuck in traffic and the gate had closed by the time we reached the airport. We couldn't board and consequently, we missed our flight.

Of course, this particular morning, not only were we not held up in traffic, but we sailed through passport control as the place was almost empty. It was the same at the scanning machine. We walked into the departures lounge three and a half hours before the scheduled take-off time. Phil wasn't too cross about it. He was too relieved to be getting away from the cold and the Christmas hustle and bustle. By the time we'd had a coffee and gone around the Duty Free shop, we were still left with three hours, during which time I began to feel worse and worse. My throat was horribly sore. The closer we got to our destination, the worse I felt.

Arriving at our rental property we both realised we had made a mistake. I think the photographs I had found on the internet of it had been taken several years, or even decades before. In front of us stood a crumbling, poorly painted house. Chickens and cockerels strutted about the front terrace eyeing us warily. Empty broken pots were strewn around. Weeds forced their way up through cracked paving slabs.

"This can't possibly be the place,' muttered Phil in complete disbelief, pulling out the printed copies of the villa that I had downloaded from the computer. He groaned.

"Maybe it's better inside."

We retrieved the key from its hiding place and shoved the aged door open. In the shuttered gloom we made out the living quarters. It was, at best, adequate. Phil was agog.

"Phone the villa company and get us moved out of here."

I got the answer phone:

'Thank you for calling *Happy Villas*. Our offices have shut for the festive season. Please phone again after January 5th. Thank you for booking one of our happy villas. Merry Christmas.'

We were stuck there.

The villa was bitingly cold. No one lived nearby. The view of the mountains, which had looked so engaging in the photos, was obscured by the clouds that loomed about them bringing in rain and icy temperatures. The heating refused to work, except in the lounge, where a large box puffed out warmish air. There was insufficient water for a shower, let alone a bath and the bedroom was like the interior of an igloo.

It was too late to find alternative accommodation and I was, by now, feeling the full effects of Tom's bug. I could hardly stand up. Phil poured kettle after kettle of hot water into a bath for me, where I sat shivering until finally collapsing into the bed with six blankets on top of me. Inevitably, Phil too became ill, and we held each other for warmth, shivering and coughing for six days, too weak to do anything.

When we finally managed to get up, we discovered the satellite television could only offer *Sky News*. We watched news bulletins about the lousy weather in the UK, as rain thundered onto our roof overhead, and water leaked through the ceiling, dripping continuously into the seven pans we had strategically placed around the room. Mallorca was experiencing its worse weather in decades. At the end of ten days, and several pounds lighter, we were more than ready to come home.

Tom met us at the airport, wearing a red nose, and a pair of felt reindeer antlers.

"Ho, ho, ho!" he said jovially."Did you have a good time? You look well. You look thinner but not very suntanned. I bet you were glad to not have this snow we've been having. It's been dreadful. I thought I might be unable to fetch you if it snowed again. And, Mum, you'll be glad to know, I feel **much** better. Think I might have had a touch of flu that time," he announced, as he put our bag into the car, whistling 'Jingle Bells' and checked his phone for the inevitable text message.
Posted by Facing50Blog.com - 2 Comments
SexyFitChick said... Bummer. Should have come here doll.
Lostforwords said... Ah! Shame.

Saturday 25th

Happy Christmas to everyone who is reading this. Hope you all have a super time. I'm looking forward to it. It has to b better than last year.

Posted by Facing50Blog.com - 6 Comments

Fairie Queene said...And to you. And to your Mum.

YoungFreeSingleandSane said...Happy Christmas everyone. I'm out with friends for lunch. Hope you all have a great day.

The Merry Divorcee said...Happy Christmas Honey. Hope Phil pulls your cracker – if you know what I mean.

SexyFitChick said...Merry Christmas. I always find it weird eating turkey on the beach. Hope it goes better than last year f you.

Vera said...My grandchildren are coming over so I won't be online tomorrow. Happy Christmas.

Serene Siren said...Christmas Blessings.

MammaMia6 said...I'm dreading it Christmas lunch for fifteen. I'm going away next year too.

Sunday 26th

Well, the forward planning worked. The frozen vegetables bought before we left for Mallorca actually had flavour, and there was not a single Brussels sprout to be seen. Phil was in charge of meat this year, which meant we had enough duck to feed a third of the entire village. Tom actually managed to heave himself out of his bed before lunchtime, and had the grace to sit and wait for the family stocking present opening, without once checking his mobile phone. He only had a couple of gifts for us. He apologised and explained finances were a bi tight for him.

"No point in wasting your money on rubbish," agreed Phil. "Just because it's Christmas, it doesn't mean we need to spend all our hard money buying gifts for people."

I quite liked my *Grumpy Old Women* book he had bought, with the half price sticker still stuck on it. It didn't matter that he had had no money for wrapping paper, and had given it to me in a supermarket bag. Phil got a bottle of beer, also in a supermarket bag, and a bar of chocolate with its sell by date almost expired.

"What does he find to spend his money on?" grumbled Phil, after Tom had left the room. "He doesn't pay rent or bills!"

Tom offered to help prepare lunch. We declined his offer. He would be more of a hindrance than help. He closeted himself in his bedroom to talk to Tiffany, to discuss arrangements for later. Lunch was okay, but Tom didn't eat as much as usual, as he was to have an afternoon Christmas meal at Tiffany's house.

"More duck, Tom?"

"No thanks I want to leave some room for dinner with Tiffany. We're having a large cock," he said snorting.

"I don't think Mr Henderson-Smthe will appreciate crude cock related jokes," I reprimanded primly, aware that Mr Henderson-Smythe was not too fond of his eldest daughter's boyfriend.

"Me and Jez get on fine," declared Tom, slugging at his glass of lager.

Phil looked unconvinced. Jeremy Henderson-Smythe was an eminent plastic surgeon at a prestigious private clinic. I'm sure he wouldn't appreciate an upstart like Tom, calling him 'Jez'.

"Nah, it's cool. I've been joking about him sharing his cock at Christmas with me, and he thinks it's funny."

Phil raised his eyebrows. I decided to pursue the topic no further. Tom will have to find out about life the hard way. I can't imagine Jeremy and Emelda Henderson-Smythe laughing raucously at a half cut young man, who dropped out of university, and who has no obvious job prospects, even if he can be quite charming at times. The meal was wolfed down and cleared away in less than ten minutes. It hardly seemed worth the effort. There was still a pile of washing up, which was immediately tackled by Phil. It was only quarter past one.

Tom went off for a shower before going to Tiffany's house. Phil gets cross that he spends so much time in the shower draining the tank of hot water. I always point out that, unlike many young men, at least he's clean. Phil and I took a glass of wine into the lounge where, just as we raised the glasses and said 'Cheers!' the phone rang.

"Hello? Hello? Can you hear me? Merry Christmas," shouted my mother.

In the background I could hear John Lennon's hit, *'Happy Christmas (War is over)'* being murdered by someone on a karaoke machine.

"Yes, I can hear you. Happy Christmas, Mum!" I yelled back, so she could hear me above the din in the background.

"'N so this is Christmas, 'n what 'av you done? A nuffer year over, 'n a new one jus' begun...." was being screamed to a cheering crowd.

"I thought I'd see how you were as I've not spoken to you for a while. I'm out with friends at a karaoke party. I'm on soon. I couldn't decide between, Shirley Bassey's, *'Hey Big*

Spender' and Tina Turner's, *'Nutbush City Limits'*. I think I'll go for Tina Turner. I can dance like she does too."
There was a pause while someone shouted something to her. She replied. "No, I'm okay thanks, Tony just bought me one and I've got two waiting."
In the background someone had taken over the microphone and I could hear voices joining in with

"New York, New York."

"Thank you for the lovely brooch. It matches the necklace that Grego bought me rather nicely. Oh, sorry I can't stop. Helena, Dorothy and I have to practise our moves for The Weather Girls, 'It's Raining Men'. Angelo has just signalled that it's my turn to sing next apparently, and I need to hitch my skirt up a bit, to create the right effect to look more like Tina. Merry Christmas!"

"She having a good time?" asked Phil as I came off the phone looking bemused.

"Yes, at least she's with friends and not stuck at home on her own." I offered.

"Yes, and more importantly, she's not here," added Phil with a raise of his glass.

Tom peered around the door surrounded by a thick cloud of the latest Boss aftershave which I had bought for him.

"Thanks for the prezzies. I'm off now."
He shook Phil's hand, which was held out somewhat reluctantly. I got a bear hug and a peck on the cheek.

"Happy Crimbo both. Have a lovely afternoon.'"

Peeking out from the curtained window to wave him goodbye, I watched Tom struggling up the path to his car, carrying an enormous bag of beautifully wrapped presents, and an object that looked suspiciously like a magnum of champagne. I closed the curtains. It was probably best to not le him know I'd seen.

Phil and I went for a decidedly non-festive walk around the village, under grey skies. We marched around in silence. Phil seemed to be in a world of his own. Wearing a Santa hat, Mrs Turnpike shot past us on her mobility scooter, tinsel hanging from its handlebars.

"Beep, beep! Merry Christmas," she shouted, as she raced by.

For a village mostly populated by older people, there seemed to be quite a bit of festive fun going on. There were several rows of cars parked outside the little cottages which lin the streets. Obviously, relatives had come to visit. Christmas tree lights twinkled in windows. In some houses through the misted up windows you could see people eating Christmas Dinner, talking animatedly, and wearing paper hats.

It was a far cry from our hastily eaten, uninteresting lunch. Phil had said virtually nothing all meal. He'd sat silently spearing carrots and throwing them into his mouth as if bored by it all. I felt empty. Phil managed to compound that feeling by commenting,

"Silly Buggers! What do they think they look like? Glad I didn't look as stupid as that."

I didn't feel like putting up with his sense of humour today I felt deflated. What had happened to those years of sitting around our table as a family, with Phil reading out the stupid jokes from the crackers, and giggling with Tom? Phil had even refused to put up our Christmas tree this year, claiming it was a waste of time. I unearthed a tiny ornamental tree yesterday and put miniscule lights on it, just so I would have something to remind me that Christmas used to be fun. Maybe this is what happens. You lose enthusiasm for it all. Phil certainly had.

We made our way back home with the wind blowing in our faces. The local pub was shut for once. Maybe the landlord and landlady had cashed up, and gone to South Africa with all the profit from sales of alcohol to Tom and his friends. Maybe they'd joined the butcher and his wife there.

Of course, as you'd expect, Phil dozed off on his return. He always does after a glass of wine. I couldn't face watching *The Sound of Music* which was being broadcast yet again, for the fifth year in a row. I tiptoed to the office and the computer while Phil snored.

Inbox 5 messages:

'I've chartered a yacht and am sailing off New South Wales. Lying on deck wishing you were here with me to pull my cracker.'

'Happy Christmas, Gorgeous. I'd love to be able to give you a kiss under the mistletoe.'

'I'm sunbathing naked. Pity you are not here to rub oil on my back. Just watched a pod of dolphins playing next to the boat.'

'Hope you have had an exciting day. Have you been a good girl for Santa?'

'I appear to have a rather large present here for you.'

I slugged a glass of wine I'd taken with me, and typed a message back:

'Bit quiet here. Wish I was on board too. It might be more fun than the gloomy UK.'

The inbox light flashed immediately.

'There you are! I've been waiting.'

'Waiting for what?'

'To tell you what your present is'.

'Oh yes. What is it?'

'Me! I'm coming over next May, to my nephew's wedding, and I want to see you again. You are always on my mind and I need to see you desperately.'

Oh goodness me. I felt the familiar warm tingling, but also warning bells were sounding.

'I'm not sure.'

'Think about it. There are no strings attached. I promise. By the way what underwear are you wearing?'

'You randy devil!' I wrote, smiling widely.

'I'm alone in the ocean on a huge yacht. What am I supposed to do?'

'Happy Christmas. I'll think about meeting you.'

'Happy Christmas. May all your dreams come true. XX'

'What are you doing?' demanded Phil testily as he walked into the office.

I hadn't heard him. I slammed the laptop shut.

'I was just seeing if there was anyone about today.'

'Only sad lonely sods will be on the computer today.'

'Yes, only sad lonely sods.'

Posted by Facing50Blog.com - 6 Comments

SexyFitChick said... I was on the internet all day, and I'm not sad, or lonely.

Serene Siren said... Oh dear!

Faerie Queene said... Don't worry about Phil, Sweetie. It's just his age. The male menopause it's called. It's the same as the female menopause, but they manage to get even grumpier.

YoungFreeSingleandSane said... Man on yacht in sun watching dolphins, or snoring man in chair watching *Sound of Music,* no contest!
The Merry Divorcee said... I keep warning you. Stay away from the good looking one. At least your man is predictable. That's good.
PhillyFilly said...Christmas is an emotional time. Think about it after the New Year, and then decide to meet up with him. At least you'll have plenty of time to get in shape. You could join me here at the clinic if you need any touching up to be done.

Wednesday 29th

It's been pretty flat here since Christmas Day. The bonus has been the noticeable absence of heavy good vehicles tearing through the village. In spite of the reduction in nose Phil is fed up because there is not much movement on the financial markets over the festive season, and he can't go through his funds daily. There are no financial programmes to watch on television, and we are down to watching our emergency DVDs. We have been forced to watch the entire series of *Fawlty Towers*, which Phil happens to love, and can watch time after time. He knows every line by heart and will say them before the character does. I find it all repetitive and have to force my laughter now. Still, it keeps Phil happy and it's better than watching the dreadful offerings on the television at the moment.

He must be getting desperate financial withdrawals though because I found him counting out all the pennies in the giant savings jar where we put all our lose change and putting them into neat piles. He also keeps going through his filing cabinet where he keeps his financial papers, contract notes etc. and rereading them as if committing the accounts to memory. I really must get him interested in something else. I've got a couple of days to write out a 'New Year's Resolution' list for us both and come up with some ideas.

Posted by Facing50Blog.com - 2 Comments

Vera said....It gets worse each year. I'm fed up with the repeat on television, which is why I spend all my time online reading blogs. They are far more entertaining.

Faerie Queene said...It's flat here too. It's been a terrible end to the year, what with Albert going. I hope next year brings fu and happiness for us both. By the way I love *The Sound of Music*; I could watch it time and time again.

CHAPTER 7 – JANUARY

Wednesday 5th

"I've got a text from Tom, at last," I mentioned to Phil as he read the front page of the Financial Times for the umpteenth time.

"It says 'Happy New Year'. Much love, and thanks for everything. Tom.XX"

Phil looked unimpressed.

"At least now we know he's alright."

Phil slammed his paper onto the table.

"Mandy, he went out on December 31st to celebrate the New Year. It is now the 5th of January, and despite you sending at least thirty texts, yes, I know you've been worried about him, and been trying to reach him," he added as he saw me about to protest. "He has not had the decency to contact us since. He has not bothered to let us know where he is, or what he's doing. He has no doubt spent the last six days completely out of his skull. I've decided that I no longer care what he does. It's one of my new year's resolutions, 'Give up on Tom'. He treats the place like it's a hotel, no, like it's a hostel. He's inconsiderate. He's lazy. He's bone idle. He's utterly useless. His room is a disgusting tip, in spite of any efforts you make to clean it, and we never know where he is or what time he'll be in."

The rant over, Phil picked up his paper again and resumed reading.

"Tell him it's four o' clock in the afternoon, and he should be up by now. I heard him come home at about five this morning. He's in his room."

He saw the look in my eyes of confusion.

"Yes, he's texted you from his bedroom. See what I mean?
I walked upstairs and banged on Tom's door.

"Tom we know you are in there. Get up!"

"Morning Mum," said Tom peering sleepily through heavi lidded eyes. I recoiled as a particularly nasty aroma escaped from the room.

"Happy New Year," he added. "Did you have a good time?

Phil and I spent New Year's Eve in front of the television watching a 1974 episode of *The Morecombe and Wise Show* until, at nine o' clock; Phil announced he was going to bed.
"It's New Year's Eve," I wheedled.
"So what? You stay up. You say 'Happy New Year'. You go t bed tired, or if you are stupid, you go to bed drunk, and wake up with a hangover the next day. You can stay up if you want to."
I uncorked an expensive bottle of red wine and quoffed two glasses in quick succession. What the hell was wrong with Phil? We used to go out on New Year's Eve.

One year we went to a party where it was obligatory to perform, as part of the evenings' entertainment. Apparently, I am tone deaf and sing off key. I didn't believe people when they told me that. I thought I had a great voice. I wasn't put of when I failed school music auditions, or when I was thrown ou of the church choir because I was putting everyone else off wi my lousy alto. Phil, like me, sings off key. We probably sound like a couple of cats fighting on a fence when we sing togethe Anyway this particular year we were to join up with another couple and perform Abba's hit *Money, Money, Money.* I was very enthusiastic.

My friend had auburn hair. I had long blonde hair at the time, so it was obvious who would dress up as Agnetha, and who would be Frieda. Phil and I practised the lyrics religiously after work, in preparation for our first dry run with the other couple, which was to be the night before the big party. The dress rehearsal day arrived. The other couple had managed to procure a keyboard and a guitar too, so we would really look the part. There were wigs for Benny and Bjorn and short sexy tunics for the girls. We stood up on 'our stage' and played the CD ready to sing along.

"I work all night, I work all day, to pay the bills I have to pay," sang my friend in a husky voice.

"Ain't it sad?" I howled.

After fifteen minutes we were ready to perform for the following day. She was to be Frieda, Her husband was to be Bjorn.I was relegated to role of Benny behind the keyboard, where I was to pretend to play, and wasn't allowed to sing. Phil was Agnetha. We got plenty of laughs and applause and I have to admit Phil looked much better in that short tunic than me. Nowadays, he has no joie de vivre. His mojo has gone. He won't drink. He won't go out, and he won't stay up past nine o'clock.

To add insult, to my misery, my mother phoned me at nine-thirty from Cyprus.

"I'm going to wish you a Happy New Year now, just in case I can't get a signal later. I'm at a 'knees up' at the Marina. It's the full works: fireworks, champagne and I believe a prize for the best fancy dress costume. I'm a Hawaiian dancer. My lei are going down well here," she added coquettishly. "Are you going out?"

“No Mum, we’re having a quiet night. Phil isn’t feeling too well.”

“Bad luck. Never mind there’ll be plenty more years to enjoy. Oh, there’s Grego. Talk soon. Bye”

I tried very hard to stay away from my Inbox, but with *Scottish Hogmanay* and bagpipes on the television and a fourth glass of wine under my belt, I thought I’d check for messages. Of course there was a message from Todd. He seems to think about me all the time. I get emails from him daily now. He had already seen the New Year in. He spent it watching the fireworks at Sydney Harbour Bridge with a group of surfing friends. They went on to a nightclub and then breakfasted on the beach. His New Year’s Resolution was ‘To rectify past mistakes.’ He ended the message with:

‘I’m looking forward to the New Year and what (or who) it may bring my way.’

“Mum!” shouted Tom bringing me back to the present day.

“Oh, sorry.”

“Any chance of some breakfast? I’ve not eaten properly for the last few days.”

He looked at me pleadingly and his eyes twinkled with charm. I trotted off to cook him some eggs and bacon. Phil grunted at me and turned back to his paper.

Posted by Facing50Blog.com - 5 Comments

Vera said... I hope your Mum won first prize at the Fancy Dress.

SexyFitChick said... Those fireworks at Sydney harbour were pretty impressive. I saw some fit guys in tight shorts. Maybe Todd was one of them. Send me a photo and I’ll check my mobile which I used to snap them - well, they were fit!

The Merry Divorcee said... I know the name of a good divorce lawyer

YoungFreeSingleandSane said... Phil was right. I had a rotten hangover for three days. You were right to stay at home. Maybe next year, I'll try it too and watch television instead.

Faerie Queene said... We danced all night and I have horrendous blisters on my feet. Next year, I'm going to watch the television too.

Thursday 6th

Oh dear what a bad start to the day! I blame the insomnia. Phil blames old age.

As you know, like many women of my age, I seem to have forgotten how to sleep. I can still manage to fall asleep and conk out, somewhere between drawing back the sheets and my head hitting the pillow, but staying asleep is proving nigh on impossible. At best, I'll manage two hours sleep, and at worst about fifteen minutes. Then, a switch in my head goes click and my brain fires up to its maximum capacity and decides it's going to work the night shift. It whirs away taking inventory of everything I've done in the day and should do the next day. It talks to me all night, puzzles over pointless things, worries over others and generally waffles away (a bit like I sometimes do on paper) until 5.30 am when the switch drops and it prepares to go into a dormant mode for the rest of the day. At which time Phil wakes up, yawns, shuffles about and generally fidgets. After many sighs he throws back the covers forcing me to also arise and drag my fatigued body out of bed.

Phil noticed a few weeks ago that the bags under my eyes had become larger than normal. I explained I was having sleeping difficulties. 'Mr early to bed and early to rise' was very understanding about it. He suggested that the next morning I should have a lie in when he got up. Maybe I'd be able to drop off to sleep for an hour or two.

The next morning just as my nattering mind finally shut off Phil awoke and gave me a sharp nudge.

"You awake?" he whispered loudly.

" I s'pose so," I huffed crossly.

"Okay, I'll leave you to try and get some sleep," he said considerately and tiptoed out of bed and into the bathroom. With the door left slightly ajar, he managed to illuminate half of the bedroom. He then serenaded me with running taps and flushing toilets for a full ten minutes until he finally extinguished the light, which clicked loudly, and tiptoed out of the room. I snuggled back down into the comfortable bed. Phil crashed about in the kitchen like a herd of elephants having a disco. He reappeared several minutes later.

"I've made you a cup of tea, would you like it in bed?" he asked.

Well how can you be angry at such consideration?

"No, it's alright thanks. I'm awake so I'll get up and join you," I replied.

And so, every night I go to bed at ten o'clock, and about ha an hour later I wake up. I know the doctor said that it is stress related but I can hardly go on a yoga retreat and learn how to calm down, can I? I tried some relaxation techniques from the internet. They help me get to sleep initially if I have trouble. The main problem is that I can't stay asleep. My brain is like a small dog which wants to go outside at an inconvenient time o night.

"Please, can I nip outside quickly?" It'll ask.

"Only for a short while and then you must come in and lie down on your blanket."

"Okay, I'll just go for a quick sniff. Oh, this smells nice. Oh, what's that over there?" and off it'll go. I never manage to coax it to calm down and doze off. It has other ideas and wants to explore or investigate. Last night was one of those nights. Hence, this morning I was more than bleary eyed.

Recently, we have been doing our supermarket shopping on-line. Phil is delighted because he doesn't have to carry so much shopping to the car and I'm delighted because it has prevented Phil from buying any more of his bargains. I've still got seventeen boxes of mini *Shredded Wheat* to eat from the last time he went out on his own to the supermarket.

To ensure you get the delivery day and time you want, you must book the van in advance, and secure your time by placing an order of any size or amount. This can be added to any time up to 11pm the evening before your delivery. Phil was a complete nuisance last time we ordered and every hour he thought of something else he wanted. I had to go back online, reorder and put my card payment through again and again. This time I booked my slot, secured it by requesting some milk and told Phil to write everything he would need on the pad in the kitchen. I would do the final order the morning before the delivery, still giving us a few hours to add to it, if we'd forgotten anything.

The list was lengthy by Tuesday morning. Phil had added cocoa powder and chocolate and cake. The usual essentials that help prevent him from becoming a permanent 'Grumpy'.

"Have you done the order yet?" he asked.

"I've got plenty of time. I've got another couple of days ye I'll do it the day before, don't worry."

"Good, because I really need some more cocoa powder and lime jelly. I fancy lime jelly," he repeated looking like a ten year old. I added lime jelly to the list.

This morning after attempting to smooth the bags under my eyes away with my magic eye pen (it doesn't work by the way Phil suggested we had a walk to wake me up.

"Okay, I'll do the shopping order when I get back," I said.

"Good, and don't forget my cocoa."

We trudged out over the muddy fields at the back of our house. After a while the freezing cold temperatures were having an effect and I felt more alert. As we neared home Phil noticed a flash of bright orange.

"There's someone near our house in a high visibility jacket he said.

We increased our pace. I could see a speck moving about near the back door.

"There's a van parked at the bottom of the driveway too," h added ominously.

"Oh no!" I ran as fast as I could over the field towards the house. Hussain Bolt would have had a job to catch me. I managed to clear the fence into our garden, surprisingly, in on leap and puffed into the driveway just as the delivery man was about to leave.

"Hello, Mrs Wilson," he said cheerfully. "I'm glad I caught you. I thought it was strange you'd not be in for your delivery.

"I thought the delivery was for Thursday," I panted in disbelief.

“Ha, ha, very funny,” he replied, opening the back of the van, and taking out the shopping I had ordered to secure the delivery. “Today is Thursday. You’ve haven’t got a bit mixed up, what with all these Christmas and New Year holidays, have you? It throws you out. You don’t seem to have ordered much this week. Are you on a diet for new year?”
He handed me the delivery form to sign and a plastic bag containing only four pints of milk.

At that point Phil arrived having strolled back to the house. He gave me a withering look. Without a word he went inside to get his car keys to go and do the shopping. As for me, well after writing this, I think I’ll try and get forty winks.

Posted by Facing50Blog.com - 5 Comments
Faerie Queene said...Oh no, you poor thing. Try some lavender oil on your pillow tonight. It works for me.
SexyFitChick said...What a bugger! I bet Phil was in a right old mood after that caper. At least he’d have been able to buy his lime jelly. I didn’t know you actually ate that stuff.
Vera said...I think you should go back to the doctor. You probably need some medication to help you. I thought it was just old people like me who got forgetful. Still at least you made us all smile at this episode. All but Phil.
YoungFreeSingleandSane said...I don’t need my food delivered. I only need meals for one. It wouldn’t be worth their while.
PhillyFilly said...Good news! You did manage to run and clear the fence. See you are not as past it at you thought.

Monday 10th

Todd sent an email asking if I'd made a decision about seeing him. He sent some photographs of sunsets on the beach. They reminded me of the sunsets in Morocco when he and I would sit and watch the sky turn purple. He'd written a caption under them. 'They are nowhere near as beautiful when you watch them alone.' I haven't decided yet. It's too soon. I told him I needed quite a bit more time. 'I can wait' He replied.

Tom seemed unusually quiet today. Maybe he can sense that Phil has hit rock bottom with him. He keeps staring at his mobile, which isn't unusual in itself, but it's the way that he's staring at it that seems peculiar. Also, he hasn't gone out this evening. He hasn't been to visit Tiffany, and he hasn't been down the pub. He's probably had so much alcohol recently that he's sick of it, or maybe he's coming down with an illness. I'll have to watch out and keep him out of Phil's way. Call it mother's intuition, but I know something is wrong.

Posted by Facing50Blog.com - 1 comment

Vera said... He's probably worried about something

Saturday 15th

I always think that a new year is comparable to when you were younger and would get a brand new exercise book at school. You would always start off in your best handwriting and make the first few pages neat and tidy, but by page eight it started to get ink splodges on it. By page fourteen, you had ripped some of the pages out, scrawled over others. Someone had had the audacity to correct your work with red ink, and written 'should try harder' on it. Halfway through the book you'd given up using your nice fountain pen, used any old drooling biro, and had written the name of your favourite pop group, or latest crush, in bubble writing on the front cover.

And, so it is with New Year resolutions. Every year, like so many, I make the same old resolutions: I'll lose weight, I'll learn Spanish, and I'll try and cook exciting recipes. By February, I'm sitting in the office eating chocolate, my Spanish CDs lying in their wrappers untouched, and wondering which ready meal I should buy from the supermarket.

This year will be different for both me, now fifty years old, and Phil who will soon be sixty. I've written out a New Year's resolution list that resembles a lengthy 'Bucket List':

-Get fit and look after ourselves which includes cutting down on alcohol consumption.

-Swim with dolphins.

-Take up a hobby e.g. painting for me, photography or cookery for Phil. (Not local art classes though)

-Learn to play an instrument.

-Learn a language.

-Cuddle a koala bear - although since I wrote that I've discovered they smell horrible, have extremely sharp claws, will only allow you to hold them when they are knocked out on eucalyptus leaves, and you can only do it in Australia.

-Try and get Phil to do a 'financial blog'.

-Teach Phil how to use 'Word' first before above resolution (maybe).

-Visit my mother at some point this year if she manages to stay in the UK long enough for me to see her.

-Be nicer to my mother.

-Try and encourage Tom to become more independent Teach him to cook?

The list goes on. It isn't in any order and so, I have decided to start, by booking a golf lesson for us both. There's a special offer for couples at the golf course near us. Maybe Phil will enjoy it enough to take it up as a hobby. I'd really like to be a golf widow. Just think of all the freedom I would be able to enjoy again: days out with the girls, shopping, loafing about with my dressing gown after a nice long hot bath with bubbles

To be on the safe side I didn't tell him where we were headed, so by the time we pulled into Sandy Acres Golf Academy, it was too late for him to protest. We were met by Max, a suntanned South African Golf Pro, with an immensely strong handshake.

"Hi! Welcome to the best Golf Academy in the UK. Ever played golf before, Mr W?"

"No, it's not something I've considered," replied Phil. stiffly.

"It's completely addictive,' declared Max confidently, and jumped onto a buggy with the ease of a gazelle, gesturing for u to climb aboard. We then haired around the golf course, at breakneck speed; while Max shouted out names of famous golfers who'd trained here, and pointed out various tricky holes.

I was totally occupied in maintaining my balance. I clung onto the buggy sides, while Phil sat comfortably, looking completely unimpressed. We passed several groups men, all dressed in the most outrageous outfits, of frightening coloured jumpers teamed with checked trousers. They looked like clowns who had escaped from a circus, missing only very larg shoes and red noses. Some were walking with serious expressions, while remote controlled trolleys followed them faithfully to the next hole.

Eventually, after the tour of the course, and a visit to the 'Nineteenth Hole', the exclusive bar adjoining the golf course, which appeared to be stuffed full of more clowns in similar ridiculous attire, we were taken to the driving range for our lesson. This involved Max patiently attempting to get us to hold a stick, or as he called it, an iron. The only iron I'm familiar with, is the one I use to get creases out of my clothes, and it is a lot easier to handle that the golfing iron. You can't actually hold it as you would expect. Oh no, you have to wrap your hands around it in a complicated fashion, and entwine your hands so your fingers are touching in a certain way. It's like a weird Masonic handshake. Then you have to stand in the most peculiar position which seems to involve leaning forward stiffly, with your backside held high.

Next, comes the swing. Once again, you can't just hit the ball. You must raise your arm backwards, but bent at the elbow so it feels very uncomfortable. You look ahead, not at the ball which should be balancing precariously on a tiny pin, known in golfing terms as a tee (not the sort you drink). Now, you attempt to hit it even though you have no idea where it is. Max demonstrated several times taking a relaxed position and effortlessly smashing the ball into the distance as he swung his torso round. It was then my turn. Max made it look ridiculously easy. It was not easy. I was immensely uncomfortable. My back protested immediately I could get the hang of the swing at all. I resembled an unbendable marionette. The whole process was further complicated by the fact that Max stood right behind me, adjusting my hand position, my arms, and my shoulders and trying to get me to swing with him. I was totally aware of his taut body behind mine and tensed up even more with embarrassment. I felt ridiculous and was relieved when he decided to leave me to it. He dropped a basket of balls in front of me to practise with.

"See if you can hit any of these, Mrs W," he said kindly, both of us knowing that that would be extremely unlikely.

The stupid ball wouldn't balance on the tee. I cast a quick glance over the partition at Phil in the next booth. He looked a uncomfortable as I felt. I got the ball balanced at last and took up the ridiculous position. I couldn't hit the ball for love nor money. I cheated and swung back my iron like a hockey stick. It connected. The ball dribbled forward and landed in front of the range.

"Well done!" encouraged Max, who seemed to be manipulatin and manoeuvring a reddening, infuriated Phil, who also kept missing the ball. At that moment his mobile rang.

"Sorry folks, I've got to take this call. Mr W. See if you can hi a few balls."

And with that he dropped another basket of balls, similar to mine, next to Phil. It was quiet for a few minutes and I half heartedly tried to hit another ball, this time ensuring my elbow stayed in the correct position and following Max's instructions Phil's balls meanwhile were hurtling out all over the range. They shot past the 50 metre mark, 100 metres, 250 metres and right out onto the border.

"Thwack, thwack, thwack."

I peered over the separator. Phil had lined up all his balls in a row and was attacking them like a man possessed. He certainly wasn't adopting any golf position I had encountered.

Just as he whacked his last ball into the distance, I could see Max returning. I hurriedly tipped all my balls out so they rolled away in front of the driving range.

"Wow Mr W!" He exclaimed looking at all of Phil's balls scattered around. "You'll make a fantastic golfer with that ability. Some of those balls have gone way beyond a beginner's ability. I hope you'd like to sign up and become a member of the club."

Phil looked at Max and smiled charmingly.

"That's very tempting Max, but I don't think I have enough time to commit to golf what with work and all my other hobbies. Maybe later, when I retire."

I kept very quiet until we had said goodbye to Max, who I noted didn't invite me to become a member.

"Well, what was that all about? You have stacks of free time," I queried after we had driven away.

"Yes, but I don't want to spend them dressed like Coco the clown, standing for hours, attempting to get a small ball, into an even smaller hole. Anyway, golf spoils a good walk."

Right, if it's a good walk he wants, I'll sign him up for the village weekly 'Heigh Ho' brigade who walk around all the fields and village, carrying ski poles and large rucksacks, containing maps, bottles of water and Kendal's mint cake bars in case they get famished or marooned up in Farmer Thompson's field.

Posted by Facing50Blog.com - 2 Comments

SexyFitChick said... Don't you just love golfer's bottoms?

Faerie Queene said... My boyfriend played golf for a year, and then ran off with Roger, the golf pro. I think he became his caddy.

Monday 17th

The woman was staring hard at me through the racks of sale shoes. She was almost glowering at me. At first, I didn't mind. I'm used to this happening.

Normally, as I have mentioned before, I walk around under a cloak of invisibility. The same cloak that most people over the age of forty find themselves wearing. You know the one. You'll try to go through a door, and the person in front of you will shut it in your face. Or a gaggle of young mothers pushing pushchairs, will march directly towards you, until you dive for cover before you get run over. No one seems to see you once you become middle aged. You turn into an invisible person.

However, periodically I'll be walking along the street and someone will stop and stare at me. Not because I'm stunningly attractive but for one of two reasons: I am usually smiling and that unnerves people. They are just not used to women smiling at them and presume you are quite simply mad. After all who smiles at anyone nowadays? They probably think I've escaped from an asylum and stare worryingly at me in case I attempt to engage them in conversation. I smile because it's nice to be smiled at – that's all. Or, and this is the most popular reason, they think they recognise me.

I am regularly told by complete strangers that they 'know me from somewhere.' I am well aware that I've never seen these people before in my life, but they insist they know me. I remind them of someone. It's been happening for years. I'll get stopped at the airport or in the street. Out there in the world are lots of people who I resemble – poor souls.

Now, depending on how wicked I feel on the day, my reply to this will vary. I used to say

"Oh no I just remind you of someone else; apparently I have a familiar looking face."

But that didn't satisfy these people. They'd insist until it became embarrassing. Now, I'll chance my luck with various ridiculous statements like

"Oh you probably recognise me from my modelling in women's magazines."

Or

"I used to be on television."

I did in fact appear on the local news once. I walked behind a man who was being filmed for a documentary. I hadn't realised what was going on and stopped to tie my scarf up properly. I was in shot for quite a few minutes as I ferreted about getting my bright pink scarf adjusted and picking up my bag again. They didn't cut it out and after it had been shown on the news, several of my friends phoned up, to congratulate me on my new television show.

Recently I've been getting more and more outrageous in my claims when people ask:

"Do I know you?"

I'll reply, "You might have seen me in *Star Trek* sitting to the right of Captain Kirk."

The people will nod and say, "That'll be it," and wander off looking satisfied that the mystery is solved. I told a woman a few weeks ago that she might have watched me presenting the weather the night before, but not to blame me for the rain we were having. I convinced a couple from Birmingham, that they'd seen me at a Madonna concert, where I was quite probably one of the backing singers. I'm waiting to see if I can get away with claiming to be one of the judges from *X Factor* or "I'm married to that Prince Charles chap but I've left him at 'Buck Pal' today talking to his cucumbers."

This week I bustled into the shoe shop to look for a pair of boots in the sale. I've had to throw my old ones out. Phil said I could have new ones but I had to get them in the sale. As I hav large feet, finding sale items in the shoe department, is not normally a problem. I selected three styles. A young fresh face girl disappeared into the room at the back, to find the correct sizes for me. What on earth is behind the door that keeps those assistants for so long? There must be a giant mountain of shoe and boots, through which the girls must seek out a matching pair of shoes, because she was gone for ages. And, I do mean ages. The shop was sweltering so I removed my coat, scarf, an cardigan and rolled up the sleeves on my white blouse.

The manageress was standing behind the counter with two trainees. They were learning how to dust shelves. Observing m removing all my clothes, she commented on hot flushes, and how she was always getting hot. I always think that it costs nothing to be polite to people, and we enjoyed a chat about the joys of getting older. We laughed jovially, about some of the problems and embarrassments, which occur at this time in our lives. It was at about this point I noticed a sharp face observing me from behind a rack of shoes. A peevish woman, holding an ugly brown shoe, was staring at me. I smiled at her. She glowered at me. I went back to my conversation.

The manageress told a rather amusing story about having gone out to dinner, had a hot flush attack, and in taking off her jumper, managed to not only lift her blouse off that was underneath, but also remove her bra surprising all the guests around the table. The woman continued to stare while holding the shoe. She didn't laugh even though I looked her way, in a half attempt to include her. She just looked annoyed. At that moment I realised why she was staring. She obviously needed an assistant, and as I was commandeering the manageress's attention, she was undoubtedly frustrated. I would resolve the problem. I smiled again and mouthed

"Do you want the other shoe to that one?"

She nodded curtly and scowled. I mentioned to the manageress, who by now was explaining mid life crises to the two girls, that she had a customer lurking behind the racks, who required assistance. She sent one of the girls to deal with her.

After a few minutes she came back red-faced.

"The lady doesn't want me to help her. She refused and said she wanted the other one."

Poor girl. She went back to her dusting, and the younger of the two assistants, was dispatched to the mean spirited woman.

"Sorry about the wait," said the manageress.

"Oh it's okay. I expect it's been manic what with the sales and Christmas."

"You wouldn't believe it," she replied. "The stockroom is just chaos. We've been so busy we haven't had time to tidy it up. Thank you for being patient."

"No problems," I replied.

The younger of the two assistants returned looking frightened.

"She told me to go away. She wants the 'lazy, loud mouthed one' to serve her," she said cheeks blazing.

The manageress pulled herself up to her full height, and marched over to deal with the rude woman, who glared in our

general direction. At that moment, my assistant finally emerge
from the room clutching several boots of various colours, non
of which looking like the ones I'd asked her for.

"But Madam," I heard the manageress say loudly. "She can't serve you."

The woman complained and waved her shoe about in a semi-threatening manner.

"She can't serve you, because, Madam, she's also a customer."

I turned away and kept my head down. I tried on a pair of maroon boots with nice thick soles made from heavy duty recycled materials– ideal for wet weather and kicking miserab people in the ankle.

"Yes, these are great, I'll take them," I said.

Back at the till, I noticed that the querulous woman had departed, leaving the brown shoe on the floor.

"Well," said the manageress with a smile. "If ever you wan a job, you'd be welcome here. You are nice and friendly whic makes a change from most of the people we deal with," she said. "And, you'd obviously be in demand with the customers, she added and laughed slipping in a free pot of shoe cream. It pays to make an effort after all.

Posted by Facing50Blog.com - 3 Comments

Faerie Queene said...I used to work in a shoe shop. It was crazy out back. It's so difficult to find matching pairs and size I'd have liked you as a customer. There just aren't enough people who smile out there. ☺

PhillyFilly said...I'd have speared the miserable woman with my Manolo Blahnik heels.
Vera said...A little kindness always goes a long way. I expect Phil was pleased with the free gift.

Thursday 20th

Yet another New Year's Resolution has been struck off the list. Inside it is as gloomy and grey as it is outside. I've been back on my social networking sites. I didn't bother so much last month, what with the trip to Mallorca, and then general apathy over the holiday period. It's amazing how nothing seems to have changed from before Christmas. Pre-Christmas everyone was writing about the weather and how excited they were that it was going to be Christmas. Now, almost everyone I know is moaning about the weather and Christmas. They are complaining about how it didn't go the way they planned. Many of them seem to be off work with flu, although surprisingly, they all seem well enough to log on and tell us all about it.

My absence has resulted in my virtual crops dying, my virtual cafe going bankrupt and my game scores being beaten. I've had a productive few days getting back into the top ten on the scoreboards. I won't be beaten by some lazy student who has nothing better to do but surf the net all day.

I've neglected my exercise regime that I promised myself I'd follow when I hit fifty last year. It was okay when the weather was better, but now it has become so windy and awful outside, neither Phil nor I, have even been out for a walk. It's making us sluggish and lethargic and that's why I've decided to enrol us in a trial day at a gym and spa some twenty miles away. Phil can barely tear himself away from *The Financial Times*, or the internet, or from the phone where he checks in every day with his long suffering, pension-handling, stock broker. The gym will occupy us and help our physical well-being.

I told Phil the good news and he looked at me with dismay.

"Do we have to do?"

"Yes, it's all booked. We have a gym session in the morning, followed by an aerobics class, then a swim and then we can use the spa facilities all afternoon. It's free, all of it is free," I added.

"Okay," he grudgingly replied. "If you really want to go, then we'll go."

So, yesterday morning we set off. Phil was wearing some old trainers, shorts and a t-shirt bearing the logo 'I'm with Dopey'. It has an arrow pointing at whoever is standing next to him i.e. me. My mother gave it to him one Christmas years ago. She thought it was hilarious and made Phil put it on straight away, then proceeded to take loads of photos of me standing in the appropriate position, next to him.

"It's the only t-shirt I own," he explained, with a shrug.

I had a nice pair of leggings and matching designer top, which I'd just happened to notice when I was at the shops last week. Well, I don't want to look out of place. It is a chic spa, after all

We pulled up at the smart resort and duly disembarked to the reception, where some very elegant girls escorted us to the separate changing rooms. Phil, of course, was already changed so only had to dump his bag, containing a change of clothes an swimwear, in a locker. I took my time to make sure that I looked presentable. Also, in the dressing room was a crowd of extremely fit women. Aged between thirty and forty, they oozed confidence and were all so shapely and toned; I had to get dressed behind my towel so they wouldn't see how blubbery I was. They were even wearing makeup. Wouldn't that come off when you sweat? Maybe they don't sweat because they are so fit.

"Hi! I'm Tina," called out the most glamorous of the group. "You're new here."

"Yes, just a trial day. Hopefully we'll join up after today."

"It's super here. It's loads of fun and we're all very friendly."

The other women waved and smiled.

"We're off to a toning class. Then we're hanging out in the Jacuzzi for a while. Come and join us when you're finished. I'll introduce you to the other girls and then maybe you'd like to come for coffee," continued the blonde bombshell.

It was like being back at school and being asked to join the 'Cool Kids' gang.

"I'd love to," I stuttered.

Great, I'd be able to have some friends at last if I joined; well it was a done deal as far as I was concerned. I skipped off to the gym only to find Phil sitting with a questionnaire, struggling to read it without his glasses.

"Why do they need to know how much we drink?" he hissed. "Or, if we've had any of the following illnesses? We're only here for a day."

"I suppose it's for Health and Safety," I replied and before he could launch into a massive grump about that, I called out to our beefy trainer for the day and had him take the form away.

Simon, the trainer, an ex-military man weighed us, measured our fat and took our blood pressure. Phil recovered quickly from his strop because Simon told him he had, next to no extra fat on him, and a blood pressure of a twenty year old. won't tell you what he said about me, but I had a little way to go before I could be considered as fit. It was probably a mistak to boost Phil's ego like that because he was so thrilled with himself, that he didn't really pay attention to Simon demonstrating the techniques required to use the machines safely, and just kept holding up twenty fingers and grinning at me. Simon showed us all the equipment and tried us out on some of the most appropriate machines.

We had a go on the treadmill, but Phil got bored walking o the flat. Once Simon became distracted, helping a slim brunett with her rowing technique, he pressed the button to give himself a bit of an incline. The button stuck and the incline ke increasing with alacrity until Phil was going upwards verticall He clung onto the handle bar across the middle for dear life. Simon looked up, raced over, pounded on the machine to stop and grabbed Phil from it before he fell off. Next, we tried the rowing machine, which had been vacated by the brunette. The some machines with pulleys and weights. Eventually, Simon decided he had shown us enough and left us to get his protein drink, or check his muscles or something, after setting us up o a couple of easy cardio-vascular machines, to get us warmed up. I wobbled about on the cross trainer gently next to Phil, who pumped his up to a hard level, and was going for it like th twenty-year-old he suddenly thought he'd become.

Fifteen minutes later, a red faced Phil spotted some buff blokes in the corner, working out with dumbbells, and thought he'd like a go at it too. I could see him in the reflection of the mirrors surrounding the gym. He loaded up a weight bar, laid down on the bench and attempted to bench press about sixty kilos. On the seventh attempt, I had to leap down from the cross trainer and over to Phil who was gasping for air. He could no longer lift the weights due to muscle fatigue and was in danger of causing himself serious damage. The weight bar hovered dangerously close to his windpipe. Between us, we managed to lift it back into position. His blood pressure had definitely gone up a few notches and when he stood up he grimaced.

"Maybe we'll skip the class and go for a Jacuzzi instead," I suggested.

Phil nodded. A large vein throbbed at the side of his head.

We found our way back to the changing rooms and agreed to meet at the pool, which was reached via the changing rooms. To get poolside you have to walk the length of the changing rooms, passing the showers slightly hidden on the left, and through a door which is unmarked but leads directly to the pool area. Directly in front of you are two showers so you can shower off the chlorine from the pool. From here, you can turn to your right, where you will find two large Jacuzzis and then the pool, which is front of the Jacuzzis.

I changed into my costume and headed out to the pool area where the two Jacuzzis were full of the same women I had met earlier.

"Over here!" shouted Tina who was seated in the nearest Jacuzzi with a prime view of the changing room doors. She had recognised me as I emerged, clutching my towel around me. I nervously introduced myself to the group, all still wearing their makeup and managing to look like supermodels, as they sat in the warm frothy water. I dropped in beside Tina, who moved u a little for me to join them. It was definitely like suddenly becoming friends with the most popular girl in the school. The girls were indeed friendly and I relaxed immediately into my new group of chums. I laid back, shut my eyes and enjoyed the warmth of the tub.

"Would you look at that!" piped up Tina suddenly. "There' a naked man under the shower." she yelped gleefully.

I opened one eye and there, to my dismay, was Phil soaping his body with his shower gel, back to the Jacuzzis, stark naked and completely unaware of the fact that he'd bypassed the showers in the changing room.

"He's not bad either, is he?" Squealed one of the women.

"Nah, he's not much to look at," I replied. I moved towards the steps of the Jacuzzi and positioned myself to grab my towe and get back to the changing rooms as quickly as possible whi the girls were distracted.

"No, he's definitely fit," gurgled Tina appreciatively.

"Go on, turn around," another urged sotto voce.

Further appreciative comments ensued, along with little growls and whistles, which started to escalate into cheers. I legged it as fast as I could in his direction. Phil, completely oblivious to the situation and no doubt with shampoo in his ears, looked around from the shower. Confusion spread across his face as he saw me heading towards him, slipping about on the wet floor.

"Boo!" chorused the girls in the Jacuzzi as I chucked my towel at him.

"Reception, ten minutes," I hissed and dashed off to get dressed.

“I don’t know what I was thinking,” he humbly admitted when we sped away from the spa. We’d only spent two hours there in total and I knew I couldn’t show my face there again.

“I met a chap in the changing room and we were chatting about the stock markets. Then I went to get showered and...” he spluttered.

He looked so completely dejected that I couldn’t be cross with him.

“...And I’ve hurt my back,” he grumbled.

Okay, I could be a little cross with him.

“If you hadn’t tried to behave like a macho man, you’d have been fine.”

“It was your idea. I don’t like gyms anyway,” he protested. “They don’t do you any good at my age, and most of the people there are posers.”

It went quiet.

“Did that pretty blonde woman in the Jacuzzi really say I looked fit?” He enquired more cheerfully.

We drove home in silence. I don’t think I’ll encourage that particular hobby.

Posted by Facing50Blog.com - 1 Comment

SexyFitChick said... I dream of finding a naked man under my shower.

Wednesday 26th

I’ve given up on fitness type hobbies. I’ll leave fitness to Todd who has gone off on a kick boxing course. Honestly, you’d think he was thirty years old. He sent a photograph of Digit looking cute with his head on one side and a speech bubble coming out of his mouth. ‘Well? How about it?’ It said.

I can't think about it yet. I am far too busy to consider the question.

The college in our nearest town is running language lessons. You can study French, Spanish, Italian or even Japanese for th term. I'm a language enthusiast. I love being able to speak some of the native language if I'm on holiday. I also like to understand at least some of what is being said to me. Not wanting to blow my own trumpet, but I'm quite good at pickin up languages. I can speak French and German already. I know few basic sentences in Italian but I've never learned Spanish and Phil, who can also speak some French, seems to be quite interested in putting his brain into gear, and having a go at basi Spanish.

"Nothing too difficult though," he insisted. "I only want to be able to say hello, order a beer and a sandwich on holiday, and ask where the toilet is."

I telephoned the college and arranged for us to start the course which began yesterday. The class was from six until eight in the evening. At first, Phil was reluctant because he'd miss his six o' clock meal and alcohol free beer, but I persuaded him by offering sandwiches early, or extra cake for afternoon tea. Then he was concerned he'd miss his favourite business programme on CNN. I convinced him that I would definitely record it for him so in the end he acquiesced, somewhat reluctantly.

Notoriously late for every event, Phil was reminded constantly yesterday of the need to be at the college for the star of the course, which began at six o' clock, on the dot. I'd been advised by the registrar to arrive early.

"It's a very intensive course and if you miss a class, particularly the first class, you will never catch up."

"Phil, you do know that we have to leave at five to miss the evening traffic and get a parking space, don't you?"

"Hmmm?"

"You haven't forgotten have you?"

"No, no."

"Okay, so we'll leave at five."

"Mmmm?"

Even going to a college for a language class, warranted an effort on my part. Going out is a rarity to be enjoyed. I sorted out my outfit and then spent most of the afternoon shaking my hands to dry the nails. I really should have bought that quick drying nail polish. In an attempt to speed up Phil, I laid a shirt and trousers on the bed. He takes ten times longer than me to decide what to put on. How difficult can it be? He only has to choose a shirt and a pair of trousers. He doesn't have to worry about his makeup or which earrings he should wear. Being Phil, he has to also wear a pair of matching socks, an appropriate belt and colour coordinated shoes.

Staggeringly, Phil owns thirty pairs of shoes. Twenty-four of which only come out of their boxes to be polished and lovingly returned, wrapped in soft dusters, and with shoe trees so they'll keep their shape. He loves beautiful hand-made shoes. Consequently, he faces a dilemma each time he gets dressed, about which pair to put on. He'll pull them all out and try them on with his outfit, ultimately settling on one of the six pairs he always wears. When I asked why he never chooses one of the other twenty-four pairs, he announced he didn't want to ruin them.

By four-fifty there was no sign of Phil. His clothes remaine on the bed. I yelled for him but he wasn't in the house. He surely wouldn't be washing the car? No. Propped against the far wall was a ladder. Up on the roof was a grubby Phil. He wa straightening some tiles which had obviously slipped during last night's winds.

"I'll just be a moment," he shouted, adjusting the tiles back into neat rows.

"It's five o' clock," I screeched in annoyance.

"Don't nag! We've got plenty of time."

He continued with his work, checking and fussing over the rows. At last he descended.

"I'll just put the ladder away."

"No," I wailed. "I'll do it, we'll be late. Please, just get ready."

Phil shrugged and disappeared. I staggered to the shed to replace the ladder in its allotted spot, not one millimetre out, o Phil would move it back to its correct position. I raced back to the house. The shower was running.

"Phil!"

"Five minutes."

I paced the kitchen floor for a further fifteen minutes. As soon as I heard him coming downstairs, I grabbed the car keys and ran outside to get it started.

We pulled into the college car park at six-fifteen. I scurried to reception. No one was there as classes had already begun. There was a note pinned to the notice board by reception. I squinted and read: Spanish Room 16. Charging down the corridor with a reluctant Phil behind me, I found the room and tapped on the door. Twenty heads swivelled around to look at me as the door opened creakily.

"I'm so sorry." I apologised to the fierce looking woman who was obviously taking the class.

"Traffic," I added as Phil joined me.

"Right," said the scary teacher sternly. "Normally, we don't allow latecomers as it disturbs the flow of the class, but on this occasion I'll overlook it. I've just told the class they must not speak any English. We're introducing ourselves. Please come and sit down and attempt to catch up."

Phil and I glanced around sheepishly. We slipped into the only two remaining seats, right at the front of the class, under the watchful eye of the teacher.

"Watashi no namae wa Smith desu. Dozo yoroshiku," said a bald headed man seated next to Phil.

"Hajime mashite."

"Watashi no namae wa Goodman desu. Dozo yoroshiku," came a voice from behind.

I looked puzzled. This didn't resemble any language I recognised. I thought Spanish would be more like French, or Italian. Phil looked blankly at me. I shrugged. The teacher had done the round of the class who had all said something completely unintelligible. She frowned at Phil.

"Dozo yoroshiku," she said and bowed slightly.

Phil looked terrified. I couldn't help. She turned to me and repeated herself and bowed again. The light in my brain illuminated. Somehow, we'd stumbled into the Japanese class. I put my hand up. Someone giggled behind me. The teacher glowered at me.

"Hai?" She said crossly.

"Oh sorry," I started to say trying to rectify the situation and get us out of here. She shook her head angrily.

"Eigo ga hanase nai," she said and refused to let me continue.

We sat for the duration of the class, in fear of the ferocious little teacher who refused to let any of us off. Even Phil tried, and succeeded, in introducing himself in halting Japanese. The fierce teacher packed her bag up at eight o' clock, bowed, and thanked us:

"Domo arigato." Then she left.

Phil now looked completely baffled.

"Wow, Spanish is a lot harder than I thought it would be," he concluded and then smirked wickedly.

"Maybe we should give it up and stay home next week. We could watch the business programme on CNN," he suggested.

"I think you may be right," I said.

"Domo arigato," he added and bowed.

Posted by Facing50Blog.com - 4 Comments

Vera said... Well done Phil. You should be proud of his achievement.

Fairie Queene said... Thirty pairs of shoes.....I love your man.

YoungFreeSingleandSane said... If you go to Japan, will Phil be able to order a beer and sandwich and find his way to the toilet?

SexyFitChick said... I agree with Fairie Queene. I love shoes and smartly dressed men.

Sunday 30th

I'm tired of sorting out hobbies for Phil. Everything seems to backfire. I'm sure he could find something to keep him occupied if he tried. Some days though, I'm quite glad that he's become anti-social and withdrawn.

A few days ago, whilst walking around the village, we bumped into 'Bunny' Warren, literally. He was staggering out of the local pub wearing his coat inside out, ruddy cheeked and cheerful as ever as he crashed into Phil.

"How the devil are you?" he exclaimed to Phil breathing fumes of alcohol over us both.

Phil has known 'Bunny' for years and years, through work but since he retired, and went into hiding in our house, he's not been in touch with his old pals from days of yore.

"Listen, old chap," continued Bunny attempting to extract a packet of cigarettes from his coat pocket, which was proving impossible as his coat wasn't on properly."We're having a bit of a get-together at the weekend. Some of the chaps and chapesses can't make it - flu or something- so there's loads of space for you next week at the Point to Point. We're gathering at 10am at my place and going in convoy to the meet. Bring the Missus of course," he added giving me a lascivious wink.

"Bunty's going to come along. Some of the other girlies are joining in as well. No arguments," he continued as we tried to protest. 'Been a long time old boy, it'd be nice to catch up. See you Saturday at nine-forty-five. Now, where the Hell did I leave my ciggies?" He muttered and crashed back into the bar where a load roar of approval erupted from the bar flies inside, or as Phil calls them, the 'local pissheads'.

I wasn't keen to go at all and told Phil about my reservations. Bunny is notorious for his ability to drink and Phil is not. Phil shrugged.

"Can't let Bunny down, I suppose."

So that was that. We were going to a Point to Point whatever that may be. I knew it was to do with horses but that was all. At least we were doing something different. I should have known though that if it involved Bunny it would be terrible.

Yesterday, aware of the crowd Bunny hangs out with, I dressed in my best smart suede fur lined boots. They are for special occasions only. I can't remember when we last went to a social event let alone a sporting event. This was a special occasion. In fact, going out anywhere constitutes a special occasion in my book. I put on my matching coat. There was no sign of Phil. I stomped down to the bedroom at nine-thirty to find him still puzzling over what to wear. The usual array of matching jumpers and socks were laid out on the bed. It drives me insane every time we go out we have this palaver. I grabbed a blue green jumper and some blue cord trousers.

"Those, wear those," I insisted.

"You're not going in that nice coat are you? It's your best one. Or those smart boots? We'll be in a filthy field. It'll be full of mud. Take them off. You'll ruin them," he said as he dragged on his trousers.

I looked sulkily at him.

"Well if you wear them you'll be very sorry," he continued. "I'm taking my wellington boots and I suggest you do the same."

I threw my coat off in a mega huff as only a woman can, and changed into my only other coat, an old grubby anorak. My wellington boots are grotty. I've had them for years. The clip hangs off on one side and they are scuffed but I guess he had a point. The fields are muddy at the moment and incredibly wet.

Phil appeared eventually in a rather nice leather coat. I bought it for him some time ago. It had a nice beaten look. He looked very good in it and his non shabby wellington boots. He looked like a smart landowner or landed gentry. I looked like someone who was going to clean out the stables.

"Erm, I think you might want to remove those too," Phil remarked as we left. "They look out of place."

I yanked off the diamond earrings and sulked some more.

Almost an hour later than planned we arrived at the Warren mansion. It is humungous. Range Rovers and 4X4 vehicles adorned the lengthy driveway. We added our car to the array of expensive cars haphazardly parked and clattered on the door.

Judging by the laughter I would say people had been drinking heavily for about two hours.

"Come in, come in," boomed Bunny, and in we traipsed. Never before have I seen so many glamorous women. They were dressed as if we were going to an evening out at the Ritz hotel.

"This is Cynthia Palmer Huntingdon," said Bunny looking flushed and smelling of booze. He introduced me. He pronounced Amanda – Amarnda. A glittering hand full of flashing diamonds was thrust out at me, and I shrank six inches as her cool grey eyes took in my anorak and wellington boots. Her Jimmy Choo ankle boots glistened and her tight Armani jeans hugged her slim figure. She wore a coat similar to the one Phil had made me remove. I glowered at him and he turned away quickly to talk to the men.

"Okey dokey, peeps," shouted Bunny. "We're all here, at last," he announced his glance lingering in my direction. I shrank a little more.

"Girlies, you can all go with Cynthia and Bunty and Bee in the 4X4's. Us chaps will go in the other vehicles and meet you in the marquee.

"Marquee?" I whispered to Cynthia.

"Oh yes, we don't want everyone messing up their nice clothes in a muddy field do we? We always like to make a goo[d] impression. You don't think I'd wear a £495 pair of Jimmy Choo 24:7 boots to a dirty old field do you?"

I tried to find Phil to stare daggers at him but he was hiding in the crowd of men.

"You wait," I thought.

After much giggling from the 'girlies', and some appalling driving, we arrived at the event. There were stacks of people dressed in anoraks and wellington boots around a large racecourse on which were fences for the horses to jump. The Range Rovers and 4X4's parped their horns noisily and raced through the people, cutting a swathe before arriving at a huge marquee. Tables set up inside, were groaning with champagne, wine and beer. It seemed Point to Point was going to consist of getting completely bladdered and missing the fun. Bunny and his chums, including a slightly flushed Phil, charged into the tent making "haw, haw, haw" noises. I disappeared out at the back, while everyone was air kissing each other, and headed of[f] towards the course. I spotted Phil in the middle of male huddle with a glass in his hand looking anxious as I sneaked off.

Outside it was rather interesting and atmospheric. There wa[s] a convivial spirit amongst the spectators. There were also lots of very nice craft stalls and I squelched up to one displaying some lovely hats. I tried a couple on.

"Hello," said a voice behind me. "You like them?"

"They're really nice. I love this purple one."

"I made them myself, well with help from Mum," said the woman who had been talking.

We struck up a conversation and, obviously, I bought the knitted hat which looked rather fetching with my boots and mud caked wellies. She introduced me to her husband and family, all positioned behind their car, using the tailgate as a table. Food was laid out.

"Care to join us?" they asked. I looked up at the Marquee. There were gales of laughter coming from the tent. I think I saw Bunny trying to relieve himself beside it, but I couldn't be sure.

"Oh dear, you're not with Bunny's crowd are you?"

"I'm afraid so.'"

"It might be better, then, if you join us. You'll at least see the races."

And, so I did. It was great fun. I even bet on one of them and won ten pounds. I bought some Candy Floss for the children. The entire experience was very enjoyable. Whole families were out for the day, all watching the horses, or visiting the craft stalls.

At the end of the afternoon I thanked my new friends and suggested I go back to the tent.

"Oh don't worry. You can stay with us. It's the same every year with Bunny's mob. They all get so drunk in there that the rest of us have to help pull their Range Rovers out of the mud, or ditches and even take them home because they are far too inebriated to drive. We'd probably be giving you a lift anyway. Is there anyone in particular in there you'd like us to collect?"

I thought about Phil. He hates drinking too much. He can't take it at all. He'd have a dreadful hangover the next day and he

would probably already be deeply regretting going to the even
He'd love to be extracted. I thought for a moment and looked down at my dirty wellington boots and my aged anorak.
"No," I said. "No, it's just me."
Posted by Facing50Blog.com - 4 Comments
Vera said...You wicked girl. Chuckle chuckle.
Faerie Queene said...Jimmy Choo 24:7 boots. Ooooh!
SexyFitChick said...Power to you. Well done. I bet the jockey were much more fun to look at than that drunken bunch. Don' you just love their bums?
MammaMia6 said...Quite right too. I'd have done the same.

Monday 31st

Phil looks terrible. He has spent all morning in the toilet groaning. He says he never wants to drink ever again and he's bloody glad he doesn't know anyone any more. He prefers being retired. He doesn't remember how he got home so I'm well in the clear. Every time I mention the words, beer, wine o lager to him he groans. It's most entertaining.
Posted by Facing50Blog.com - 2 Comments
SexyFitChick said...Ha ha!
MammaMia6 said...He should know better at his age anyway

CHAPTER 8 – FEBRUARY

Sunday 6th

"Hello Pet!"

"Hi Mum, how are you coping being back in the UK?"

"It's miserable."

I should think it was miserable after two months of high jinks and fun in the sunshine. I heard the sound of a wine glass being refilled.

"I'm so cold after the warmth of Cyprus," she continued, obviously with a cigarette hanging out of the side of her mouth

"I really hate these cold months," she continued.

"Have you booked to go back to Cyprus yet?"

"Not yet. I thought I'd spend some time here. I have a few things I need to sort out and catch up on."

I can't imagine what she might be catching up on, not unless she has planned a mammoth wine making session. The conversation turned to soap operas on the television. She started to tell me about the exploits of the characters from her favourite soap opera, one I've never watched. I listened while she regaled me with tales of the characters and their shenanigans, adding "Oh really" periodically, and pondered as to why we all watch soap operas. I suppose they serve to remind us that the drudgery we experience in our lives is completely normal. Having said that, some of the characters from the soap opera my mother watches, seem to be having a surprisingly interesting time spicing their lives up with torrid affairs and secret assignations. Of course, that led me to think about the delicious Todd, now back from his trip. He emailed me some photographs of him cycling in Thailand. Gorgeous doesn't even begin to describe him. He looks so content too.

"I expect Grego will enjoy the soaps when he comes over to stay," continued my mother.

"Grego? Stay? When?" I stammered inarticulately. Todd was instantly vaporised.

"Next week. I'm going to drive down to Heathrow and collect him. He can drive back."

This was going from bad to worse. Mum is lethal behind a wheel. She hasn't driven on a motorway since 1980. She always hated motorways, a fact that was demonstrated the last time she drove the length of the M25, on the hard shoulder, doing 40mph, in an attempt to stay away from the traffic which frightened her.

"Are you sure about this? Couldn't he just get a taxi?" I asked.

"I suppose so but I want to collect him in my new car."

"New car?" I spluttered.

Mum has had the same car, an old Honda Civic, for over thirty years. She's always maintained she would never get rid of it as she only travels two miles, twice a week, to the supermarket and back.

"I treated myself to a new car, last Thursday," she continued. "I thought it was about time I replaced the old girl. I got a good trade in price for her."

Good, at least she'd bought another Honda; she'd be safe in that. Nearly all older people in the country drive Hondas, as they are reliable and practical.

"Yes, I've bought another Honda. It's only done 4,000 miles. Now what model is it? Wait a minute I'll go and get the brochure."
There was a lot of coughing in the background. The receiver was picked up again.

"It's called an s2000."

"Mum, that's a soft top sports car," I groaned.

Phil loves cars and we'd looked at that particular model a few years ago.

"It's pretty powerful, and not terribly practical for the shops," I added.

"I know, but it's a bit of a head turner. Men stop and stare at it when I get out of it. Grego thinks it's an excellent choice. I've put him on the insurance while he's here so he can drive it too."

This is becoming incredibly surreal. My mother has now purchased a sports car and a swarthy suntanned toy boy appears to be coming over to stay with her. I smell a rat. What is Grego up to? More to the point, what is my mother thinking of?
Posted by Facing50Blog.com - 3 Comments
Vera said... She's probably just trying to have fun. What's wrong with a Honda s2000 at least it's not boring?
Angelique said... I wish my mother would get an exciting life. She seems to spend all her time with her cat and crocheting tablecloths for me. I have an entire drawer filled with them.
Lostforwords... I think you shouldn't jump to conclusions. I agree with Vera, she's probably just trying to have fun.

Wednesday 9th

Tom came in tonight in a dreadful mood. He slammed open the back door and threw his lunchbox on the kitchen top without a word.

"Hi Tom," I ventured. "You okay?"

He mumbled something unintelligible and stormed off to his room shutting the door firmly. I tiptoed upstairs and heard low mumblings as he spoke to someone on his mobile. I couldn't hear what he was saying even when I tried the old trick of putting a glass against the door to amplify the sound, and listen through it. Phil caught me attempting to eavesdrop and reprimanded me.

"Leave the boy alone. He doesn't want you noseying in his affairs. His private life is his private life."

And, with that, he took my glass away from me. That'll teach me to be concerned. Well maybe I was being a little bit nosey. It's very hard being a mother if your offspring refuses to tell you what's going on in their lives.

Posted by Facing50Blog.com - 2 Comments

Lostforwords said... Did you ever tell your mother what was going on?

Facing50 said... No, I didn't because I didn't want her to know or comment about my life. Okay, you have a point. I hadn't thought about it in that way. Thanks.

Thursday 10th

What a day! Tom refused to eat his usual half a kilo of sugary cereal for breakfast saying he wasn't hungry, and headed straight out to work without his sandwiches. I ran after him but he had already sped off like Sebastian Loeb, the rally driver, tyres spinning and gravel pinging in all directions. I hope he's not in danger of losing his job, or has failed his college work. Phil will go ape if he has. I decided to take his lunch to work for him, and check he was alright. Obviously, Phil was set against that idea.

"If he's stupid enough to go without it..." he started to say, but I insisted. Having worked out that he would be able to combine the trip with one to the Garden Centre for coffee and cake, and some specially reduced bird seed, since it was on our way, Phil decided to accompany me. I sent texts to warn Tom of our arrival. We turned up during his coffee break. Tom was resting against his car with a cigarette in one hand, a habit we both detest, talking intently into his mobile. He put up his hand to acknowledge us. I pointed at the sandwich box, placing it on his car roof.

"Thanks," he mumbled. "No, not you, no, just the 'Rents. They're dropping off something for me."

He went back to his mumblings. Phil wasn't too impressed. He doesn't like being called a 'Rent'. He thinks people who talk on the phone when they should be having a conversation with you, are ignorant.

"He should have thanked us properly instead of holding a conversation with his mates," he grumbled. "He's always on that ruddy phone wasting time. I should take it off him." However, I'd seen the look on Tom's face as he spoke to whoever was on the end of the phone. He was a young man in some distress.

We drove to the Garden Centre, a Mecca for old people on coach trips, and mothers with noisy offspring. There is so much more here than just things for the garden. There's a gigantic cafeteria where they serve cheap lunches. As soon as the food is laid out under hot plates at half past eleven, coach loads of people appear from nowhere and form an orderly queue in excited anticipation of the two for one lunch offer. There's a playground for the children - not the old aged pensioners

You can buy almost anything imaginable there, obviously a highly inflated prices: delicatessen goodies, clothes, candles, toys, books, jewellery, fish for your aquarium or pond, bird feed of all descriptions, conservatories, benches, Birthday card and of course plants for your garden.

Apart from the cafeteria, Phil hates the place. He considers to be full of old rubbish. I'm always surprised by the array of goods for sale, a personalised jar of jam or some special Lebkuchen biscuits from Germany. It's all beautifully laid out I'm as attracted to it as a Jackdaw is to shiny objects.

Today there were four coach loads of pensioners, all out on day trips. There was a large group of them sorting through the left over bargains from Christmas. They were piling almost ou of date Christmas cakes, mince pies and chocolate Santas into their wire baskets as if they were going out of fashion, and cackling loudly.

Phil headed towards the bird feeding section, where there were more pensioners buying small stick on bird feeders, to adorn their windows. Phil is extremely conscientious about feeding the birds and we always have fat balls, seeds and mealworms to put out for them over winter. He is very kind when it comes to animals and nature. He always catches the spiders in the house for me. He puts them outside gently rathe than let me suck them up in the vacuum cleaner. He takes grea care not to throw ladybirds away on the compost heap by mistake, by checking each and every leaf when he collects them, as they lay fallen from the trees in autumn. He particularly likes birds. Over the years he has managed to attract many varieties into our garden. I often find him staring out, watching them feed, and looking wistful.

The garden centre was overrun by people in wheelchairs, some with Zimmer frames, and some with sticks pushing others in wheelchairs. There were ten long tables set up for lunch for them in the cafeteria. They were all delighted to be out for the day, but it made us both feel a little melancholy.

"That'll be us in a few years time," Phil declared gloomily. "The highlight of our week will be coming here for coffee and cake, and a bargain purchase."

"Not so different from now then," I commented as we queued behind chuckling ladies with baskets full of cake, holding our two bags of half price bird seed.

Posted by Facing50Blog.com - 3 Comments

Vera said... It sounds quite fun really.

Lostforwords said...You really need to get out more.

SexyFitChick said... I'm warming to Phil. He likes birds. He'd be great with my galah. It's a greedy little devil when it comes to food. Last night it tried to peck at my toenails after I painted them purple. He thought they were raisins.

Friday 11th

Last night after the depressing visit to the garden centre, I logged onto my usual site. My Inbox contained four messages from Todd:

'Sitting naked by the Scrabble board waiting for my playmate to join me. It's very hot here. I've been to the beach and played volleyball for the first time in ages and it made me feel young again. Remember the last time we played?'

'I've just logged on in case you are around but you don't seem to be. I hope you are doing something exciting and fun. I've just come back from a long walk with Digit and watched the sun going down. It's nowhere near as romantic on your own.'

'You must be very busy as you are still not around. I hope you haven't forgotten about me.' 'I'm off to Hanoi next week for a short trip. You'd love it there.'

I logged onto the Scrabble board where the play icon was flashing. Todd had played 'excite' I added '–ment' to it. That's just what my life lacks at the moment.

Posted by Facing50Blog.com - 3 Comments

SexyFitChick said... Hurray your blog is spicing up again. Hanoi or garden centre? Tough choice!

Lostforwords said... 'All that glitters is not gold'.

Facing50 said... I'm confused by that last comment.

Saturday 12th

Well the first tentative signs of spring are here. No, I haven spotted crocus pushing their way through the soil or the first cuckoo of the year (not unless you count the one I see in the mirror every morning) no, more obvious signs than that have started to appear.

It began last weekend when we had half an hour of sunshin The rays shining through the window alerted Phil to the fact that the bathroom wall required painting. He duly went to the shed and chipped the layer of ice of an old tin of paint and set to it. Naturally, my assistance was required, and I spent most o

Saturday holed in the bathroom, with an increasingly frustrated husband who stood precariously perched on a ladder, whilst I held an enormous tin of paint for him. Painting is not his favourite occupation but after several hours he was quietly pleased with the result. He was even more pleased that he hadn't needed to employ the services of a professional painter.

Spurred on by the painting I decided to turf out my wardrobe. It is in desperate need of cleaning out. I hung the fallen blouses back onto hangers. I put my shoes into order in boxes and labelled the boxes. I tidied the makeup bags up. Finally, I bagged up a load of stuff I didn't need or want any more, for the charity shop, and cleaned all the shelves. I'm very good at throwing old clothes out. Well, I have to make room for all the new ones don't I?

I showed the new gleaming tidy wardrobe to Phil who glumly decided he really should sort through his old suits from when he worked, and dispose of clothes he would no longer need. This of course, was as they say, easier said than done.

When Phil worked he would drive off each day looking like the top executive he was. He would be kitted out in his smart suit and shining Italian leather shoes. His tie and shirt would match perfectly. He would have a matching handkerchief in his pocket. In short, he looked like a male model or famous film star.

Since he retired he has no use whatsoever for these clothes. He can hardly go around the supermarket in a Cashmere camel coat and loafers. He can't wear a two piece soft grey handmade suit in the garden. His ties are redundant. His handsome shoes are also redundant. He too is now redundant. Well, that is how he feels. He has had his 'useful' time and the clothes represent

what he used to be; an important businessman. In getting rid o
them, he'll be getting rid of part of his identity. He spent most
of his life as a businessman and disposing of such lovely (and
expensive) clothes is very hard for him. I completely
understand.

When I gave up work I too had to dispose of the designer
clothes, the power suits and the matching accessories. It was a
wrench to let them go and I did it with a heavy heart. As for
Phil, well, I think it is even more difficult. Up until now I've
left his clothes hanging in the wardrobe. He needed to be read
to sort through them. I left him contemplating his vast and
colour coded wardrobe and answered the phone.

It was my mother. Being someone who doesn't like to sit
still, she'd certainly been busy.

"Sorry, I've not phoned this week, I've been in the attic,"
she explained.

"What on earth were you doing up there?"

"I thought it was time to clear it out. I thought I'd do it
before Grego gets here." she replied.

The attic, typical of attics in many homes, houses everythin
we ever owned as a family. The attic is a dreadful place,
reached only by some pull down steps, and loosely boarded so
anyone could fall through the ceiling if they dared to go up
there. My mother had decided she would take on the challenge

"I've been up there all week," she added. I had visions of
her trapped up there unable to descend but she meant it had
taken her all week to go through some of the tons of stuff that
there.

"I've been reading your school reports from 1970."
Inward groan.

"Amanda is a vivacious student who always has something to say," she read out.

Don't you just hate being reminded of how bad or naughty you were at school? I felt myself regressing to my youth. I was no longer a mature woman. I was a child being reprimanded by my mother again.

"Maths – could try harder," she said, puffing on her cigarette, making me squirm even more.

"Music: I'm sure Amanda would be an able student if she paid more attention to the subject and wasn't so easily distracted."

I almost felt like apologising. Mercifully, she stopped reading out every entry, took a further drag on her cigarette, and announced:

"I found your *Wurzel Gummidge* scarecrow costume I made you for the school fancy dress competition. Do you want it?"

"I can't think when I might next need it, Mum. I can't see me wearing it to the shops," I replied.

"Yes, I thought you'd say something clever like that," she said crossly, making me fidget as I held on to the phone. I didn't really want her to get cross with me. How can mothers manage to make you feel so juvenile?

"Anyway," she added. "It's probably far too small for you."

"Well, I was eleven when you made it, so I'm guessing I might be a little larger now." Oops. I shouldn't have said that. The silence hung in the air for a while and I squirmed some more.

"I found your old Enid Blyton books: the entire series of *The Famous Five* and *The Secret Seven*. I gave them to the neighbours' children along with all your old games."

She then went through each item she had discovered at length.

"Oh do you remember....? Well, I found that too."

The entire conversation turned into a trip down memory lane. We recalled events from decades before. We chatted about old times when I lived at home.

"Anyway the attic is now empty. I've had everything removed and disposed of. It's all gone apart from the photograph albums. I couldn't part with those, she said finally.

"Mum," I asked, when I could finally interject. "Why have you cleared the attic?"

"It's time. It's been almost ten years since your father died. have to let go at some point. I have my memories. I don't need things or objects or memorabilia to remind me of my happy life, or of your dear father."

My mother had spring-cleaned her life. She wasn't too sad about it. The final part of the cleaning out process had been th conversation. Talking to me about everything that she had discovered had undoubtedly helped.

I returned to the bedroom after an exceedingly long chat with her. Phil was still staring wistfully at his clothes. He'd pu two pairs of grey socks out and had shuffled some boxes abou

"Look you don't have to do this. Just because I've thrown things out doesn't mean you have to," I said. "Let's call it a day."

I shut the wardrobe door. Phil looked relieved. He'll clear it out when he's ready. Maybe next spring!

Posted by Facing50Blog.com - 5 Comments

Vera said...That was a very touching post my dear. It sounded as if you and your mother had a nice time reminiscing.

Facing50 said...Thank you Vera. Yes, for once I felt a little closer to her. We didn't seem to get on each other's nerves today. I suppose she will be back to her usual self when I next hear from her though. Grego arrives very soon. I hope she isn't thinking of starting afresh with him.
Vera said...Oh my! That would be quite something wouldn't it?
Serene Siren said...You have motivated me into sorting out my wardrobe.
MammaMia6 said...Men are hopeless at throwing out their clothes. I chucked all of husband's pants and jackets out when he got too fat to wear them. I haven't had to bother with the second one's closet though. He only seems to wear vests and t-shirts. At least there is has been plenty of room for my stuff.

Tuesday 15th

It was Valentine's Day yesterday. Phil hasn't always hated Valentine's Day. In bygone times, not only did he once get me a card (admittedly that was our first Valentine's Day together, and many years ago) but he used to buy me flowers. He would wait until the day itself, or the day after, and get the flowers reduced.

"No need to pay hyped up prices!"

He would return with a gleeful look on his face having bagged a bargain. He's right, of course, Valentine's Day is, like so many occasions, a commercial excuse for consumerism. And yes, only romantic doltish youngsters like Tom, are mug enough to take their loved ones out for a Valentine's Day meal.

"Twenty pounds and no wine, you must be joking!"

Especially, when their loved one can cook a meal at home for a
fraction of the price, and if they are very lucky, will have some
tea lights on the table.

However, some of us have romanticism in our soul and so against my better judgement I had decided to embrace the day. I bought him a postcard with a cloud on it in the shape of a heart - not a proper card because that's too sloppy and it would evoke some comment about wasting money. I got some foil wrapped, heart-shaped chocolates – he adores chocolate so I was on a winner there, and some special shower gel; something practical but thoughtful.

The day dawned brightly and cheerily. The sun was rising and the birds were singing, well, actually they were squawking but better that than the rain and grey that had been forecast. Th signs weren't good in the grumpy department though. Phil was looking his usual cantankerous self as he drained his coffee cup, then thundered down to the shower, casting a glowering look in my direction as he went. Oh well, in for a penny.... I go breakfast and set the table, laying the chocolates out in the shape of a heart, and standing his card upright against his cup.

Twenty minutes in the shower had improved his mood. He only just managed to suppress the look of pleasure on his face when he saw his gift and the chocolate hearts on the table. No, he didn't get me anything. There was no card, or surprise bunc of flowers, or even a kiss of appreciation but for a few hours that day Phil was less grumpy than normal. At lunchtime he was verging on cheerful and he prepared a Valentine's Day lunch: a poached egg on crumpet (almost in the shape of a heart) and I do declare that I heard him whistling as he went outside to clean his car. Who said Valentine's Day was a waste of time?

I admit that although I was pleased that Phil was slightly less crabby than normal, I felt a little flat. Todd had sent me a singing email card for Valentine's Day. When you clicked on it, a video of the artist and song played. He'd chosen Jacques Brel's *Ne me quitte pas;* a song I adore. It's full of passion. The singer begs his love not to leave him. There's an English version called *If you go away,* but I prefer the original, which means 'Do not leave me'. It was very romantic. Todd had added a heart after it. Phil wandered in after cleaning his car and saw me watching it.

"Haven't you got anything better to do?" he moaned.

"No, not really," I replied, staring mistily at the screen, transported again to my youth.

Posted by Facing50Blog.com - 2 Comments

SexyFitChick said... Wow he really knows how to woo a lady!

Lostforwords said... You don't need a silly day thought up by card manufacturers to show you care for someone.

Wednesday 16th

Tom has had nothing to say about his wonderful romantic night on Valentine's Day. He'd saved his money for the occasion and was very excited about it. He'd planned it for weeks. He'd even booked the best table at a pricey restaurant. He'd arranged for flowers and a bottle of champagne to be at the table. He had taken a day off work to buy Tiffany a special present.

"Do you think she'll like them?" he'd asked me anxiously, showing me a large teddy bear holding a cushion with the words 'I love you' embroidered on it, and a box with a pretty necklace in it.

"Sweetie, she'll love it. It's beautiful. She's lucky to have someone who cares about her so much."

He hugged me spontaneously and beamed. My heart ached for him and his youthful romanticism. I hope she doesn't break hi heart. I'd hate him to become hardened against affection.

My mother, on the other hand, had plenty to say.

"I've had the best Valentine's Day I've had in a long time," she declared, having phoned me yesterday evening because sh was too busy to phone on Sunday. "Grego cooked us a speciality dish from Cyprus, 'meze'. There were lots and lots little dishes of delicious food. We had 'keftedes' which are meat balls and what were those sausages called, Grego?"

The muffled reply was inaudible and she giggled, yes my mother giggled.

"'Loukanika', really lovely sausages in red wine, too much red wine," she added and giggled again.

I heard a manly chuckle in the background.

"Oh, and 'moussaka' and 'kalamari' and 'zucchini,'' she continued.

It was starting to sound like she was reading from a menu in a Greek restaurant.

"Grego set the table with candles and petals from pink rose He even bought a very nice Greek CD *'Roots of Greek Music, Volume 4: Romantic Ballads: Kira Georgina (Mrs Georgina),* '" she read, obviously holding the CD in front of her.

In the background I could hear typical Greek music which all sounds the same to me.

"We've got it on now," she explained.

It didn't seem to be a very romantic ballad, more like smash your plates along to this song, but hey, she was enjoying it.

"Grego even bought me a little present, a thank you, for showing him the sights."

I wondered what sights my Mother might have shown him. To my knowledge there was only a supermarket, a Coop funeral parlour and a huge housing estate in the area. He'd be alright if he liked train spotting as Mum lives slap bang next to a railway line. The trains to London rattle by every half an hour, all day and all through the night. Living beside our busy road is bad enough but when a train whistles past her house you cannot hear a thing. Conversation completely ceases until the train has passed through. The entire house trembles when the heavy trains go by, and you have to leap up and grab various pictures, or more importantly her antique copper warming pan, which is hanging on the lounge wall, to prevent it from clattering to the floor. Mum doesn't hear the trains any more. She carries on as if they are not there.

"Sorry Mum, what did you say? I couldn't hear you for the train going by."

"What train?" She'll reply.

I hope Grego likes rolling stock. He'll certainly have enjoyed plenty of it. I drained my wine glass and stared out of the window. My mother's chatter continued in the background.

"So we went to Covent Garden and saw *La Boheme* which is, as you know, is one of my favourite operas. When Rudolfo sings to Mimi *Che gelida manina* (Your tiny hand is frozen) we were spellbound. It was so moving. At the end, when Mimi dies of consumption, we both sobbed into the box of Kleenex. I've

not been to the opera for decades. Your dear father didn't enjo
it too much so I didn't go. Grego and I are thinking of trying
Sadler Wells Ballet next week. I think *Swan Lake* is on.'

I wanted to voice my suspicions about Grego, but how could I? She was going out to theatres and ballets. She was enjoying herself for the first time in a long time, and doing things she was passionate about. I had forgotten how much she loved opera. All she ever had at home were a few books about it, and some old records, which she listened to all the time when Dad was away. I recall the look on her face as she listened to her records every weekend, trying to get her ungrateful daughter to appreciate the beauty of *Pagliaci* or *Madame Butterfly* when all I wanted to listen to, was 'The Bay City Rollers' or 'Wings'. I refused to like opera in my youth, on the basis that my mother loved it so much. We never want to copy our parents do we?

Fluent in Italian, because she spent her youth in Rome, my mother would sing along to the arias and particularly loved *O mio babbino caro.* She'd always sing it to me after a few glasses of wine and cry. I only realised many years later it means 'My dear father'. It probably held special connotations for her. I found myself humming the said aria from Puccini's opera. Anyway, I really hope Grego isn't up to something. I voiced my concerns to Phil after the call.

"Yes," he agreed. "It is pretty suspicious. What man likes Opera, ballet and cooking?"

True, after all, Phil only likes Abba, business programmes and cake.

Posted by Facing50Blog.com - 2 Comments

Fairie Queene said: I like opera and I'm a man. Albert and I had a large collection of opera classics. He took them with him when he went off with that golf professional, the ingrate. I can't imagine Roger appreciating the beauty of Puccini like I did. I like ballet too.
Lostforwords said: It was only a night out. Don't worry. I'm sure Grego behaved like a true gentleman. He sounds delightful company.

Monday 21st

With all the unprecedented weather we have had over winter this year, we haven't been out in our car as much as we normally would. Temperatures, which plummeted to minus thirteen centigrade on several occasions, have also had an effect on it, and the car has begun to show signs of winter wear.

For the last couple of weeks the battery has been discharging. The alarm will suddenly go off. Or, we can't open it on the key fob, and have to get the key itself out to unlock it. I took this to mean that the battery would need replacing but Phil insisted that it was due to the cold snap we were once again experiencing, and if he could nurse it through the next month, it would recover. I bowed down to Phil's superior knowledge of all things mechanical, after all, he bows down to my superior knowledge of all things technical.

Every other day, Phil has been going out with an old battery charger to trickle power into the car battery. Each time, the old thing coughs into life, and a triumphant Phil swaggers back to the house, happy that it will not cost him a replacement battery.

Friday, rather unusually, we decided to go to town. We've done away with getting our food delivered, now that we are no longer snowed in, and Phil has missed his routine of searching out bargains. He loves to buy the offers, and reduced items, an has been getting serious withdrawal symptoms. Since the *Shredded Wheat* episode he hasn't been allowed to go shoppin on his own, but he was so enthusiastic to round up some deals last week, that I caved in and agreed we would go shopping. The car, which had been on charge the night before, started fir time.

"See, I told you it would improve if the weather got better," he announced proudly. "The forty-five minute run to town wil help recharge the battery too," he explained.

I beetled off, to look at all the lovely goodies in the shop windows, and browse through books and CDs. Phil was on strict instructions to buy nothing until I met up with him much later. I had a very enjoyable time browsing through rails of Spring Collection clothes, checking out the makeup counters, reading Birthday cards and looking at the latest DVD releases. noticed Phil standing in a newsagents' shop reading a magazine.

We met at the supermarket. Phil checked to make sure I hadn't spent any money and proudly announced he too had spent nothing so far. He looked very pleased with himself. We'd spent an entire morning in town and had made no silly purchases. Just what a grumpy husband likes best. We shoppe together. Phil pounced on all the offers like a man possessed.

"No, I don't think we actually need ten bottles of bleach."

"But they're only 85 pence a bottle. They won't go off."

"Why have you put fourteen boxes of *After Eight* peppermint chocolates into this trolley?"

"Half price," he said gleefully.

"No, no, no! We do not need any more boxes of cereal."

"We eat a lot of cereal and look, the milk is on offer," he said shoving eight plastic bottles into an already full trolley.

"There is no point grabbing all those frozen peas? It'll take months to eat them."

"Buy one get one free," he said gleefully. "They'll sit in the freezer until we need them."

We checked out, our arms straining under the weight of the bags of food.

"It's a good thing you came to join me," he acknowledged. "I'd have had a job carrying this lot back on my own."

I kept quiet. I needed all my energy to carry the heavy bags.

I was cheesed off by the time we reached the car. My arms ached. The car was parked on floor seven, the top floor. Phil insists on parking it as far away as possible from everyone, and as only the ground floor, and floor one, had any cars on them, seven was a pretty sure safe bet. The lift didn't work so we had had to climb the stairs.

I let the bags fall to the floor. Phil did the same as he ferreted about for the car key. He pointed it at the door to unlock it. The car door wouldn't open. He got out the little key and tried. The car wouldn't open. He tried again. The back window came down halfway but the door wouldn't unlock. He tried the key again. The car alarm started to warble feebly then gradually died off as the battery went flat. The car had effectively died on us.

Fortunately, I have the number of the garage programmed into the phone, so Phil phoned to explain our predicament. They would come to our rescue. Unfortunately, they were rather busy with a couple of heavy jobs, so they would be a couple of hours or so.

Two to three hours, with bags sprawled beside the car, and back window half open. There was little we could do except wait. After thirty minutes we were both bored and fractious. I decided we would split the watch. One of us would stay by the car with the phone and the other would go back to the shops fc something to do. I took first shift. Within ten minutes Phil was back. He didn't want to go around the shops any more. He would wait with the car. I didn't protest, after all if he'd changed the battery as I suggested we wouldn't be stuck on floor seven of a car park. I disappeared for a good couple of hours.

On my return, mercifully the rescue team from the garage were there, fitting the new battery. Phil was fussing about his car. Some of the shopping had slowly defrosted. There were small puddles developing beneath the plastic bags. Sometime later, the men brought the car back to life. Several hours after our arrival, we could finally leave.

After several hours in the car park, the parking fee had amassed to rather a significant amount. Phil had received a bill for over a couple of hundred pounds for the call out and new battery. And I had sneaked a rather expensive purchase, from the dress shop in town, into the car when he wasn't looking. Well, what is a girl to do; stuck in town for over two hours on her own?

Posted by Facing50Blog.com - 3 Comments

Lostforwords said...That won't help your financial position will it?

Facing50 said...No, but it helped my mood.

Faerie Queene said...I spluttered coffee all over my screen when I read this. Oh, it is too funny. Your poor husband.

Tuesday 22nd

Tom has been even more recalcitrant than usual. He's on his mobile from the second he gets up, to the last second before he falls asleep. I know, because we still pay his phone bill. We took out a contract for him, in Phil's name, when he went to university. We thought he would struggle to pay for a phone what with books, student equipment and of course beer. Because it's not due up for renewal until the beginning of next month, we've been mugs enough to keep paying the bill.

He should have 600 minutes of free talk time and 1000 text messages but amazingly he keeps going over the limit, which means we've consistently had to pay more than we expected, which is difficult when you are on a strict budget. Phil was so furious last month when he saw the enormous bill; he threatened to break the phone into little pieces. We explained the situation to Tom who nodded, apologised and said he would definitely keep to his limits. When he's drunk too much it's terrifying the number of texts he sends. These are usually to just one number, his girlfriend's. The bill comes addressed to us every month. It has reached telephone book status in terms of how much it weighs. I'm surprised the postman can squeeze it through the letterbox. Every call and text is itemised with a date and time. It'd be quicker to read Tolstoy's *War and Peace* or all seven volumes of Proust's *A la Recherche du Temps Perdu*.

This months' bill arrived yesterday and I scoured it. It was £145.87p. Phil would blow up spectacularly when he found out. Here we were, supposedly watching our household expenditures, and Tom's bill was £115.87p more than we had expected. Why? Because he's been texting his girlfriend all day, and most of the night, for three whole weeks. Isn't that stalking? I had to find out why he'd sent so many texts. He must have known he was out of free ones. Before I told Phil, I hid the bill in my wardrobe and waited for Tom to come in.

Phil has been very unhappy with the performance of his banking shares. They no longer yield a dividend and they're n recovering from the massive losses they took last year. The pension fund has suffered hugely because most of investments were in banking shares, which, at the time, gave good yields. I was with Phil who was trawling through a list of funds and shares, trying to work out where to put his eradicated funds, when I heard Tom banging down his lunch box on the kitchen top. I tried to head him off before he reached his room, but no such luck, which meant I'd have to take the plunge and enter The Pit.

I retrieved the bill from its hiding place, took a deep breath banged on his bedroom door and barged in. Tom was sitting dejectedly on his bed, phone in his hand. I looked at him stern and waved the bill at him. He jumped up.

"I knew you'd mention that soon," he said resigned to my wrath which was about to be released. "I can explain."

"No need," I snapped furiously, "I can see why it's this ridiculous amount."

I pointed to the large total at the bottom of the page and wavec the pages of itemised numbers at him.

"You've hounded that poor girl like a stalker. What do you think you were playing at texting her all day and all night ever two minutes? She must be sick of hearing from you. You just send text after text. If I were her father, I'd get the police involved for harassment," I continued, getting angrier, "And you've taken your father's generosity for granted. You thoughtless..."

It was the sob that made me stop abruptly. Tears were welling in Tom's eyes. He oozed abject misery. Some maternal instinct kicked in and I rushed up to him, all six foot of him, and tried to hug him. He cried on my shoulder.

"Tiffany's dumped me," he sobbed. "I've tried and tried to get her to explain why, or give me another chance. I kept texting her in the hope she would reply. She won't answer any of them, not one. I don't understand why. We've been together for ages. I thought she felt the same way about me as I do her. And, now I've let Dad down too. I want him to be proud of me and I've made it impossible for him to trust me. He'll be so fed up with me. I don't take him for granted, not anymore," he croaked between sobs. 'Why won't she at least answer my texts?'

Tears poured down his face. Sitting behind him, on a shoebox in his open wardrobe, sat the lovely little bear he had bought her for Valentine's Day. I felt a sharp pain. My heart ached for him. I wanted to cry for him, and smack Tiffany hard for hurting my boy so badly.

"Don't worry. I'll sort out the bill. Look Tom, I know you hurt dreadfully. I know you think I don't understand the hurt you are feeling, but I do. I remember clearly how it feels like to have someone you are bonkers about, suddenly decide they don't feel the same about you, even though you were convinced that they did. It feels like the worst thing imaginable in the world. The pain is immense. The hurt indescribable, but honestly son, it will get easier in time. I promise."

I held his head in my hands and looked him in the eyes. He looked back at me with such misery and hurt that I forgot the annoyance, frustration and pain he'd caused recently. This was just Tom, my son, who needed love and care and putting back together again.

"One day, when you don't expect it, you'll start to feel better. Then you'll start noticing people again. You'll forget the hurt, and in the future, maybe even this time next year, there will be someone else in your life who will make you feel good about yourself again. Someone who will make you smile. Someone who will make you laugh. Someone who will care for you and love you," I looked at him earnestly, "Just like I found your father."

He gave me a quizzical look but said nothing. He looked dreadful but at least the sobbing was easing. I told him I would give him some space to sort himself out, but if he wanted to talk I'd be downstairs. Honestly! Growing pains. Who needs them?

Phil was still surrounded by sheets of paper in the lounge oblivious to the drama.

"I don't know whether I should pull the funds out of Lloyds and put them in Shell or pharmaceuticals maybe GlaxoSmithKline," he pondered out loud.

"Maybe you should invest in telecoms," I ventured and, brandishing the phone bill. I explained the situation to Phil, fully expecting him explode about the amount showing on the phone bill. I told him about heartbroken Tom. Phil's face clouded over darkly. He took a deep breath.

"Bloody women! They're always trouble," he growled. I was dismissed as he rummaged through some more pieces of paper.

Posted by Facing50Blog.com - 3 Comments

Vera said... The poor boy. Tell him there are plenty more fish in the sea.

YoungFreeSingleandSane said... How old is he? I've got loads of friends who are single. I could set him up on a blind date.

Fairie Queene said... I know how he feels. Since Albert went, I've had no confidence. I don't even like going out any more.

Wednesday 23rd

Following on from Tom's dreadful heartbreak, I have decided that for his birthday next month, we are going to send him on a ten day break to Tenerife. He was going to spend it with Tiffany. I asked him what he wanted to do now about it. He is going to be twenty-one and that is worth celebrating. He replied he didn't want to celebrate it anymore and maybe he'd just go out with his friend Dave, who funnily enough, had also just split up with his girlfriend. I've been on the internet and booked a super self catering apartment. I checked thoroughly, especially after that debacle in Mallorca, but all the write ups on it are excellent. It should be ideal. I've managed to contact Dave via *Facebook* to see if he'd like to go with him. He's 'well up for it'.

Phil has contacted Tom's boss at work who more than happy to give Tom time off from work for a surprise birthday trip. He said he was delighted with Tom's efforts , and announced he has three weeks holiday owing to him anyway, which he

needed to take before the right to take it expired. I'm pleased about it and so is Phil, firstly, because it will only cost four hundred pounds, which is an exceptionally good price, and secondly, because Tom will be out of the house for ten whole days. Of course, Tom doesn't know anything about it, which also means that he hasn't got any appropriate clothes to take away so Phil and I are going to treat him to some holiday clothes. Well he is going to be twenty-one years old after all.
Posted by Facing50Blog.com - 1 Comment
YoungFreeSingleandSane said... Don't forget to buy him some condoms. You know what these young men are like on holiday.

Friday 25th

I checked through Tom's wardrobe, well floor really, to work out what was decent enough to take away and removed it from the messy pile. Tom will never notice if something is missing. If he does, he'll just think he's lost it. It happens all the time these days. He's always leaving clothes at friend's houses, and Tiffany appears to have most of his collection of t-shirts. We needed to buy him some t-shirts, flip-flops and shorts. I even managed to remove Tom's college card from his room, as you can get a discount for students, and every little helps. Phil and I went together to one of those trendy shops that have all the young labels: *Bench*, *Animal*, *Henley* etc. Phil yelped in horror as he picked up one of the t-shirts and turned over the price tag.

"Thirty-five pounds for this rag?" he squealed, holding up a *Bench* t-shirt with lettering on it that was deliberately faded.

"I could buy a whole suit for that," he moaned quite loudly, attracting a little too much attention from fellow shoppers, all aged about seventeen. He mooched about growling at the prices until his eyes alighted upon a pile of brightly coloured t-shirts, with no logos, and a sign above them, announcing you could buy three for twenty pounds.

"That's more like it," he declared, rifling through the pile of t-shirts for an extra large one. Fortunately, there were quite a lot of XL sizes and we managed to get six rather decent shirts.

"Six for the price of one and a bit," sighed Phil looking again at the first t-shirt he had held up. 'That's more like it."

Next, we had difficulty in finding some shorts. There really isn't a lot of demand for shorts in February. Phil had a rather loud pair of multicoloured floral shorts in one hand, and a pair of blue and white ones in the other, when a sales assistant appeared. He looked about fifteen years old, and was sporting a stud in his nose – very trendy.

"Can I help you Madam?" he asked politely.

Being called Madam makes me feel old. As polite as it may be, it conjures up pictures of maturity for me.

"I'm cool," I replied trying to look as if I fitted in the trendy store. "We are just trying to decide which pair of shorts we should buy our son."

"Well Madam," continued the young chap, "Those," he said, pointing to the loud floral shorts that Phil was holding, "Are a little bright, in the short department."

"Unlike our son," continued Phil now beaming. "Who is a little short, in the bright department."

He started chortling, which made me laugh, and behaving like two seventeen year olds ourselves, we headed off to the counter to buy the t-shirts, along with the blue and white shorts, snickering at Phil's wit.

Posted by Facing50Blog.com - 4 Comments

Lostforwords said... You see, Phil can be fun.

YoungFreeSingleandSane said... Did you remember the condoms?

SexyFitChick said... Damn, I missed a few of your posts because I was on a fitness course. Just catching up. When are they going on holiday? I might book a flight and join them. How old is Dave?

Facing50 said...Lostforwords – I suppose he has his moments. He always used to make me laugh.

YFSS – No, I forgot. Should I send Phil in to get them?

SFC – LOL. Leave them alone. They need time to mend their bruised hearts and egos. Besides, Dave isn't your type. Actually, come to think of it neither is Tom.

Monday 28th

Phil and I were ensconced this evening in a programme about the Great Financial Crash of 1929. No, Phil was ensconced, and I was fantasizing about lying on a warm beach drinking Mojitos, looking young, suntanned and slim. I think the muscular bronzed male body lying next to me might have belonged to Todd. In reality, I am old, pale, and chubby and bundled up in four layers of clothes. I'm feeling cold and I have a blue nose that keeps running. Tom crashed into the room in a slightly animated fashion. Tom only normally works on two speeds, slow and slower. Considering he was also cut up about the great break up with Tiffany, he seemed surprisingly pepped up. He had a large carryall over his shoulder.

"Evening Papa."

Phil nodded at the greeting. He's been a bit nicer to him recently. He even speaks to him now on occasion.

"Mum I'm off out. Don't know when I'll be back. I've joined the local football team."

Phil looked at me and I looked at him. We started laughing simultaneously.

"Haw, haw, haw!" we snorted.

"Well, that should dilute the average age of the team to about seventy," we scoffed, holding our sides in mirth, and imaging all the old folk of the village playing football.

"Do they allow Zimmer frames on the pitch?" we continued childishly, as tears rolled down my face.

"There are some young people in the village, you know? Actually, you wouldn't know, as you are always incarcerated in this house. An exciting night for you two is an alcohol free beer and a Marks and Spencer's pie," he reprimanded.

"I like M&S pies," huffed Phil.

"There are other people your age in this village too. They go out occasionally. Some of them play cricket for the village too. Many go to the pub, eat out, attend quiz nights and have a life," he emphasized. "That's what I'm trying to do. It's difficult enough being twenty-one. It's hard having virtually no money to live on. And, on top of it all, living at home with two old fogies who do absolutely nothing with their free time. And, I live in a village, in the middle of nowhere, where there is very little to do. There are no nightclubs, bars, theatres, galleries or restaurants. It sucks, but at least I am trying to have a life," he concluded glowering at us as we sank back in our chairs.

"Sorry Tom," I muttered.

Tom good naturedly forgave us straight away. He's not one to bear a grudge and grinned amiably.
"Right, I'm off to footie training. You two want to do a bit more with your lives before you need a Zimmer frame yourselves. Bye Papa. Bye Mum. See you both tomorrow. I expect you'll be in bed in an hour or so, won't you?" and with wink in my direction he went off whistling.
"I like Marks and Spencer's pies," reiterated Phil turning the volume back up on the television.
Posted by Facing50Blog.com - 2 Comments
Vera said... Well Tom has got a point, hasn't he?
Fairie Queene said... !!!!!

CHAPTER 9 –MARCH

Wednesday 2nd

I received an email this morning:

'Well, will you? Say you will. Please. Go on, go on, go on, go on, go on, go on. Please. Pretty please. Pretty, pretty please. It would just make my day if you say you'll meet me. No strings.'

Then he sent some photographs of Hanoi for me to look at. They were stunning. What a magical place. He'd put a caption at the bottom of one of them.

'I wish I could have shared this beautiful place with a beautiful woman - you.'

Posted by Facing50Blog.com - 6 Comments

YoungFreeSingleandSane said ...bleurgh! He is so soppy.

Facing50 said ...More romantic than soppy.

SexyFitChick said...Romantic, sexy, wealthy and fit. I really can't see the problem.

Vera said...How exotic. I'd love to have visited Hanoi. I managed Singapore and Hong Kong in my youth but not Hanoi.

Faerie Queene said...He's persistent, I'll give him that. I expect he's trying to break your will and make you succumb. I read about it in one of Albert's Psychology Self Help books.

Lostforwords said...I think he's trying too hard. I'm not convinced of his sincerity.

Saturday 5th

Today, we surprised Tom. We had his new clothes, including ten pairs of pants. I couldn't bring myself to send him abroad with aged pants, containing name tags from his school days. I'd put in suntan oil and passport and so on. It was all packed away in our room. Tom thought Dave was coming to take him out for the day. I could hear loud thudding music emitting from his room. It reverberates all around the house even with the door shut. How I long for the old days when it was Tubby you could hear, not all this loud noise.

One parent's evening, when Tom was a young lad, his Music master had called us to one side and informed us that Tom would make a very good tuba player. He asked if he coul give him private music lessons as he showed huge potential. Phil snorted, but the thought that Tom had potential in anythin at all, was incentive enough to allow him to give permission fc Tom to try it for a term, at the cost of five pounds a lesson. We both thought Tom would quickly lose interest, but no, the term became a year. Before long Tom parped his way through a music competition winning the music cup.

The master in question proclaimed him a natural. Tom was now sufficiently proficient to play an E Flat tuba, but the scho didn't own one. If Tom were to continue, we would have to bu a tuba for him. The master managed to find us a second-hand one, which we purchased and brought home. Phil lovingly attended to it, and each month, he took it to bits, cleaned it and oiled the valves then rubbed it over with polish until it gleame Every weekend, we were rewarded with Tubby, as he became known, parping his melodies and vibrating the house windows

It was a nightmare to cart about, of course. It would have been a lot easier if Tom had learned to play the flute or a recorder. I had to lay the seats flat in my car every time it had to be transported. It also meant I couldn't give any of Tom's friends a lift home, nor indeed could any of the mothers help me out, by taking Tom home when I was late at work. But, it didn't matter because Tubby became part of our lives. Tom and Tubby won another music cup for his rendition of the *Horn Pipe*. They gave solo performances. They became an important part of the school concert band and orchestra, where they would play to packed out auditoriums.

Christmas time was extra special. The orchestra members would be in their best suits and bow ties, while Tubby and his brass friends, would all be decked in tinsel. They played rousing Carols and the audience loved it. We all loved Tubby. We would listen to Tom practising for hours. When Tom left school he didn't want anything further to do with music, or, indeed, the tuba.

"It belongs in the past Mum," he declared.

Phil and I had to drive Tubby down to the shop, where we had first bought him, and ask them to resell it. It was like losing a favourite pet. Worse still, we had lost our little boy. He had suddenly grown up. He had moved on from those school days, and happy times. We no longer were his audience. He no longer needed us, or Tubby. Tubby found a new home almost immediately. It joined a circus. Apparently, E Flat tubas like that one, in such good condition, thank you Phil, are rare. Some days, I think about those days and I imagine it now, being played melodically, in a misty field beside a huge circus tent, and lovingly cared for by a man with a large red nose.

Dave arrived at ten o' clock with both of his parents. I could see them from where I stood, partly hidden behind the curtain at the front window. Dave's Mum was hugging him as if he were leaving for ever. She was obviously checking that he had everything because he would nod and point to a pocket or his backpack or his case.

"Have you got your wallet dear?"

Pat, pat as he tapped his pocket in his coat.

"Have you got your phone?"

I knew the conversation. I've had it hundreds of times with Tom. Just when do we let go of our children properly and stop worrying about them? Dave's father looked awkward and kept fidgeting from one foot to the other. Then, obviously, it was time to go and they did that sort of father and son dance. The one where they give each other a manly handshake, followed by a half hug-half back pat, the same dance that Phil and Tom very occasionally perform. Dave's father looked embarrassed and shoved a twenty pound note into his son's hand. Dave took it and hug- patted his father again. Mum and Dad got back into the car. They wouldn't leave until Dave was standing at our door. Mum had tears in her eyes and was waving like mad. I opened the door.

"Phew! Hello Mrs Wilson. I thought they'd never go. Is Tom ready?"

I had to go and bang loudly on Tom's door as there was no point in shouting. He'd never hear me above that row. Issy Miyake oozed from under the door.

"Dave's here."

"Great!"

The CD player was switched off by the remote control, no doubt, onto standby mode. I'd have to go back later and turn it and all his other appliances off properly. Tom thumped downstairs.

"Alright mate?" he beamed at Dave.

“Yeah, sound Mate,” replied Dave holding out two t-shirts.

Phil emerged from the sitting room and we stood grinning stupidly. Tom held up his bright yellow t-shirt. ‘Tom’s 21st Birthday Tour- Tenerife here we come’ was written on the front. On the back it stated ‘I’m Tom. It’s my birthday and I’m 21!’ Dave had a similar t-shirt but on the back was written ‘I’m Dave – Tom’s only mate so buy him a drink please’ Tom’s mouth just opened and closed silently, like a fish, and a huge smile spread over his face.

We took the boys to the airport after explaining the plan to Tom. He was more like the Tom of old, the Tom he had been before he came back from university. I insisted on walking them to check in. Once there, Phil gave Tom a wallet of Euros for the trip. They did the same half hand shake, half hug that Dave and his dad had done. I hugged Tom tightly, then Dave, then Tom again.

“Your birthday presents, only little things though, and your cards are in your bag,” I half choked.

”Yeah, yeah, cool Mum. This is awesome though. This is a fantastic present.”

I hugged him yet again.

“Have you got your passp...?’ I started to say but caught myself in time. “Have a great time both. Phone if there’s a problem.”

They waved cheerily and headed off to through the gate towards Departures. It really is quite hard to watch your children grow up, and away from you, even if they are a complete pain. Phil however had shed years in those few moments.

“Race you back to the car!” He shouted scampering off like a teenager.

Posted by Facing50Blog.com - 1 Comment

YoungFreeSingleandSane said... And, did you remember the condoms?

Sunday 6th

“He could have come here for his birthday,” growled my mother. She’s just gone back to Cyprus with Grego in tow. He insisted that she return with him for a week.

“Why didn’t you tell me?”

What a great idea that would have been; two twenty-somethin year olds, under the watchful eye of my drunken, partying, nor stop smoking mother. I don’t know who would end up looking after whom.

“I think there’s a slightly younger scene in Tenerife Mum,” replied.

“There’s a younger scene here too. My friends from Paphos are only fifty-five and Grego is only fifty-nine,” she retorted.

What can you say? Luckily for me, her pay as you go card wa running out, and the phone kept making beeping noises.

“Well, I probably wouldn’t have had time to look after then anyway what with my own party to organise. By the way I’ve extended my stay by a further three weeks.”

She may as well move over there permanently. The phone made some more noises. I could hear her complaining about th ‘confounded thing’. The phone made bip, bip, bip noises and then went dead. Just when you really want to talk to your mother she’s suddenly out of contact. Her mobile just kept going to answer phone and she didn’t reply to any of my texts.

Posted by Facing50Blog.com - 2 Comments
Vera said... I say!
Fairie Queene said... I hope you can get hold of her. I love hearing about her adventures.

Saturday 12th

I've been rather busy this week. I cleaned Tom's room thoroughly, disinfected it, sprayed it, and washed everything in it. It took three days but it was worth it. The house smelt nice again and clean. The bathroom was mine. There was no left over toothpaste spit in the sink, or on the mirror, when I went in to wash my face. There were no unflushed toilets with the seat up and indeed no nasty stench. We didn't have the anxiety of waiting for Tom to come in at all hours. We didn't miss him leaving a mess anywhere. We certainly didn't miss his friends who turn up just as you are serving dinner and then stay to eat it. We weren't subjected to the noise of his loud music while trying to watch television. It was wonderfully quiet and calm. Phil's face lost some of the lines that have been appearing on his brow. He even smiled a couple of times.

We spoke to Tom of course on his birthday; after all he was twenty-one years old. He sent us forty texts thanking us for the trip, twenty-three of them between two and five in the morning, while he was out clubbing.

It has been more peaceful without Tom and there has been less anxiety. Phil has still been his normal self, but at least he hasn't got as worked up about things as he does when Tom is at home. It would be so nice if we could achieve this level of calm more often. It might even help our relationship. I had hoped with Tom out of the way Phil might feel friskier. Alas, no. I

tried to get him in the mood by wearing a clinging dress at dinner time and playing soft music on the stereo. Phil spent th meal glowering at his steak in pepper sauce as if it were going to suddenly moo at him, and then commented that either he wa going deaf or I hadn't put the music on loudly enough. We probably need more than ten days to rekindle the flame.
Posted by Facing50Blog.com - 3 Comments
SexyFitChick said...You should give him a black eye for not noticing you. That'd made him appreciate the steak more.
Faerie Queene said...Maybe he's becoming a vegetarian.
Facing50 said...Guess he just wasn't in the mood. The clingin dress probably put him off. I have quite a lot for it to cling to.

Monday 14th

I grabbed a few minutes today to check *Scrabble*. Todd had managed to fill the entire conversation panel beside the board with the word' please'. He'd also played 'hopeful'.
Adding an -ly to the end of that, I logged off. Well, it wouldn' hurt to see him.
Posted by Facing50Blog.com - 2 Comments
SexyFitChick said...Glad you are listening to me. You'll neve know how you feel if you don't see him again.
Facing50 said...I'm now wishing I hadn't played that. I really don't know if I should see him.

Saturday 19th

Spring is definitely here. Nature of course is doing her bit. The birds are singing in the mornings. Small yellow flowers ar dotted about the garden. The nights are drawing out and we ar no longer huddled in front of the log burner at four o'clock in the afternoon. But the real signs of spring are much more obvious. It doesn't take much does it? A few rays of sunshine and we go barmy.

I went a bit loopy myself this week, baked a cake, and cleaned the house from top to bottom. Then I washed all the windows, inside and outside. Phil went a bit mad too, cleaned all the window ledges then gardened like a man possessed.

Next, on his to do list, was his filing cabinet containing all his paperwork. He was completely absorbed, which left me free to get on with those very important chores, or in my case trying to write this post. I had no sooner got my muse into gear when I noticed two strangers in our garden. They were muffled up in military type coats and seemed to be waving about metal detectors. Was it the police?

"Someone in our garden," I shouted to Phil.

"Sort it out. I'm busy," he replied.

I marched off into the garden, vexed at having my train of thought interrupted and determined to reprimand the trespassers.

"If you're looking for my husband's body it isn't here, I buried him under the patio after I murdered him," I said arms folded staring at the undercover policemen.

Turned out they weren't policemen at all. They were friends of the farmer who owns the field next door. He had given them permission to hunt for treasure in his field. They had got the wrong directions and ended up in our garden instead. I don't really see how, as they had to come through a gate to get into it, and there are flowers in it...actually looking at the garden I can see how they thought it was the field as there are still mole hills from months ago. Which reminds me, I forgot to tell you all that the mole man caught the female mole who escaped from her trap. He got her the following week so since then, we've been a mole free garden. Anyway, these guys were hardly likely to find golden ducats around here, so I sent them on the way. Honestly, as soon as the sun comes out people do the strangest things.

Next morning, Phil decided to wash and polish his car. Fou hours later he finished. Yes, I know, four hours to wash a car. think he must have licked it clean. It certainly gleamed. Infused with spring like enthusiasm, he spent the afternoon sanding down all the exterior wood on our large conservatory. The dust settled all over my clean windows leaving smeary brown marks. By the end of a very long day, the conservatory looked fabulous, all freshly painted with gleaming windows which I had washed again. We were both very pleased with th result.

Yesterday, was 'Comic Relief' day. People all over the country put on red noses, and did madcap things, to raise money for charity. Phil, now in a better mood, agreed to go to town as the sun was shining. We passed several cars sporting large plastic red noses, and many individuals in town who wer dressed in fancy dress, clattering buckets at us to throw money into.

Standing in the supermarket, being served at the cheese counter by a woman wearing a large red nose and a bright red wig, a voice came over the tannoy system:

"Ladies and Gentlemen if you would like to make your wa over to the cigarette counter you will be able to see the store manager getting his legs waxed for 'Comic Relief'. Please come and sponsor him.

The old ladies standing in the queue all tittered.

"Oh, come on, Gertrude," said one. "Let's go and watch."
'We don't have much time, it's nearly half past,' said the other chuckling and off they went arm in arm.

The atmosphere in town was so positive that it bounced onto you and lifted your spirits. That is apart from 'Marks and Spencer' where there was an ugly scene developing. Gangs of teenagers? No, crowds of old age pensioners annoyed that the shelves were emptying of the 'Dine in for £10' offer. I half expected a security guard to be called in. The chuntering got louder. People jostled each other for the remaining food. One old woman was elbowing an equally elderly man away from the last remaining haddock gratin that she had her eye on. Clearly annoyed that he had it within his grasp, she squared up to him and shoved her way in front of him, emerging from the scuffle waving the readymade meal victoriously. The elderly man almost growled at her. He was clutching the last bottle of Zinfandel Sparkling rose wine. They were just about to smack each other over the heads with their broccoli spears when, fortunately, a staff member turned up with a fresh plastic case of readymade meals. Some of which were haddock gratin. It was like a feeding frenzy as people pounced on the meals.

On our return, feeling as energetic as a new born spring lamb, Phil decided we would pressure wash the patio. It's a job I detest as it takes hours and I get filthy from it. Still in a spring like mode he dragged out the pressure washer from the shed where it hibernates all winter and connected all the necessary hoses together. It is a terrible palaver. Finally, he was all hitched up and ready for action. I went to seek out my old clothes to wear. The machine started up. It makes an awful noise. The wretched thing was obviously getting old and crotchety because the noise was worse than usual. I came outside to help, only to discover a fountain of water gushing ou of the top of the pressure washer. Phil, who had his back to it and was trying to clean the slabs, had no idea. I screamed at him to stop but he couldn't hear me above the noise of the machine. Water continued to shoot out of the machine like a geyser erupting. Dirty brown water was shooting in every direction, particularly all over the newly painted and cleaned conservatory, making it look as grubby and old as it did before we painted it.

Spring is definitely on its way. Blossom is beginning to unfurl on the trees. Birds sing cheerily. And that groaning, grumbling sound you can hear in the distance is the sound of a Mad March Phil.

Posted by Facing50Blog.com - 6 Comments

MammaMia6 said...I can't stop laughing. What a scene.

YoungFreeSingleandSane said... I knew there was an advantage to living in a flat – no patio. Hope you get it all cleaned up. I feel quite exhausted reading about all the things you did.

PhillyFilly said...Comic Relief day sounds fun. I'd love to come and join in that day. After the last lot of surgery I had, m nose would fit in a treat.

SexyFitChick said...Have you heard from your Mum yet?

Facing50 said...Thank you all. SFC No, I haven't.

SexyFitChick said...She's obviously having more fun than yo then. Bet she isn't cleaning patios and windows.

Sunday 20th

Tom and Dave have returned, all too soon. They are refreshed, bronzed and full of beans. They had a phenomenal time, much of which I gather, centred on nightclubs, reps, girls, sleeping and drinking. I saw Dave's photographs of the holiday on *Facebook* this afternoon and I realised that sending Tom off was a great idea. His confidence has been somewhat restored. He's certainly seems to have got over the initial hurt of breaking up with Tiffany.

He slightly impressed Phil by announcing that he is going to take on his own phone contract. He feels that it will help him control his impulsive texting if he actually has to pay his own bill. He's worked out that he can afford thirty-five pounds a month if he knocks out one night's drinking a month.

Phil has immediately become withdrawn and miserable again. I can't understand why. Tom is behaving well at the moment. Phil just keeps muttering that Tom's attitude will soon change again. He thinks this is just a flash in the pan. So, everything is just the same as before Tom's holiday, except Tom is happier. Oh well! It's a start.

Posted by Facing50Blog.com - 1 Comment

Vera said...Maybe you should send Phil on a holiday!

Thursday 24th

What is causing Phil to mutter under his breath and stomp to the shed? What has made him bad tempered, even though the sky is blue and the birds are singing? No, it's not Tom this time. Tom is behaving marginally better, presumably because he is still on a high after his birthday trip. No, it isn't the continued fall of his shares. It's worse than that.

The answer, dear friends, is *Taraxacum*, which means, 'useful to man' in Latin. We know it as the common dandelion. In my opinion the dandelion gets bad press. Even the French call it 'pis en lit' which means wet the bed. Personally, I like the jolly little chaps which appear during spring. I still take childish delight in blowing the seeds from a dandelion clock to tell the time. Phil despises them. They ruin all his hard efforts to make his lawn the greenest, neatest lawn in the village. He spends hours cutting the grass to achieve bowling green perfection. One of his greatest pleasures is to sit back with a cold beer after he has finished, and admire his handiwork. Being such a neat man, he demands neatness surrounds him. The dandelions ruin the effect. I suggested he put down a type of grass enhancer weed killer.

"Why would I want to pay money for that when I can pull them up for free?" he exclaimed in horror.

Consequently, last Sunday, he spent all morning tugging out the yellow offenders. Each time he extracted a few, a Mexican wave of yellow would appear behind him in defiance, each waving their leaves at him and sticking out their little yellow tongues. He kept finding more and more of them. For each one he yanked out, two more would appear. Finally, he got out all that were visible, all 249 of them, roots and all. I silently booed at him from behind the window.

The afternoon was spent mowing the grass and trimming the edges with shears. Three hours later the lawn was fit for a croquet match. It was immaculate. Not one blade of grass was out of place.

He went for a shower to cool off after his efforts. Coming back outside to hang his towel out to dry he noticed three rebels. They glared at him. He marched to the shed, brandished his fork at them and hauled them out ignoring their protests. He nipped back to the bathroom to wash his hands of all the gunky yellow brown mess they leave behind. I got him a beer and installed him in his favourite chair overlooking the garden.

The beer spluttered almost instantly.

"I don't believe it!" He screeched in true Victor Meldrew fashion.

A yellow face beamed at him from just outside the window.

"Leave it," I soothed. "It'll wait until morning."

Phil, being Phil, couldn't wait. He stomped back to the shed, emerged with his trowel, heaved the hooligan out of the ground and smacked the earth back into place, and jumped over the ground, exuding irritation. He walked backwards and forwards, scrutinising the lawn for any more yellow devils. They all hid their faces under their leaves and sniggered.

By morning the garden was dotted with cheerful bright yellow faces.

"Morning!" they all chorused to Phil who choked on his bowl of muesli.

They waved, and blew raspberries at him. (Okay, I admit. I'm getting carried away here. They didn't blow raspberries. I'm making that up.)

He dropped his bowl into the sink and went on the attack. He yanked each and every one out, including all those lurking in the field behind the shed, in case they advanced forwards. The compost bin was stuffed with wilted dandelions. I didn't see him again until lunchtime when he plodded back into the house and had another shower. The garden looked perfect. Not a dandelion to be seen. Phil had won. His hands were red and sore but he was victorious.

He had another check of the garden and satisfied he had removed them all he announced we would go out to the shops

I got dressed with rapidity, slapped my lipstick on, and we headed off. Phil went to open the gate for me as I was driving. As I left the garage and started off down the drive I saw one little head look up and smirk. I'm sure it was laughing and no doubt saying

"Okay, chaps, all clear. You can come up now!"

Posted by Facing50Blog.com - 5 Comments

Vera said...What an amusing story. You are obviously in a cheerful mood today. Poor Phil. You really must buy him som weed killer.

Facing50 said...I felt light hearted today. I'm fed up with moaning about everything. Spring is here and I have things to look forward to.

SexyFitChick said...And we know what they might be, don't we?

Facing50 said...No; I just thought you'd all be sick of my complaints. It was time to write a funny post.

SexyFitChick said...Why don't I believe you?

Saturday 26th

"Is Dad okay?" asked Tom as he sat shovelling *Crunchy N Cornflakes* into his mouth at two o' clock this Saturday afternoon.

"Yes, Fine I think," I wondered if Tom was finally detectin the frostiness that seems to emanate from Phil these days. "Why do you ask?" I continued in the hope that I'd have an entire conversation with Tom, instead of his usual grunts. Often, I get monosyllabic responses to my barrage of quite frankly pointless questions like:

"How was work?"

Usually, the response to that one is a shrug.

"Are you going out?" (Duh, of course he is if he smells of aftershave).

"Have you lost your razor?"

I can get him to shave by constantly referring to him as a Garden Gnome, or pretend to sit on a toadstool and hold a fishing rod, until he gets the message. Today, I was in for a treat. Tom was going to actually converse with me.

"It's nothing important just he's getting a long face, you know like an old man. He's got thinning hair on top and a thin long face," he revealed. "And, he's getting thin," he added.

Gosh, not only had Tom been looking at his father, but more importantly had noted he was looking different. I hadn't noticed Phil with anything other than a miserable face, is that the same thing as a long face? Tom got up with a clatter, taking half the table cloth with him, and disappeared, leaving me to clean up the mess of splattered milk that had formed all around the place mat. Do they grow out of throwing food everywhere? I sought out Phil who was frowning at the computer screen. Tom was absolutely right. Phil looked 'drawn'. How come I hadn't noticed that?

Posted by Facing50Blog.com - 1 Comment

The Merry Divorcee said... Sounds odd to me.

Sunday 27th

I had hoped that after we had the secondary glazing fitted, that my nights of sleeplessness would be over, but that doesn't seem to be the case. The noise of the traffic has been successfully deadened. I get to sleep immediately, but wake up some twenty minutes to two hours later, absolutely wide awak It's as if my brain is set on a clock timer and clicks into life at some ridiculous hour of the night. It will then proceed to whir away at high speed. I have to listen to its crazy talk all night until five-thirty when the off switch drops, my brain voice shu up, and my body or Phil, or both, decide to wake instead. I wis someone could synchronise my settings. I wouldn't mind too much if only my brain could come up with something useful overnight but it seems to be stuck in a groove and rambles on about the same old things night after night.

I still worry about Tom and his attitude towards life. Phil was right. He has slipped back into his old ways. He's got a new phone which he pays for but he still treats the house like a dumping ground. I saw his coursework file thrown on the floo of his bedroom yesterday. If I were marking his work and I would be wondering if a five year old had written it. It's gibberish. I fear he won't pass his exams and we'll be back to square one with him. I daren't interfere. He doesn't listen to m advice at the best of times.

I worry about seeing Todd in May. I dread him looking at me and saying:

"Yuck, what happened to you? You're not how I imagined. Who said the camera never lies. Your photos must have been taken years ago."

And, what if, deep down, I still have some feelings for him? If I relight that flame the consequences are appealing and yet frightening. What would happen?

I worry about how quickly life is passing by. I puzzle over how to get through to Phil and cheer him up. Why is he so glum? Is he getting fed up with me? Then the thoughts get out of hand. Should I go on a diet? Did I shut the fridge door properly? Did I lock the back door? My mind incessantly rambles without a pause until I'm exhausted.

However, it doesn't just seem to be me who is having trouble sleeping. Phil tosses and turns for hours. I know he's awake because he sighs loudly and then hurls himself about the bed tossing and turning like a whirling dervish, until he's gathered the entire duvet around him, and I'm left freezing cold. I, on the other hand, lie perfectly still all night and make no noise. I figure if my brain is going to go ballistic each night then my body may as well try and rest as much as possible.

It's unlike Phil to be awake. He normally conks out and snores away merrily until five when he leaps out of bed quite cheerfully, unusual in someone who spends the rest of the day in a complete grump. Phil is looking very tired and worn out. I always look like a fatigued panda with my dark bags but Phil is also looking weary. He's been using that eye gel stuff again too. I know because he doesn't rub it in properly and it looks like copper sulphate under his eyes. I asked him if he was feeling alright. He snapped back at me so I figured he must be.

Posted by Facing50Blog.com - 2 Comments

The Merry Divorcee said...Why is he using eye cream? Is he seeing someone?

SexyFitChick said...He needs to take up Tai Chi. That will help him calm down and relax. Visit my website for the relevant exercises.

Monday 28th

I have decided to see Todd in May. Of course, I couldn't possibly arrange to see Todd without telling Phil. When I say, tell Phil, I mean:

"I think I'd like to meet up with an old friend I used to wor with when I lived in Morocco. I've not seen them for twenty-five years. They live in Australia but they are coming over to the UK in May."

"Oh yes?" piped up Phil suddenly interested, probably imagining a nubile female Aussie.

We have never discussed our love lives before we met each other. It never seemed relevant to do so. So Phil has never heard of Todd.

"Yes, he's over for his nephew's wedding," I added.

Phil's slight enthusiasm waned. He mistakenly believes that al male teachers wear thick wire rimmed glasses and cardigans, and should be doing something more useful with their time, li being a captain of industry, an explorer or an astronaut. I suppose it stems from a bad time at school. He left school as soon as legally possible and went straight out to work. Anywa he soon lost interest in my friend from Australia muttering something about:

"Why would you want to catch up with a boring old teacher?"

So, I have put the plans into place, now I just have to have the courage to carry them through. I sent Todd a quick message:

‘The answer is yes. When are you coming over?’

I hope I haven’t made the wrong decision. I mean, why am I agreeing to meet up with him again after all this time? It’s not as if there is anything to be gained by it is there? I really don’t know why I would want to see him again. We’ve both changed so much. Well, I’ve certainly changed. The last time he saw me I had long blonde hair that cascaded to my waist, which was a narrow and shapely 23 inches, with blemish free skin and sparkling eyes. Now, I have short greying hair and resemble a ‘Telly Tubby’. I have wrinkles deeper that ravines etched deeply into my forehead and around my eyes, and massive bags under my eyes. Make that, large suitcases, not bags. He’ll run a mile when he sees me.

Maybe I should make some effort. I’ll try and lose some weight and regain my svelte figure from years ago. I’ve not worried about being plump in recent years, or about the fact that my body is losing its fight with gravity, because Phil doesn’t seem to mind or notice that I’m not skinny. Call me Mrs Insecure but I used to badger him constantly about my appearance:

“Does this dress suit me? Do I look fat in this skirt? Do I look okay?”

I would ask him every time I got ready, until one night, after I’d primped and preened in front of him in a sexy dress for an evening out. He was trying to put on his socks as I waffled

“Do you think I should wear these earrings with this dress? Is it too tight?”

“Look do we have to go through this every time we go out? If you looked awful I would tell you you looked awful. Just accept you look nice unless I tell you.”

Since then I've never asked and I never get told so I suppo
I must look okay. I have become more worried about my weight recently. In spite of not eating no more than normal m waist size has increased hugely. It's like the joke – I'm the same weight I was in my thirties but now it's all around my waist. It must be my age or hormones. A few weeks ago, Phil and I met a couple of new people who looked us up and down and commented on how slim Phil was whilst giving me that look. The look that says: 'We know who eats all the pies in your house.'

Since then I've become more paranoid, what with being larger around the waist, and blowing up every month with water retention, I'm beginning to become despondent. Todd will loathe the way I look now. He was always very keen on fitness and staying slim. I've let my standards go and must do something about it.

Posted by Facing50Blog.com - 3 Comments

SexyFitChick said...Come over to my blog. I'll sort you out i no time. You'll look super sexy by the time I've finished.

Lostforwords said...Don't be too hasty. Think hard about seeing Todd. I'm sure you don't look too fat.

The Merry Divorcee said...Ha! Hubby number 5 found a new friend on the internet and ran off with her...he fell in love with her avatar!

Tuesday 29th

I've decided to take up jogging. It wasn't my first choice though. I found a very helpful website aimed at middle-aged women. The fitness instructor on the site advocated dancing f ten minutes, three times a day, while at home. It's so difficult fit in exercising with Phil at home. He absolutely hates me wasting time doing exercise, and believes we should all just be active, like him. He only approves of walking. He insists that exercise of any other type at our age is dangerous and could easily result in injury. He's a great example of staying active and not eating much. He's slim and toned. It must be from carrying all those supermarket bags up seven flights of stairs to the car. Or, from pushing the mower up and down the field, instead of buying one of those self propulsion ones. He looks really good, where as I look, how can I put it, well I look middle-aged?

The website suggested putting on music that you thoroughly enjoy and bopping to it. I sneaked off to my workroom/dressing room/junk room and put on my old trainers from years ago to avoid injury. In years gone by, I would have danced all night in ridiculously high heels, something I can't even contemplate now what with these corns. I chose some upbeat music on my player. I had borrowed it from Tom's collection of noise that passes for music these days. I turned on the mp3 player and danced in front of my dressing room mirror.

What an idiot I looked. Whatever happened to the great dance moves I used to perform? I considered myself a really good dancer when I was younger, but now, I only seem to be able to step from side to side in a type of demented shuffle in time to the music, and wave my arms around a little. This was never going to help with losing weight. I jumped up and down for a while and did some star jumps, kicked my legs like a can can dancer, waved my arms some more, tried to remember the moves to *Macarena* and gave up. Dancing is no fun on your own, when you are sober and wearing earphones which keep getting tangled up. I emerged from the room frustrated and slightly pink-faced. Phil was standing in the hall.

"Been doing some cleaning, have you?"

After the lousy dancing session I awoke ready for my jogging today. I found yet another useful website which allow you to work out a jogging programme for yourself. You input loads of data, age, weight, (don't lie), exercise level, medical information and so on and they send back a programme, whic if followed correctly, should help you become a proper runner or jogger. I also contacted a couple of trainers on Twitter who gave me some very good advice, so armed with my new found knowledge, after all how difficult is it to run, I was ready for today?

I intended telling Phil I was going to the Post Office, that way I'd ensure he wouldn't come with me as he hates standin in the queue there. Then I'd take the back lane to it and go for jog.

"I'm off now to the PO. It'll no doubt take a while, so don' expect me back too soon!" I yelled up the stairs to Phil who was ensconced on the BBC share site.

I shut the door and strolled nonchalantly to the drive wavin my letter in case Phil glanced out of the window then, instead of crossing the road and turning left, I turned right. My programme had suggested I warm up with a brisk walk for fifteen minutes, energetically swinging my arms, break into a jog for two minutes then back to a brisk walk for two minutes and so on. It started well; I marched out and soon felt warmer, broke into a little trot and checked my watch for time. I had forgotten that the lane was actually on a steep incline, so it didn't take very long before I was wheezing. I almost made it the full two minutes but had to give up. I marched, as briskly as possible, but my breath continued to come in short pants.

The lane climbed unendingly upwards. Blip, the watch alerted me to the next two minute jogging session. I managed one minute ten seconds, then thirty seconds the next time, and then fifteen seconds, then I gave up running completely. Boy was I out of condition. As I neared the back lane, which arrives at the post office, I was brought to a sharp halt by the farmer who decided to let his cows cross the road at the very moment I wanted to go past his farm. I stood, hopping from one foot to the other, while he calmly took his time walking Daisy and her friends across the road, causing a traffic jam consisting of two motorbikes, eight cars, six vans, a caravan and a milk lorry. I finally reached the post office, threw my letters into the box, turned around and headed back the way I had come.

Running downhill was much easier and I'd just managed to get into a steady stride when a small dog hurtled out of the hedgerow almost causing me to fall. It was Edna's dog Rufus who proceeded to bite my shoe laces and nip my ankles.

"Hello Edna," I puffed slowing down to walk beside her in the hope she would disentangle Rufus from my feet. "You don't normally come this way."

"No, Rufus decided he'd like a change of scenery. Didn't you dear?" Rufus ignored her, intent on growling at me and biting the top of my sock.

"Are you doing some keep fit?"

"Oh no, just felt a burst of energy coming on and thought I'd give way to it. I'm a little too old to be jogging," I laughed, surreptitiously swiping Rufus from my shoes.

“Yes, people of your age always look quite uncomfortable when they try to run, don’t they? They puff away like steam trains. I often see them trying to run up this hill with faces as red as beetroots. I think there comes a time in life, when one should just slow down, and accept we are not as young as we once were. Oh bless him! Rufus seems to have chewn off the end of your lace and is playing with it. Naughty Boy,” she chastised him affectionately and scooped him up lovingly into her arms. “I’m just going to let him run around the field for a while. It helps burn off his energy you see and then maybe he’ settle down tonight, and let me watch the television in peace. Goodbye Dear.”

I stopped even trying to run at that point. Edna could see m after all. She’s right. There comes an age when you shouldn’t overdo it. I’ll probably try some light skipping instead tomorrow. I saw a website that says it’s very good for your le and bottom. I used to love skipping when I was a girl. I’ll give that a go instead.

Posted by Facing50Blog.com - 2 Comments

SexyFitChick said...Two minutes, not five, two minutes. You didn’t read my post properly you wombat! No wonder you couldn’t manage it.

Facing50 said Doh! What a banana I am. I still don’t think I’d have managed two minutes. I’m not built for running. I wobbl too much.

Wednesday 30th

My latest venture into the happy pastime of skipping isn’t producing much success either. I dragged my new, ultra cool blue plastic rope out of its packaging, which was in itself sufficient exercise for the day. I couldn't get it out and the plastic binding the whole thing together wouldn't cut with normal scissors. I had to sneak Phil's Stanley knife out and cut through, almost chopping my hand off in the attempt....now, that would have made skipping difficult.

It looked much more impressive than my old rope with wooden handles that I owned decades ago. I twirled it around and it made a swishing noise. It has a counter on the end so I can see how many twirls or jumps I've made and how many calories I have worked out of my system. The twirling didn't seem to burn any off.

As a young girl I could skip all day. I would skip after school, when I wasn't playing my recorder. If I could have perfected the art of playing the recorder, whilst simultaneously wearing roller skates and skipping, it would have been in my idea of heaven. I would skip all weekend. I didn't walk, I skipped everywhere. I would skip to school, either with or without a rope, and I couldn't wait for playtimes. Every playtime, the boys would run around and make noise, and the girls would queue to join in a skipathon. There would be a girl at each end of a long rope twirling, with the rest of us trying to synchronise our jumping, and see how many skips we could achieve as a group. One girl would start off and then another would join in and so on. We would chant in unison:

"Salt, pepper, vinegar, mustard"

In the end, they'd be about fifteen or twenty of us, all jumping in perfect synchronisation. We were all passionate about it, that, and handstands.

Several twirls into my solo effort today and I tied myself up in knots. Several more twirls, and I'd managed to whip the backs of my legs with the plastic rope. It stung. I don't remember doing that when I was a girl. Still, I was never one t give up easily and so I started again. The counter read ten twirls. I was hardly going to get fit at this rate. I stretched a little and started again.

"Jelly on a plate, jelly on a plate, wibble wobble, wibble wobble," I chanted and then smacked the back of my leg with the cold surprisingly hard rope. It brought me up short.

"Ow, ow, ow," I rubbed the back of my, by now, very red leg.

This was not going to beat me. Not me, the champion skipper of Tiddleswade County Primary School. I persevered for a while and, finally, got a rhythm of sorts going. I counted the turns of the rope and successful jumps.

"Twenty-three, twenty-four, ow!"

My face turned red to match my legs rather rapidly, probably due to frustration and to cap it all I started to feel a strain in my left calf muscle. The more I persevered the worse the muscle became. The rope became my enemy and lashed m legs some more. At one point it managed to smack me in the face. It was punishing my incompetence.

"Two hundred, two hundred and one..." I puffed and then gave up. The calf muscle was definitely pulling. I needed to stretch it. I took a look at the super doper calorie counter to se what I'd burned off with my efforts. I'd managed a paltry eigh calories. I probably weighed less though due to all the flesh I' stripped from my legs. The rope went back in the cupboard an I spent the morning rubbing cream into my stinging flesh.

So I'm not enjoying much success with my new exercise regime. I think I shall have to try and follow Phil's example and just be more active. Wonder if I'm too old to try handstands?
Posted by Facing50Blog.com - 3 Comments
SexyFitChick said...You need a personal trainer to sort you out. Self help isn't working is it? Eight calories? That thing doesn't work properly.
Fairie Queene said...Give up. He should love you for who you are. That's what I use to say to Albert. I loved him for the way he was.
Lostforwords said...Are you sure you need to do all this exercise?

Thursday 31st

Can you believe it? Tom has just sauntered into the living room with a gleam in his eyes. Phil was glued to a discussion on *Russia Today* about US employment figures when Tom swaggered in, followed by a pretty, slim girl, with very long blonde hair.

"Hi Mum, this is Alice. And, this is my Mum!" he announced, as if there might be some doubt, and I was, in fact, the Romanian housekeeper.

"And this," he said building up the introduction more than a compere would an act on a talent show.
Phil pointedly turned up the volume on the television set.

"This is my Dad!" he finished, waiting for a round of applause.

"How are you Papa?"

Phil gave him his best scowl while managing to stay fixed on the television. Tom waited but no response. I tried to compensate by waving hello and grinning in a friendly manne from my chair. I probably looked like a simpleton.

"Don't worry," said Tom after a couple of minutes. "He's always grouchy."

A petite Alice stood holding onto his hand tightly. She was lovely. She had large shining eyes and an engaging perfect smile.

"Hello Mrs Wilson," she said holding out her hand politely "It's a pleasure to meet you."

"Hello, Mr Wilson," continued Alice. "Tom told me you were a little partial to cake so I've taken the liberty of bringing you one from my range of homemade cakes. I bake them and sell them at football and cricket matches."

That got Phil's attention. A girl who can not only converse properly, but can bake cakes, and clearly has an entrepreneuri spirit.

"Thank you, er, Alice. You can call me Phil," he muttered, looking expectantly in the cake box. "Chocolate muffins, my favourite," he announced pulling one out and biting into it. "Mmm, delicious."

Tom and Alice sat for a while chatting to us about how the had got together. They had known each other quite a while, having first met at the pub, where Alice had been doing some temporary work. Alice had always liked Tom, but it had taken while for him to notice her. She was a staunch supporter of the local team and turned up to all the football matches with her cakes and sandwiches. Eventually, she won Tom's attention. Phil even turned the television down for once to listen to them I liked her instantly, not because she could bake cakes, was clever, pretty, cheerful and was sensible but because she had put the light back in Tom's eyes. I have a feeling that this relationship will be okay.

Posted by Facing50Blog.com - 1 Comment

Lostforwords said.... Ah, bless him!

CHAPTER 10 – APRIL

Friday 1st

I always dread April 1st - April Fool's Day.

I hate people playing tricks on each other, or winding them up, and the simple reason for that is that I am a completely gullible fool.

It started decades ago when I was a youngster. I scampered into the kitchen one morning to find a stranger there instead of my mother. She resembled my mother but instead of her usual brown hair this woman had a blonde bob haircut, a pair of huge glasses and didn't speak like my mother.

"Where's Mum?" I asked somewhat in awe.

"She's gone away, Cobber," said this woman. "I'm her long lost sister all the way from Australia. I'm going to look after you."

I didn't like this idea at all. I wanted my mum . After about ten minutes I burst into tears. The woman pulled off her hair to reveal my mother.

"Ha ha, April Fool, You didn't really think I was my own sister, did you?" she said and laughed herself senseless.

But I had. I had believed her.

I was always the one that people chose to play pranks on as I got older. I was, after all, the one who would fall for the stupid things. I sat on tin tacks placed on chairs. Buckets of water fell on my head when I opened the door. My friends would laugh and cheer. If you can't beat them, join them. So, I would laugh at my naivety and carry on behaving like a clown.

Later, when I became a responsible teacher I became wary at this time of year. It's one thing being regarded as a chump

when you are a schoolchild, but quite another, when you are t
actual teacher.

My first year in teaching was an intense one. I taught all ages and levels. I had a particularly enjoyable but demanding class of Sixth form students (aged 17-18 years old). We were currently working through Chaucer's *The Canterbury Tales* a
as these students were all shining lights hoping to go to Oxfor
University I had to plan those lessons meticulously.

However, this particular morning I had 2B, a class of twel
year olds who had just finished an essay about a day in their lives. I had marked their efforts and was in my classroom waiting to hand back the work and teach them some Gramma
The door opened and my Sixth Formers rolled in.

"Morning Miss," they said and took their seats. I was horrified. I thought I was supposed to be teaching 2B.

"Morning class," I gulped trying to look like I knew what was going on. How on earth could I swing this? I didn't even have my copy of the text with me.

"Uhm, I am supposed to be teaching you today?" I asked nonchalantly. Don't I usually teach you on a Wednesday morning?

"It is Wednesday today, Miss," they said straight-faced. I racked my brains. I did often lose track of the days but this was disastrous.

Convinced that I should be teaching them I quickly regained my composure. One of them had just offered to lend me his copy of Chaucer when there was a knock at the door and the Art teacher poked his head round.

"I think I have something here that belongs to you," he sai
jovially.

Behind him stood my grinning class of twelve year olds.

"They tried this trick last year too," he said pointing to the senior students. "Come on you lot, back to the art room we have some catching up to do."

My Sixth form class stood up smiling.

"April Fool, Miss," said the last one out and winked.

My mother loved that story when I told her. She recounted it to all her friends. Since that day I have been on red alert every April the first. Both Tom and Phil know not to try and trick me. Phil attempted it one year when he left an old banger of a car outside on the drive. He told me was to be my new car. He had to confess when I actually got in it, and tried to drive it, that it was an old fleet car which he was supposed to be taking to the garage.

I haven't needed to worry about any pranks this year. Tom is at work. He recently became a full-time employee. We no longer have to put up with him being at home on a Friday. Phil has been quietly ensconced in front of the computer today. He didn't even come out of the room for morning coffee and cake. I took him a cup to him when he didn't appear, and noticed he was on the Bush craft website, no doubt genning up for his impending weekend.

Posted By Facing50Bllog.com - 4 Comments

Vera said...How ingenious of your class. I hope they all got into good universities.

Facing50 said...They all managed to get places at Oxford and Cambridge. The one who thought up the whole prank is now a professional comedian. Two of the others are now actors. No surprises there. They obviously had the ability to act from an early age.

Faerie Queene said... I hated school. I went to an all boy's school. I didn't quite fit in because I didn't like football. I muc preferred drama. I'd have loved to have been in your class.
SexyFitChick said... Fancy being fooled by those kids. Lol Good on your Ma for trying to be an Aussie. She should have worn a hat with corks hanging from it – that would have swun it.

Monday 2nd

'Hello Beautiful. I'm off to Thailand today. I'm sitting in Qantas first class lounge checking to see if you are available f a quickie.'

I logged onto *Scrabble* to give him a good beating before h disappeared for days again. The events section was winking a message:

'I'm ready and waiting. It's time for you to take your turn.'
He'd played 'sex' and added a message:

'I couldn't resist playing that word. I never could resist you in the morning,' he'd added.
I added a 'y' onto 'sex' and played 'yawn'. That would calm him down.

'You wouldn't be yawning if I were there,' he wrote cockily, making me suddenly spark into life.

'Cheeky. What time's your flight?'

'In about an hour. I'm going to an elephant orphanage to help with some baby elephants for a few days'

Yet another one of my 'bucket list' desires. I have always adored elephants and have always wanted to help out at an orphanage. Todd and I had often spoken about what we would do when we had the money and time to do it. This had been one of my hopes.

'I would just love to do that,'
I stated impotently, thinking what a dull life I had. How could washing windows and feeding the family compare to playing with baby elephants?

'Well, come and join me.'
He played the word 'wish' on 'yawn'.

'Not likely is it? I'm far too busy at the moment and I can't see Phil agreeing.'
I played 'hopeful'.

'Oh well, who knows what the future will bring,' he added. 'I'll hug an 'elly' for you and send you some photos of it. Apparently, they love to play soccer (oh dear he was becoming very Australian). Maybe I'll be able to train them to a good enough standard to play in next year's World Cup,' he joked.

I smiled in spite of all the longing. It would be fabulous to go somewhere like Thailand and be with baby elephants. If we'd stayed together we'd have done all those things and more. Still, my life is good enough isn't it? I'm extremely lucky really. Think about all those poor Japanese people whose lives were washed away in the awful Tsunami this month and whose lives will be blighted by radiation. Those who survived have nothing. And, look how dignified they behave. I have Tom and Phil and I live in a nice village.

I beat Todd 230 points to 115. His flight was called and he left me with a line of kisses in my message box. I set about checking out elephants on the internet. I found a company that sponsors elephants and helps them recover from awful experiences in captivity. They look after them and ensure they have freedom now. Each elephant has a sad story to tell about their lives before they were saved. You can purchase a 'date' with them. For £30 you get a DVD of all the elephants. You chose one and he/she will write two love letters to you. They'l send you a Valentine's Day poem on recycled elephant poo paper, along with a photo of themselves. The money goes towards feeding and looking after them, and to the elephant family project, which helps in many ways.

I decided to date one. I chose Nong-Dah whose descriptio read:

'Where are you? My love is lost along with everything else in my suitcase. Find me! Please find me and love me.'

It was the closest I'd get to helping them, or getting to Thailand. Oh well.

Posted by Facing50Blog.com - 6 Comments

Fairie Queene said... How adorable, I must date one. Please tell me how.

The Merry Divorcee said... I bet the elephant behaves better on a date than my ex number 4 did. He had terrible table manners.

SexyFitChick said... Would you go to Thailand if you could afford it?

Facing50 said... I can't afford it so I can't consider it, can I?

SexyFitChick said... You are not really answering the questio

Facing50 said... Well, I have to say I would be tempted, but what about Phil?

Wednesday 3rd

We went to town yesterday and bought Phil some sensible walking boots. Now he'll be able to avoid standing on puff adders and walk over damp forest floors, without ruining his leather loafers, which are the only other type of shoe he possesses. He insisted on buying plenty of shoe cream protector for them and proceeded to spend the rest of the day coating them liberally with various creams and lotions. He wanted to ensure the damp will not seep through and ruin them.

Fortunately, we haven't had to buy much else. We discovered quite a haul of goodies in Tom's old school pile. At one point, we'd invested in 1000 mile socks, thermal vests, compasses, walking pole, rucksack, sleeping bag, gas stove and so on for Tom to do his Duke of Edinburgh Award. He got his Silver Award but didn't want to do the Gold Award as he claimed he needed the time 'to focus on his studies'. We both suspected that the real reason he didn't want to pursue it was because he didn't want to give up his precious weekend lie-ins. Consequently, we have had a pile of outward bound clothing, gathering dust in the wardrobes, ever since. I had hoped that Tom would have a change of heart and continue with the Duke of Edinburgh after he had finished school but that wasn't to be either.

How much money we have spent on that boy is anybody's guess. Not only has it been expensive to keep him clothed and fed, but every activity he has taken up, like tennis or skiing has cost us a fortune. Still, at least this lot would now get some use. We sifted through the unused clothing sorting out what might be ideal for Phil's weekend. I spent the rest of the day unpicking all the name tags that had been carefully and thoroughly sewn into each item. I'm not very good at sewing, but after many years of practice, I am a dab hand at sewing in labels so they will not come out. My fingers almost bled from trying to get the name tags back out.

Phil seems quite enthusiastic about the weekend. It is difficult to ascertain if Phil is enthusiastic or content at any tir as the gloom cloud that generally surrounds him tends to shiel any emotion. Given that he wasn't complaining, or wasn't snarling about something, then I can safely assume he was se content. I think I might even have heard him humming at one point in the afternoon. No, that was probably my imagination.

Well, if he is looking forward to it he cannot be looking forward to it as much as I am. An entire weekend of 'me' time I really cannot wait. I can't make my mind up what to do yet. I'd like a lie-in; not be woken up at 5am. Maybe a lie-in followed by a long hot bubble bath. My nails could do with some pampering so maybe I'll go to the shops and have them done, or a facial, or even get my hair done. I'll be able to eat what I want, as opposed to what Phil wants, so definitely past for tea then. I'll be able to watch what I want on the televisior instead of documentaries or news programmes and I can put r music on the stereo, loudly. Really, I cannot wait.

Posted by Facing50Blog.com - 10 Comments

SexyFitChick said... Why don't you go clubbing?

Vera said... You can't beat settling down with a good book.

The Merry Divorcee said...Enjoy it. It's so nice to have some peace and quiet when they're not around. I loved your Fool story. I'm anti pranks too. My third ex husband served divorce papers on me on an April 1st. I didn't believe they were real to start with. I got my own back though. I made him have custod of the children.

YoungFreeSingleandSane said...You can't beat a night in with a tub of ice cream and a good film. Better than sex.
SexyFitChick said...YoungfreeSinglaandSane - Don't be ridiculous! Ice cream and sex is much more entertaining than a film.
Faerie Queene said...No, I agree with her. A good chick flick and ice cream works for me too. Albert and I spent one night watching *P.S. I Love You* with a giant sized tub of cookie dough flavoured ice cream. It was one of the best evenings we spent together. I still love that film. I hate April Fool's day too. Some jokes can be funny, like the one your mother played. Some are too cruel. Hope you enjoy your weekend.
Facing50 said...I shall certainly check out the films. I loved that film too Faerie Queene. I'm not too keen on ice cream though. I'll probably settle for a glass, or two, of wine.
The Merry Widow said...Don't eat too much pasta Honey. It'll go straight to your hips and then your man won't fancy you anymore.
Facing50 said...He doesn't seem to fancy me anyway.
Lostforwords said...I don't suppose your mother meant any harm with her little joke. She probably just wanted to make you laugh.

Saturday 9th

And so, Phil left yesterday evening. His bag was neatly packed and he looked, well, how I can put it, happy? Yes, he smiled and even pecked me on the cheek which is, for Phil, the height of passion. As he pulled away I let out a yelp of delight, put my new Brandon Flowers CD on the stereo loudly, poured a glass of wine and flicked through the TV channels. Would you believe it, there wasn't anything worthwhile watching. I ended up watching the CNN business programme so I'd have something to tell Phil when he came back. I ran a bath but soo got bored and wondered if Phil had got to his destination. He refused to take a mobile phone as it wasn't appropriate for life in the wild. He didn't want the *Great Escape* ringtone I'd put on it for him, ringing out loudly while they were learning to ru sticks together.

I came online but everyone seemed to be out probably having a good time. There was no one available to chat to online. Todd was unavailable. The Scrabble board lay untouched. His icon was flashing indicating it was his turn to play. Tom was staying at Alice's house all weekend and I suddenly felt horribly alone. I no longer have girl friends and I don't know anyone in the village to go out with, apart from Edna and Rufus, but I doubt they'd be up for a party. I realised the full extent of my loneliness.

All my friends live in my laptop. You are all great friends. You give me advice and listen to me, but I can't nip round to your houses for a drink and a catch up. I can't suggest we go to the cinema together and on to a pizza parlour. We can't go to the salon together to get our nails done and then go shopping together. We can't even have a good gossip. You're all too far away. We even live in different time zones, so when I'm in be you're reading what I've written and vice versa. I'm so glad you are all there but my only' real' friend is Phil and he wasn' around.

The lethargy, which crept in last night, stayed with me all today. I had wanted to have a lie in but habit made me wake u at 5am. I hated finding Phil's side of the bed empty and cold. I missed the noise of him clattering about in the kitchen first thing, making a cup of tea for me, and a coffee for him. Breakfast was pointless. I skipped it. I headed out to the shops to cheer myself up but found myself wondering around unfocused and wondering what Phil might be doing. I missed waiting for him at the department store, until he arrived with his damn cake in a bag, and I almost cried at afternoon tea time when I sat at the table with a slice of cherry cake and no Phil.

What is the matter with me? He's only away for a couple of days. I've got so used to being with him all the time that I've forgotten how to function without him. I hadn't realised how much I actually need him. He's there when I feel unhappy. He may spend most of his day stuck behind the newspaper or the internet or on the phone time, but at least he is there, and we actually do chat a lot in the daytime. I missed him moaning about the economy or Tom or the news. I missed seeing him outside checking the car or chopping logs or just doing things.

Posted by Facing50Blog.com - 7 Comments

SexyFitChick said...I think you should have gone to a night club and let your hair down. Fancy staying in and watching TV what a dull girl!

Lostforwords said...Appreciate what you have now because one day you could lose it forever.

Angelique said...I think Lostforwords is right. When he gets back tell him you love him.

Facing50 said... Whoa Angelique! This is Phil we're talking about. He doesn't do touchy feely sloppy. Maybe I'll just buy him a large chocolate cake instead.

Faerie Queene said...I thought Albert was my soul mate. I shed a little tear today at your blog. Hope he's missed you as much as you've missed him. Maybe even more, having spent all that time on a damp forest floor, with no cake.

The Merry Divorcee said...Aw that's sweet. His is an emotion that is kind of alien to me!

Sunday 10th

Today was as bad a Saturday. I cleaned the house from top to bottom to keep my mind off the loneliness. It was quite therapeutic really. I should do it more often instead of sitting around feeling sorry for myself. I logged on again. There was no Todd. He knew Phil was going away so I'm surprised he hasn't taken advantage of my free time to chat and play *Scrabble*. He's probably too busy kicking footballs with the little elephants.

I even missed my afternoon chat with my mother. She didn't phone me at four. I gave her a call but the phone just rang out. It's unusual, as she's always at home. Still, she's probably tearing down the local high street in her new sports car. For heaven's sake! Why has she bought that thing? She's never been shown any interest before in cars.

I expected Phil home by four. I paced from the kitchen to the lounge and back again. Twenty paces to the conservatory, where I stared out. Forty paces back to the lounge. I checked the clock. I know he's a grumpy old man, but he's 'my' grumpy old man and I have missed him. I laid out the large chocolate cake I'd bought for him. I paced some more. I drew a large letter 'P' in the cake's icing. The car finally pulled up. Phil emerged looking a little rough, having not shaved. I threw the door open and jumped up and down in glee.

"Did you have a good time?" I asked, before he'd even had time to remove his shoes.

"Yes it was very interesting."

"Did you learn to make wooden tools?"

"Yes."

"Did you make your own shelter to sleep in?"

"Sort of."

"Did you kill any animals and cook them for dinner?"

"It was a Bush craft weekend Mandy, not an episode of *I'm a Celebrity, let me out of here*."

I felt suitably chastened. I was being childish, but I couldn't help it, I was so pleased to see him. I suppose a dog that has been inside all day feels like this when its master comes home. I wanted to fetch his slippers, lie by his feet and lick his face. Well, maybe not actually lick his face.

"Did you miss me?" I asked.

"I didn't really have any time to miss you. It was full on all weekend," he replied and shrugged by way of an apology.

I stood by the kitchen top waiting for him to notice the large chocolate cake but he seemed oblivious to it.

"I really need a shower. Then, I think I'll check the internet to see what was written in the weekend press about the markets, and get an early night," he said picking up his rucksack.

"Oh okay. I'm glad you're back," I offered in a final desperate plea to get his attention. He didn't reply. I put the cake back in the box.

Posted by Facing50Blog.com - 2 Comments

The Merry Widow said...I hope he didn't 'discover himself' while he was away. Husband number two did that and then

before I could say 'discover what?' we were in the divorce court.
Vera said...Don't worry. He was probably just tired.
Lostforwords said...Did you not think that your mother might have just not heard the phone?

Monday 11th

Phil hasn't had much to say about the weekend. I am very surprised. He was definitely looking forward to it. I thought he'd be full of enthusiasm but it's as if he hasn't been away. He's more distant than ever and I'm starting to wonder if there may be a problem in our marriage. It's been pretty lacklustre for some time. What if has he met someone on the weekend that interested him more than boring old me? I bet there were lots of female outdoor types who could chat effortlessly about flora and fauna. I bet they could throw up a shelter made of wood in no time. They most certainly would be more interesting than me. I can only converse about things that don't interest Phil. I tried to get him to talk over the chocolate cake, which was a little dry, having sat out for too long yesterday.

"Did you meet anyone interesting at the weekend?"

"Yes, there were one or two nice people. They were from all sorts of backgrounds. It was surprising who is interested in nature and going back to basics."

"Any men your age?"

"A couple."

"Any women?"

"Yes. Three. One was about your age. One of them lives near us."

I felt a rise of panic.

"Did you all have to bunk down together?" I persisted.

"Mandy, I hope you are not taking this conversation where I think you may be trying to take it," he warned.

"Oh no," I said breezily. "Just getting a picture of what it was like. Maybe I should go on a weekend.

"No, you'd hate it," he said, terminating the conversation. I hope Phil doesn't intend keeping in touch with this 'woman from nearby' and swap camp fire stories with her.

Posted by Facing50Blog.com - 2 Comments

SexyFitChick said... Aren't Sheilas, who go on that sort of thing, a bit butch?

Facing50 said... I hope so.

Wednesday 13th

I've given up with the exercise for now. Todd will just have to accept the way I look. Phil does. Talking of Phil, he still looks worn out. He was tired enough before the weekend away but he looked worse this morning. I'm sure he's bought some more eye gel because a new pot has appeared in the bathroom cabinet, hidden right at the back, behind his foot file and deodorant. I tried to read the label but without my glasses, it was impossible, and then he nearly caught me.

"What are you doing in my cabinet?"

"Just cleaning it."

"Well you don't need to. I do it frequently. Leave it alone. I know where everything is, and it's in order, so I don't want it disturbed."

Anyway, I've had my mind taken off Phil, Tom and Todd too as it's that time of the year, when for a brief spell, the village bursts into life. Technically, it begins in March, when posters are stapled to every wooden telegraph post and are plastered on every available surface. There are four stuck to th side of the village bus shelter, five in the post office, two on th hairdresser's window and almost every house in the high stree is displaying one:

'Snittington Open Gardens Easter Event - Saturday Apri 23rd and Sunday 24th.

Prizes awarded for the best gardens and displays.'

The elders in the village adore 'Open Gardens' weekend an prepare for it months in advance. For one weekend a year, the general public is invited from far and wide, to visit the garden in Snittington. They can choose which ones to visit. At each they pay a small entrance fee which goes to charity. They can also buy plants, flower displays and homemade jams from some of the residents. It is taken extremely seriously. Not only is everyone in the village expected to sort out their gardens, an tidy them, but they are expected to put on magnificent display of flowers and shrubs and allow complete strangers to walk around them. This is so odd, given that the rest of the time; yo never seem to see the residents.

The prizes for the gardens are more coveted than the Oscar here. The oldest members of the village have been doing this for decades. They plant out seedlings in greenhouses during winter ready to produce phenomenally bright and healthy species, of all sorts of flowers, which you wouldn't normally find in the local garden centres at this time of year. It's like Chelsea Garden Show here. The villagers are frightfully protective over what they will be displaying. They won't even tell their best, and most trusted friends, who at this time of yea become their adversaries.

The village square is adorned with large wooden barrels filled with colourful flowers. Last year, some 'n'er do well' made off with the contents of one of the barrels. I have my suspicions as to who that may have been. The day after the tubs were emptied, I found some petals in the pockets of Tom's jeans, which he had been wearing to a party at the pub the night before. The jeans appeared to be rather grubby even by his standards.

I haven't mentioned the episode, as the 'n'er do well' left a couple of trays of pansies beside the tub the following afternoon, along with a note with the word 'Sorry' written on it. Mrs Fetherstowe, who had lovingly nurtured the plants for the tub, remained inconsolable and threatened not to plant them this year. After several glasses of sherry at the pub, and a good chat with the committee, she was encouraged to do them but she demanded the installation of CCTV cameras above the planted tubs. The committee compromised, and Mr Druid, the school caretaker, will come by on his bike a few times a day, just to make sure they are alright this year.

I am so horticulturally inept that it would be complete folly to open up our garden. That is unless people want to look at prickly bushes, lavender, which has not yet got past the woody stage, and grass. I have absolutely no idea about plants. Poor Phil has had all his work cut out trying to cut the grass. So, we have never 'opened our garden'.

I'd been thinking about Tom's outburst earlier this year and how we make no attempt to participate in village events. Tom is trying to make an effort by being on the local football team and getting to know people, so this year, I'm going to buy some

flowers from the garden centre. Today I'm off to the village hall to sign up our garden.
Posted by Facing50Blog.com - 3 Comments
Vera said... Why don't you ask your mother about plants? She plants out a lot of containers doesn't she? You wrote about it in a July blog.
Facing50 said... You're right Vera. I hadn't thought to ask her.
SexyFitChick said...Geez, your life is one never-ending party isn't it? Nah, seriously, I think it's quite sweet. I love quaint old English gardens. I prefer quaint old English men but gardens are nice too.

Friday 15th

Thanks to Vera, I phoned my mother about flowers. She turned out to be an absolute fountain of knowledge. She gave me the names of flowers that would look the best at this time of year. She also suggested I put some mixed grasses in my borders to break up the flowers. We had a long and interesting conversation. I hadn't realised she was so good at that sort of thing. She never used to do the garden when my father was alive.

Since she got back from Cyprus, she's been rubbing down wooden benches and a wooden arch. She's going to paint them both blue and put them in a part of her garden which she is going to call a Mediterranean garden. She's going to put down some large grey pebbles and plant lavender and rosemary there. Then, she'll be able to sit on the bench during summer, and listen to the bees, while she drinks her morning coffee, and pretend she is abroad.

Having been to the garden centre, and after much deliberation, I am now in possession of some stunning hanging baskets, filled with spring flowers, along with a couple of large standing planters, also brimming with colourful flowers. I can't take the credit for those. The garden centre had a spring section where you bought the planters and plants. They arranged them for you. It couldn't be easier. They must be used to us villagers charging up there at the last moment to get plants. They appeared to have a large section of ready to plant mature plants, so now I also have lots of pretty plants in my borders. I won't bore you with all their Latin names. I don't know how gardeners remember them all anyway. I still call them the yellow plant, the green one with berries and so on.

I know some of them. There are, for example, some bright shiny red leaved plants called *Photinia fraseri* 'Red Robin'. And, I have mixed *Helleborus* 'Harvington Shades of the Night' with spring flowers, although I understand hellebore is toxic. According to the internet, they have been used for years in all sorts of herbal remedies. It has been said that the humble hellebore caused the demise of Alexander the Great so I'd better be wary of it. My mother suggested getting it as she thought it looked very striking. Phil has his own ideas about why she suggested it.

I've also chose some very pretty plants called *Cicentra spectabilis* for the shady spot by the shed. Looking at the label that accompanied them, they have heart shaped flowers that dangle from pendulous arching sprays, although mine don't seem to have many yet. They just seemed romantic plants to me. Now, don't I sound like a proper gardener?

Tom has been most interested in the whole event. I'm not sure if that is because the pub will be joining in and hosting a weekend of games and frivolity. The football team has been coerced into putting on some family activities. They're doing a car wash on the Saturday. On Sunday, they will be participatin in a tug-of-war with a rival team from the pub in the next village. There are to be other activities which will no doubt culminate in a drinking contest. Tom's new girlfriend, Alice has also been extremely helpful. Her father sent over some of his prize-winning periwinkles. She made Tom pressure wash the patio and plant them near it. I like her more and more each day.

Tom and Alice have all the local gossip too. I learnt that there is huge rivalry going on between some of the contestants Mr Wetherspode is retarding the growth of his primulas so the will flower late, by keeping them in the cold. Mrs Featherlight has gone to extraordinary lengths to procure some wild flower from some Peninsula in Puglia, Italy, famous for its rare orchids, to display in her front garden. At present, it is all bein hidden by large panels ready for the big event next weekend.

The landlord of the pub has bought a huge old wooden dray painted it green, and filled it with large pots of flowers. It's definitely garden fever here in Snittington. The village is looking delightful. I've never fully appreciated it before. Everyone seems to be looking forward to it. I cajoled Phil into helping too. Reluctantly he mowed all of the field and the garden, complaining all the while, that he had' better things to do'. I trimmed the edges, so it looks as neat as I've ever seen it.

Both sets of neighbours are going to be away for Easter. Fred is taking Ethel to Wales on the back of their motorbike. *Robocat* was going to go too but, mercifully, he is now going to stay with their children.

"Shame, said Fred. "He'd have loved the trip on the bike. Pity he's too old for it."

Cedric and Shirley are going to Spain. Cedric is disgruntled because the temperature here is set to be warmer than there. I have volunteered to look after and water all their plants while they are absent. Consequently, I probably won't be able to post for a while.

Posted by Facing50Blog.com - 6 Comments

Vera said... I'm glad your Mum could help.

Facing50 said... Yes thank you Vera. It was nice to talk to her. Made a change for me to phone her out of the blue. I think it surprised her.

SexyFitChick said... Any fit blokes going to be looking around your garden?

Facing50 said... I hardly think so. I don't think fit blokes are into village gardens.

SexyFitChick said... No but they might be into the pub games afterwards.

Fairie Queene said... Albert and I had a beautiful courtyard. We used to have candlelit dinners listening to the tinkling of the fountain we had installed which cascaded over small pebbles. Sigh, how I miss his company.

Sunday 17th

I know I said I probably wouldn't be able to post but once more I have been left completely bewildered. My mother, who is off yet again to Cyprus, seemed to be in a nostalgic mood, but not in her usual maudlin way,

"I can't chat long. I'm in a rush to get everything organised My neighbours are coming around soon and I need to pack as I'm leaving at midnight tonight for Cyprus," she said breathlessly when I phoned her today, but then she proceeded to chat non-stop for fifty minutes.

She was cheerily talking about clothes. Mum used to be an accomplished dress maker. It derived from necessity. In her youth, if she wanted an outfit, the only way she would be able to afford it would be to buy some material and make it herself. She started buying dress patterns but, not only were they quite expensive, they were not always youthful. So, she started goin to boutiques to check out at the latest styles and fashion. On h return home she would make her own design based on what sh had seen. The result, in retrospect, was astonishingly good.

She'd been sifting through some old photographs of us whe I was about three or four years old. She used to make us matching outfits. I remember seeing some rather cute pictures of my very stylish mother wearing a cape and cap, with me holding her hand, in a tiny matching cape and cap. She used to make all my clothes when I was young. I adored the beautiful dresses that were miniature grown up dresses which she produced, sitting by her sewing machine night after night, unti the early hours of the morning.

Once I hit teenage years, I was much less appreciative, and certainly didn't want to be her smaller clone. I ached to wear the same clothes as my school friends. I hated the smart outfits perfectly made skirts and stylish trouser suits with matching hats or scarves. My friends were wearing jeans and wide legged cords.

I'd forgotten all about the midi and maxi suede skirts, the pillar box hat with a veil, little bolero jacket and the delightful lemon dress in embroidery anglaise that she had made me for my birthday. I had been a micro copy of my beautiful glamorous mother. We enjoyed a lengthy chat about those times.

As she chatted, I recalled some of those later years. She would crawl around the floor, her mouth full of pins, pinning material together. I used to stand still, for what seemed like hours, while she fitted me for an outfit, ungratefully holding my breath, as she pinned me up in between cigarette puffs. I hadn't thought about it for years. I had been lucky enough to have my own tailoress and bespoke outfits and hadn't appreciated it. What I would give now to have someone make me designer outfits. Alas, I can't sew. Mum never showed me and declared me too clumsy to use her precious sewing machine. I can just about sew on a button but that's the limit of my ability.

In the end she detected my reluctance to have her make my clothes, and so she made them for friends instead. She made a wedding dress for a lady with whom she worked. Everyone seemed to clamour for one of her outfits, but she never took it up professionally, or took money from her friends. It was just something she enjoyed doing, and she didn't want to spoil the enjoyment. So the conversation raced by today. I began to feel slightly nostalgic by the end of it.

"Just before I go," she added with a lengthy suck of her cigarette. "I thought I should let you know that Grego has asked me to..."

At that precise moment the 5 o'clock express train to Paddington went rattling past, whistling loudly. I couldn't hea what she was saying.

"So I told him I needed time to think about it. After all it's very important decision to make at my time of life and I'll giv him my answer next week when I see him. Oh yes, my mobile phone isn't working either. I think it was when Kitty dropped in the punchbowl at the last party. I need to get a new one and unblock it so it can be used abroad. I can only do that at the fortnightly market, so I won't be able to talk to you for a coup of weeks or so. Sorry, that's the doorbell ringing. Oh goodnes is that the time? I must dash. I'll talk to you when I next can. Bye Mandy."

"Mum, Grego asked what?"

The phone buzzed as she'd already hung up. I pondered for a while and then phoned her back. There was no answer. I suppose she'd nipped out to the neighbours and would soon b off to the airport. What could Grego have asked her? Surely not? He wouldn't, would he? Would he have 'popped the question'?

"How is the old witch?" asked Phil glancing over top of th financial section of the paper and seeing my puzzled expression.

"Casting serious spells over some people."

Posted by Facing50Blog.com - 3 Comments

SexyFitChick said... Your Mother rocks!

YoungFreeSingleandSane said... Wow, would she make me cape and a cap. They are back in fashion you know?

Fairie Queene said...Me too!

Wednesday 20th

I woke up last night wondering if Grego may have actually asked my mother to marry him. I know that sounds daft, but it would make sense, wouldn't it? It's not as if she behaves like an old lady. She's fun to be with. She's had all her teeth done and she's just bought a new sports car. She keeps going to Cyprus. He's stayed at her house. He might have asked her. If he has asked her, and if she accepts, I wonder how I'd feel about that. I suppose I'd be pleased for her. She deserves to be happy. I know she has missed my father enormously, so I can't deny her some affection and fun in her life. We all need someone to love and be loved by.

Romance seems to be all around at the moment. Tom is starry-eyed again. The television is full of documentaries about love and The Royal Family. We have the Royal Wedding to look forward to later this month. People have already been lining the streets in London, camping out each night, in the hope of getting the best view of the Royal couple on their big day. I remember being in London for Prince Charles' wedding. What a night! The atmosphere was so happy. I spent all night walking the streets with friends and waving at complete strangers. I hope it'll be like that this time. It's a good thing that it's been as warm as it has. The poor people would be freezing otherwise.

"That's just complete codswallop," huffed Phil as he came in during a documentary about Prince William and Kate Middleton. "Who's interested in that soppy nonsense? It's not a flipping fairy story. Look what happened to his father and Lady Diane?"

I switched it over to *Russia Today* where they were discussing Gas price increases.
Posted by Facing50Blog.com - 2 Comments
SexyFitChick said...Cheer up. Soon be May.
Facing50 said...But, he's right. Happy ever afters exist only in fairy tales.

Sunday 23rd –late evening

What a nice weekend. I wish I'd got involved before. The garden was swamped with visitors all day. They were very complimentary about the garden. That was due in part, to the vodka that Tom had sneaked into my homemade lemonade, which I was handing out, along with homemade biscuits - bought from the garden centre, of course. Tom was right. There are quite a few people our age in the village.

Phil emerged from his den and got chatting to a couple who live at the other end of Snittington. I believe the husband is something to do with finance. They spent quite some time in a huddle discussing very important issues, which I felt, had nothing to do with the primulas surrounding them. The pub was stuffed with people all weekend. The football team raised a huge amount of money with their charity car wash. Phil was agog. Tom never washes our car or even his own car, but there he was, chatting about all the extra tips he got for the good job he did. All of which he put in the charity box, of course.

The prize giving on Sunday night attracted most of the village. Phil didn't fancy it. He said he's put up with strangers in his garden all weekend. He drew the line at going to pub and mixing with some more people he didn't know. Besides, he needed to check up on some funds that Bill had mentioned to him. I guess Bill lives at the end of the village. I went with Tom and Alice. Surprisingly, Tom ordered a glass of wine for me and two coca colas for Alice and himself. Alice is having a hugely positive effect on him.

The pub was stuffed with locals. A marquee had been erected so we could all fit in. Clutching our drinks, we squeezed into it. There was a table laid out with trophies. In front of it sat the elders of the village, holding glasses of stout or sherry, waiting patiently for the announcements. Everyone else milled about saying hello to each other. I recognised one or two from the weekend and nodded as they waved at me. Tom took control and manoeuvred us towards the rest of the football team. They were in a huddle in the corner trying to hold each other up and reeking of alcohol.

After a while, the chairman of the committee thanked everybody, and announced that we had raised a superb amount of money for charity. More than last year, but he had not got the final amount, just yet. He would post the information up on the local board in the next few days, but at this stage, it looked like we had raised more than three thousand pounds collectively for our visits and produce sold. The pub erupted and people applauded loudly. A hush fell as he prepared to announce the winner of first prize for the best kept and most interesting garden. People held their breath. I noticed some of the oldest members of the community nudging each other excitedly.

"Happy Easter to you all. And now, Ladies and Gentlemen, the winner of the first prize for the Snittington Open Gardens Competition, a superb event which attracted so many people from other villages..."

"Get on with it Derek," yelled Farmer Jones, clearly worse for wear, his ruddy cheeks glowing.

"As I was saying before Thomas interrupted," continued th chairman, glowering at farmer Johnson. "It was a very difficul decision this year. My colleagues..."

"Come on Derek, get to the point," shouted Mrs Weatherspoon

"Yes, hurry up Derek, I'm missing *Coronation Street*, and it's time for Cyril's cocoa," chirped up another.

"We decided this year to award a joint prize. I am delightec to announce that our winners are Mr Weatherspode and Mrs Featherlite."

A cheer went up. A beaming Mr Weatherspode clambered t his feet and shuffled to Mrs Featherlite's chair, offered her his arm, and helped her up. Together, they collected the 'Snittington Cup' and held it aloft like captains of a football team. The local media clicked their cameras and made them pose some more until Mrs Weatherspode came up to take her husband home.

"He's had too much excitement this weekend," she grumbled, as Mr Weatherspode gave Mrs Featherlite a kiss on the cheek, all differences clearly forgotten.

Edna won the award for the best window box; a voucher fo £50 to spend at the garden centre. Rufus growled at the chairman, and licked Edna on the nose, as they posed for the camera. The pub won a special award for their stunning cart display. Two of the less drunk lads from the football team collected it for the landlord and landlady, who were rushed off their feet, serving customers. It was a meal for two at a nice quiet restaurant in town.

“Hush, Ladies and Gentlemen, a little quiet again please,” called the chairman as people were beginning to leave. “Our final category prize goes to... Mr and Mrs Wilson.”
Too surprised to even move, I sent Tom up to collect the prize for us. There was a fair amount of back slapping and, “well done, Mate,” going on. Tom seemed very much at home and proudly accepted the award.

“As some of you know the last category is called ‘The Wooden Spoon’ award and it goes to the villager who has made an effort, but needs to try harder, in order to reach the strict high standards of our village gardens,” grinned the chairman amidst the guffaws of laughter from the older members of the audience. “Better luck next time, Lad.”

Tom took the spoon, bowed to the audience graciously and was actually cheered by the crowd. His cheeks flushed pink.

“You having the usual then Tom?” shouted one of the locals and ordered him a pint.
As the tent emptied I whispered to Tom,

“I hope you’re not too embarrassed about that.”

“Nah, Mum, it’s great. Feels like we’re actually part of the village,” he replied, winked and smacked Alice on the bottom gently with the wooden spoon.
Posted by Facing50Blog.com - 1 Comment
SexyFitChick said...So, no good looking fellas then?

Thursday 28th

This is looking very bad indeed. I am consumed with anxiety about Phil. He has not slept properly since he came home. I can hear him sighing miserably. He keeps getting up. He turns away from me when I try to touch him. He has also taken to shutting himself away in his computer room, closing down the screen every time I go in as if hiding something. I tried to log onto his history page when he went outside, wher he just stands and stares into space, to find out what he'd bee up to but he'd deleted the history.

Phil who can barely send an email has discovered how to hide his trail on the internet so I have no idea what he has bee doing. He is even more recalcitrant than usual and completely oblivious to my feminine charms. Mind you, I can understand that last bit because if a wobbly walrus tried to launch itself o me, at six o clock in the morning, I'd be reluctant too.

Today, I think I discovered why. Phil suggested we went t town. I was already suspicious about his suggestion. With everyone being off work, because of the extended public holiday, town would be heaving. Phil would rather stick pins his eyes than mingle with crowds of shoppers. More unusuall he was wearing a watch, something he hasn't done since he retired. He was ready to leave at exactly ten o'clock. As you know, Phil is the world's worst time-keeper. Every week we intend leaving at ten to go to town but we never get going before eleven-fifteen. Today, he was ready and looking jolly uncomfortable. He was dressed as if going to the office.

"Why are you dressed for an interview?" I asked

"I just thought I'd give these clothes an airing since I hardl get the opportunity to wear them nowadays."

He looked very smart. Just like the successful businessma he once was, before he became a poor pensioner, with lousy share dividends to rely on.

"Are you going to the bank?" I persisted.

"Get in the car, Mandy, or we'll be late."

He drove speedily to town; a trip that normally takes forty-five minutes only took us thirty-five today. My radar was on full alert. When he announced he wasn't hungry, and he didn't want to start the trip with a visit to the cafeteria for cappuccino and cake, I was convinced something was up. He headed off in the direction of the bank having agreed to meet me three hours later. I followed.

Now, I've seen enough detective films to know how to tail someone and I think I did an excellent job. There's nothing like a good dose of anxiety to make you scurry along and hug the walls invisibly. Phil didn't even look back once, so I didn't have to leap into a doorway, or pretend to be admiring something in a shop window. He obviously thought I hadn't picked up on his suspicious behaviour, and had gone off to while my time shopping, like the vacant empty headed selfish person I am.

He beetled off in the opposite direction to the shops, to an area I'd never visited before. He stopped occasionally to consult a piece of paper, no doubt with directions on it. Finally, he stopped in front of a large glass fronted building. There was a huge reception area, lounge chairs in the window and gym equipment next door. It looked like a very chic gym or club. Phil sauntered in and spoke to the receptionist, then took one of the chairs in the window, where I could see him clearly from my position behind the wall in front of the buildings. Soon enough I saw a gorgeous, raven haired, tall, elegant woman emerge from the gym area. She walked up to Phil and kissed him on the cheek. My heart fell into my stomach somewhere. I guess this was the' woman from nearby'. He was having a

secret assignation with a babe. No wonder he was dressed up a
'Mr Successful'.

Phil and the 'woman from nearby' disappeared into a back room. I stumbled about and found my way back to the shops. I slumped on a nearby bench, tormented myself with thoughts of what they may be up to, and waited for Phil to meet me. He came back on time whistling and holding a bag with a cake in it.

"Did you have a good time?" He asked. "See anything interesting?"

"No, not really," I replied.

I feel like someone has knocked the wind out of me and I just don't know what to do.

Posted by Facing50Blog.com - 7 Comments

The Merry Divorcee... I'm so sorry. I know how you feel.

Fairie Queene...Oh Mandy, I cried when I read this. It reminded me of how I felt when Albert left me.

Angelique said ... Men!

YoungFreeSingleandSane said... And that is why I'm staying single. So sorry, Mandy. Big hug.

SexyFitChick said... Fancy a break? Come and visit me. I'll take you to a few clubs and we'll sort out a new man for you.

Vera said... Don't jump to any conclusions yet Mandy, you may be wrong.

Lostforwords said...Stop feeling sorry for yourself. If you love him fight for him.

CHAPTER 11 – MAY

Thursday 5th

It's been a long holiday for most people. What with Easter, The Royal Wedding and May Bank Holiday, I expect most people will be dreading going back to work. Tom went back today. He really has become a different young man. Ironic isn't it? I've wanted this for so long and it yet it's happening at a point when it isn't going to help my relationship with Phil. We won't benefit from this change, not the way things are going.

It's been the most beautiful weather too. Instead of sitting together outside enjoying the warmth, Phil has been ensconced in his room. He doesn't seem to want to come out for any reason. I tried to get him to come for a walk over the fields with me today. There are calves in the field next door. It is charming. Phil refused and grunted he was busy.

Tom has some exams tomorrow for his HNC. I know, because Alice told me. She has been helping him revise. He spends quite a lot of time at her house. Her parents adore him. He goes out with her father to the pub and plays darts with him. Shame it isn't with Phil.

I haven't bothered with *Facebook* recently. I haven't got any interest in virtual harvesting at the moment. Someone called Big Wally beat my game score on my regular game. I've slid to fifteenth place. I don't think I care anymore.

Todd has still been sending emails. I got one from him a couple of days ago. He'd been to a vineyard.

'Been sampling some great local Aussie wines. You'd have a spiffy time – or do I mean squiffy?
As I recall you always liked a good Pinot...'

At least it raised a smile. I joined him, in a virtual sense, and had a couple of glasses in the lounge while watching the film *Up.* It made me cry.

Posted by Facing50Blog.com - 4 Comments

Lostforwords said...Amanda, please pull yourself together. The answer is not to be found in the bottom of a glass.

The Merry Divorcee said... It gets easier. I didn't even feel s after husband number four.

YoungFreeSingleandSane said...If it does get to the you-know-what stage, I can assure you that being on your own is quite good fun. Honest!

Facing50 said...Thanks for the support. I appreciate it.

Thursday 12th

I decided today that I needed to try and sort out this mess with Phil. At first, I thought he'd maybe just have a fling and then come back to me. I'd forgive him if he did. I never realis before how much Phil means to me. He has always accepted me for who I am and put up with my nonsense. I can't be that much fun to live with. I spend all my time on the internet, mostly because Phil is busy doing other things, and I've just taken him for granted. Why didn't I try harder before? I've been so obsessed with getting older and hitting fifty that I haven't thought at all about what Phil might have wanted. I ju presumed he was content in his own miserable way. I suppose also thought no one else would be interested in him.

I know you are supportive but I need someone to talk to. M mother, well she'll probably just cheer when she hears that th relationship is headed for disaster, and say "I told you so." Anyway, she's extended her trip in Cyprus again by a few day so I can't talk to her. She sent a text with a smiley face on it, saying all was well, and she'd talk to me when she had some time and news. I had to grin. What seventy-seven year old sends a smiley face? I seem to be aging and she seems to be getting more youthful.

It's like a corrupt enactment of *Picture of Dorian Gray* by Oscar Wilde. Dorian hides a painting of himself in the attic, which shows the signs of aging due to his debauchery, but he keeps his youthful beauty. I am the picture in the attic. My mother goes out and has fun. I exhibit the signs of aging.

It will be Phil's birthday tomorrow. As he always loathes his birthday. I no longer make a fuss about it. In the early days when we were together I once surprised him by organising a get-together with his friends at a Michelin starred restaurant. He was picked up in a limousine that one of his best friends organised. Everyone else was waiting at the restaurant ready to surprise him. He refused to get into the limousine until I told him exactly what was going on. He told me that, although he appreciated my attempts to make his birthday special, he really would prefer to ignore it altogether. He had to feign surprise at seeing all his friends. To be honest he isn't a very good actor, so I'm sure they knew that he had found out. We had a jolly enough time but I accepted then that Phil didn't appreciate or enjoy birthdays like some of us do.

This year I had made a memorabilia box for him. It contained a few things to remind him of all that's happened in his life. I've been making it for months. It's like getting a big red book with *This is your Life* on it but in a box. I thought he should remember all the good things that had happened in his life. It holds photographs and booklets detailing his achievements. As you may have gathered, he is not keen on commercialism, but I thought this would show care, love and appreciation for him.

Also I've drawn up a lengthy list, written in my best calligraphy pen handwriting, of some historical events that ha coincided with his time here on planet Earth. For example the year he started up his business was also the same year Margar Thatcher became Prime Minister. I had some DVDs of his favourite shows from years ago: *Dallas* which he used to love watching when he first started up the business, and a couple o James Bond films. I have written out a list of every music number 1 hit, from his birthday to the present day, and downloaded the ones I thought he'd like onto a CD. I'd managed to get a signed photograph of his favourite group; Abba.

There were photos of the family, his parents, us and Tom a a young boy, then as an older boy. I hope he isn't still fed up with Tom. Well, he has been much better since he met Alice and not nearly as inconsiderate. Yesterday, he even offered to wash up and managed to shave without me hinting. He's been getting up for work without a struggle, although I think I have to give Alice the credit for that too. Her parents used to be farmers so they all still get up at the crack of dawn, and I think Alice texts Tom, to make sure he's up in time for breakfast an work. I painted a picture of Phil's first car, a Ford Capri in purple. I copied one faithfully from the internet and was very pleased with the result. It almost looked professional.

Somehow though, today, my heart is no longer in it. He probably won't be that excited by my pathetic efforts. I can't help but wonder what gift he might be receiving from the 'woman nearby'.

Posted by Facing50Blog.com - 2 Comments

Fairie Queene said...I used to love *Dallas*, Joan Collins was beautiful and those shoulder pads were to die for.

Lostforwords said...Well, if you made all that effort you must love him. Now stop being so soppy and sort your marriage out.

Friday 13th

I made Phil a special cake for his birthday. It was in the shape of one of the heavy goods vehicles he used to own. I laboured over it all day getting the right coloured icing on it. He loved his vehicles and was proud of the blue and yellow curtains they sported. They were always clean. How very typical of Phil.

In the morning he claimed that he needed to go out without me. How unusual is that? I didn't even ask why. I could guess where he was going; to see the 'woman from nearby'. He looked mightily relieved that he wasn't getting the inquisition that he clearly expected. I used the time constructively to bake the cake. I'd been planning it anyway, and had the recipe and picture ready, along with the ingredients. I made the number plate so it read 'Phil 59'. It might be the last time I do anything special for him and, in spite of the dreadful melancholy I'm experiencing, I felt I owed him a nice birthday. He has been good to me over the years.

He got up at the usual time and prowled around the kitchen trying to pretend it was a normal day. He wasn't allowed to think it for long, because I burst in singing *Happy Birthday* in my usual off-key voice, and gave him his card. He smiled and thanked me, then gave the usual speech about how he didn't want a fuss, and how he particularly didn't want a fuss this year, because next year he'd be sixty and that was scary. I nodded and carried on as if everything were normal.

Tom got up an extra half an hour early, no doubt prompted by Alice's text. He also sang to him, in a perfect baritone. He gave him a funny card and a bottle of wine in a Homer Simps bottle bag. Phil actually looked delighted. They even slapped each other on the back for a while, laughing at the card, which had some rude comment about being an old git on it.

Tom left and so did the levity. Phil muttered something about having to go out again, but not for too long, and refused to look me in the eyes. I almost said something. I almost gave in and revealed what I knew, but it was his birthday, what did matter if I waited a little longer?

Phil left, looking very smart again in his old suit. No prizes fo guessing where.

I logged onto *Scrabble* to find a message from Todd. He w full of apologies for not chatting to me much before but he ha had trouble getting internet. He had sent some fantastic photos of the elephants he had met at the orphanage and there were several of them all playing football. He had written:

'I am so excited about seeing you next week I can't get my trousers on.'

With everything that had been happening here recently I h entirely forgotten about our meeting next week. Well, who knows, he could be meeting a single woman by next week? How strange life is. I played the word 'fate'. It seemed appropriate.

Phil came back looking much happier. He breezed into the kitchen. His meeting with the 'woman from nearby' had obviously done him the world of good. I decided to treat his birthday as our Swan song. I would make it as nice as possible. At least he would have one nice memory of me to take away with him, when he drove off to his new raven-haired beauty.

I prepared a tasty meal of 'confit de canard', thanks largely to Marks and Spencer bistro section and opened a chilled crisp Chablis wine. We clinked glasses in front of the log burner and listened to some Abba music. Phil seemed relaxed and less stressed than he had been for weeks.

I fetched his box of gifts. There was the usual,

"Oh you shouldn't. You know I don't bother with birthdays." But he opened it enthusiastically, all the same. As he unwrapped each present, his face fell a little more. He unfurled the list of events and stared at it.

"This must have taken you hours. No, probably weeks to prepare," he said sadly.

"You hate it, don't you?" I asked

"No, no."

He opened the other gifts without saying a word and then, when he looked at the painting I had done, he stared at me intently. He looked so unhappy. What had I done?

"I'm so sorry. I should have bought you something instead. They're rubbish gifts. I'm really sorry," I burbled.

"No, no, not at all. They're so thoughtful. How could you have thought to do something like this? I'm just surprised and well I suppose I'm nostalgic. How did you know about my first car? It was before we even met."

"You used to talk about it."

"And this DVD. You remembered I liked *Dallas* in 1979." He sounded amazed.

"Well, yes, I've been with you a while now and I remembe all sorts of useless things."

He stood up and gave me a hug. Normally, I would have been delighted to receive such affection but I knew it was just gratitude.

"Oh you're welcome," I said flustered and went to fetch th cake.

If he was surprised by the presents, he was even more surprise by the cake.

"The colours are just perfect," he praised as he attempted t chew a piece of rock hard icing sugar.

When I told you all that I made the cake I neglected to say tha I'm not very good at making cakes.

"This is so thoughtful. You've brought back so many memories for me," he paused. "I think you and I need to have chat."

This was it. It was going to be the 'I really appreciate everything you've done but I've met someone else' speech. I just knew it would happen. I wish I hadn't made him feel he had to get it over with now. I held my breath and listened.

"I've been keeping something from you," he started hesitantly. "I haven't been easy to live with for some time, I know, and you must have days when you wish you were free and single."

"No, not at all. I accept that it's been very difficult for you. What with giving up your business, your raison d'être, and wi the shares performing so badly that we barely scrape any income from them. I do understand. Honestly I do. You aren't

difficult. You can be really funny sometimes and well, I'd miss you if anything happened and you weren't here."
He looked at me quizzically.

"If anything happened and I wasn't here. What do you mean? How much do you know exactly?"

"I know you've met someone else who you really like. Someone, who makes you happy and you are going to leave me."
Phil looked amused. That wasn't the reaction I was expecting. Then he laughed.

"Oh Mandy, your imagination really does run riot at times."

"No, I saw you," I continued feeling close to tears. "I saw you at that gym in town, being kissed by that beautiful woman. The one who you met on your Bush craft weekend."
Phil looked more and more amused. He glugged his wine in one and poured another glass.

"I didn't meet her on the Bush craft weekend. She is the wife of a **man** I met on the Bush craft weekend. She's called Giselle and is a consultant, of the medical variety."

"Er, okay."

"I met up with her because I have been having terrible heart palpitations for quite a few months. They keep me awake at night and as you know I will not go to our local GP. I've been anxious because heart disease runs in my family and well; I'm not getting any younger. I met a chap called Tony on the weekend. We got on really well and shared a tent together. We were talking about getting older. I confided in him about the heart palpitations and how my heart will suddenly beat nonstop, out of rhythm. I know," he said as I started to protest and say he should have told me. "You have had your own fair share of

difficulties this year. I know you've been worried about hittin
fifty and had a few female problems. I also know you've been
awake and almost ill with worry about Tom for months. You'
looked so tired. I really didn't want to give you extra anxiety.
You've been fretting about your mother. And, you are never o
that internet checking out remedies for this, that, and the other
It's difficult getting older, Mandy, I know. You're only fifty,
but I am nearly sixty, and I feel I'm turning into a useless
wreck."

"You're not useless," I sobbed.

"Your present tonight was lovely. However, it served to
remind me I've done so many things and had so many
experiences and now I'm frightened that there's nothing left f
me to enjoy."

"The consultant, tell me about the consultant."

"Oh yes, well, Tony arranged for me to see his wife, Gisel
who is a specialist in heart conditions. I met her briefly, when
she collected Tony, at the end of the weekend. That wasn't a
gym or a club you saw, it's a brand new BUPA centre where
they can check out your health. It's not quite finished yet so
there are no signs up. I had various tests for my heart and
examinations to try and work out what was wrong with me. I
couldn't let you come with me; you'd have only got worked u
I had to have an ECG which showed arrhythmic patterns in m
heart. Then, I had to wear a heart monitor for a day to track th
irregular patterns. I had X-rays and blood tests and, in short, I
got my results today. That's where I went."

"And?"

"I have an extra ventricular systole."

"Is it serious?"

"No, just jolly uncomfortable. My heart is working off its own electrical impulses. It will just beat like a drum, or stop beating for a few beats, and then after a day or longer it will sort itself out. It's made me really tired, and of course, I was pretty worried."

"Can we do anything to help you?"

"I can take Beater Blockers or maybe we could try something that I've been researching on the internet; Omega 3 and 6 oils. You find them in seeds. Apparently, they can help rebalance the heart."

"We'll try whatever we can, but not the Beater Blockers yet. Let's try the alternative first. By the way what's caused it?"

He looked at me sheepishly.

"Too much stress and anxiety. I think I got too worked up about our finances. Andworked up over Tom, of course."

We finished the wine and listened to some more Abba. Phil deliberately didn't watch the finance programme. Judging by the snoring later I'd say he slept alright too.

Posted by Facing50Blog.com - 6 Comments

The Merry Divorcee said... Well thank goodness for that. No, I don't mean that he has a heart condition; just that he isn't going to leave you. You seem good together.

Angelique said... Men, they are never in touch with their emotions.

Fairie Queene said... I'm so happy he's not having an affair. It really is dreadful when that happens. I hope he gets better. I'm sure he'll recover with the love of a good woman, and I don't mean the 'woman from nearby'.

Lostforwords said... At least all's well that ends well. Now what about Todd?

SexyFitChick said... Put some Abba on and let him dance around a bit he'll soon sort out his heart rate. Or, maybe you can think of another way to raise it.
Facing50 said... SFC you are very cheeky.

Sunday 15th

So, no more anxieties about Phil and I. Phil certainly appears to be less crabby and worked up. He even spoke to Tom last night. Surprisingly, he was the first one to speak. I think even Tom was surprised. More surprising was the conversation with my mother today. Back from Cyprus again she had a lot to tell me.

"I suppose I ought to let you know what's been going on," she wheezed and coughed for an age. "I've been in Cyprus because of Grego. He had a proposition to make."
So he had asked her to marry him.

"As I told you before I left, he wanted me to become his partner," she continued, pausing for a quick hack.

"That's a novel way of putting it," I commented.

"What do you mean? He wanted me to become his partner in his new venture. He has a boutique in Larnaca selling upmarket, bespoke dresses. He wanted me to become one of h partners and advisors. I thought I'd explained this to you. You should try and listen more when I'm talking to you on the phone. You always were a dreamer. I suppose your mind was elsewhere. He's a dress designer."
I was flabbergasted.

"You're very quiet. Have you heard me?"

"Let me get this right. Grego makes dresses. He wanted you to join him to help him, not only design them, but supervise their production."

"Yes, exactly. I met him the night I had the all-night party. He was one of those who came down to complain about the noise. We hit it off straight away. He admired the caftan I was wearing. You might remember it; the one with all the fringing. I told him I had designed and made it and then told him about my interest in sewing. He came over to the UK and stayed with me so he could see what else I had made. He wanted to look at my fabric collection. I showed him my collection of patterns I had designed over the years too. I also demonstrated how I put together the wedding dress I designed and made for Deirdre, who I used to work with. He loved it. He wants to sell some like it. So, I went back to Cyprus with the patterns and some more ideas I have been working on recently. He absolutely adored my work. He thinks I'm very creative, He wanted me to advise his staff and even assist with fashion shows. Fancy that, at my age too. I had to think long and hard about it. I was really tempted, but well, I'm not getting younger and my eyesight isn't what it used to be."

"So he hasn't asked you to marry him?"

"Marry? I hardly think so. He's only fifty-nine you know?"

"Yes, but you seem so close and enjoy the same things together, good food, sewing, opera..."

"Absolutely, and he is fabulous company. I have had such fun with him. He makes me feel fifty-nine myself. No, Mandy I wouldn't marry him even if he did ask. I loved your father. He was, and still is, the only man for me. When you find someone like that, someone who makes you feel complete, you will

never be able to replace them. They make you whole. Togethe
you are one whole person, and without them you are a shell or
fragment. I miss your father every hour of every day. Grego
helped to distract me from my loneliness. Thanks to him I hav
met some fascinating and fun people. I have even had a life
again for a while. I felt I was useful again. But Mandy, I
wouldn't marry Grego, as adorable as he is, and he wouldn't
ask because Mandy, Grego is gay."

How do you follow that? The last few days and weeks have
been some of the strangest in my life and yet I have learned so
much. My mother is not a miserable complaining old woman.
She is just like me, only older. She gets lonely too. She has the
same and anxieties as me and just wants to enjoy life while sh
can. It's taken quite a few years for me to realise. Maybe, I've
started to grow up at last.

Posted by Facing50Blog.com - 2 Comments

SexyFitChick said... Well I never. Gay?

Vera said.... I'm very pleased for your Mum. She could
probably do with her daughter being her friend again.

Thursday 19th

Today was 'Todd Day'. I know you are all dying to know
what happened, but I need to build up the picture first. While I
was agonising over Phil, I received two messages last week,
both of them terribly suggestive. Todd told me he just couldn't
wait to see me. He had arrived in the UK. He was going to hav
one day to get over his jet lag and catch up with some old
friends. He was then attending his nephews' wedding on
Tuesday 17th, allowing himself a day to sober up, and then me
me today. The email told me where and when to meet him, It

was too late to send a reply and cancel the rendezvous. He might not receive the message and be stuck at the hotel reception like an idiot. I couldn't be that cruel.

I couldn't sleep last night, at all. I couldn't decide if I was excited or very anxious. I was only going to see him for old time's sake. After all, I had realised that Phil was the man for me. Yet part of me still bubbled with excitement at the prospect of seeing him again. Of course, it was only a meal and a catch up. There was no doubt in my mind about that, but deep within, the younger me was buzzing. I'd had my outfit ready for weeks. I'd bought a very sexy dress in black which hugged my curves, yes; I've accepted that I'll never be a size ten again.

I got up at six ran a bath and shaved my legs. A girl should never go out for an assignation without shaving her legs. Even if it is just with a friend, and indeed that's what today would be, a meeting with a friend. I applied my makeup carefully. I employed the minking technique I picked up months ago. My eyes looked smouldering. Phil was downstairs with a cup of coffee whistling *Dancing Queen'* when I appeared.

"You look very nice indeed," he said and gave me an appreciative look.

Well, that completely threw me. I've forgotten when Phil last noticed what I wore or looked like. I could parade around wearing nothing but a pinafore and carrying a feather duster, and he'd ignore me but today, probably because he's less worried about his health, he actually seemed interested in me.

"It's nice for you to get out and meet people again," he continued. "I think you've been too insular, stuck at home all the time, with a miserable old man."

"No, I rather like being at home with you."

And guess what? I do. I missed him over that weekend he went away. I was terrified I would lose him to some woman h had met. Then, there had been that possibility that he might have been seriously ill, and I would have lost him forever. My mother's words echoed in my ears,
'When you find someone like that, someone who makes you feel complete, you will never be able to replace them. They make you whole. Together you are one whole person and without them you are a shell or a fragment.'
She had hit the proverbial nail on the head.

"Do you know what? I don't think I want to meet up with a boring old teacher from way back when. Why don't you and I have a hot cocoa together and then go out for lunch in the Pea District. It's a lovely sunny day. I'll phone my friend and call the meeting off. He won't mind. He was only being polite."

"Well, if you're sure. Fancy a brownie with your cocoa?"

So, I didn't go. I tried not to think about how upset Todd would be. I pictured him arriving, probably with a bunch of flowers, and waiting for me, checking his watch and wonderin when I would be arriving. I phoned the hotel and left a messa for him:

'I'm so, so sorry but I can't do this. I'll probably regret it, but at the moment I can't go through with it. Sorry.'

Phil and I went out and enjoyed a pub lunch in the pretty hills of The Peak District. The pub rang with our giggles as w laughed at the ridiculous walkers, who came armed with ski poles, dressed as if they were climbing Ben Nevis.

I don't know how Todd will react and I feel dreadfully guilty. I've led him on. I've flirted terribly with him. Even if Phil and I had parted, Todd would never be right for me. He is in love with the person I used to be, the young carefree girl who wanted nothing more than to play at life. I've changed since then, and not just physically. If I'm honest, Todd would make me feel inadequate, and once I'd rushed about the world a little, what would I be left with? Phil has never tried to change me, nor the way I look, or behave. He restored my confidence just as Alice has restored Tom's He put meaning back into my life. I wouldn't want to hurt him, or cheat on him or leave him, even if he is a grouch at times. My eyes are finally open. Wow! What a month of revelations it's been.

Posted by Facing50Blog.com - 8 Comments

SexyFitChick said... I just don't believe it. You turn down an Aussie stud muffin for a cake eating old crock. Oh well, you know what you're doing I suppose.

Angelique said... Now Phil is feeling better, maybe he will be less grumpy.

Facing50 said... No, I don't think Phil will change much but I'm used to him, and he's not an old crock, just yet. LOL

The Merry Divorcee said... Well that's a relief. I was sure you'd run off with that Todd and it would all end in tears. I ran off with hubbies 4, 5, 6 and 7 and they all ended in disaster. Still, I do seem to have a lot of houses, nice cars and diamond rings that came out of various divorce settlements to keep me cheerful.

Facing50 said... Luckily I have become older and wiser in time.

Lostforwords said.... Todd would have been a dreadful choice he's too fond of himself to have really cared about you.

YoungFreeSingleAndSane said... Good choice...you know which side your bread is buttered. At least you know Phil well.

You shared lots of history together, and you've had Tom, of course.

Fairie Queene said... I am sniffing into my hanky as I read. I'm so glad you didn't leave Phil. I've got quite fond of him over the last few months I've been following your blog. I'm s happy your mum helped you to see sense. I wish I still had m mother.

Friday 27th

So much has happened this month, that you'd expect me t be posting that I'm skipping hand in hand in the garden with Phil. Alas, that is not the case. Phil is still absorbed by his sha portfolio and I have to drag him away from it periodically to stop him sinking into a depression. I have to keep thinking of things to distract him. He is slightly more cheerful but, well, Phil is Phil.

The car needed taxing again and once we got over the sho of how much we had to pay this year we flipped a coin to see who would be the unlucky person who had to take the forms t the Post Office.

Living in a small village has its benefits but the local Post Office is not necessarily one of them. I have written before about how long it takes to get there and indeed get served. No that I know a few more people in the village, thanks to the 'Open Gardens' event it'll probably take me all day to get the and back. Phil refuses to go and I can't say I'm keen on it.

I pointed out that I had the pleasure of going last year and took me two hours, so we agreed as I had called 'heads' and lost, that I would take it instead to the Post Office in the town where they have one of those machines that gives you a ticket with a number on it, and you wait for your number to be called. I had the misfortune of going there at Christmas with a parcel for my mother. I collected my ticket – number 188 and stood by the cards to wait. The first cashier called for the next customer

"Ticket number 97 please."

I stood miserably for ages waiting for my ticket. Moral of the story. Don't go to the Post Office at Christmas.

I didn't have much planned for town. I only had to collect a jacket that had been repaired from my very favourite dress shop and I even allowed Phil to do the food shopping. I thought he'd be safer looking for bargains, and terrorising old ladies, than standing with me in the Post Office. Armed with a list of provisions that we required, Phil beetled off on a mission to get them at the cheapest price possible. I headed off to my favourite dress shop.

"Hello! How are you? We are so sorry you couldn't make out little event. You missed a splendid evening here," boomed the owner. The day I was supposed to meet Todd, the shop had held an evening for their special customers. It involved a makeup expert who had worked on a television makeover show here in the UK. One of those shows where someone who looks sixty comes on. They are dressed by a professional, get a haircut and have make up properly applied to them. The next time you see them they are completely unrecognisable and look forty years old. I would have enjoyed that evening. Phil probably would have vetoed it anyway though. He'd have presumed it was just a way to get women in and spending their money. The expert came to give tips on how to make yourself look younger. She held a demonstration on how to use the makeup and there was champagne and canapés. Fascinated to learn what the evening had been like, I entered the shop. The owner said

"Fancy a glass of champagne? We have some left over."

Me, champagne? Of course I wanted one and I accepted a large glass, tried on a couple of lovely t-shirts while I was there, and scoffed some left over smoked salmon sandwiches. The girls, who weren't overly busy selling clothes, divulged al the secrets that the makeup expert had given them. I told them was made over in the makeup department of a shop earlier in the year.

"Those girls on the counters are just girls who play with makeup," they sneered. "This woman is an expert."

I had another glass of champagne; after all they had opened a fresh bottle for me, and listened intently.

"Right, firstly what colour mascara do you wear?" asked Libby one of the girls (When I say girls I mean about forty years old)

"Brown, and black" I answered pleased with myself becaus I know all about minking, don't I?

"No," said Libby. "You mustn't wear black. It's very aging for women of a certain age"

I sipped my champagne interested in what she had to say.

"You need dark blue or purple. Look!" and she fluttered he eyelashes at me. Quite honestly by then, they could have been bright pink, and I wouldn't have noticed. Bad eyes and champagne make everything even fuzzier.

I learned that I needed to put concealer on around my jaw line and up into my cheeks and then put a primer on.

"Primer? Paint?" I scoffed. Clearly, the champagne was making me squiffy.

"No, proper face primer, one with an SPF factor. Then brush, yes brush, your foundation lightly over the area. You must always use a brush."

"Eyeliner?" continued Libby.

"I can't see to put on eyeliner," I commented.

"No, you'll be able to. You do it like this," and she tilted her head in a strange fashion backwards.

"You put it on only 'iris to iris'. Not the whole underneath of your eye. Just the width of your iris."

She then gave me a lesson in how to put on eye shadow. By now, I was fully into how to look younger. The secret is less is more. Keep it light and natural. Cover the blemishes. Wear little eye shadow and keep those eyelashes a nice shade of dark blue.

I took a last glass of champagne and chatted about makeup and eyesight. Apparently, the lady is coming back to do one to one tutorials. She even has a class for partially sighted people so I should present no problem for her. The girls at the shop are going to book me in for a session. Finally, I collected my repaired jacket and staggered out.

Next door is my optician. Since I nearly lost Phil to another woman, okay, that was only in my head, I have been thinking about getting laser treatment. Well, you know how squeamish I am about eyes but emboldened by the fizz I asked about eye surgery. They gave me a number for the clinic to make an appointment.

I navigated a path around all the shoppers milling about. I must have looked like a complete drunk trying to weave around everyone and whiffing of booze. I stopped off and bought some

mints which I scoffed in one go so I didn't make people stare
me and woozily waited for Phil at the usual meeting point.

He arrived with dozens of plastic bags containing half pric
chocolate mints and farmhouse bread. I guessed they must ha
been on offer. They certainly weren't on the shopping list. He
looked decidedly chuffed with himself and we raced upstairs
the car just before the car park ticket ran out.

"Did you have to wait long at the Post Office for the tax?"
He asked.

"Oh bugger!"

"You forgot didn't you?"

"Yes, well, I went to get my jacket and they gave me
champagne and..."

Phil wasn't pleased. However, he knows what I'm like abo
champagne. I burbled away at high speed about makeup and
champagne and eye surgery to the point where he just looked
confused.

"Well," he said, when he could finally get a word in. I suppos
you managed to spend two hours in the dress shop and got
something for nothing. At least you didn't spend a fortune lik
you normally do in there. Makes a nice change."

I smiled enigmatically.

"I tell you what," I offered. "I'll go up to the village Post
Office when we get home."

Phil agreed and, happy in the knowledge that he had bagged
some bargains, he drove home. I sat quietly nursing my
handbag, in the bottom of which, nestled a brand new purchas
a very nice coloured t-shirt.

Posted by Facing50Blog.com - 4 Comments

PhillyFilly said...I have made a note of your tips and am off to get some blue mascara. I had my eyelashes lengthened last year so I expect blue will look good on them.
Vera said...Tut, tut. I hope you are going to take it back and get a refund or you'll never be able to afford eye surgery.
Facing50 said...Once I sobered up I went off the idea again. I think I'd rather have the t-shirt.
Faierie Queene said...I would love to appear on one of those makeover shows. They could change my whole life for me.

Monday 30th

I have found out some useful information on 'extra ventricular systole' and bought pumpkin seeds, linseeds and sunflower seeds which I grind down and mix into Phil's cereal each day. I am delighted to report that he is having fewer attacks and therefore is a lot less morose. I think it will take some time to get his heart settled but if it keeps him off other medication then it will have been worth it. I just wish he'd get an interest and stop fretting over the stock markets. 'Che sera sera.'
Posted by Facing50Blog.com - 2 Comments
Vera said... He'll find something to interest him in time.
Angelique said....Why doesn't he write a financial blog?

CHAPTER 12 – JUNE

Friday 3rd

"No, I'll do it. You don't want to get oil over that nice top," insisted Phil as he moved me, in a determined fashion, away from the stove and removed the frying pan from the cupboard.

It's nice of him to take over the cooking but when he gets hold of the frying pan he becomes a man possessed. It's the same come that time of the year when we can consider having a barbecue. Fortunately, it rains so much in this country that we don't get too many opportunities to barbecue but when it's a bright day Phil leaps up and down with the excited expectation that he will be allowed to cook.

It is all planned out with military precision. At four-thirty the poor old metal barbecue unit is dragged out from the tangle of plastic chairs and sun beds that never escape the shed. Phil attentively brushes off the cobwebs from it, and cleans it thoroughly in preparation. The necessary coal and lighting fuel is also extracted from hiding places amongst the tins of paints and many boxes of screws. You never know when you'll need a spare nut or bolt. We have thousands of them, should there ever be a shortage, and someone needs one.

All the required 'barbecue preparation' equipment is aligned neatly on a plastic table, once a suitable position for the barbecue itself, based on wind direction, has been established. Phil will then lay out each coal or 'brique' with measured care, coat them liberally with the lighting fluid, and wait until that has soaked in. At five, on the dot, he will strike the first match, look triumphant and wait for his fire to light. His face crumbles, as by the fifth attempt, it still won't have lit successfully and he has had to move it around into another position, blaming the wind for putting out the struggling flames.

By six it will have gone out several times, Phil will have used up his entire bottle of lighting fluid and will be looking somewhat peeved. He will be cursing and blaming the barbecue. At this point, I usually get him a cold beer. You will now be able to observe him supping his beer, simultaneously fanning the flames in an agitated fashion, with an aged copy of *The Financial Times,* until the wretched thing finally is warming up and the coals are glowing.
By half seven, Phil will be reading the old copy of *The Financial Times* with an intensity that astounds me. The coals will be hot enough for us to cook the two sausages and piece of chicken that we are having for our meal. By eight we will have finished eating. Phil will finally tear himself away from the old newspaper and exclaim that the barbecue is 'just right to use.' He'll claim it's a waste to not use it, and will set about removing all the chilled food in the fridge and cooking it, in a sort of 'Cookfest', looking like a dog in a butcher's shop. We will spend the rest of the week eating cold barbequed food.

In training for all the barbecues to come, Phil decided last night that he'd like to practise his culinary skills. Once he discovered I was going to cook salmon, he thought that he would like to be chef. The frying pan was put on the highest gas flame possible and oil added. Phil had one of those gleams in his eyes; a look of satisfaction. He was in charge. The pan started to smoke and he dropped in the salmon steaks.

"Don't let them get too hot. They're pieces of salmon not large steaks," I offered.
He gave me a withering look.

"Who's in charge here?" he barked.

"You dear," I replied and snuck off with a glass of wine into the lounge.

Salmon really shouldn't take very long to cook, and it didn't. Within a few minutes I heard the high pitched wail of the smoke alarms. I scooted out to discover billowing smoke and the aroma of charred fish. Phil had opened up the back door to let in some fresh air.

"Dinner's ready," he proudly announced. The alarm continued to wail.

"Don't worry. It'll stop in a minute," he said putting the cremated pieces of fish onto a boiling hot plate. He insists that the plate must be hot no matter what we eat.

The alarm continued to howl, as smoke continued to snake about the kitchen and hall. He assured me it would stop soon. Fresh air came in displacing the acrid smoke. We ate our meal. We washed up and sprayed the kitchen liberally with some air freshener. Now it smelt worse, but chef was pleased with himself, and content that he had been useful. As we sat down in front of the television, the alarm mercifully ceased howling, although my ears rang for quite a while afterwards. The evening passed normally and Phil, worn out by the excitement of cooking, went to bed early.

At 2.22 am we were awoken by a high pitched screaming noise.

"Holy.... what's going on?"

"Smoke alarm, in the hall," replied Phil leaping out of bed.

"It's not gone off again, has it?"

"No, the battery has died in it. It makes that noise when the battery is failing," shouted Phil, trying to leap up and down to reach the alarm. "It must have run down earlier when it went off because of the smoke," he continued, still unable to reach as he stood on the stool I'd pulled out for him. I got a chair. That was no good either. It was too low. Phil jumped up and down on it but couldn't grab the alarm box.

"I need the step ladder," he grunted. I beetled off to get it. The shrieking noise was dreadful. When I came back he was still jumping about on the chair. I took the chair from him and he put up the ladders. He climbed up and extracted the battery The revolting shrieking noise ceased.

"Well, that's doesn't seem to be much of a story or a problem," I hear you comment. No, it isn't, except Phil doesn wear pyjamas to bed so he performed all of this in nothing more than his birthday suit.

"Oh well, that must have been fun for you," you may say. Yes, it was. But it was even more fun for Ethel, our neighbou who was also up at that time and was looking out from her kitchen window, where she had a splendid view of him jumpi up and down, first on a stool, then a chair and finally a ladder right in front of the window, where earlier I had forgotten to draw the curtains. She saw me looking and gave me the thum up. Nice to know her eyesight is still good at her age. I hope that wasn't a mobile phone she was pointing in our direction.

On reflection it would be better to only let him cook when we have a barbeque. However, I'm sure Ethel wouldn't mind I let him lose with the frying pan again.

Posted by Facing50Blog.com - 6 Comments

SexyFitChick said...He's a right flasher isn't he? First, at the gym and now in front of your neighbours. I can only presume by your neighbour's thumbs up, that he is worth seeing in the nude. No wonder you didn't want to lose him.

MammaMia6 said...I hooted with laughter at this post. I even shared it with hubs. He thinks you are all ravers in the UK.
Faerie Queene said...How funny! I'd have enjoyed seeing him leap up and down too. I most certainly would have videoed him. You can get good money for those videos on television.
Facing50 said...Groan! I hope Ethel hasn't recorded him. She'll show it to all her friends at the golf club. Oh well, at least you are never too old to appreciate such shenanigans.
Vera said...My dear Horace always wore a nightgown. He said it was more comfortable as it let the air flow around. Lucky that Phil didn't have one of those – that would have just looked ridiculous.
The Merry Divorcee said...I never wear anything to bed – just my latest man to drape over me should I get cold.

Saturday 5th

What a turn up for the books. There I was hiding in my computer room pretending to be working, but secretly writing my blog, and eating chocolate fudge, when I get a message from SexyFitChick who has awarded me the 'Most Entertaining Blogger Award'. What can I say....cough cough...I would firstly like to thank my dear new friend SexyFitChick from www.keepfitandsexy.com She has been a great follower, always writing enlightening and sometimes very saucy comments on my blog. She has made me smile when I have felt down. She has given me advice and supported me when I needed it. In short I consider her a true friend.

I should thank my family for being the butt of most of my jokes and posts. Thankfully, they are unaware of what I say about them. Thank you to Lee, the young man at the department store for putting up with Phil's demands and for selling us what has become my invaluable laptop. I hope you recovered from the whole episode and are now off the medication.

Thank you to my blogging friends and those who stop by t read my drivel. And, lastly my very grateful thanks to you, my followers. You have held my hand through a turbulent year. I truly don't know what I would have done without your little comments and words of encouragement.

There, that's the dry run and now I'm ready for my Oscar award speech.

Rules for accepting this award are:
1 Thank and link back to the person who awarded you this.
2. Share 3 things about yourself.
3. Pay it forward to 5 recently discovered great bloggers.
Here are 3 things about me:
-I adore pasta. I once won a pasta eating competition where I polished off fifteen plates of it in record time. I won a pasta plate.
-I watch *Desperate Housewives* when Phil is in bed. I would love to be like the character Gabrielle Solis. I liked her quote: 'I'm married and can't shop. The worst of all possible worlds.
-I have a secret - I do 'Sudoko' puzzles online. I'm actually pretty poor at maths, and when it comes to multiplication, I flounder without my fingers to use, but I'm a dab hand at thes puzzles. Last week I had the fastest finishing time for a 'diabolical puzzle'. I'm giving up though now because I find them too easy. I shan't tell Phil though. He thinks spending hours putting numbers in order in boxes is worse than watchi paint dry. He can't see the sense in it.

I would like to forward this award to:
Vera @ www.meetagain.co.uk
Faerie Queene @ www.literarylover.com
Angelique @ www.recipes4nondomesticgoddesses.com
The Merry Divorcee@ www.themerrydivorcee.com
YoungFreeSingleandSane @
www.funandfrolicsonmyown.com

Thanks to you all, I no longer feel completely alone. I have been amazed by the friendship and openness that surrounds bloggers and their blogs. Everyone tells a story. I feel you have all been part of mine.

Posted by Facing50Blog.com - 5 Comments

The Merry Divorcee said... Thank you and congrats. You have poured out your heart on this blog and I feel I really know you. You may live miles away but you are beside me every day when I log on and read your posts

Vera said...Thank you dear. I appreciate the accolade. I've enjoyed being part of your life. I feel like your auntie.

Angelique said...Well done, and thank you for the forward. I have made many friends since I started blogging and it's true you realise that you are not alone on the world. I'm so glad you visit my blog as often as you do. I hope the recipes are helping. If you need any more just email me.

Fairie Queene said...Oh I'm thrilled. I love your adventures and reading your blog has really helped me get over Albert leaving me. Thank you.

YoungFreeSingleandSane said...Cheers! It's great that you've got an award and I'm 'chuffed' (one of your words that I have learned since I've been reading your blog) with mine. I'm not sure if I'll be blogging much though as I've met a really nice

guy and I think my time might be taken up with other activitie
I might have to change my name if it all goes well.
SexyFitChick said...You are my best blogging buddy. The firs thing I do each morning is check to see if you have posted. You've been a large part of my life too.

Friday 10th

I got an email from Todd this morning. He is back in Australia. I couldn't open it at first in case it was full of hurt and retribution. I have been worried about how upset he'll be. have felt guilty ever since I stood him up. The third time I logged on I finally got up the courage to open the email:

'Hi Mandy,

I don't really know how to begin this email. I am sorry, tru sorry that I didn't turn up to our meeting. I hope you didn't wa there too long for me. I would have phoned the hotel but my phone was dead. Hopefully, the bottle of champagne I had arranged will have been of some consolation. I found myself unable to come and meet you due to all the pressure on me from my family who hadn't seen me for so long. After the wedding, they had arranged for me to visit relatives, and go on outings with cousins I haven't seen in years. I just couldn't let them down as they were so pleased to see me. You understand that, don't you? My mother was in tears. I've not seen her for so long. It was almost pitiful they way she clung to me. I couldn't race off again and leave her, not now she is so frail. I was all extremely awkward. I realise I have let you down, but well, maybe you could come and see me here in Sydney. Or, maybe we could meet up when I next come over, probably in year's time, when my niece gets hitched.

I hope you are not too disappointed. I would have loved to have seen you. Did you wear black lace knickers as I requested? Now that thought has got me mighty excited.

Take care and look after yourself. I'll see you on the Scrabble Board.

Loads of love

Todd xxxxxxxxxxxx

P.S. You're still the sexiest vixen I know'

I couldn't help myself but I laughed. I don't know why I thought he would be any different. Oh well, his family would have been delighted to see him after so long and I'm completely over him now anyway. I'm glad Phil is reliable. I logged on to *Scrabble* where my icon was flashing. He obviously presumed that he would charm me again, and had set up a board for us. He had played the word 'forgive'. Under the events section he had written 'forgive me? Please?' I added the letters 'end' to play both 'forgiven' and 'end' then clicked off for the last time.

Posted by Facing50Blog.com - 3 Comments

SexyFitChick said... You will not believe this but I know the truth of the story. That email is a bunch of crap. My cousin, Mathilda, who migrated to the UK a few years ago, was one of the bridesmaids at that wedding! I was completely blown away by that little fact when I found out. She's known Todd's nephew's new wife for years. She and I have always stayed in contact since she left home. We're quite close I suppose, funny since we live miles apart. Last week we were on Skype and she told me that had met a bloke at a wedding. She had fallen for him instantly. She laughed and said normally the bridesmaid should get off with the Best Man, not the groom's uncle.

She's always preferred older men though and she certainly liked this one. She was going on about him being very sexy a charming. She then said the thing that clinched it for me. She told me the uncle lived in Oz and what a shame she had move to the UK. She'd have loved to have seen more of him. I pushed her a bit further and she finally told me his name; Tod Bradshaw. Todd came onto her at the reception after the wedding. He told her she was the most beautiful woman he h ever met, and incredibly sexy. The sleazebag.

She and Todd spent the next three days in bed together, at her apartment. They weren't catching up on their sleep either, you know what I mean. She hasn't heard from him since though. Even though he promised he'd stay in touch. I think you might well have made the right decision.

He'd better not turn up in my neighbourhood or I'll set my galah on him.

Lostforwords said...I knew right from the start that you couldn't trust him. Never trust a man who wears his collars turned up.

Facing50 said...Well, well, well, SexyFitChick what can I say The leopard has definitely not changed his spots. Lostforword how do you know he wears his collars up?

Saturday 11th

Phil and I are completely gobsmacked. We were outside attempting to get the garden into some form of order. I waste the first hour listening to Phil complaining about the rabbits. Yes, we got rid of the moles and now the garden is like the se of *Watership Down.* It is over run by small medium and large rabbits.

They've been breeding under next doors' shed and have
ecently all emerged into our garden. They keep multiplying by
he week. The trouble is that the smallest bunnies are really
ute and quite tame. I was weeding beside the patio with my
rowel and one came and sat next to me, nose twitching, and its
ittle eyes looking at me

"Whack it over the head with your trowel," yelled Phil from
he far side of the garden.

Of course I refused, and now the little perisher, along with
is hundreds of brothers and sisters, have scuffed up Phil's
reshly cut grass, and chewed the leaves off my nice flowering
ostas. Phil is not amused. I haven't noticed him trying to get
id of them though, and I'm sure he stopped mowing, just so a
articularly tiny rabbit could finish a blade of grass it was
njoying.

I put on my personal music player to drown out Phil. This is
what it must be like for him all the time. I'll jabber away and he
ears nothing. I should wear it more often. It would be nice to
give him a dose of his own medicine occasionally. I almost
nissed Tom and Alice who had arrived in Tom's car and were
aking out a bucket of water to wash it. Phil was amazed.

"Tom, are you feeling alright?" He asked.

"Ha ha! I thought it was about time I cleaned the car. I can't
xpect you to do it with all the work you have to do here."

Phil rubbed his eyes, no he wasn't dreaming. Nevertheless,
e insisted on supervising Tom and put away the mower.

"You need hotter water than that Tom," he called, and went
off to fetch his best car shampoo in honour of Tom's first
attempt to wash his own car. Alice and I stood to one side and
watched the show.

“Make sure you get it sufficiently wet before you clean it with the sponge. It’s very grimy and you don’t want to scratc the paint.”
Tom hosed it down thoroughly and began to soap it.

“Oh look Tom,” called Phil. “It’s a red one,” he announce gleefully as the muck came away from the car.

“Highly amusing, Papa!”

Alice and I giggled. Tom hosed us both and we chucked hi sponge at him. It was all very silly but fun. It was certainly th first time we’ve washed the car together. Tom and Phil becam serious after that and cleaned it thoroughly, and even vacuum it all out. Phil bashed the mats clean. Alice and I cleaned the interior dashboard and windows.

After we had cleared everything away Tom said he wante to talk to us, which is always a bad sign. I suppose, that was why he cleaned his car, to butter us up. Phil’s face set sternly he prepared himself for some bad news.

“Alice and I, well me really. Well, er, I think it’s time I became more responsible. I’ve not been very good with, er, money for ages. I just, well, I just spend it. If I have it in my pocket then I think it’s okay to spend it. I need to have some, er, boundaries. Like the phone contract. I’ve been much bette with my texting since I got my phone. I think if I had to fend for myself more, I’d learn more quickly, and well, you both need some time alone. You could do with some space...” Tom burbled at high speed.

“Tom, slow down. What are you trying to say?”

“I want to move out into rented accommodation.”

“Oh yes, and where do you propose to live?”

"There's a flat for rent over the hairdresser's shop in the village. It'll be available at the end of the month. I've been to see it and it's very nice. I wouldn't be far, so if you needed a hand with anything..."

"Stop right there, Tom. How much is the rent for this flat?"

"£400 a month. I can afford that."

Phil took a deep breath and got ready to explain to Tom how this really wouldn't be possible.

"Tom, you will need money not only for your monthly rent, but to pay for the electricity, the gas, the council tax, the water rates, and, you will also have to pay a deposit for the flat. You can barely afford £400 a month. You would have no money left at all, certainly nothing for fags, booze and barely enough for food."

Tom smiled broadly.

"No, I can afford it. Not only am I working the full five days a week now, but I got promoted last week, along with a decent pay rise. I'm going to be a supervisor. I'll get extra training too and future promotions if I stick at it. I didn't want to tell you until I had all the details and knew I could afford to live alone."

The word ecstatic doesn't even begin to describe how we felt. Tom, lazy old good for nothing Tom, had been promoted. The euphoria wore off rapidly though.

"Tom that is just fantastic news but you'll need to buy furniture for the place and put down three months rent as a deposit. Even if you chose to live in a bare flat you'll still be stretching yourself. I don't think you can afford to do this just yet. Maybe later, when you have saved a little money."

I expected Tom to be disappointed, instead he continued to grin.

“No, I can afford it. I can afford to buy a bed, table, and settee and put down a deposit. Really, I can. Grandma gave me £3000 for my twenty-first birthday. She said I wasn’t to tell you yet. We discussed spending it on me moving out. She said that you were at that time of your life when you probably needed to start spending time together, doing things before it was too late and you needed your Zimmer frames, and that it would do me good to branch out. She knew I’d been spending recklessly, but she understood that, after all I’m young. She thought if I took on a few responsibilities it would do me good. It was her suggestion that I looked for somewhere to move to. She said something quite funny,” he laughed. “She said ‘After all, you don’t want to be stuck at home forever with those two old fogies, who do nothing with their free time, except sit on the internet or mope around eating cake.’ She’s pretty funny, isn’t she?”

My antennae pricked up.

“You’ve been talking to Grandma?”

“Yes, she phones me regularly. I gave her my number when I got my new phone. She usually texts or phones me on a Sunday.”

And so, my mother is to be thanked for restoring calm to our household. We need to arrange for Tom to move out. Phil will go to the letting agents with him, to help sort it all, but already the mood is much lighter in the house and Phil is looking younger by the hour.

Posted by Facing50Blog.com - 7 Comments

YoungFreeSingleandSane said... Wow! Hope my Mom is as understanding and helpful as that.

Vera said...The young man deserves a chance doesn’t he?

SexyFitChick said...You are so lucky to have a cool Ma like that.

Faerie Queene said...Hurrah for your mother. Hurrah that Tom has finally begun to see sense. It's funny how we don't always take advice from our parents but can listen to our grandparents. My Nana always understood me. She used to let me bake cakes with her and wear her yellow pinny to make them.

Looking60feeling30 said...Us older people are still in touch with the young you know. Your mother is a fine example. Good luck to your son.

Lostforwords said... I'm glad it's working out at last for you.

Facing50 said...Thank you everyone, especially Lostforwords. I have a funny feeling you and I need to talk about your involvement when we chat on Sunday.

Sunday 12th

Mum and I have just had a long chat. As she is no doubt reading this post I'd better be careful what I put. For the rest of you in the dark still, the conversation went as follows:

"Hello Sweetheart!"

"Hello Lostforwords. I should have guessed when you called me 'Amanda' in the comments. Only a mother would use her daughter's full name. Just how long have you had the internet? How long have you been following my blog? And, how on earth did you ever find it?"

All I could hear was 'cough, cough'. Give the cigarettes up, Mum.

"I've had a computer for a couple of years now. I was so lonely and bored here; that I thought it would help me get in touch with others, like me. I had some lessons from a neighbour's son and I soon picked it up. I can email all my friends in Cyprus too when I'm not there. I met Vera in Cypru She told me all about her blog named after the Vera Lynn son *We'll meet Again*. As you know it's all about life in the thirtie and forties with reminisces, and recipes, and photographs. I used to read it regularly. She told me about a blog she'd found which she was enjoying reading, so I linked into it.

I didn't realise it was you at first but I soon worked it out. I opened my eyes, shall we say. Incidentally, I'm sorry you felt was just phoning you to blether on. I really wanted to talk to you but didn't know what to say as you're normally so recalcitrant. Rather than listen to silence I would just fill it. I just didn't want to get off the phone, because that would mear I'd have to wait another week, before I could talk to you agair Anyway, that's why I phoned you every week."

"I'm sorry too Mum. I should have included you more in m life. I have no excuses. I've been a lousy daughter. Anyway, I really enjoy our chats now; we have more to talk about."

"I read your blog whenever I could. I had to let you get things out of your system, but I can't tell you how relieved I was, that you decided not to see Todd. I was on the point of coming clean and telling you my worries. I may not have always expressed my approval of Phil, but you and he are goo together, and you have been together for twenty two years so that must count for something."

"Absolutely."

"I enjoyed reading because I actually got to find out about the real you. You never tell me anything anymore. You've ke me at arm's length ever since you left home, and I just didn't know you anymore. This allowed me to rediscover you. I didr always approve of what you said or did, but then again, it looks like you felt the same about me."

"You know I'll write this conversation down on my blog don't you?"

"Yes, and you can add this. I am proud of my daughter. If there was an award for 'Most Fun Daughter' I'd award it to you. You're not as stuffy or dull as you think. You have managed to inherit some fun genes."

"Thanks Mum, and thanks for helping to sort out Tom. It'll give Phil and me a chance to get on with our lives and stop worrying about him."

"Oh you never stop worrying about your children Mandy, no matter how old, or independent they become."

Posted by Facing50Blog.com - 7 Comments

Vera said... I'm delighted you two have made it up.

Fairie Queene said... I need to thank your Mum publically too. She has been my fairy Godmother. She introduced me to Grego. We got on like a house on fire. It turns out that we both love designer clothes, candlelit restaurants and opera so I am going to visit him in Cyprus next month.

Facing50 said... Did you Mum?

Lostforwords said... Yes, Spencer, sorry I mean, Fairie Queene, and I have been emailing each other for ages. I thought he and Grego would make a nice couple when I read his comments here on your blog. They had a day together when Grego visited me. I think they had a good time together. Spencer is going to stay at my flat when he comes over. I always fancied having a son as well as a daughter.

PhillyFilly said...What a small world. I wonder what will happen next. I wonder if I could turn out to be your long lost sister separated at birth from you. Tee hee!
SexyFitChick said...Can your mother sort my love life out to• I seem to have lost my pulling ability. Maybe it's my age. I don't think sixty-three is too old, do you?
SexyFitChick said...Only joking! LOL

Thursday 16th

I love that line in *Fawlty Towers* when Sybil Fawlty is ask how long she's been married to Basil:

"Oh, since 1485," she replies wearily.

I know how she feels. I can't seem to remember how long Phi and I have been together. Some days it feels a short time and other days it feels like an eternity. Yesterday heralded anothe wedding anniversary.

"Oh how sweet!" I hear you cry. Yes, I suppose so but as you know now the words 'Phil', 'Anniversary' and 'celebration' don't ordinarily, fit into the same sentence, unle: you add a negative which can only mean one thing, the same thing as every year; 'nothing'.

I don't rant about it anymore. Especially given that I appreciate him much more now. I'm resigned to the fact that whilst a lot of women get flowers or gifts or are taken out in celebration of another year of marriage I get, well how can I p this? Oh yes, forgotten, or at best he'll say 'Happy Anniversary' as he bounds out of bed which is almost worse than being ignored. He just isn't a romantic kind of chap.

I suppose I am still a die-hard romantic at heart. Whatever Phil may say or think, after all these years, I still make an effc and this year was to be no exception. In fact, I felt it was more important than usual to make an effort. I put small heart shaped candles on the breakfast table along with a card. I bought him a book by his favourite author, and left it on the table, in front of his place setting. I put on some romantic music and waited for him to emerge from the bathroom. He walked into the kitchen, eyebrows furrowed in confusion.

He had completely forgotten what day it was. It hadn't even hit his radar this year. After the events of recent weeks, I suppose I shouldn't be too surprised. Disappointed, but not surprised. Phil hasn't changed. He is just slightly happier at the thought of Tom moving on. You could see the proverbial penny eventually drop.

"Oh thanks," he said through a mouthful of muesli as he unwrapped his book. "Happy Anniversary," he added thoughtfully, and carried on chomping on his toasted grains of wheat, oblivious to my slight frustration that he hadn't even remembered the day. After the initial disappointment I got over it. What's the point in being glum? I should know what he's like by now. A leopard doesn't change its spots. Some men are just not romantic, and Phil has other plus points.

In fact, the more I thought about it, the more I realised I was actually very fortunate. He is probably the only person who completely understands me and my mad ways. He's fastidiously tidy – who wouldn't want that in a man? He makes me lemon hot water when I get up every day. He never tells me I look overweight even when I do. He doesn't watch sport on television and drive me mad trying to explain the 'off-side' rule.

I suppose he's right not to remember the 'big' day, after all I did bulldozer him into it. One minute he was happily dancing along to *Let's Do The Time Warp* from *The Rocky Horror Picture Show* dressed appropriately at a fancy dress all-night party and next thing I'd cornered him, waving my empty champagne glass about, dangerously close to his face and asking "Well, how about it?" He probably thought I meant something else and agreed. Two weeks later, as he found himself being frogmarched up the aisle, he realised his mistak but by then it was too late, and he's been lumbered with me ever since.

In appreciation of the fact that he has been very good to me over the years I made him a delicious meal – actually that is a complete lie. 'I heated up a delicious readymade meal' is more accurate. I prepared (got out of the fridge) a specially cooked (bought from the bakery) apple strudel for desert. I dressed up (I changed from my usual jeans into a dress). Phil looked ever more confused when he came in from his shed, where he had been hiding all day. Still, he pushed the boat out, got changed himself, lit some candles on the table and had an entire glass c wine to celebrate with his meal. After dinner, credit where it is due, Phil started on the washing up. He often does this even though we have a dishwasher. He started humming along to th music on the CD player.

"Turn it up will you," he asked. "I like this one."

"You're my one, shining moment," he sang along to Diana Ross.

"I didn't know you knew the lyrics to this," I commented, drying cloth in hand.

"Oh yes," he said. "You light up for me all the empty places..." he continued.

"Actually," he said interrupting his song. "It makes me think of you."

"Does it?"

"Uhm," he said embarrassed that he'd been so unusually romantic. "Yes." He rinsed a glass off under the tap until it shone and carried on singing.

"If I never met another, I'm glad that I've known you."

A lump rose in my throat. Who needs a present or a meal out or flowers to celebrate? Every day is a celebration.

We went into the lounge after dinner where I found he had lit some more tea lights. On my chair was a box inside which were some rather wonderful bath products.

"I thought you might like to feel a bit pampered in the bath,' he said watching the television and feigning disinterest. "It's just a little something. Nothing special. Oh, by the way, don't get too excited because I got you something this year. Don't think it's going to become a regular occurrence," he warned.

I just sat starry eyed with my box on my knees. Who said 'leopards couldn't change their spots?'

Posted by Facing50Blog.com - 16 Comments

SexyFitChick said...Well, blow me down. The old fox. I bet you needed that Horny Goat's Weed later too, didn't you?

Facing50 said...Funnily enough we didn't need it. We managed perfectly well without it. Phil says it pongs so I chucked it out. I don't think it'll be necessary from now on.

SerenSiren said...How romantic. Singing to you and buying you gifts. You're a lucky lady.

Facing50 said...Yes, today I feel fortunate.

Vera said... Congratulations on your Wedding Anniversary. I hope you have many more happy years together.
Blue Moon said... Congratulations from me too. It's our twentieth in a couple of weeks. I hope Hubs sings to me too.
Facing 50 said...Ah thank you both. I hope your husband can sing better than mine Blue Moon! LOL
PhillyFilly said...I got breast implants for our fifteenth Wedding Anniversary. For my sixteenth I got a new boyfrien Glad you had a good time.
The Merry Divorcee said...I can't remember all the dates of my anniversaries. I've been married so many times I get up now and presume it must be one of my anniversaries that wee Congratulations Honey, Nice to hear you are still together aft all this time.
Facing50 said PhillyFilly – You are so funny! Thank you for the smile you have just given me. You've done nothing for m laughter lines though. They've got worse. I'll have to come a see your surgeon if you keep creasing me up like this. The Merry Divorcee – Good luck to you. I read on your blog you' getting married again next month. Hope this one is for keeps.
YoungFreeSingleandSane said...I hope I have as much fun with whoever I end up with.
Facing50 said...Me too. I'm sure you will.
Looking60feeling30 said...Doug and I have been together sin forever too. He always forgets our anniversary. I just get my own present now. I wouldn't swap him though.
Emptynest2 said...Our daughter left the nest last year. We ha enjoyed so much together since she went. I hope you too have as good a time as us. We've been married about the same tim think too so well done on getting this far.

Faerie Queene said...How lovely. What smellies did you get. I adore that Molton Brown stuff. You can't go wrong with a few bubbles. Happy Anniversary to you both. Hugs

Facing50 said...Looking60feeling30 – thank you. Sounds like congratulations are in order for you too. Emptynest2 – I can't wait to get. I hope Phil is up for some fun. Faerie Queene – I agree. I got Molton Brown so bubbly bath – here I come.

Friday 24th

The month is shooting by rapidly and I haven't posted for a while because it's been quite crazy again recently. Phil and I have made some important decisions. Following on from Tom's revelation that he wanted to and was ready to move out, once and for all, Phil shut himself away in his room for a couple of days. I thought he was lost in the world of finance once again, but it seemed not.

"Mandy I've been thinking."

"What about? Don't tell me you're going to sell the emerging market fund and buy into a more defensive fund now that markets are rising in case they fall rapidly?"

"No, although I probably will. I've been thinking about how time goes by so quickly. I have been retired for over a year now. During that time we haven't really done anything, except worry about Tom, and get anxious about getting older. I think we need a challenge."

"I've been trying to get you to take up a hobby for ages."

"A hobby isn't a challenge. I spent years building up a successful business. It was a huge part of my life. It was my incentive to get up in the morning. It was my goal. It was what made me me, if you know what I mean."

"Yes," I replied wondering where the conversation was headed, surely he wasn't going to attempt to start another business.

"Since I sold it I haven't felt plugged in any more. The closest I get to feeling useful is when I sort out the finances, read up on funds and work out where to place them. Admittedly, with not a huge amount of success this year, it ha to be said, but they will rally in time. I need something extra though."

"Well what have you thought about doing?"

"It's an idea I have had for a while. Since going on the Bu craft weekend I realised that I really like the outdoor life and being in touch with nature."

"Oh please don't tell me you're going to live in tent in the wilderness."

"Not quite. I've been looking at some very interesting site on the internet. I think we should take a gap year and go travelling."

"Travel? We can't afford to go travelling?"

"Actually, we can. I have found a second hand motor hom for sale. It has everything we need in it, a shower, a lounge area, a double bed, sink, and kitchen. We just need to pay for fuel and food. We pay for that here, so why not abroad? I've planned to see it tomorrow, and I've already mapped out a route through Europe, which looks great fun. We'll be able to park wherever we like, within reason of course. We could eve park beside the sea in the South of France and watch the stars night. What do you think?"

He looked eager and resembled the Phil I had met years ag full of optimism again.

“I think it sounds like an interesting, no make that an exciting idea. Let me see the motor home though first, before I say yes.”

“Great. You’ll love it. I’ll just go and get the route map I’ve drawn out.”

“Hang on. You expect to be away for a year. What about this house?”

“Ah I thought about that too. I thought we’d let Tom have it for a year, rent free, on the proviso that he saves the money he got from your Mum, along with what he would have paid in rent and outgoings, for a deposit to buy his own place when we get back. If the funds do well, we might even add to the money he saves. If he doesn’t save enough money, then he’ll be stuck here, with us old fogies, won’t he? I think that’ll be incentive enough to get him saving, especially after having the freedom of the place for the year.”

Posted by Facing 50Blog.com - 5 Comments

Faerie Queene said...How exciting. Clever Phil

YoungFreeSingleandSane said...I wish I had you two as my parents.

PhillyFilly said...Get a bigger trailer and come and visit me. I’ll show you both a good time here and we’ll squeeze in a few procedures together.

SexyFitChick said... I went all round Oz in a camper van when I was younger. Happy days! I think you should give it a go. Chose something a bit bigger than the VW I had though. You’ll need one that can fit in a big bed.

TheWanderer said...I can highly recommend it. I’ve been in a motor home for three years now. You can read all about it on my blog. I wouldn’t swap it for a real house now. Who knows?

You might never want to go back to your house. Good luck. Hope you like the motor home.

Sunday 26th

We travelled to Gloucester yesterday to look at a Burstner Elegance motor home. It was amazing. It has rotating seats at the front where you drive so you feel like one of the members of Star Trek sitting in front of the controls at flight command. was tempted to swing around in my seat and shout;

"Captain, there are Klingons off the starboard bow."

But, Phil and the owner of the motor home, were being very serious about engine size and fuel consumption, so it seemed inappropriate. I had a good look around it taking in all the luxury.

It wasn't a van. It was a designer tardis. There was air conditioning and blinds for goodness sake. In the kitchen was 150-litre refrigerator. I'd be able to fit in all of Phil's alcohol free beers in that. The lounge had plush leather furniture. It wa more comfortable than our beaten up old chairs. I found a remote control. When I pressed the red button, the top of the smart wooden cabinet whirred open, and a flat screen TV emerged from it, settling itself back onto the cabinet. How coo is that? The king-sized bed –yes, king-sized- unfolds at the push of another button. The room was perfect. There was ever a dressing table and a wardrobe. The kitchen was styled in oak with designer fittings and I just loved it.

It was like being on a fantastic yacht, without the water. Fo me the most exciting bit was the reversing camera. I'd be able to see if there was anything behind when I reversed. I don't suppose Phil would want me to do much driving though, judging by the boyish smile that was playing on his face. It was a fabulous vehicle. It was smarter than our house. The man selling it had not had it for long, but had loved travelling in it so much, he was buying the next model up and going to tour around the USA for a year.

"Something for you to aim for next year," he quipped, as Phil and he shook hands on the deal.

"Are you sure we can afford it?" I asked Phil as we clambered back into the car and headed home.

"Yeah, I got a good price on this old girl," he said referring to his precious Mercedes. "It belongs to the past and we need to be looking at the future now. I also sold my 'Sainsbury' shares in my personal portfolio and made a tidy profit on them. No point in saving it for Tom to waste it. We may as well get some enjoyment ourselves. I figured that we'd get most of the money back on this motor home anyway, if we sell it in a year when we come back, so it will hardly have cost us anything to go travelling."

"**If** we sell it. We might enjoy it enough to go the States too or Mexico," I laughed.

"Or Australia," added Phil.

"No, I don't think I fancy going to Australia, but maybe New Zealand or Canada," I continued.

We spent the return journey chatting animatedly about our forthcoming year feeling younger than we had for many years.

Posted by Facing50Blog.com - 12 Comments

Fairie Queene said...Come to Cyprus and visit Grego and me and your Mum.

Facing50 said...We're going to visit Mum this week. All of us are going, including Alice and Tom; we've not been for so long

I'll probably have forgotten how to find her house? She says she's looking forward to seeing you and Grego at the launch c his next designer collection and she's especially looking forward to the after party next month.

The Merry Divorcee said...I hope you don't fall out being wi each other 24/7. Husband number six and I got on each other' nerves after a week's holiday in Tenerife and the next thing I knew we were in the divorce courts.

Vera said...Hope you have a lovely time and don't forget to take your laptop so we all know what you're up to.

SexyFitChick said...I am so excited for you. I might come an join you. It'd be a great way to meet some hunky foreign men Is there a spare room?

Charismatic said....I pass by regularly but I don't normally leave a comment. I thought I would today. I'm very happy for you both. Your plans sound very exciting. I shall eagerly awa your posts.

PhillyFilly said...I'm sure you'd make a great job of reversin it. Personally I'd rather sit on that leather sofa and watch the television and let Phil do the driving. You don't want to chip your nail varnish on the big old steering wheel, do you?

Serene Siren said...Waiting to hear all about your trips eager

RodeoBob said...We had one of those RV vehicles. It was mighty good. Good choice. Let me know if you need any advice about it. I still have the old manual for it.

Fortifyingyourfifties said...Wow! What a great idea. I'm goi to run that one past my husband. We need to put some oomph back into our olden years too.

Trinny said...At least you won't have to worry about Phil anc clothes. The closet won't be large enough to house all his clothes. It'll make it much easier. Just think, no more boxes of leather loafers piled up, no more stacks of jumpers, belts and ties. Instant declutter!

Facing 50 said...Thank you all. Sorry I can't reply individually to you. I'm a bit busy at the moment, packing away and the like. I'll email you all later in the week though.

Thursday 30th

This will be my last post as facing50withhumour. I didn't think when I started this blog that I would end up feeling so much part of a community, a blogging community where people understand you. Thank you all, (wow, 250 followers now) for not only giving me the encouragement to carry on writing, but also for listening to me.

Getting older is difficult for all of us, but it's nice to know that the challenges we face, are faced by all of us. When I turned fifty this year and began this blog I didn't realise that I still needed to grow up. Now that I finally have, I can start a new phase of my life, and a new blog, so I hope you will all join me at www.gapyearsforfogies.blogspot.com where I shall recount all our adventures over the coming year.

At least this year we'll be going somewhere nice and sunny for my birthday. That is, unless Phil has started the travel itinerary in Germany.

Posted by Facing50Blog.com - 72 Comments

Lightning Source UK Ltd.
Milton Keynes UK
UKOW051647231111

182584UK00001B/6/P